O9-BTN-147

WITHDRAWN

Baldwinsville Public Library
33 East Genesee Street
Baldwinsville NY 13027-2575

MAY 18 2010

The Lady and the Poet

WITHDRAWN
Baldwinsville Public Library
33 East Genesee Street
Baldwinsville, NY 13027-2575

Maeve Haran

THE LADY AND THE POET

St. Martin's Press

NEW YORK

This is a work of fiction. All of the characters, organizations, and events portrayed in this novel are either products of the author's imagination or are used fictitiously.

MAY 1 8 2010

THE LADY AND THE POET. *Copyright © 2009 by Maeve Haran.*
All rights reserved. Printed in the United States of America.
For information, address St. Martin's Press,
175 Fifth Avenue, New York, N.Y. 10010.

www.stmartins.com

Library of Congress Cataloging-in-Publication Data

Haran, Maeve
   The lady and the poet / Maeve Haran. — 1st U.S. ed.
      p. cm.
   ISBN 978-0-312-55415-6
   1. Donne, John, 1572–1631–Fiction.   2. London (England)–History–16th century–Fiction.   I. Title
   PR9199. 4. H3626L33 2009
   813'.6–dc22   2009017050

First published in Great Britain by Pan Books,
an imprint of Pan Macmillan Ltd.

First U.S. Edition: March 2010

10   9   8   7   6   5   4   3   2   1

For AG my JD

THE GOOD MORROW

I wonder by my troth, what thou, and I
Did, till we loved? Were we not weaned till then,
But sucked on country pleasures, childishly?
Or snorted we in the seven sleepers' den?
'Twas so; but this, all pleasures fancies be.
If ever any beauty I did see,
Which I desired, and got, 'twas but a dream of thee.

And now good morrow to our waking souls,
Which watch not one another out of fear;
For love, all love of other sights controls,
And makes one little room, an everywhere.
Let sea-discoverers to new worlds have gone,
Let maps to others, worlds on worlds have shown,
Let us possess one world, each hath one, and is one.

My face in thine eye, thine in mine appears,
And true plain hearts do in the faces rest,
Where can we find two better hemispheres
Without sharp north, without declining west?
Whatever dies, was not mixed equally;
If our two loves be one, or, thou and I
Love so alike, that none can slacken, none can die.

The Lady and the Poet

Chapter 1

'THIS IS YOUR fault, Mistress Elizabeth More!'

I poked my sister awake in the great bed we shared and she smiled at me, her eyes full of sleep and contentment. 'For the sake of your stupid marriage we must vacate the house today that they may sweeten it.' I imitated the haughty tones of my grandmother. '"I will not have the county's nobility hold their noses while they relieve themselves in my privy." So thanks to you, Bett, they are to empty the house of offices and strew herbs and fresh rushes on every floor.'

'Has Father forgiven me for wanting the marriage here and not in London where Queen Elizabeth might attend?' Bett reached out her hand and gently pushed a strand of my busy auburn curls back inside my cap. They will never stay there.

I laughed. 'Oh, he agreed soon enough when Grandfather offered to charge the wedding to his own expense.'

My father, though plentifully rich, is apt to be careful with his money.

Looking across at my sister's lovely face, which I have woken up to see each morning of my life, I felt a sudden sadness swooping down upon me. She is the one, since our mother's loss when I was but a maid of tender years, whom I have held closest to my heart.

And yet by temperament we are like distant continents. While I am fire and air, ever ready to argue and dispute when I should be humble, my dearest Bett is earth and water. She is as calm as a chapel in the stillness of the day, and her eyes hold that same clear brightness of sunlight on the sea. And she is so kind! While my temper is tried by the smallest trifle—the bread with our daily soup being hard, pricking my finger on a needle, my grandmother's eternal chivvying—Bett is ever sweet and smiling. And when Frances, our youngest sister, although but ten years old, drives me to distraction with her tidying and sermonizing, Bett tells me that it is Frances, not I, who is the model for a good Christian wife and I must hold my peace.

Marriage holds no fears for Bett. She cares nothing that her betrothed, Sir John, is portly and pompous, and that he wants a wife more for her dowry and her docility than her sweetness or her spirit. It does not stir Bett to anger, as it does me, that daughters can be bought and bargained over like cows at a market place, and that the first questions before any betrothal are how large is the marriage portion and how advantageous is the settlement. These things are natural, according to my lady grandmother. What is not natural is love.

My grandmother says love cools, leaving nothing but a burned-out pot that others must clean. Perhaps Bett will be happy then with her husband, who cares more for hawking and hunting than for the joys of a new bride.

The house beneath us began to stir. It was Sunday so there would be no morning prayers, since we go to church. The servants were already stowing away the pallets they had slept on in the Great Hall and lighting the fire before all must leave for worship. Soon the whole house would be busy. Sometimes, I think, with fifty servants, not to mention we five, and passing guests who must be given a bed, there is no nook or cranny in my grandfather's house where it is possible to be alone.

Even in bed.

As I thought of Bett's marriage I wondered for a moment what it would be like to climb beneath the covers with a man whose eyes were afire not with thoughts of dowries or of marriage negotiations but with love and desire, and I felt suddenly stirred. Across the pillow Bett looked at me.

'What a strange smile, Ann. As if you had tasted a ripe peach from our grandfather's hothouse and the juice was running down your chin.'

I laughed in shyness at the accuracy of her words. 'What will I do when you have left me, Bett?'

'You will come often to Camois Court and visit me. It is not so far away. Half a day's ride, no more, on your sturdy old cob.'

'Half a day! That sounds like half an eternity!'

I pulled back the curtains of the bed, our private world, as pale light filtered into the big, cold room. We are fortunate, I know, to have our own chamber. Sometimes, when the house is full, five or six must be accommodated here, often sharing a bed with a stranger, the visiting servants abed in the passageways or sleeping on truckles with their master or mistress.

The old manor house of Loseley, near Guildford in the county of Surrey, was built by my great-grandfather, Sir Christopher More, and my grandfather inherited it. My grandfather might have gone on dwelling there, since it was a solid old house, if somewhat lacking in luxuries, but Queen Elizabeth chided him. He needed a fine new house, she said, so that she might come and stay with him on one of her summer progresses.

Queen Elizabeth's subjects do not need to be told her wishes twice. So my grandfather, Sir William More, built a fine new house using the stone from nearby Waverley Abbey, a Cistercian monastery before the Dissolution. Being a careful man he supervised the building himself at cost of £1,640 19s and 7d and still has the account books to prove it. Yet I think my grandfather regretted his largesse when the Queen and all her retinue of servants and courtiers, three hundred in all, with more than a hundred cartloads of belongings, even with their own hangings and furniture lest ours was not good enough, came to stay three times more. Some gentlemen, I have heard tell, were made bankrupt by the Queen's visits, with all the food and fine wine her followers insisted upon, and the masques that had to be performed, the musicians provided, and all at the host's own expense. And each time she came the Queen insisted my grandfather remove us, his family, to another place and lay straw along the roads so that her coach would not jolt her uncomfortably. He must needs take with him, she commanded, any female servant, since she liked not the whiny voices of women. Even when my grandfather pleaded illness the Queen ignored him and moved in anyway, telling him that Loseley must be left cleaner than the last time.

The house, long and wide, with many great chimneys, is faced with twenty-two loads of stone that have been quarried in nearby Guildford then cut in half, and has pillars built of rock from Hascome Hill. It has three storeys, the lowest of which houses the Great Hall, withdrawing chamber and my grandfather's library, as well as kitchens, pantries and scullery. Above are the bedchambers, looking out over rolling pasture, and on the highest floor are quarters for the servants and less important guests. It is a plain house compared to some newer, showier mansions, more glass than wall, built by ambitious upstarts who have prospered under the Queen, but my grandfather says it has a quiet and distinguished air as befits a gentleman's abode.

As my grandmother reminds us often, we are privileged to live in a house with fine furniture, warm wainscoting on the walls, which has been carved by master carvers, and rich tapestries to keep the wind from whistling through any cracks in the stonework.

Loseley has a great green parkland all round it, with deer nibbling at the grass—when they are not the quarry of my brother Robert's hunting—and a kitchen garden behind leading back to a moat and stewpond, where fish are kept for the table. There is even said to be a secret passage to the cellars which we all hunted for as children, yet never found.

Bett and I dressed hurriedly, helping each other to lace up our stomachers and to tie our sleeves to our gowns, glad they were made of the fine wool of England. Prudence, our tire-woman, had laid out bread and small beer that we might break our fast. After a last check in the glass above the press I went and looked for my grandmother.

I have always lived in this house, yet my father, George More, lives not here with us which some consider strange. The truth is, he cannot get on with his father, our grandfather, for he wishes to have his own way in the running of the place, yet my grandfather feels himself to be still master here. 'The trouble with the Mores,' my father once said sharply under his breath, 'is that they live too damned long.'

When our mother died he married swiftly again, and with his new wife's money built another mansion nearby at Baynard's. He took our brother Robert, his heir, to live with him but left us five girls here at Loseley with our grandparents, Sir William and the lady Margaret.

I love my grandparents staunchly, but I was sore hurt by this election. I knew it was much to do with my father's new wife, Constance, a shrewish woman who wanted children of her own to replace us in our father's affections. 'For who would want a great brood of daughters cluttering up the hall?' we heard her ask her guests on more than one occasion. To which my eldest sister Mary, who is elemented with fire even more than I, remarked, 'And who would want a stepmother who is as soft and appealing as the sow of a boar?'

I must confess to kneeling by my bed and imploring God who is our Saviour to send my stepmother only female children, and to my great, though possibly impious, satisfaction he has sent her none at all. So my brother Robert remains sole heir.

Perhaps to assuage his guilt at our abandonment, and to Constance's great anger and resentment, our father set aside the profits of several rents and leases to be used by my grandfather solely for the advancement and education of myself and my four sisters. Since my grandfather is a learned man, equally at home with the works of Seneca or Aristotle, he has tried to pass his learning on to us, feeble women though we are.

I cannot help but smile at our differing responses. My sister Mary, the eldest of us, was an apt pupil, quickly learning to speak in French and Italian, though fonder of reading the love poems of the troubadours than the history of the Roman Empire. My sister Margaret simply sighed and stated there was no rhyme or reason why a woman should wish to know any tongue but her own, and that she would rather learn the skills of my grandmother in the herb garden or the cook in the kitchen. My beloved Bett tried to listen, but her mind was ever wandering to the sunshine outside, or the sound of the birds singing. My sister Frances was too young for schooling, and so happily sewed her samplers, choosing the worthiest mottoes she could find.

That left myself. And I was different from the rest. I felt for all the world like a plant that had been withering away and was given a sudden dose of water and sunshine, so that I bloomed and bloomed. Indeed, I worked so hard at my lessons that my grandmother had to stop me, telling me I would lose my eyesight, or acquire a brain fever. Normally a dutiful wife, my grandmother castigated her husband for creating a strange freakish thing—a woman too educated for her own good. 'For what man,' she asked him angrily, 'will want a wife who can quote philosophers yet her servants run idle and her meats burn in the fire?'

My grandfather listened, for my grandmother, when roused, is a fearsome lady. Indeed, I once heard a groom of the Great Chamber say her face was like to a statue carved from granite and that the sternness of her lips made him think of the general of an army. And yet, beneath all, there is a kindness she seeks hard to conceal. After that I was forbidden to study after the hour of three in the afternoon.

I walked down to the Great Hall, a fine large room with windows running from floor to ceiling looking out over the park. The windows are adorned in stained glass with the More coat of arms so that when the slanting sun shines through them, a light like rubies and emeralds plays on the wood of the floor. My favourite piece of glass, no more than four or five inches long, shows a lord and lady sitting at the table in their great hall, eating. It is like a tiny world in miniature of our own. It must have made the artisan who fashioned it laugh to think there would be two tables and two sets of lords and ladies eating in this room, the Mores, and these tiny creations caught in glass.

On all the wainscoted walls fine family portraits look down upon us. The floor in this room is wooden, strewn with fresh rushes thrice a week. A busy fire roars next to a likeness of King Edward, the boy King, and a vast candleholder, already blazing with light at this early hour, hangs from the dark beams, lighting up a fine plaster ceiling. By the great front door we could hear a loud commotion announcing that my father has arrived and is already in hot debate with my grandfather. It made me remember what a good scheme it had been that they lived not together in the same house.

'Greetings, Father,' I saluted him. Even when he is riding out in Surrey, twenty-five miles from the Court or Parliament, my father likes to dress according to his rank. His doublet is of black velvet, adorned with wide runnels of gold thread, his hose are elaborately worked in a similar pattern, and these are topped with a wide black hat which, like most gentlemen, he keeps on even during meals. He would argue that he has a position to keep up, as a member of Parliament and a busy local official.

'Ann. Good morrow.' Piercing grey eyes shone out from a long but fine-featured face with a wisp of moustache and a pale, gingery beard.

It was my father's habit to decry men with full beards, yet I know secretly he envied the dashing square-cut beard of the Earl of Essex, still the idol of the age to most, though his standing with the Queen seems to change like a weathercock depending on news of the campaigning abroad. 'Are your sisters yet arrived?'

'No, Father. I had thought the sound of your horse might be their approach.'

'Your sister Mary is no doubt in two minds which of her jewels to dazzle us with,' my father answered rudely, 'when I know that husband of hers has not two angels to rub together. That young man has been a severe disappointment to me. He may have expectations, but expectations can be empty as a rattling gourd unless they lead to wealth and power. Any jewels she wears will have been borrowed against three times over.' I felt a moment's sorrow for Mary, who thought she would indeed impress us rustics with her displays of finery, not knowing my father would have unmasked her so completely.

Mary's husband, Nicholas Throckmorton, comes from a good family but had the misfortune to be a younger son. He does, though, have connections, his sister Bess being married to Sir Walter Ralegh. And connections, in these days when advancement rests on the good word of one in power for another, were hard currency. It was his connections that had persuaded my father to agree to Mary's marriage. But as yet, to my father's violent choler, no advantage to our family had been forthcoming. In fact, Nicholas had made the severe error of asking my father to lend him money.

The most noticeable thing about my father is his height. Or rather, lack of it. When my grandfather and father stand side by side it is hard to see that they are father and son. My father is so small of stature that he can never stand pall-bearer at funerals lest the coffin slip untimely into the grave. Yet he is forever ready to fire up if he thinks himself the victim of a slight, while my grandfather, who is taller and thickset, with eyes that are kind yet sharp, and a long white beard, forked at the tip as is the fashion, seems to possess all the calmness of God the Father, if that be not blasphemous, and much of his patience. Which is needed often when dealing with my father. My grandfather was not always so calm. In his youth, I have heard, he turned against the

Romish religion which he had followed and became a fierce scourge of all the Papists, who rightly feared him.

Now they fell to discussing whether to add swags of herbs and red berries to the carved ceiling of the Great Hall for Bett's marriage feast.

'Yes, yes,' insisted my father, 'you need some colour to cheer up the gloom of this great old-fashioned cavern. If we were at my home we could feast in the gallery. I cannot believe, Father,' he shook his head in amazement, 'how you can do without a gallery and that you dine still in this hall, with all the servants, and have no privacy for discourse or witty conversation. At Baynard's we have given up dining in the hall for a comfortable dining chamber and have the upstairs gallery where we can walk and talk while the sun streams in and warms us all year round.'

I could see my grandfather wrestled with telling him to go back to his treasured Baynard's and be done with it. 'I do not need to eat privately from my servants,' Grandfather informed him. 'My servants are part of my family and will always be so. Next you will be advocating the groom of my bedchamber no longer sleeps outside my door or that, for the sake of privacy, I lead not the household in prayers thrice a day. I am the head of the house and such traditions are important to me, as they ought to be to you.'

My father, with his usual tact, ignored him. 'Comfort's the thing nowadays, Father. We don't have to live like beasts of the field or poor peasant farmers. Take those great hard beds of yours. You should replace them all with feather mattresses.'

'Forget your feather beds,' Grandfather replied, containing his anger with difficulty. 'In my father's day they slept on straw pallets with covers of dogswain or hopharlots, and a good round log under their head instead of a pillow. A pillow was only for women in childbed. If he had acquired a mattress after seven years of marriage a man thought himself well set up. Not like your bed, eh, George?' This was a subject of some delicacy since my father had spent a deal of Constance's money on the bedchamber. Grandfather smiled slyly to himself. 'I hear yours is topped with a gilded coronet and seven plumes of egrets' feathers like the Queen's. A good thing the sumptuary laws regulate clothing and not the lavishness of the bedchamber, eh?'

All around us in the Great Hall servants scurried, weighed down with armloads of cloths, silver chargers and pewter trenchers, candle-sticks and silver plate, and a vast Turkey carpet to lay upon the great table at one end of the room for the wedding feast.

'You will never fit all the guests in here,' announced my father with a hint of satisfaction.

'Why, Father,' I almost asked, 'perhaps we should be holding the wedding feast at Baynard's instead?' But I held my peace. My father expects respect from his daughters and it is not worth risking my sister's happiness by challenging him.

'Which is why we have five tents being erected outside in the park,' answered my grandfather shortly. 'Each decorated with painted hangings from Italy as Great Harry used in his tents on the battlefield. The musicians will play in one and the masque is to be performed in another.'

A sudden wailing from outside the scullery made us all turn to see what was amiss. As well as the sweetening of the floors and privies, today is the day my grandmother has appointed as washday for the great tablecloths needed for the wedding feast, and for the small towel each guest will place over his shoulder or arm to wipe his hands during the meal.

Miriam, one of the washer maids, was standing next to the great buck tubs, made of half-barrels, cradling her face and crying because my grandmother has just boxed her ears. 'The stupid girl has forgotten to empty the piss-pot into the ley,' accused my grandmother, pointing to the tubs where the cloths had been carefully folded with sticks supporting each layer so that water may filter through. 'How does she expect us to shift these stains without the aid of urine? Silly girl! Do you think we keep the piss for our own pleasure, to sniff at it like some posy?'

Miriam cowered in the corner. 'Go and find fresh piss from one of the bedchambers and bring it to me direct. I will supervise the next wash since you have not the wits to do it. One more mistake and I will send you home to your farm where you can break your back picking turnips and lay your stupid head down in the midden instead of on a clean straw pallet in a gentleman's house!'

My father, bored by household drama, spied my sister Bett, who had just come downstairs to assist us.

'Ah, here is Elizabeth, our comely bride.' He turned to me. 'A shame that you did not inherit your mother's beauty, Ann, as Elizabeth has.'

Even after all these years my father's cruelty wounds like the sting of a wasp. I know I am not as lovely as my sister, but do not the soul and the mind have beauty too?

My sister, all happiness, noticed none of the acrimony and kissed my father prettily. 'Thank you for the fur, Father. I shall be as grand as any rich Court lady.'

My father bristled. 'The Mores are as honourable as any at Court, Elizabeth. And more gentle than many favourites who have come lately.'

This I knew to be only partly true. The More fortunes had risen with my great-grandfather. He too was a new man, not noble, but elevated in the service of the crown, yet we were high enough now and would go higher if my father had his way.

My grandmother emerged from the scullery wiping her hands. 'George. The very person I was hoping to see. Will you be going to London between now and the marriage day? I am out of all humour with the clerk of the kitchen who has forgotten to order sugar for the Hippocras wine. How can we have a wedding toast without that? And no more currants, either, to sweeten our meats.'

My father shrugged, wanting to hold on to the subject of the honour of the Mores as a dog does a bone. 'I have no plans to visit the city until next week when I sit on three committees, but I have a man in Cheapside who will send you sugar and currants if you pay for a messenger.'

'Thank you, my son,' my grandmother nodded. 'I will certainly apply to him. Robert, the clerk, believes our last supply was eaten by rats, though it may be he covers up his own bad ordering. Now he has strung all our sweet fruit for the marriage feast in a basket four feet from the ground.'

As if in endorsement of the clerk's claim we heard a loud shout coming from the kitchen and saw a rat scurry past us, pursued by a crowd of shouting grooms and ushers, all milling helplessly about like virgins at the sight of an invading army.

Impatiently I grabbed the wooden bucking spade used to turn the clothing in the wash barrels and laid about the rat with it. I know not who was more surprised, the rat or I. Until I caught him square on, as a mallet catches a croquet ball at Hampton Court, and he spun up into the air then landed with a thud, dead, at our feet.

'Ann, Ann,' protested my father, 'truly I despair of you. When will you ever learn to behave like a gentlewoman?'

'Am I supposed to climb upon a stool when I see a rat and shout until I am rescued like a maiden saved from the dragon by some brave St George? Is that the act of a gentlewoman? Then you are right, Father, I am no gentlewoman.'

At the far end of the path to Loseley we heard the ring of horseshoes on the road and round the bend from the south my sister Mary, slender as a willow reed in smart riding habit and feathered hat, rode into view on a chestnut mare. Behind her, stouter even than when I saw her last, was my sister Margaret, the happiest girl I ever knew. Margaret was happy with all things: her husband Thomas Grymes, her home in Peckham, her new tapestries, her baby son, even her dogs were the best dogs ever owned.

'Bett! Ann!' called Mary as she jumped gracefully out of the saddle. 'Bett, you are as lovely as ever and hardly old enough to be a bride!' She held my sister at arm's length. 'To think, from now on you will look like Margaret, a happy barrel, carrying a baby every year until you are forty!'

'My sister is envious,' Margaret announced calmly, even though she needed two grooms of the horse to lift her down. 'Since I am content with my babe and my Thomas while her husband gambles, goes ever to cocking, or the playhouse and the bowling alley, and rarely spends time enough at home with her even to change his hose.'

'Aye. But then your Thomas is as dull as an attorney's clerk.'

'Hush, Mary, you ever had a forward tongue.' My grandmother nodded her head towards the group of servants who had appeared from nowhere at the approach of horses' hooves to welcome my sisters back to their family home.

'Besides,' I could not resist adding in a voice too low for Grandmother to catch, 'you manage not to be always with child yourself, Mary.'

'Tis a great skill,' Mary winked. 'I have two babes and intend to give my husband his heir and one to spare so I need not forever be a brood mare for the Throckmortons.'

'A dangerous practice.' My grandmother's ears were sharper than we had thought. 'My kitchen cat has more sense than that. She knows disease can wipe out her young so she has many litters.'

'Worry not, my lady grandmother,' Mary replied. 'I intend more kittens later. At the moment I am having a rest. From breeding. And from husbands.'

'Then keep your eye on the tom cat,' my grandmother said as she shook out the cleaning clout. 'He may seek his cream elsewhere.'

The remaining days before Bett's marriage passed in the busy bustle of servants, the shouts of my grandmother ordering furniture to be moved from one room to another, the arrival of what seemed like storerooms' worth of provisions, and the cook filling every larder and scullery with pies, sweetmeats and marchpanes for my sister's celebration. The tablecloths, with the piss now added, lay drying on bushes in the park, pewter chargers were scrubbed with sharp river sand or horsetails picked from the garden. Plate was polished, and trenchers were carved out of four-day-old rye bread for the meats to be served to my sister's guests.

Even though it was summer the weather was so cold that there was a fire in the Great Hall night and day, and the servants who slept there on pallets were glad of its glow. I was glad, too, of Bett's warm body close to mine, lying next to each other in the big curtained bed. Unlike I, who was always restless and eager for the morn to arrive, she slept like an angel, often with a smile on her face. Softly, I touched her cheek. Did she, as my father said, share the features of our lost mother?

If our mother still lived how different things would be. My father, without a shrewish wife at his side, would have been softer, our mother a balm to his bitterness and bile. And we five girls would have had a mother's love and a mother's lore to help us through life. My grandmother, I knew, had done her best to mother us, but she was so brisk, so caught up with the daily necessities of life, that she had scant time for mothering, and it was not in her nature to pet and indulge. At least Bett, Margaret, Mary and I had known our mother a little. Poor Frances, our youngest sister, who lived while our mother lost her life in childbed, had not known her at all. Hard though it might be, I resolved to be gentler with Frances. And today, the occasion of her wedding, I would help Bett to think only of happy things.

As the first light of dawn filtered through the windows on the great day I slipped from the bed. It was a sunny morning but the rays did not warm us since our room faced north, always accounted the healthiest direction, the belief being that none of the diseases from the Continent could blow therefore into the bedchamber. My feet froze with nothing but rushes to warm the cold wooden floor.

Hearing me move around, Bett opened her eyes. Usually she could sleep all morning in her nest of covers, almost until the midday meat was on the table, unless my grandmother came to scold her for her idleness.

'Only a few more hours,' I said softly to her. 'And you will be my lady Mills.'

'And no longer a maid.'

'Are you frightened of that?' Myself, I thought it sounded a great adventure. 'Mary says it can be a duty or a pleasure, depending on the skill of your husband.'

I pictured heavy Sir John, with his thoughts of hunting the hart and filling his trencher. It did not bode well.

'And Margaret says I must view it like putting grease on the wheel of a farmyard cart. All moves better when it is done.'

We both laughed at our sister Margaret's prosaic turn of mind. 'Practical Meg. How poetical! She must have been studying the lyrical verses of Sir Philip Sidney!'

Now that the day had finally come I almost cried. Instead I bit back my salt tears and helped Bett into her bridal attire. Since children we had helped each other with the elaborate rituals of a gentlewoman's wardrobe. Clean linen shift first, and for today silken stockings worked in silver stitching, then into the hooped farthingale petticoat, afterwards lacing up her velvet stomacher, stitched with tiny seed pearls, before tying on the skirts of her red taffeta gown, its sleeves adorned with my father's gift of fur. Next came the dainty slippers with their elaborate shoe roses in white and red. Lastly I took down the starched ruff, as delicate as a spider's web, from the curtain where last night I had pinned it, that it might keep its stiffness and not be crushed. I attached it tenderly, smiling at Bett's small white breasts, like two white half-moons, spilling from her dress. After today, as a married woman, they would be covered from the gaze of other men.

With Prudence's help I combed her hair and left it hanging loose and shining like a pale river of silk, as only a virgin is entitled to wear it.

She looked lovelier than I had ever seen her.

I, too, had tried to look my best, in a kirtle and gown of yellow silk that I fancied brought out the burnished colours of my hair and eyes.

Bett turned to me. 'I wish our mother were here this day,' she sighed.

I held my sister so close I could feel her heart beating close to mine. 'She will be, Bett. If we believe in the immortality of souls, then hers will be here with us this day.'

We descended the great staircase. My father stood waiting at the foot.

'Bett, you are truly beautiful.' I saw no sign of his wife, Constance, and hoped he had left her at home with the other sows from his piggery.

'Thank you, Father.'

To my surprise he turned to me. 'I know you are no beauty, Ann, but you have the Poynings' eyes. Warm and nut brown like the shiny seed of the chestnut that boys so love to play with.'

It was mixed enough as flattery goes, yet it brought a lump to my throat for compliments from my father were as thin upon the ground as rose petals in winter. I stored this one up as a squirrel does his autumn store. 'Thank you, Father, I am happy you think so.'

And so we processed down to the church, my sisters Margaret and Mary, my brother Robert, and silly Frances, my father and Constance, who had now appeared decked out in as much finery as if it were she who was the bride in Bett's place, as well as my grandparents and the noisily sniffing Prudence. My cousin Francis had just arrived from London, but without his mother, my aunt Elizabeth.

Sir John, the groom, looking for all the world like a fat sausage encased in black velvet, stood waiting for his bride at the church door. There, according to the old traditions, he and Bett exchanged vows and rings where all could see, to a great cheer from the guests within and from my grandfather's servants who had gathered in the churchyard as thick as the faithful on Christmas morning.

After this as many as could fit inside went to see them blessed and shared the toast of Hippocras wine, sweetened by the good offices of the merchant my father had recommended in Cheapside, who had sent the sugar down on horseback with his wishes for their happiness together with a large bill.

Once they had exchanged their vows and were blessed Bett took it on herself to say a prayer, which she read out in a clear and sweet voice. 'Give me the Grace, Lord, to acknowledge my husband to be my head, to reverence him, obey him, to please him and be ruled by him in all things. Amen.'

I caught Mary's eye and saw that she was shaking her head. 'Forgive her, Father,' she whispered softly, 'she knows not yet that husbands need no encouraging.'

After the vows the Hippocras wine was passed round all the pews before my grandfather led his guests away from the church to the Great Hall and tents arranged in the park for feasting and jollity.

There was such a weight of food that you would think an army was expected. Three oxen were turning on giant spits, while six sheep had lain two days in hot ashes. There were peacocks stuffed with pheasant and other small birds. There were boiled capons in lemon sauce, baked rabbit with pickled cowcumbers, spinach tart, stewed oysters, all to be washed down with sweet wines, small beer and lemon mead especially for the wedding pair and followed up with preserved fruits, macaroons and baked custards.

The final centrepiece was a vast marzipan confection gilded with gold leaf and bearing birds, beasts, twists of sugar rope and the coats of arms of both the More and Mills families entwined, which had taken my grandmother's pastry cook three days, eight pounds of almonds, a pint of rose water and a restorative gallon of strong ale to complete.

At every guest's place there was a favour of perfumed gloves, scented soap, sweet bags for the linen closet, or water distilled from rose petal, dried orange peel, musk, civet, precious gums and oil of jessamine.

My sister Mary had slipped away after the blessing and changed her gown into one that showed off the flashing jewels my father had told us were borrowed three times against, which took away some of their lustre.

Margaret piled her plate with sweetmeats, then surprised us all by dancing a galliard with her husband Thomas, with all the grace of a thistledown on the summer wind.

It was, I had to admit, a gathering grand and glorious enough to please even my father's demanding tastes. The women wore silk, brocade or cloth of gold, some encrusted with garnets or aquamarines, others with heavily worked silver thread or coloured embroidery. As the dancers whirled by to the sound of harps, lutes and drums, the diamonds and emeralds pinned in their hair flashed like sun lighting the stained-glass windows in the hall.

Mary appeared at my side, slyly pointing to the bridegroom. 'Have you seen that thing in Sir John's ear?' Our portly new relation, apart from his unflattering velvet hose, was sporting a vast pearl earring, which threatened almost to tear the lobe away, were it not so firmly bulked by Sir John's jowly flesh. 'Poor man, he thinks to copy Nick's brother-in-law, Sir Walter Ralegh, without an ounce of his charm! You could as much put a pearl in a pig's ear, it would look as fine. The man must weigh more than three great sacks of lime. Tonight poor Bett will be crushed like grain under a millstone!'

'Mary!' I dug her in her ribs, which were well laced in, causing her breasts to stick very much out under their filmy covering. If Mary could have displayed them openly, she would. I had heard her moaning—discreetly, thank the Almighty, or we would all be in the Tower—that despite all of her sixty-five years, Queen Elizabeth could still show off her bosoms, since she might at least claim to be a virgin, yet no one would want to look at them.

'Ssssh, Mary! Sir John is standing by.' I saw my sister's new husband approach us with a gleam in his eye that was not entirely brotherly. 'God's blood, I wish I did not have to choose between you, but could take you all to my bed.'

'Except that I have a husband already,' Mary's wicked eyes sparkled, 'and my sister Margaret could not be parted from her marchpane cake, and Ann here thinks men are poor creatures only interested in their horses and their hounds, do you not, Ann?'

'How proud must you be, Sir John,' I steered the subject away from such dangerous waters, 'that this day is finally come.'

'Certain, I am proud,' he quaffed another tankard of mead, 'for it is a special day indeed. This very morning out hunting I brought down two white harts on the hunting field. You don't see that every day of the week.'

I had to stifle my laughter and avoid the merry looks from my sister Mary.

What an oaf the man is.

Two of his retinue came lumbering up from one of the other tents. 'Sir John,' slurred the first in drunken tones, 'I've just heard an apt saying for you: "A wife, a spaniel, a walnut tree; the more you beat them, the better they be."'

They all laughed with great gusto. The next fool decided to embroider the theme. 'As my father was wont to tell my mother, "Women and horses must be well governed."'

'Apt indeed,' I replied, my voice all maidenly sweetness. 'And our grandmother has a saying also. "The happiest day of a woman's life is when she becomes a wife—and the second happiest is when she is made a widow!"'

At this the gentlemen staggered off to find more ale and sweeter company.

'Tsk, tsk, Ann,' Mary chided, taking my arm, 'you will never find a husband that way.'

The night was drawing on into the early hours. Torches flickered in their sconces and the candles were burning low. The grooms of the Great Chamber tried to hide their yawns. Even my grandfather's dogs were creeping to the fireside. The musicians, knowing their vail would be the greater if they kept the festivities going as long as possible, struck up another air.

Everyone knew that the time of the bedding was getting closer. Sir John summoned the cupbearer for a final filling of his tankard with mead. 'Come, wife,' he grabbed Bett by her wrist, half rough, half playful, 'time for you and I to climb the stairs together now that we are well and truly wed.'

At this news there was a great crash on the drums and all in the hall and outlying tents started to follow the blushing Bett and her husband through the Withdrawing Room, up the stairs and along the passage thence right up to the door of their bedchamber.

Mary, Margaret and I then shut the guests and bridegroom out, Frances for once losing her holy looks when told she was too young for such practices, and helped our sister undress. We arrayed her in her new nightgown, with its collar of fine cobweb lace, and laid her gently on the bed.

'Ann! Mary!' she suddenly beseeched us. 'Don't leave me here!'

Mary soothed her, sitting down next to her on the great bed. 'Don't fret. With luck he'll have had too much mead to do his work.'

'Let's hope she's had enough herself not to notice,' added Margaret.

Mary began to giggle as, behind her, an apparition appeared. It was Sir John, dressed in his nightshirt, led by his two friends, while his family stood at the door cheering him on as if he were a nag running in some horse race.

I bit my lip. Under the fine lawn of his shirt his member stood stiffly to attention.

'Oh dear,' Margaret whispered, 'the mead has fired him up instead of damping him down.'

At that my grandmother arrived, carrying two pewter mugs. 'Make way for the bridegroom's caudle! A little wine mixed with milk and cinnamon, sugar and nutmeg to keep your strength up!' She noticed the state of Sir John's member under its white linen nightshirt and shouted with laughter. 'Not that by the looks of things you need it! Let us leave the happy couple to their sport!'

I tried to catch Bett's eye to offer my sympathy that she should be subjected to so undignified a charade. Practices as bawdy as this, after all, had been abandoned by the more elevated of the gentry. I could hardly see London lords and ladies subjecting themselves to mummers' rites. Yet my grandfather liked to respect old ways and country habits and, marvellous to account, my sister seemed quite happy with all the antics and even smiled when the stocking was thrown to mark the wedding night.

At the door of the chamber, beaming like a Cornish pixie, and not much taller either, stood my father.

'Come, everyone. There are more victuals to enjoy downstairs. We need not stay here waiting to inspect the sheets as they did in my grandfather's day. May God grant their union prosper.' He turned to me as we all began to troop downstairs towards the hall and its great warming fire. 'You next, Ann, or as you see, your sister Frances will overtake you in the marriage stakes.'

'Frances is but ten years old, Father,' I reminded him.

'All the better. Old enough to be betrothed and young enough not to cavil at my choice.' He looked at me levelly. 'Unlike some young women.'

'Yes, Ann,' murmured Mary archly, 'you wouldn't wish to find yourself an old maid, would you?'

'If otherwise I must have such a husband as yours, who buries you in worry and debt, then I would rather stay unwed!' the Devil prompted me to reply. Yet I resisted as I knew Mary fretted about her husband's extravagant ways. 'Of course I want a husband. I am not so strange and freakish as to turn entirely from the joys of hearth and home. But can I have no say in what manner of man he is? Must he be chosen simply for the advancement of the More family?'

That night as I knelt, alone, to say my prayers, I tried not to let my mind roam to what was unfolding in Bett's bridal chamber.

'O Lord, dear Lord and Saviour,' I whispered into the empty darkness, 'if I must have a husband let him neither dolt nor debtor be, nor dullard either. For it seems to me, Lord, that these are the fates of my dear sisters.'

Chapter 2

THE NEXT DAY dawned warm and glorious and yet the thought of Bett's departure dulled the golden light of morning more than the blackest of clouds. No longer would I wake each day with my beloved sister.

From this day on I would have to share a bed with Frances, who could not stay still one moment, except when she knelt in prayer for longer than a martyred saint. Even now with the sun hardly up she had risen from our bed and stood gazing at a picture I had always hated. It was the painted figure of a woman holding a finger to her lips, denoting modesty and silence, a set of keys at her waist to signify household efficiency, standing of all things on a tethered tortoise, which—my grandmother once explained to me—meant that, like the tortoise, she would never roam. This was the supposed portrait of an ideal wife.

'I long to be married,' sighed Frances. 'To have a husband and a household of my own to look after. Do not you, Ann?'

I had lain in bed last night thinking of these things also. And had concluded that the husband for me was one who allowed me a soul to feel and a brain to think with. And sometimes I wondered where on this earth I might ever find him.

I admired my sister Mary for her easy acceptance of the married state, even though she is married to a spendthrift. She has such natural ease, a way of handling all things—household, husband, dogs, servants, that I could not but envy. All do exactly as she bids them. She even seems to relish the ambition and scheming of the Throckmortons and is dazzled by their nearness to Court life.

And Margaret is simply Margaret, not so very much older than I in years but like a settled goodwife, relishing the rocklike safety her Thomas affords her and the peace of living in Peckham, near enough to London but also far enough away, unshakeable in her contentment.

'It would serve you right,' Frances intoned, her piety slipping to reveal a fissure of malice beneath, 'if Father found you a husband who demanded obedience and shamefast modesty in his lady.'

'And it would serve *you* right if Father decided he and Constance needed someone to look after them in their ageing years, and that you, the youngest daughter, should forgo the joys of marriage and family and be the one to do it.'

Frances looked so stricken I had to take pity on her. 'You do not truly think they would do so?'

'No. Father is too ambitious. He wants good marriages for all of us because his own standing requires it. If we marry not at all or—worse— marry badly then in the world's eyes all the family is diminished, or so he says. That is why he is so angry with Mary's husband. With his connections he should have got far. But Nick prefers his own amusement to advancing the family interests.'

Frances studied me, as if she possessed some valuable piece of information still denied to me, like the cat that had got to the cream first.

'What, Frances? Spit it out or I will pull your cap off and throw it from the window.'

Frances' hand went to her head as if to hold her cap in place. 'I heard Father talking to some old man the other day about his son's prospects. They mentioned your name also.'

All of a sudden my heart beat fast, and my mouth was dry with fear.

'Frances! I am sure eavesdropping like some servant at the keyhole is not God's work. I am surprised at you.'

Frances looked mutinous. 'God's ways are many and various. I thought you would want to know of any marriage negotiations.'

In spite of myself I asked, 'And what was this old man's name?'

She looked at me with her disconcerting pale blue eyes. 'I think my father called him Manners.'

I knew I had to run, to get outside, away from this house which my grandfather had built and which represented, stone by stone, the honour and status of my family.

'Bett is leaving at midday,' she called to my retreating back. 'I heard her tell my grandmother so last night. You'd better be back for that.'

'I will.'

I ran down the back stairs, not towards the open parkland at the front of the house where the revellers from last night might still be sleeping, but towards the moat where the carp swam sleepily amongst the tall reeds. I climbed onto the high wall which separated the kitchen garden from the moat and walked dizzily along it. Everywhere around me nature was breaking forth into leaf and bud and for some strange reason it made me want to weep. I too was tender and green, waiting for the sun to warm me into womanhood, eager and hopeful. Yet I was blessed—or cursed—because though I had passed but fourteen summers, I knew what I did *not* want.

And yet all around me told me I had no power, that I had to simply obey and bend my will to my father's as a dutiful daughter must.

As if in endorsement of this I hear my sister Frances' voice, not pious now, but excited and jealous. 'Ann! Ann!' she calls. 'Bett is leaving! And you are to go to London! To be trained for the Court! Our lady aunt has invited you to live with her and Father has accepted!'

I jumped down from the wall. London and the Court felt like a glittering reprieve from marrying someone I knew not. If I was to go to London the marriage negotiations between my father and this Master Manners's father must have come to naught. Perhaps he wanted a dowry bigger than my father was ready to provide. I knew from the haranguing over my sisters' portions and jointures that marriage negotiations could take longer than fitting out a ship to sail to the Indies and were just as risky. They were often long and bitter and broke down in acrimony, even after months of discussion. With luck, the same had happened here.

Breathlessly I returned with Frances to the house, which was crowded with servants, departing guests and their grooms as well as my sister Bett, her new husband and all his family, who were preparing to journey to his manor at Camois Court.

The sadness at losing her overcame my excitement at going to London.

'Bett, beloved Bett,' I wrapped her in my strongest embrace, 'I can hardly bear to say goodbye.'

'Dearest Ann. It is not as if I leave for a new-found land. I go to Sussex not America! I will write to you weekly. You have my word on it.'

'Time will pass in a trice,' interrupts my grandmother. 'In the wink of an eye Bett will be calling upon you to her childbed, to hold pillows to her head and soothe her brow with chamomile.'

Bett blushed prettily.

'Indeed I am sure she has already made a start!' My grandmother pinched Bett's cheek. 'A fine son to inherit from Sir John.'

Always sons.

Six queens had been married to King Henry and only one son born between them, and he had lived but a few years while our Queen Elizabeth, a mere woman, had reigned over us for forty and brought both peace and stability. And now it started over again, since she had no male heir and everywhere, though it was treason to do so, her people whispered about who would take the crown when she died.

'Farewell, my Ann.' Bett held me fast. 'You will soon forget me in the lures of London. I will be but a country mouse of no interest to a fine Court lady such as you will be.'

I watched outside the great front door, the More coat of arms emblazoned in stone above it to announce our family's stature, until Bett's coach was out of sight. Then I went to look for my grandfather, for it was he, rather than my father, who had studied me closest and most nearly understood my heart.

I found him in his library, my favourite room. Panelled in finest English oak, whose wooden glory had been so carefully crafted by London carpenters to his detailed design, the library was covered on all four sides by shelves, and with small heads of Grandfather's favourite writers peering out as if to say 'Read me!' My grandfather was passing proud of his collection since few individuals possessed libraries, and none so splendid and well stocked as his. From my first years he had encouraged me to read whatever I chose.

Since many books were in Latin or Greek it took me some years of study before I accepted his offer, but once I had acquired some learning in these I would sit in one corner where there was a long low window seat and lose myself in stories of the heroic tales of Ulysses or Hector. Now and then I would stop to look out at the unfolding landscape when the mist lay over the valley or some lone pheasant had strayed out across the lawn, his silly croaking cry belying the finery of his gold and red feathers.

Above the mantelpiece the arms and initials of Queen Elizabeth were carved, to commemorate her various visits to Loseley and to remind us of our important place in the scheme of things.

My grandfather sat in his favourite chair, dozing underneath his portrait painted by one Lucas de Heere, whose work he had admired in Flanders. My sisters shuddered at this image since, alongside the depiction of Grandfather, all clad in black as he ever was, it also contained a grinning skull, resembling Grandfather in every feature, staring back fit to terrify the onlooker.

Yet it was Grandfather who had taken me on his knee, not long after my mother died when I was so young a maid, and smiled at me tenderly. 'In life, death is always with us, Ann, which is why I like this picture. Yet your mother will never leave you. One day you will marry a noble man and have fine children of your own. And you will remember your mother, whom you were named after, and she will smile down upon your children from Heaven where she resides with our eternal Father.'

Ever after, I loved the portrait that scared my sisters so, for it linked me to the love of my grandfather and my lost mother also.

Although he was busy with his work as sheriff of Surrey and Sussex and subsidy commissioner on behalf of Her Majesty, Grandfather took two naps a day, as regular as the tick of his beloved clocks. Sometimes I would be there when he awoke to bring him a tankard of small beer to ease his thirst on awaking.

I did so today. The smile he gave me was of such sweetness.

'Good afternoon, granddaughter,' he greeted me. 'Are you recovered from your galliards and your corantos last night?'

'Grandfather, I am. Have you heard the news?'

'That your sister has left or that you are to go to London?'

I laughed. Of course he would know. Grandfather knew everything. He had, in his youth, been one of the most trusted advisors of the Crown, seeing so much of the Queen that she, making sport with him over the sombre clothes he always wore, dubbed him her 'black husband'—much to the stormy looks from my grandmother, though she hid them from Her Majesty.

'That I am to go to London.'

'A little wounding that my granddaughter looks so happy to be leaving us behind in our provincial hovel while she seeks the gilded guise of the courtier.'

'My lord grandfather! You know I have no time for Court doings. But Loseley will be flat without my dearest sister, Bett.'

'And flatter still without you, sweet Ann. But I have a bone to pick with you, young woman. I find neither my Ovid nor my Catullus and unless your sisters have hired a Latin master or your grandmother has taken to reading the classics instead of receipt books on the pickling of cowcumbers, then the culprit must be you.'

'I am sorry. I will return them to your shelves at once.'

'Thank you, Ann.' And then as an afterthought: 'Tell not your father of your reading habits though. There are passages in Ovid that a young girl's eyes should not be exposed to.'

I knew he talked of the *Ars Amatoria* which indeed had brought a flush to my cheek when I delved discreetly into it, yet I pretended I knew not what he referred to.

'If he thought you had read such passages of Ovid your father would choke on his plate of meats.'

'But the Queen reads Ovid, Grandfather, and has done since she was my own age. My cousin Francis told me so. His father was her Latin Secretary so he must be right.'

'The Queen can do what she likes. The same is not true of all her subjects. I hope I have done the right thing to encourage you to read as widely as I have.'

'Of course you have, Grandfather. How can learning and knowledge ever be a bad thing?'

'In men, yes. But women? Learning is dangerous in women; many say it makes them cunning, like foxes.'

I kissed my grandfather's brow. 'Then I will be cunning as a fox and hide my learning from all but you.'

'I fear it will curb your taste for ordinary life.'

'And frighten off husbands?'

'God ordained women to be wives and mothers. It is an important estate.'

'I know, Grandfather. Yet perhaps it might frighten off the wrong kind of husband.'

'Your grandmother and I will miss you.'

I took his hand, all seamed with veins, and kissed it.

'After all, who will be Ratcatcher in Chief when you are gone?'

The thought of Frances' revelation about my suitor came into my mind, the one shadow on my newly sunny horizon. 'Grandfather . . .' The hesitation in my voice made him look up.

'Yes, Ann?'

'Do you know of a gentleman called Manners?'

The expression in his eyes, like that of a weasel with someone's pet mouse in its jaws, told me all.

'Ann, my Ann,' he replied gently, the paper thinness of his skin suddenly reminding me of the skull in the portrait. 'You have to wed some time. There is no other calling for a woman.'

I walked out into the grounds to imprint them on my memory. I loved this house, its peace and stark grey beauty. But I knew also that life was not as easy for others as it had been for us. I had seen the hordes of wandering beggars, driven off their land by enclosures for sheep, and how they ended up being shuffled from parish to parish, or chased away with sticks, since no one wanted to pay for their upkeep. Some of them ended up in the manor courts my grandfather presided over. I had witnessed the bad harvests also, four of them in cruel succession, that had blighted the life of the villagers, making them thin and pale and anxious, only kept from starving by the pigs they each kept in their small cottages.

Indeed there was so little corn that the Privy Council had instructed my grandfather as sheriff to impose a ban on the unneedful use of it in the brewing of strong beer and to order the closure of the many ale and tippling houses—an unpopular measure if ever there were one.

I knew that life in England was divided and nowhere so much as at the Court, where I would be visiting. And yet I could not suppress a thrill of excitement. London seemed not so much twenty-five miles away, as the other side of the world.

Life for me was about to change and I was glad of it because, truth to tell, now that Bett had become a married woman I knew even less what I wished or how I might achieve it.

I took one last look at the green valleys, the blackthorn hedges a froth of white as if for nature's own wedding party, and sighed. Loseley was my childhood. The gilded glamour of London was both frightening and alluring in equal measure, and while I felt a shiver of excitement at the thought, it also filled me with fear, and the temptation, strange and contradictory though it might be, to stay here and remain a child forever.

Back in the house I called Prudence to help me with my packing. I had a fine new gown of leaf-green taffeta to wear in the city and a new kirtle the colour of burnished brass, both paid for by my grandmother. 'Saved up by the offices of my good hens,' she confided, and it was clear to me that this gave her extra delight.

In both manor house and hovel, money from egg laying belonged by tradition to the woman of the house.

'Give thanks to my Buff Sussex bantams, the ones your grandfather said looked like drunken slatterns who would never lay an egg to save their lives.' My grandmother's stony face, which one of the dairymaids had whispered could turn the butter rancid, softened into a proud smile. 'They have just started to lay again after their winter resting.' She chucked my cheek. 'My silly hens would be glad to have helped make you pretty. They knew there was no hope for me,' she shrugged, laughing at the same time, 'even if they laid for a lifetime.'

I held her to me at that, moved to my heart at her kindness. 'Thank you, Grandmother. Not for this alone, but all you have done for me.'

I took one last look at the bedchamber I had shared with Bett since I was in short coats. I knew we two had been blessed. It is the custom for children, no matter how gently born, to be sent from an early age to be brought up in other people's houses, so that they might learn the ways of their betters, and to further the advancement of their families. I was fortunate mine had waited so long to be paid back for their much-delayed investment in me.

I looked at the familiar bed with its green and blue hangings, the tapestry behind it of Ruth, standing exiled in her field of corn, and wondered if London would feel like the distant land Ruth had been sent to or a world of wonderful opportunity. I emptied the presses where I had kept my gowns and the coffers where my few jewels were stowed. The room had seemed mournful without Bett. Now Frances would sleep in it alone, giving it up to grander guests when any came to stay here.

'See, Ann,' Frances' voice behind me made me turn, 'I have made a parting gift for you to take to London.'

It was a package, all wrapped in silk with a ribbon I had seen in Frances' hair.

I opened it to reveal a sampler, sewn with perfect delicate stitching, as neat and clear as if it had been illuminated by a monk in some long-gone abbey. I turned it over. The sign of good stitching is at the back. Mine looked always like a nest of vipers. Frances' stitching was as perfect behind as in front.

'Do you like the text?' she asked me eagerly. 'I found it in Grandmother's book on needlework.'

I looked down at the sampler in my hand and read aloud:

'Virtue is the chiefest Beauty of the Mind
The noblest Ornament of Womankind;
Virtue's our Safeguard, our guiding Star
That stirs up Reason when our Senses err.'

I felt moved that she had taken so much trouble for me, and yet strangely shaken at the message she had chosen. It seemed to foretell of an adult world where virtue and the senses were forever pitched against each other in battle. A world I had not yet encountered. All of a sudden a frightening sensation flooded through my very soul. Was this a lesson I would one day need to learn?

'Thank you, Frances. I will read your homily if ever my senses try to lead me astray.'

'I am glad of it,' replied my pious little sister. 'I have heard that the Court is a very ungodly place.'

'Then I will have to be doubly virtuous.'

And then my saintly sister took me by surprise.

'I will miss you, Ann.'

I took her hand. Her face was so serious, her great dark eyes like those of a dog that watches, waiting for its master's return. It would be lonely here for the last child, but then Frances was hardly a child at all, despite her tender years.

'I know that great bed will seem empty at first. Bett and I were often glad of each other's company on winter nights. Yet it is also a magical place, your own world, a castle, or a great ship, to take you off to wondrous places of your own imagining.'

'I shall try to remember that on the darkest nights. Yet I am not one to yearn for ships and castles. I am happiest at home by the fireside. You are the fearless one, Ann. You can kill a rat or brave Father's anger, and Grandmother's sternness, as if they had no power over you as they do over the rest of us.'

'More fool me, perhaps, for they do have power over me. I have no house or money of my own. But I do have strength of will.' I held her to me for a moment. 'Though I am not sure it is always such a blessing. Come, help me take down my basket and we will ask the usher of the bedchamber to carry down the trunks.'

My grandfather and grandmother, together with Prudence, all the gentlemen servants and grooms, had gathered in the Great Hall to bid me farewell. My father had already arrived on horseback to accompany me to his sister's house in London.

'Goodbye, Ann.' My grandmother kissed me on my cheek. 'Some words of advice. Be chaste, silent and obedient.'

My grandfather was waiting behind her. 'Be the first at least,' he said to me softly. 'Asking you to be silent and obedient would be like asking the stars not to shine in the sky.'

'Goodbye, Grandfather.' I felt a sudden wrench of pain and fear along with my excitement. All my short life my grandparents had been my rock, now I would have to sail into the treacherous ocean of womanhood alone.

Chapter 3

I FELT MORTIFIED that I had never visited London before.

My father went often, as a member of Parliament and to carry out his other official duties, and my aunt, Lady Elizabeth Wolley, the mother of my cousin Francis, lived in the capital for much of her time when she was not accompanying the Queen on one of her summer progresses. My aunt was a Lady of the Privy Chamber to Queen Elizabeth, second only in importance to the Ladies of the Bedchamber, and the Queen called my aunt her 'sweet apple'.

We were fortunate that this year the weather had been dry and the road from Loseley to London was passable for my father and me on horseback, together with the carrier in his cart, so we avoided being bogged down by water or with mud. Last year there were floods and our neighbour Lady Montague needed six pairs of oxen to pull her coach from the mire each day to get to church. When we climbed the Hog's Back near Guildford some three hours past, half the county was laid out before us, sparkling like a jewelled wedding veil, and our ride was broken only by the song of birds and the occasional cursing of the carrier when one of the wheels of his cart lodged itself in the narrow track.

How different from what we saw once we approached London.

We rode for a half-hour through Southwark, a wild area just south of London Bridge, inhabited by many foreigners and strangers, with bear pits and theatres, noisy clanging from a hundred workshops; courts and alleys thick with the stench of wine, piss and cooking fat.

Everywhere there were stray dogs and huge bands of wandering children, many of them dirty and in rags that barely covered their decency, with great begging eyes, all clamouring with their hands up, saying, 'Give us a groat, kind mistress,' and making gargoyle faces and pretending to throw stones at us when we did not. And I was shocked at the sight of the oldest and poorest lying in the street on straw pallets but feet away from the filth of the midden. And everywhere yet more children.

'Are there so many children on the streets as this always?' I asked the carrier. 'Have they no homes to go to?'

The carrier laughed. 'Children are like vermin, mistress. They come out of the gutters and swarm everywhere. Sometimes I think we have more children in London than rats or fleas.'

As we approached the city the carrier, a native of Cheapside, dour as a pall-bearer until now, grew more and more cheerful so that by the time we reached London Bridge he was as gossipy as a wench at a wassail.

Near to the bridge, and from nowhere, a smell so overwhelming assailed us that I caught my breath. I, who thought nothing of white-wash mixed with pig's blood or the odour of animal excrement spread over the fields by farmers, indeed who laughed at the town dwellers who covered their noses at it, found myself choking like a child with the whooping cough.

It was like nothing I had ever encountered. Rotting and rank. Fume laden. It smelled like the overflow of a thousand privies, burning the nostrils and making the eyes water. I thought of my precious Loseley with a flower garden and green meadows and wondered how our heaven could smell so different from this hell.

'Aaah,' said our friend the carrier, breathing in deeply as if he were scenting a batch of new-baked bread, 'the London stink! Home!'

And then we were on the bridge. On every side of us the crowds swelled, not just with people but with herds of cows and flocks of sheep, all heading for the single entry to the great city, apart from by river, from the south.

But the stink was not the worst thing.

From the first gateway of the bridge, twenty skulls grinned down at us, all beheaded or executed for treason.

I was torn, half fascinated, half repulsed that we, a country that had produced art and song and poetry, could be guilty of such barbarism.

'Only twenty of 'em! Not like the old days under her father,' grunted our carrier with regret. 'There used to be hundreds then. Made an example of, for taking arms against the Crown, to encourage the other nobles to keep their swords in their scabbards.' He shook his head at the eternal folly of his betters. 'Yet I've heard young gentlemen pointing up at them skulls and showing off with "That were my uncle," or "He be my father-in-law," as if it were something to be proud of that their relations ended up with their bowels on a skewer!' He laughed and spat. 'They'd better be careful, mind, or they'll end up there themselves. Since the Pope made the Queen a heretic even the walls inform round here.'

I shuddered and looked away. We were so protected from such things at Loseley. Poor men that died for their beliefs, only to be the object of a cheap boast by their descendants. I remembered hearing the story about Thomas More, whose name we share and are distantly related to by marriage, a fact my father and grandfather chose often to forget. I remembered how his daughter did not boast but went secretly and took his head down from its pike. She must have been a brave woman. Would I do that for my father?

I glanced across at him, tiny and stiff-backed on his horse. I knew my father greatly disliked Papists and often spoke enthusiastically against them in the Parliament, yet I believed this was because he was a pragmatist rather than a man of principle, acting more out of frustrated annoyance that they could not see what was good for them than from any cruelty or love of doctrine. Yet recently he wrote his own personal defence of the protestant faith, *A Demonstration of God in His Works*, so I had to believe his religion mattered much to him.

It was a slow time to get the horses and the carrier through the jostling crowd. I tried not to stare like a country wench as we passed right under a house with four gilded turrets in the centre of the bridge, adorned with a dome and elaborately carved galleries which hung out many feet over the river. It was wonderful, a proper palace, but in miniature. Yet the idea of sitting in one of those galleries with such a sinister view of skulls would never hold an appeal to me. Perhaps Londoners got used to such sights, but I hoped I never did. To accept brutal death as normal in the midst of all this teeming life seemed to me a loss of humanity.

'Nonsuch House,' the carrier informed us, pointing out the miniature castle we were riding beneath, clearly delighting in having found an innocent such as I to ply with copious information. 'Modelled on King Henry's old palace, they do say.'

After the little palace we passed between tall houses, six storeys high, on either side of the bridge with haberdashers' or mercers' shops on the ground floor. I watched enthralled as the goodwives of London pushed past crowds and sheep and cows and ducks that had to walk so far to market that they wore leather shoes on their feet, to reach the shops in search of their ribbons and gewgaws.

'Rich merchants,' confided our friend the carrier. 'They live above the shop. And there was a tale to tell in that one.' He leaned towards me as if I hung on his every word and pointed to a long narrow house whose balcony stretched dizzyingly out over the water beneath. 'Used to be lived in by Sir William Hewet, who became Lord Mayor of London, great estate of six thousand pounds a year, he had, and a little daughter called Anne, just like you. One day the nurse was playing with her out of the window and dropped the little lass bang smack into the water. Everyone thought she'd gone to her Maker. Except this young lad who worked for Sir William, name of Edward Osborne. He jumped right in and rescued her. And do you know what?'

'No,' I replied, 'but I believe you are going to tell me.'

'Her father gave him Anne in marriage *and* an enormous dowry.'

'If it were me,' I pointed out prosaically, 'I would have punished the nurse first. I hope little Anne dried off and was old enough to consent.'

The carrier was disappointed by my lack of wonder.

'And Edward Osborne,' he added limply, 'became Lord Mayor after him.'

'This fellow's stories are better than a play actor's,' commented my father, directing his horse out of the channel of filth that ran down the middle of the bridge.

The carrier looked injured. 'God's honest truth, your worship. I travel this way so often I make a habit of taking in my surroundings.'

We had come to one of three gaps in the line of houses on the bridge and suddenly, sparkling through the river mist, there was the white stone of the Tower of London, with dozens and dozens of wherries plying their trade in front of it, like a pond full of water boatmen.

Even in broad daylight the Tower evoked a sense of dread. I had heard enough whispered tales of the rack and other terrible fates that awaited men inside those white walls. It would have been in the Tower that all those men whose skulls were on spikes would have spent their last days. I shuddered at the thought.

It took us the best part of an hour to get across the bridge which measured but a third of a mile. We continued our passage down Fish Street and Bread Street, passing round the back of St Paul's Cathedral, its spire still missing since it was struck by lightning many years ago. I craned my neck to see Paul's Cross next to the great church, where the famous sermons were preached to crowds of thousands. From there we passed through Ludgate and across the Fleet Bridge into Fleet Street, still so thronged with street sellers calling their wares, sightseers come to see the cathedral or worship there, and more gangs of children, that our passage was slow indeed.

Halfway along Fleet Street the crowds eased and the carrier was able to pull the cart to a stop to let the horses drink from the conduit there.

'Listen, mistress,' the carrier held a finger to his lips, 'it is three of the clock.'

From inside the fountain, which was carved with a statue of St Christopher standing atop a band of stone angels, all carrying bells, there came the sound of a clicking and a whirring and to my delight sweet-sounding bells began to gently chime a hymn. As if the fountain were the key that turned a lock, all of a sudden from all around us church bells began to toll so loudly it was like being trapped inside a belltower.

'You'll get used to that, mistress,' confided the carrier. 'In London we ring bells for everything, the hour, when someone is married, or dying, and then again when they're dead. There's a different toll for whether it's man, woman or child if you know how to listen for it.'

'How sad. Are deaths so common in London even when the plague is not rife?' I knew the plague struck often, badly enough to fill the graveyards to overflowing not five years since.

'Death's an everyday thing here, mistress.' He glanced back at Ludgate to where, high above the ground, a metal cage hung, and in it was the rotting torso of a body being picked at by crows. I had to look away before I retched. 'Though they do say a man's lucky here to live to five and thirty.' He clearly deemed this some manner of achievement.

'That's enough from you, sirrah!' my father admonished. 'You would do well to learn to keep your tales to yourself instead of scaring young women with them. The only people who are punished are felons and traitors to Her Majesty.'

'I'm sorry, your worship.' The man climbed back onto his cart. 'My wife says I do babble on.'

'Don't listen to my father,' I whispered, guiding my horse so that it was alongside the cart. 'You have made my journey much the livelier.'

The carrier winked.

'See, Ann,' my father commanded, looking unusually pleased with himself as we processed up the Strand with its busy shops on one side, where the mud gave way to paving stones under foot. 'York House is where your aunt is living now.' He pointed to a small and unassuming door, but I could see that the house it led to was large indeed, no doubt with a fine river frontage. 'My sister Elizabeth has just wed its tenant, Sir Thomas Egerton, the Keeper of the Great Seal, one of the most important men in all of England.'

'But she is five and forty!' I blurted before I had the sense to button my lip. I loved my aunt well but somehow, after Bett's wedding, the thought of my aunt as a new bride seemed most unnatural.

'What has age to do with it?' My father was descending from his horse and handing the reins to a liveried groom. 'She is no blushing maiden but she had a good fortune from her husband Sir John Wolley. Sir Thomas Egerton is a widower who needs a wife to organize his household. He offered her position and status. It is a good bargain for both.'

And, without waiting for any comment from me on the sensible justification for such a marriage, he swept into the house.

Small though he is, my father walks faster than any other person I know, and I had to rush to keep up with him as we made our way through the warren of rooms, past vast family portraits, enormous tapestries, suits of armour and, as was just becoming the fashion in more forward households, statues of Greek nymphs and maidens.

I was out of breath by the time we arrived at a wondrous long gallery filled with light, and I saw that beyond it the river sparkled in the afternoon sun. 'Ann! My lovely girl and favourite of all my nieces, welcome!' A figure stepped out of the light, almost like a goddess herself, and took me in her arms, a hard task since we both wore farthingales.

'My lady aunt!' I returned her embrace with equal affection. She had ever been kind to me, even though she was so busy in the Queen's service that she had not time for her own son and sent him to be raised with us at Loseley. 'I am glad to be come.'

I had to admit, though she might be five and forty, my aunt was trim and youthful, her teeth not blackened nor missing, with a straight back and a sprightly step. Her hair, which she wore wound round an Italian wire band, heart-shaped and studded with pearls, as was the fashion, was still brown, though whether by nature or artifice I knew not. And there was something different about her from when we had last met. A glow of contentment.

It was often said by other women that to be a widow, especially a wealthy one, was the best estate of all—with neither father nor husband to command you. And yet my aunt's smile told a different story. Rich widow though she may have been, she seemed as happy as a girl to be married once again and to so august a person as the Lord Keeper.

'I was sad to miss your sister's celebrations. You must recount me every detail. No point asking your father, for all he will tell me is the size of her husband's expectations.'

'Plentiful, I assure you,' I bit my lip in laughter. 'Sir John is not a thin man.' I dropped my voice. 'Mary said Bett would be like grain under a millstone in their marriage bed.'

'Ann!' My aunt pealed with laughter while my father threw me a silencing look.

'Such talk is not seemly,' he corrected me stiffly, 'above all from the lips of a young girl. You are not schooled in the ways of society. My sister will have a task in teaching you, I fear.'

I dropped him a curtsey. 'I will do my best to learn all she teaches, Father.'

Suddenly the room was full of men, all dressed in black garb down to the ground instead of the usual doublet and hose, each wearing a large black hat. I thought of that expression my grandfather had told me, looking out of the window at Loseley to where a great cawing flock of black birds roosted in the trees. 'They are called a *parliament* of crows, Ann.'

And thus seemed this group.

'Ann,' my aunt's voice interrupted my thoughts, 'this is my husband, Sir Thomas Egerton.' Her voice held a smile under its formality, which I saw returned in the eyes of a noble-looking man standing next to her. He was taller than the group around him, and his back straighter, almost with the posture of a soldier, and his clothes more ornate. In one hand he carried a small bag fashioned of cloth of gold, and I guessed with something approaching awe that this must contain the royal seal of England without which no document in the realm had the force of law.

At first his white beard brought to mind my grandfather, yet on greater studying I saw that he was a younger man than I had first imagined, his gaze clear-sighted and calm. I vowed that if ever I had to bring a case in the courts of Chancery or Star Chamber, I would trust it with this man.

'You are welcome in my house, Mistress More,' the Lord Keeper said and bowed low. 'Your aunt has told me much of your lively mind. I hope you will find company here with my son's wife and his three young daughters. They could do with some youthful diversion amongst this nest of lawyers.'

The crows all laughed as if Lord Keeper Egerton were the greatest wit in Christendom.

IF I HAD thought our house at Loseley large, it was as a cottage compared with a castle next to York House. I lost count of how many servants the Lord Keeper had, yet reckoned it was almost a hundred, and beyond that four gentlemen ushers as well as chaplain, auditor, receiver, almoner and steward, and various other noble men who served my Lord Keeper, carrying out his business at Chancery, and running for him between Queen and Court.

Then there was his son, Sir Thomas the younger, and another son,

John, who resided nearby at the Inns of Court but was much seen here also. Of the younger people my dear cousin Francis lived here, as well as the young woman, my aunt's ward, Mary, to whom he would soon be married, who brought with her the manor of Chequers in Buckinghamshire.

Francis and I had spent so long in each other's company that I considered him more nearly brother than cousin and had seen more of him than of my own true brother, Robert. There was also, I was told, a poet and friend of the young Sir Thomas, lately come to work for my Lord Keeper as a secretary, a Master Donne, but I did not encounter him at first.

I meant to write to Bett to tell her of life here and of the surprise and pleasure I felt at seeing my new chamber. Instead of sharing a bed at Loseley with my preaching little sister, Frances, I was given a grand room with fine views of the river, like an honoured guest.

The first morning I awoke as excited as a child on Christmas morn, and looked out at the shining river—at this time of day not so stinking and crowded as it would later become—and it seemed a road to excitement. It was on the river that everyone of power travelled, between the palaces of Whitehall and of Westminster, downriver to Greenwich and upriver to Hampton Court or Richmond.

I dressed carefully and went downstairs to find my aunt and break my fast with her. She sat in the smaller chamber off the Great Hall, her spaniel dog, Spratt, at her feet. He was so called because, like the dog in the children's verse, he would eat no fat, though he would happily polish off a baron of beef if he could get his paws on it. This meant that, unlike many dogs, his chops were not greasy, and my aunt therefore cosseted him and cuddled him as if he were her infant. Sir Thomas the younger was also at the table with Eleanor his wife and two of the baby girls.

Thereafter my days took on a pleasant pattern of playing with the children, venturing abroad with my aunt on various errands and in finding ways in which I could make myself useful to this busy household. And then, about three weeks after my arrival, I descended to the Great Hall, dressed as I often was, with the expectation of some small outing.

'Ann, beloved girl,' my aunt asked, a look of slight annoyance on her face, 'did you not receive my message?'

My look told her the answer.

'That stupid Mercy! Today you and I are going to the palace at Greenwich for an audience with the Queen.'

My heart leapt in my breast. I had seen Queen Elizabeth on her visits to Loseley, but only when I was a small child, and had been quickly shushed and taken back to the nursery. This time I would be an adult, and treated as such, savouring the majestic delights and extravagant glory of the greatest monarchy in Christendom.

'If we are in luck we may have a word or smile from Her Majesty. Faith, I will come with you myself to choose your gown. First impressions matter much. The Queen loves a modest maiden and this is the first step to get you a place about her, hard though that will be.'

The Queen, I knew, was the centre of our entire universe, what she wished or thought governed every person in our nation. To be a planet, however small, in her constellation would be keenly sought by all.

'Every nobleman in the land wants a place at Court for his daughter,' my aunt shrugged. 'There was a time when precedence decided who would win, with the oldest families at the top of the list, but times have sorely changed. So many new men have come up lately, all offering their fine new houses to Her Majesty for her summer pleasures, putting on masques and lavish entertainments, giving her gifts and jewels, so that precedence has been ousted by more vulgar values. The Queen no longer chooses her ladies for their virtue or breeding but because they have fought a long campaign, with prizes hidden in the trees for Her Majesty to pick like apples.' She dropped her voice as if there were ears in the linen-fold panelling, which indeed there might be. 'The Queen is ever mindful of a bargain. She inherited much pomp from her father but empty coffers. I trust we have offered her enough.'

In my innocence I had not known that even at Court favours were only given for money or gifts, like bartering in some great market place.

'Bess Throckmorton, sister to your own Mary's husband, only got her place at Court when her brother Arthur gave the Queen a jewel costing fifteen pounds.'

I was surprised to hear that even my own relations, if only by marriage, were bidding for position. I had not thought we were so ambitious as that for preferment.

'Arthur Throckmorton thought it well worth the price. A relation at Court means the whole family may rise up on their back. I will send you my own gentlewoman of the chamber to help you change. Joan!' A stately woman, her prettiness now faded by middle age, came humbly into the room. 'Ask the usher of the bedchamber to place pegs here,' my aunt pointed to panelling next to the window, 'so that Mistress Ann may hang her best gowns and not keep them all in this infernally cramped press.' She picked up one of my ruffs, an especially delicate one, almost like a spider's web, which was sewn in Brussels lace. 'And pin Mistress Ann's ruffs to the curtains, then they will need less attention from the poking stick and will therefore save our starch bill.'

I smiled that even my rich aunt, like the Queen when she stayed with her nobles in order to save money for the Exchequer, appreciated her small economies.

My aunt busied herself in appraising all my dresses. With my auburn hair and warm brown eyes I favoured the hues of autumn for my gowns. Burnished golds, the green of a new-furled leaf, the warm red-brown of cinnamon spice, newly arrived from the Indies. 'Pretty enough,' my aunt insisted, 'but none of these will do for Court. The Queen's ladies must all wear white and silver.' A naughty gleam came into my aunt's eye and she lowered her voice. 'Her Majesty must be the jewel in the crown, her ladies but foils to set off her magnificence. If any wear bright colours they find themselves sent smartly back to change.'

'What if they refuse?'

'Wake up, niece. What world live you in? None refuse the Queen. Or they find themselves back in the bosom of their families. Or worse.'

I felt like some ignorant stranger in a foreign land, unaware of either the customs or the rules. Life at Court seemed like a trick staircase I had read about in a fable; it fell away if you gave the wrong answer to some incomprehensible question.

'Ah, this one will do.' She pulled from the bottom of the press the simple white dress I had worn for my confirmation.

'But it is too tight for me,' I protested. 'And not long enough!' This was not the vision I had of myself going to Court, dressed as a twelve-year-old girl making her confirmation. 'My grandmother bade me bring it only in case you needed my help with household tasks.'

'Then you will look the more maidenly, and please the Queen the better.'

I bit my lip. No matter that the Queen was an old woman, I was beginning to see that, though none dared acknowledge it, she liked to brook no competition from younger beauties.

'Come, put on this simple strand of pearls.' My aunt handed me the necklace she had brought with her and helped me put it on. I looked at myself in the glass and saw my aunt's reflection behind me. The tenderness on her face made me wish, with a sharp pain, for the mother I had hardly known, struck down so early in childbirth. There was no portrait of my mother and she died before I was old enough to fix her face in my mind's eye, yet I did recall the eyes. Rich brown, like those of myself and my brother Robert, and direct in their gaze. Too direct, some said, for a maiden of my tender years.

And then, just as were are to leave, my aunt remembered something and led me, alone, through her bedchamber, and the two or three rooms adjoining, to her private closet.

It was a small room, wainscoted, containing little but table, chair and chest. She lifted the chest, in which were stored spare hangings, and removed a pouch of velvet.

'Take it. I came upon it amongst some old treasures and meant to give it to you before now.' She handed me the pouch and I untied the lace and discovered a silver case, inlaid with enamel filigree, a pretty thing. The catch was stiff and wanted not to open. Of a sudden it sprang apart like a Jack-in-the-box and the face I had not seen since I was four years old looked up into my eyes. My mother!

In my soul I knew such a yearning for her, as if my very heart would burst from my chest. I felt her presence, leaning over my shoulder, whispering that she had wanted to give me a mother's softness, to hold me to her, to temper my father's choler, his helplessness in dealing with such a great brood of girls. I had to hold on to a chair-back, my knuckles whitened by the force of my longing.

My lady aunt leaned over and placed her hand under my chin. 'She would be proud of you, Ann. And now, let us go to Court.'

To my great excitement we went downriver to Greenwich in the Lord Keeper's barge, with liveried servants to announce our status. I was amazed to see that the river was almost as crowded as the road had been. Stately barges ploughed their way up and down between the Queen's various palaces, past the gardens on the river bank and the vast mansions where her advisors and courtiers lived, with their private stairs down to the water. Tiny wherries darted about, a comic sight with scruffy boatmen rowing grand ladies in their gowns and ruffs, hardly able to fit their fine dresses inside the craft.

A tilt boat overtook us with well-dressed courtiers fanning themselves under a rich red canopy, a lute player sitting on the deck softly singing a melancholy song. My aunt told me that often in summer the Queen and her ladies took to the river in one of her barges and rowed up and down to feel the breeze.

'She knew that in her honour the church of Lambeth undertook to ring the church bell at her passing.' My aunt smiled at the memory. 'And sometimes she went back and forth five or six times that they might keep tolling. As I recall the vicar complained that he could not afford to keep paying the bell ringers! Her Majesty retorted that her people should want to ring the bell for her without payment!'

All along the river front were small stairs dipping vertiginously down into the water. Well-off Londoners in search of a wherry gathered here to shout 'Oars!' or 'Westward Ho!'

On the south bank we passed Southwark with its pits for bear and bull baiting, and went on towards London Bridge. Beyond were the legal quays, where I was astonished to see almost a hundred ocean craft lined up all the way from the bridge to the city, loading and unloading their cargo by way of ingenious pulleys to be assessed for customs duty.

After that we rowed on towards the daunting white stone of the Tower of London. I shivered as we passed the Traitor's Gate, thinking of all those who had entered it, not knowing if they would ever emerge. One of them, my aunt reminded me, had been the Queen herself, placed there by her own sister, Mary, and how she had gone in bravely, stopping only to announce, 'Here standeth as true a subject as ever landed at these stairs.'

I told myself we lived in kinder times than under Bloody Mary, yet the sight only a mile or two round the bend of the gibbet at Wapping, with its occupant swaying in the breeze, carrion for the crows, made me shudder all the same.

'At least he weren't a pirate, mistress,' the barge's master commented, following my eye. 'They're hanged at low water and the tide must wash over them three times.'

I was quiet after that, wondering what constituted piracy. Was it shipping the odd barrel of brandy, an occurrence which happened frequently enough in Sussex, or was it a practice that happened only in the far-flung oceans?

A few more bends and we passed the quiet village of Bermondsey with its three corn-grinding mills. Only a short time now and the palace of Greenwich would be in sight.

Out of nowhere the wind got up and the water scudded and eddied and a sheet of muddy water blew off the surface, making us wet even though we were so high.

'I envy the Queen her barge's glass windows,' my aunt said as she shook the river water from her skirts. 'This water is as brown as my mother's sere-bark potions.'

'It was a deal muddier when I was a boy,' commented the master. 'So muddy then you could catch haddock in your hand at high tide. The fish saw not where they were going!'

Any thought of mud-blind haddock was pushed from my mind as the palace, its tall lead-roofed turrets gleaming in the sloping sunshine, hove into view. It was a glorious sight indeed. The Palace of Placentia was favourite of all the Queen's palaces, and the one where she was born.

The bargemaster shouted to a groom on the river bank to look out as we slid in through a great watergate. From there we walked up the steps and through a garden and thence to a courtyard where many people crowded together, some holding petitions, all eager for what could take months or years to secure: an encounter with the Queen herself.

My heart pounded as finally we were led, with great pomp and ceremony and sound of trumpets, into the vast Presence Chamber where lay Elizabeth's great canopied throne. But the Queen herself was not there, only some of her ladies. These were dressed in great splendour, all in white and silver, as my aunt had told me, though each outdid the others in trying to make her dress more gorgeous than her rivals'.

My aunt nudged me. 'They are Ladies of the Presence Chamber, the lowest of the Queen's attendants, though believe me the competition even for that position is as fierce as a battle. If one of the ladies has a headache, some nobleman will be suggesting his daughter take her place before she recovers.'

She led me past the discreetly chattering women into another smaller room beyond. Even though its size was the less it took my breath from my body. The walls were painted in a midnight blue that glowed with richness, and on them were embellished every flower that could be found in the field, in hues of scarlet, orange, purple and gold. It put me in mind of walking inside a jewelled casket. The hangings, too, were the richest I had ever seen, of ivy and fleur de lis, picked out in dark green upon a cloth of gold.

There were several ladies reclining on great cushions opposite another throne, also canopied. My aunt nodded to them. 'These are the Ladies of the Privy Chamber. Until recently I have been among their number. The most favoured of all are those of the Bedchamber, who dress the Queen and meet her most personal needs.'

All at once I imagined the Queen calling out in the middle of the night for her close stool and some sleepy lady trying to be grateful for the honour of helping her to it. But I did not voice this for I was fast learning that it was best to keep such thoughts locked inside my breast.

'Stay here awhile, Ann, while I discover Her Majesty's whereabouts and whether it is possible that I present you.'

Suddenly shy in the presence of four pairs of inquisitive eyes, and very much aware of the dowdy nature of my gown amongst so much fashionable finery, I smiled humbly and found myself a quiet window seat.

The ladies soon forgot my presence and resumed their chattering.

'Heard you of the Earl's latest doings?' one whispered to her neighbour.

I guessed there was only one man they could be talking of: Elizabeth's dashing favourite, the Earl of Essex. In her life the Queen had had two great favourites. Robert Dudley, Earl of Leicester, whom my father served for many years when he was a young man, and he was the man she most nearly married, but for the inconvenience that he had a wife already. And when his wife was found dead at the bottom of a staircase the scandal was so great that the Queen would not wed him. Finally, to her great fury, he married one of her ladies in waiting. This lady, Lettice Knollys, had a son of her own, one Robert Devereux, now Earl of Essex. And though this Robert was thirty years the Queen's junior, he was yet the only man who could make her laugh and feel young. Or make her furious. Or so people said.

I made busy with opening my fan while the Queen's lady continued, 'Last night the Earl stayed so late playing cards with Her Majesty that the birds sang in the trees before he left for his own apartments.' The lady dropped her voice so low I could hardly hear it.

'And yet he finds time to make love to Elizabeth Brydges,' whispered another.

'And Mistress Fitton also.'

They all giggled.

'Why does she not stop him? She is the Queen. She could send him to the Tower.'

'She has too much fondness for him. Even though it is rumoured he looks beyond her reign to James, the Scottish King.'

One of the ladies looked around her stiffly, her eyes nervous as a startled bird's. 'So do many, though they would never have it known. And so they all will until she names her successor. Though none dare say so.'

'She will never do that. It would mean acknowledging the ending of her own great reign. She prefers to live in the present.'

'Silence!' said the oldest of them. 'Such talk is treasonous. It is you who will end up in the Tower not my lord Essex!'

With a glance behind them they returned to their previous topic.

'Know you the latest?' the first lady enquired in a low voice. 'Two days past the Queen saw love looks pass betwixt the Earl and Lady Mary Howard.'

'Mercy! Has the man no shame? What did Her Majesty say to him?'

'Nothing at all. He can still do no wrong in the Queen's eyes. It was the lady in question who caught her ire. Lady Mary wore a dress of fine velvet all powdered through with gold, and the Queen pulled at the stuff with her own hands demanding to know who said she, a mere lady of the Presence Chamber, could wear such finery?'

They leaned in, eager to hear the climax of the tale.

'Sssh,' one lady elbowed the other suddenly to be silent, 'here comes Mary now.'

A small and neat young woman with fair hair and glowing dark eyes, a striking combination, came slowly into the room. Taking in the knot of ladies who had fallen silent at her approach she seemed to straighten up, like a puppet whose string is pulled to make it stand. Her bearing went from meek to passing proud.

It seemed as if she would speak when, without warning, a figure in a red wig appeared from the royal bedchamber, with many jewels adorning her, wearing a dress of velvet all powdered through with gold that laced not up properly, revealing two ancient white bosoms almost to the nipple. Just as shocking, the dress hung only halfway down the calf, exposing an expanse of velvet stocking. I tried to quieten my gasp of horror. It was the Queen!

Fortunately she had eyes for none but her errant lady in waiting. 'See, now, Mary Howard!' she demanded, her voice high and wild. 'Is not this a fine dress?' Her pale eyes glinted like stone chips when the mason wields his chisel, and looked just as sharp.

I watched in horror as the other ladies scrambled to their feet. It dawned on me that this was the gown the ladies had just described, the one that had so incensed Her Majesty with its finery. The Queen was wearing Lady Mary's dress, and it exposed her stockings because she was six inches the taller!

'Tell me, Mary Howard, how does your fine dress suit me? Since you dress like a Queen, tis meet that the Queen should have your dress. Is it too short for me, Mary, what think you?' And then, not leaving the hapless Mary time to answer, she shouted furiously, 'Well, Lady Mary, if it be too short for me, it be too fine for you, so none shall wear it.'

At that the Queen turned on her jewelled heel and walked back into her bedchamber, with all the ladies save Mary in her wake.

Mary turned towards the long window at the end of the room and I heard a sob escape her.

I sat, fixed to my seat, not knowing what to do. There was still no sign of my aunt. The sobbing continued until, plucking up my courage, I laid my hand gently on her shoulder.

'I should never have worn that stupid dress. Or listened to my lord Essex's honeyed words. Except that he told me I looked so well in it. Sometimes I wonder if he does it just to taunt her, to show how great is his power over her.' She turned towards me, her large eyes glistening with tears.

It struck me that Lady Mary and I were of an age. Old enough, it seemed, to fuel a man like the Earl of Essex's desire.

'He is but a serpent sent to try me! And I have failed the test! My father bade me come to find a noble husband and instead I have lost a reputation!' She seemed to see me properly for the first time. 'You are young too, Mistress . . . ?'

'More. My name is Ann More.'

'It is so hard because the Queen is old,' she looked around in case her reputation might not be all she lost if she were heard, 'yet she keeps about her so many men and women who are young. We are summoned to wait on her. And we wait. And wait. And sometimes our eyes stray where they should not.'

'The Devil makes work for idle hands?'

Mary Howard laughed at that. 'And not just hands. The Queen does not want us to have a life, she wants all to herself. She is the Virgin Queen and she would have all her ladies be virgins too. Even the married ones! And everyone knows she will not talk of her succession, though she is well past sixty. It is why the young nobles are restless. The Queen seems to have reigned over us forever—and thank God that she does!' she added nervously. 'And yet they are wondering what will come after. The Earl of Essex perhaps?'

I wondered if this girl were not so innocent as she appeared. Did she allow the Earl to court her because people whispered that he might one day be King, after Elizabeth had left her kingdom without an heir?

Of a sudden I felt beyond my depth, as if some dangerous currents lapped at my feet. My aunt thought it such an honour, indeed the greatest honour, to wait at Court. And yet, to me the Court seemed, despite its richness, and its gilded splendour, to be a dangerous place, a quicksand where the safe banks were not clearly marked. The

Queen might not persecute her subjects for their beliefs with the fervour her sister had done, but it seemed there were other crimes just as punishable.

To my relief my aunt appeared, walking quickly from the royal bedchamber, skirts swishing angrily, her lips pursed in annoyance. 'Well, Ann, we have had a wasted journey. Due to that silly wench . . .'

Mary Howard, who had been hiding her reddened eyes by looking out of the window, turned and raised her head proudly.

'The Queen is in an evil temper and boxes the ears of sundry of her ladies. And only because they ask to bring her some soothing rose water from the still room. If I were you,' she raised a stern eyebrow at the girl, 'I would go back to my chamber and summon my lord father to come and take me home.'

'Will not the Queen forgive her if Lady Mary were to throw herself onto Her Majesty's mercy?' I enquired.

My aunt shrugged. 'Her Majesty says mercy is something a Queen cannot afford to show. It is too costly and dangerous. Come, Ann, let us return to York House. We will present you another day, when the Court is a happier place.' She stared at Lady Mary angrily. 'Now it will be weeks, months mayhap, before the Queen will take on another lady to wait on her. At present, thanks to this silly wench with her pretensions, she wishes them all damned to hell.'

I smiled at Lady Mary, trying to convey my sympathy at her plight, yet I had no choice but to follow my aunt towards the river stairs. As the barge rowed upriver my mind teemed with many things, faster than the mill race under London Bridge at high tide. I felt the power of Her Majesty in all her glory but also a sense of shock that so great a Queen should be thus reduced to spiting her rivals for the love of the young earl when she was almost the age of my grandmother.

For I could not picture my grandmother Margaret being chased after by young gallants, their codpieces scented with musk (for that is the scandalous fashion at this Court), nor playing cards with them until the birds sang in the trees as the Queen did.

At York House all was humming with busyness. Messengers came to and fro between the palace of Westminster, where the courts now sat, and the Queen's advisors at Whitehall. The Lord Keeper had fingers in many pies, sitting in the Privy Council, dealing with the Parliament, overseeing the courts of Chancery and Star Chamber and, so I had heard, beginning an investigation into lawyers and officials at Chancery for charging extortionate fees from their petitioners.

Since my aunt wanted to be sure the Queen's humour had softened, it was many days before she came to me once again to suggest we try our luck with another audience at Greenwich. In that time I had had the peace to think and even to pray; kneeling at the foot of the great bed overlooking the river, I asked the Lord our God for His guidance. By the time my aunt bid me go to Greenwich again I had made up my mind and screwed up all my courage to tell her, knowing my words would mightily displease her and all my family with her.

'I am sorry, Aunt, for you have shown me so much kindness, but I have come to see that I am not suited to the ways of the Court.'

'What nonsense is this! You will do as you are bid!' I had never seen my kind aunt so angry, even with the hapless Lady Mary. 'We have been to much trouble on your behalf. Half the young women in the realm would trade their portion to be in your position!'

'Indeed, and I thank you for it. But it is not a world whose air I could ever breathe. I am blunt, while a courtier needs to be subtle. I feel things deeply and could never learn to hold my tongue and dissemble. At Greenwich I saw clearly how a lady in waiting needs two faces, one to show to the Queen, and another in private. I heard what those ladies truly said, and thought what a brittle world the Court is, built on fear and rivalry.'

'You are not a maid in short coats, Ann.' My aunt's eyes were as cold and forbidding as a winter sea. 'You are a woman. You must learn to rein in your emotions, to be discreet. Do you think I, too, do not feel anger, fear, resentment? Yet I keep them to myself. You have a choice, niece, and it is high time you accepted it. Learn the skills of a courtier, as I have learned them, or take whatever husband your father deems suitable for you.' This time there was no softening of sympathy in my aunt's manner. Her back had become like a ramrod, and her voice deepened with a strong and harsh reality. She seemed a different woman from the one who had given me my mother's locket. 'Ann, remember this. The Queen is the sun who brightens every corner of our realm and even beyond. Without her all would be darkness. You do not choose to accept the sun or reject it.'

'Yet I do not have to serve the sun like some high priestess, making a pretence that she is young and beautiful, ever ready to do her bidding whether it is fair or not . . .' I was remembering that vision, crazed and half-naked, attacking Lady Mary.

At that my aunt struck me hard across the face.

I gasped at the pain. Never in my whole life had I been struck, even by my father in the most frenzied of his cholers.

'You put yourself too high. This is not a simple choice for you alone. I have talked to the Queen and, although she values loyalty above all and likes to keep those who are familiar about her, she is ready to entertain the idea of you in my place as I decline in years. Be mindful of what an honour that is to our family.'

'I could not, Aunt! I would be like a poor common thrush in a golden cage, beating its wings against the bars when all around called for a canary.'

'You are too fanciful, Ann.' My aunt's voice was as cold as the glint of metal when the sword flashes out of its scabbard, and just as threatening.

'But, Aunt, pray . . .' I tried to argue.

'This is no small matter, niece. The Queen expects you. Our family's name is at stake, and your father's future too. The Queen is not someone to be gainsaid because you are young and innocent. If you like not the brittleness of Court life, then learn to dissemble!'

'Aunt, it is not in my nature.' Some good angel prompted me to add the one thing that might convince her: 'I will speak out of turn or do the wrong thing and bring shame on the good name of the Mores!'

'It may not be as simple as that. Subjects do not turn down favours from the monarch. This offence is a serious one.' She held me with steady, disapproving eyes, as a hawk surveys a small animal. 'If you are not to be a gentlewoman to the Queen, then there is no other thought but marriage. It is time you learned humility. I will go to Court alone and you will start to learn the skills of running a great house, since marriage is certain to be your lot. Joan, my gentlewoman, will be your mistress and you will do exactly as she says.'

'I am sorry, Aunt, to so displease you.'

'This is no trivial matter, Ann. I fear your grandfather has too much indulged you. He was hard on his own children, your father and my sister and I; if we dared to gainsay him he would have had us whipped, yet in his dotage it seems his brains have sunk to his boots.'

She noticed the locket with the picture of my mother I was turning in my hands and flung it to the floor. 'Do you think *she* would be proud of you?'

Loneliness swept over me, and I missed my life at Loseley so much I almost wept.

I slipped to my knees when my aunt had left the room and picked up my treasured trinket. 'O Lord of Righteousness,' I beseeched, 'all-seeing God, assure me that in this I do your will, and act not out of pride and selfish arrogance, but true proper humility.'

I heard the door open and looked up, expecting Joan. But it was my sister Mary, so I rose to my feet in love and gratitude.

But Mary had not come to salve my loneliness.

Her face was almost as angry as my aunt's and her voice crackled with harsh annoyance.

'So, Ann, what is this nonsense I hear that you find the Court unpalatable to your saintly tastes? My brother-in-law Throckmorton sold lands to win his sister a place there, yet our aunt tells me you have the chance and hand it back like a hot pan that burns your delicate fingers.'

'I am sorry but I cannot . . .'

'*Cannot!* Cannot get a place that will help your whole family! You know how badly my husband and I need money and advancement, how close we are to the brink of disaster, and yet you act thus selfishly!'

'I am sorry, Mary. Perhaps I may help in other ways.'

'I greatly doubt it. Since my sister-in-law Bess is disgraced for marrying Sir Walter Ralegh, we had high hopes of you.'

'Cannot you see, Mary, why I might not want a life where disgrace or advancement depend upon the Queen's whim? When all around her wait for her to die while pretending she is the sun shining in the firmament? How, as they bow or curtsey, already they are calculating who will be the next in line to replace her?'

'Sssh, Ann, you must not talk so.' Mary looked behind her as if some spy might be lurking behind the tapestry.

I smiled. 'You see, Mary, how indiscreet I am, how ill-suited to Court life where clearly discretion is all?'

Mary shook her head, suddenly relenting and holding her arms open to me. 'What want you, then, you wild and silly girl?'

'Oh, Mary,' she was the eldest of us all, and had the mothering of us thrust upon her when she was but a child herself, after my mother died, 'I truly know not.'

'They will find you a husband, then.'

I stared out at the glittering river. 'Frances says they have already started. What do you know of a Master Manners?'

'Richard Manners? Handsome and amiable, with a reasonable income. You could do worse than he, Ann.'

'He is the protégé of our dear stepmother.'

'Ah. We should wonder what lies beneath the surface of the suggestion, then. Constance bears no tender love and maternal affection for us More girls. I will see what I can discover. By the way, good luck with the housewifery. I hear my lady aunt is to punish you by setting you to work with the servants.'

I had wondered what my punishment would be for my arrant disobedience. 'I thank you, Mary, not to look so pleased at the prospect. It is better than spending another day at Court.'

'Ann More,' her voice held a grudging tenderness as if I were a child who had stolen a sweetmeat and curtsied when caught, 'you are the most unnatural girl.'

'Yes,' I sighed, the loneliness descending again like a black crow, 'that is a fact on which all are agreed.'

Chapter 4

'COME, JOAN!' MY aunt commanded her tire-woman, her anger against me still blowing as strong as ever. It had been almost a week now since I had spoken out and there had been no sign of my aunt relenting. 'Dress Mistress Ann in plain clothing. Today she will assist you and Mercy at your tasks.'

'You'll need to take off your fancy partlet, mistress.' I could see Joan thought me one step away from Bedlam to turn down a place at Court in exchange for washing dirty linen. 'And those fine embroidered sleeves as well!' She began to unlace me and replace my green silk gown with another in plain brown, the colour of slurry, made of hard, stiff worsted that rubbed instead of comforting. My fine stockings were thrown onto the bed in favour of itchy woollen ones, and my dear pointed shoes of green velvet with black frogging replaced by galoshes that seemed to be fashioned from sweaty and discarded saddles.

It seemed to me that Joan took rather too much delight in my transformation from fine lady to skivvy. When she was satisfied with my new clothing she raised a saucy eyebrow. 'And what should I do with her hair, my lady? A maidservant would never have hair like Mistress Ann's.'

Unlike most ladies of fashion I liked to wear my hair loose. Not long and flowing like the scandalous Lady Rich, sister of the Earl of Essex, but curling below my ears, that I might feel the wind in it when I ran or rode. I hated the coifs and French headdresses so many ladies wore so that they could not feel if it were calm or windy when they went abroad.

It gave Joan especial joy to scrape my hair back so that it was invisible, a hidden treasure beneath this drab cap so that now I looked like any workaday serving girl. Even my own grandmother, I swear, would not have known me.

'Come, mistress,' Joan chided. 'We must do your aunt's bidding and see how life as a laundry maid suits those tender hands of yours.'

I knew from watching my grandmother that even gentlewomen were not spared from the most menial tasks. Idleness and luxury were sins not to be indulged in, and women's household labour was seen as God's holy work. Yet even finding my way round the dark passageways used by the servants of York House was a daunting challenge. It was so great a place, far greater than my familiar home of Loseley, with countless chambers and more than a hundred servants, all dedicated to the smooth running of one household, be it a very great one.

'Now you are one of us you'd best stay on the right side of the steward, mistress,' warned Joan, laughing at me, 'or he will fine you two pence for being late for dinner and the same for prayers.' I wondered how much servants would be paid. Not enough for fines like those, I was sure. 'And if you leave a door open, woe betide and a threepenny fine for you into the bargain. All runs on oiled wheels in this household.'

I was surprised, also, to learn that apart from Joan and Mercy almost all the servants were men, since at Loseley my grandmother liked to have women about her.

'Women servants are not thought much of in London,' Joan shrugged. 'Men can make their fortunes if they choose to serve the right lord, though they end in poverty as often. "Young servingmen, old beggars," so the saying goes.'

I saw, with a little unease, that I had never thought of the lives of those who waited on us before. They had been like part of the wainscoting on the walls, no more than the background to my comfortable home.

I had no further time to ponder on the condition of servants' lives since Joan bid me accompany her to distant Moor's Fields where the laundrywomen of London laid out their washing and we had to collect our great tablecloths. I wondered that the servants did not wash them here, as they did at Loseley.

'The Lord Keeper does not like to show his doings to the world,' Joan informed me grandly. 'If tablecloths were laid all across the bushes here, he says, it would seem as if we were running a wash-house!'

To my surprise, despite the streets being as thick with crowds as a dog's back with fleas, I greatly enjoyed myself.

Walking out dressed as a serving maid was a world away from trying to push your way through on a fine horse, being stared at and importuned by all and sundry. On foot I had time to take it all in without being the target—the costermongers calling, the water vendors, like snails, with their great bottles on their backs, the old dames selling hot codlings, and all manner of tradesmen shouting their wares, from ropes to mend your bed to new chairs for old.

Now that I was down among them, the sounds and the smells of the city seemed not threatening but exciting and exotic. London was said to be the noisiest city in the world, with the clatter of carts, the cries of the street sellers and the incessant sound of bells. We had a German guest at my uncle's table who said he had never heard so many bells as were rung in London. The apprentices sometimes ran across the town to ring them for their sport, my father said, and had bets to see who could toll the longest.

Just by the end of the Strand, hard by the maypole that stood there, we saw a milkmaid in the shade of the trees, crying, 'Milk, pretty maids!'

For a moment I envied the girl her freedom, not having to lead her life for the sake of her family's honour but having some say in her own choices. Yet perhaps I was being too innocent. Putting bread on the table governed the choices of most, not freedom. She was a tall young woman who smiled much, with a more joyous countenance than I had seen on any other woman about the streets.

'Aye,' Joan seemed to be following my thought. 'Milkmaids come and go from their villages without the say-so of a husband. Not a bad life for a woman! Gossip has it, through luck or witchery they even escape the smallpox. And the Queen herself wasn't safe from that. Instead one of her ladies, who nursed her through the worst, caught it from her, and ended up as pitted as a pumice-stone! My poor Lady Sidney, so they say, never showed her face again at Court these last forty years.'

As I pondered on the lucklessness of serving the powerful the milk-maid raised her eyes and smiled at Joan. 'Try my milk, mistress?'

'We've no time, young doxy.' Joan brushed the girl out of the way.

In sudden sympathy, I delved into the purse I kept round my waist, and handed her a coin.

The girl stared after me, which I found strange until I remembered my appearance. A servant offering charity to another of her rank? No wonder she stared so.

By the time we regained York House, carrying our heavy burden of tablecloths, I longed for my chamber. But Joan was not so easily appeased. 'Put the cloths away in that chest. Time now to show you how to air the beds.' She must have seen the droop of my shoulders because she laughed, not unkindly. 'There are but twenty bedchambers in the Lord Keeper's house. We shall not make you air them all.'

As she led me past the great portraits and rich hangings of the hall towards the oak staircase, she called for Mercy to come and help us. Already the steward was ordering his underlings to pull out the leaves of the vast table in the Great Hall and unhook the stools from underneath for midday dinner. Some scurried around with square trenchers in their arms, others with great silver jugs of wine and ale.

Joan led us into the first of the bedchambers, a large room a little like my own with carved ceiling, tapestries lining the walls and rich Turkey rugs strewn here and there on the rush floor which was weekly perfumed with rosemary. In the centre was a vast bed, hung with red taffeta fringed in gold.

'To make sure no dampness remains you must pull it back like this.' She pulled at the thick brocade bed cover, all lined with white fur, then doubled it back on itself. An insect, tiny and black, jumped out onto her arm.

'Cursed fleas! Tis the season when they do begin to bother us most.'

Mercy sat on the edge of the bed and felt it sag beneath her. 'Heigh-ho, Mistress Joan. This bed has suffered some sport!'

Joan winked broadly and pulled off, one after the other, a feather mattress then two more of canvas filled with straw and lastly a mat woven of rushes. Under this a tangle of ropes criss-crossed into holes in the side of the bed timbers like laces in a shoe. To think I had slept on such a bed every night of my life and never thought to look beneath the covers.

'You pull that end as I pull this, Mercy,' Joan commanded. 'When the ropes are tight we put back the mattresses and the bed is firm.' She winked again at Mercy. 'Until the next bout loosens them.'

After such warm work I crossed to the window hoping for air.

I glanced out, my eye attracted by a tall figure dressed only in black, his face half hidden by a broad-brimmed hat, standing a few feet below. He leaned on the moss-covered wall, smiling and shaking his head, as if observing a picture that was as full both of sadness as of merriment.

As silently as I could, and slowly, too, so that he would not look up at the sudden movement, I pushed the casement open and leaned out that I might share the object of his amusement.

The rush of warm air hit me. Inside it was cold in this vast warren of rooms and I found myself shivering at the change. Looking down I saw the sight that so amused the stranger below.

Two birds, ring-necked doves. One, the hen, pecked with sullen eye at the narrow strip of grass. The other, the cock, was so desirous of her attention that he puffed up his chest, showing to her all the glory of his rainbow neck, and strutted all around her, calling loudly like any Court gallant seeking the favours of his mistress.

Still she paid him no heed. Losing patience, the strutting bird assayed to climb aboard and have his way with her. But she was too quick for him. In a flutter of disdainful feathers she flew up to the branch of a tree.

The watching gentleman shook his head and laughed aloud. 'Alas, poor dove,' said he, as if for all the world the bird could understand him. 'It was ever thus. The fairer sex ignore us or—crueller by far— enjoy us at their will then tire of us like last year's glove that has lost its perfume.' He leaned down towards the cock, conversing as if to an old friend. 'One consolation. The city is full of pretty birds. Try another and this one will change her mind soon enough!'

I did not know that I had laughed aloud, but the man turned all at once in my direction so that I needs must duck back into the room in case he saw me, hitting my head on the wood of the frame.

My memory of that strange occasion—when I looked back on it—was to hold both laughter and pain.

'Joan,' I asked, feigning disinterest in my voice, 'who is that gentleman in the garden below?'

Joan banged the window shut and looked down at him in disapproval. 'Gentleman? Master John Donne, the Lord Keeper's secretary.' Her words sounded as if they had been dipped in vinegar. 'Aye, a handsome enough face but also, so they do say, a heretic and a writer of lewd verses.'

Down in the garden Master Donne doffed his hat as if Joan had paid him some extravagant compliment, while I hid in the shadows, smiling.

Outside in the Strand a bell tolled the hour. 'Eleven of the clock, Mistress Joan,' Mercy reminded her respectfully. Rank had to be maintained even among servants. 'Thomas the steward bid me help with the laying of the table.'

Joan sniffed the air, already fragrant with smells from the bakehouse. Soon the dining chamber and the Great Hall would be full of hungry people. 'Go, then. I need to get my lady's dress of blue damask from the press and hang it well. Mistress Ann can finish here alone.' She jerked her head towards the bed. 'Just put back the linen and pull up the brocade to cover it.'

As she went I tapped my foot in impatience. Pulling up a bed was not such a skilful task as Joan would have me believe. I smoothed the linen, enjoying the feel of the cloth taut beneath my hands until I was satisfied that no wrinkle remained. Then I shook the pillows one by one and placed them neatly at the bed's head. Lastly I pulled up the silk cover, which was richly worked with all manner of exotic birds.

I was still holding the soft fur lining to my face to remind me of my cat Perkin, left at Loseley, when I gasped. Someone was standing behind me, sliding their arms around my waist.

I tried to move but found I could not. I was held fast.

'I can think of better uses for a bed than to straighten the covers,' whispered a voice, as deep and honeyed with invitation as the serpent's was like to have been in far-off Eden.

Before I could scream or shout I was turned round and I felt lips, hard at first then soft and full, on mine.

Deep in my female core, where until this moment I had felt as calm as the cloister, I sensed a sudden tightening of desire. I should have cried out or fought. Instead, for the blink of an eye, I shuddered and closed my eyes.

Then, furious at myself and angrier still at him, I pushed him from me with all my force so that he stumbled and sprawled on the floor.

'It is a dishonour to you, sir, to take such advantage of a serving maid! Have you no sense of decency to stop you preying on the innocence of one who is not your equal?'

Master Donne picked himself up, having the grace at least to look shamefaced.

'You are correct indeed,' the passion in his eyes was now tempered with amusement, 'but who is it that rebukes me with such fiery justice? An avenging angel, perhaps, sent by the Almighty to put me on the path to righteousness?'

His laughing tone served only to stoke up the flames of my wrath. 'Jest not, sir. Adding blasphemy to selfishness will hardly win you the forgiveness of the Lord.'

'And how must I suit for *your* forgiveness?'

'By considering what consequence your sudden lust might have on the life of one so far beneath you.'

My aunt or grandmother would certainly blush at such unmaidenly directness, yet I burned still with resentment, and also guilt at my own scandalous response. 'Is it not a cruel outrage to prey on one who will lose her place if she gives in to your licentiousness? This were no great lady you might woo in your verse with clever conceits and no harm done. Think you that you are Jupiter descending on Io, sir?' In my indignation I grew a little confused in my references. 'For the effect on the girl would be far worse than turning her into a cloud.'

He looked closely at me now, grey eyes alight with laughter and also with curiosity. 'I think you will find it was Jupiter who was the cloud. Io, sadly, was turned into a cow.'

I feared he might be right and this made me more passionate yet in my condemnation.

'That is hardly to the point. Your conduct has been despicable.'

To my surprise the effect on Master Donne was immediate, akin to a bucket of cold water thrown over an amorous dog. A look of genuine contrition came into his eyes. 'Unknown mistress, your criticism is more than justified. In the court of Chancery I have been fighting against the powerful taking advantage of the weak, yet find that here I am doing the same myself. I promise I will not err again, no matter how tempting the provocation. Yet might I know the name of my fortuitous rescuer for I would guess you are no true serving maid?'

I looked into his eyes, no longer sure if his repentance were a true one. 'I do not see there is any need for that. Your conduct is between yourself and your Maker.'

'Just so that I might include you in my prayers, mistress, and give thanks to you for my timely deliverance.'

'The Lord God will know who I am.'

I gathered up the skirts of my humble dress and sped from the room, feeling his smiling eyes pursuing me, knowing that he was not the only one who must request the forgiveness of the Lord. My response to that embrace had not been that of an angel, avenging or otherwise.

In case he thought to come after me I ran down the great staircase, past a warren of rooms where men sat discussing the finer points of the law. By the time I reached the Great Hall, my shameful excitement had subsided and I began to feel nothing but righteous indignation. So caught up was I in this thought that I noticed not my father who had lately arrived to sup with the Lord Keeper.

'Ann?' The puzzlement in my father's voice made me almost lose my footing.

'Father? What brings you here all unannounced?'

'I bring you good news. Why are you clad like a serving wench? Surely the Lord Keeper has enough servants without requesting your assistance?'

'It is a long tale. What is the news you bring? Is it from Loseley or my sisters?' Of a sudden I remembered how much I had been missing them.

'All are well. My father and mother send you their good wishes.'

At this moment my father had a curious look about him, like a cockerel who knows he has one hen left, the best of all. 'Ann, go up and change into proper clothes then come and join me in the gardens. I have brought someone with me who is anxious to meet you. His name is Richard Manners.'

Chapter 5

I HAD TO vouchsafe, Master Manners was not as I had imagined.

Bett's new husband was so dull, and Margaret's so dependable. Mary's Nick, to be sure, had a spark about him, but it was this spark that seemed to lead him to the bowling alley and the cock fights and the bear baiting, and—worst of all—the gambling on all three that caused my sister so much distress.

The garden was a delightful place at any season, but now, in autumn, its colours were at their most glorious.

Against the glossy dark green of the overhanging ivy, the yellow leaves of a crab apple stood out in colourful contrast. Beyond them lay a great alley of beech trees, each one a glow of copper, and standing right in the middle of the alley, as if in a burnished arch, stood Master Richard Manners.

A garden was not his natural setting. He would, I suspected, have looked more at home in the saddle, or with a sword in his hand. Lively blue eyes shone from a strong-boned oval face, framed by ruddy brown hair which hung, shorter than is the fashion, to the length of his collar. And there was a startling addition: five or six strands of black silk hung from his ear to form a dramatic earring.

At first I almost laughed at so womanly an affectation. And yet there were no other signs of the Court gallant about him. I liked his clothes for they were fine without being too overlaid with gold or lacing. Above all, he had an air about him of decision. A man, I would say on first encounter, who got what he desired on this earth.

'Mistress More,' he bowed low, flinging back the cape of his doublet in a dramatic gesture, 'I meet you at last.'

To my surprise I found myself curtseying in return when I had intended to be cold and distant.

'How are you finding life in London? Does it please you after the peaceful fields of Surrey? And what think you of the Court? I hear you have already been presented to her Majesty.'

'It is certainly different.' Did I trust him enough to tell him of the scenes I had witnessed at the palace of Greenwich and speak my true mind about what I found there? Would he find the situations humorous or think my descriptions too close to treachery?

'I found the Court a wild place.'

'How so?'

'So much rivalry and jockeying for position.'

'And you yearn for a simpler life? There is much, I have found, to be said for the life of an English gentleman possessed of a reasonable estate, as I have in Leicestershire.' He moved a little closer to me, while I picked up the seed of an oak tree and turned it in my hand. 'But a gentleman needs a wife.'

I might like his looks and be pleasantly surprised that he was not a clod like Sir John, but this directness of purpose made me shy away.

'I hear you are a distant relation of my stepmother Constance.'

He nodded, seeming to understand my change in direction. 'Yes. My mother and she are cousins.'

I wanted to say, 'Then your mother has my sympathy,' but stayed my mouth. Perhaps, hard though it was to imagine, his mother liked her cousin.

'How do you find my cousin Constance?' he asked. 'A fine woman, is she not?' Master Manners was watching my face. A sudden smile spread across his. 'Or do you agree with my mother that Cousin Constance could try the patience of a saint?'

I relaxed at that, liking his easy sense of humour, and the way he guessed, without being told, my feelings for my stepmother.

'Are you a farmer, then, on your estate in Leicestershire?' Leicestershire sounded so far away I could hardly imagine its geography. 'I know not that county, I am sorry to say, never having left the gentle boundaries of the south.'

'Oh, we northerners are tempestuous indeed. We live in caves and kill our meat each day with clubs.'

'Indeed?' I laughed at his teasing. 'That would suit my brother, Robert. He loves nothing so much as killing God's creatures. The more the better.'

'I will have to invite him to join me. And you? What are the interests that hold the fancy of Mistress Ann More? Not the hunting field, I hazard?'

'I like to ride, but not to hunt. A hart is too beauteous to kill.'

'You disappoint me. I had heard from your stepmother of your fierce ungovernable nature. Exterminating rats was listed as your favourite occupation.'

I could not help but laugh. 'Oh, I only kill rats during the season, you understand. To do so otherwise would be most unsporting.'

'I am sure the rats at Loseley would be pleased to hear it.'

'I enjoy reading also.'

'Cousin Constance complains of Latin and Greek. She says your grandfather has mistaken you for a boy.'

The tone in which he said these words implied that he did not share this illusion and I found myself blushing, a habit I detest.

'My grandfather is a very learned man. He looked for a pupil. I was more apt than the others. Perhaps you share the common notion that learning in women should not be encouraged? It makes us as cunning as foxes, so he maintains.'

Master Manners fixed his clever blue eyes on my face. 'I have great admiration for the fox.'

To my surprise I saw my cousin Francis stride across the lawn towards us. I had not seen him since I came to London as he had remained at my aunt's house in Pyrford, some few miles from Loseley.

'Francis!' I greeted him. If I had been alone I would have run the few yards between us and flung myself on him. Francis was more to me than my brother, since we had grown up together while my own brother lived with my father and my stepmother. 'What a pleasure! When came you to London? Have you met Master Manners?'

Francis bowed. He was only a year older than I but seemed suddenly the gentleman. 'I arrived from Pyrford this morning. I came to say that your aunt, my mother, requests your help with some task indoors.'

Master Manners smiled and bowed. 'Her gain will be my loss, Mistress More.'

'That fellow has some address,' Francis whispered as he threaded his arm through mine. 'He sounds almost like a Frenchman.'

'Aye. He has a silvery tongue, but at least he is not a dull dog like Bett's husband.'

'Oho. So the suitor your father has selected is not so far from your taste after all?'

'I said not that, Francis. Simply that he has a fluency and a certain wit.'

'But wit is the quality you prize above all, Ann. I have heard you say so often.'

'As long as it is coupled with a good heart and an honourable soul.'

'You ask not much, cousin,' Francis teased me.

'Why does my aunt want me?'

'She felt you had spent long enough with the well-named Master Manners. He must not be allowed to tire of your company. And I think she feared if you were alone for too great a while, Mistress Ann More might . . .' He paused, searching for words.

'Say aught that requires a brain?'

'Ann, Ann. Outspoken as ever.'

'And what of your own courtship, Francis, with Mistress Mary Hawtrey, heiress to the manor of Chequers in Buckinghamshire?' I teased.

Francis sighed. 'Well enough for a match decided for us when we were in our cradles. Mary is an amiable young woman.'

'Yet there is no love between you?'

'What hath love to do with marriage? You are too sweet on such things, Ann. One would believe you had buried yourself in bowers of green with shepherds trilling on flutes and swains plighting love all day at Loseley. Marriage is a business arrangement, as you well know. Love can be found elsewhere.'

'And what if I like it not to be a business arrangement?'

'Very likely you will have to make the best of it, knowing the temperament of your good father.'

I shrugged, conceding that on this Francis and I would not agree. I changed the subject to avoid quarrelling. 'Tell me about Master Donne, is he as great a libertine as people say?'

'Master Donne? My stepfather's secretary? He writes clever verses, full of wit and paradox that are passed round the Inns of Court. They talk of love and witty seductions and are much prized, or so I'm told.'

'Francis,' I said, as brisk as if I ordered a batch of loaves, 'I would like you to bring me some.'

'Ann!' Francis looked as if I had announced I was a secret Papist and believed not in the Thirty Nine Articles. 'They are not for pure young gentlewomen.'

'Good.' I bit my lip and looked down demurely.

'Ann, I cannot.'

'Francis, I have done many things for you. I have lied when you were out with your roistering friends, and assured my aunt you were at your studies. I have brought you water when your head was raging after too much sack. I have even translated some of your Latin syllogisms which, as far as you understood them, could have been written in Ancient Greek.'

'I know it. But . . .'

'Francis, I will tell no one. Why should women be ever excluded from the mind of men?'

'If it were only the mind . . .' He sighed. 'I will do my best. If I can lay my hands on them.' We had reached the great door of York House. 'Ann, I hope you dip not your fingers in the fire.'

At that I looked as stern as Athena wielding the scales of justice. 'I am playing no game at all. From what I hear, Master Donne is a promiscuous and ungodly man.'

'Ever the sort ladies like, then.'

'Francis, cousin, give us more credit. Now I must seek out your mother. She is determined, if I am not to be one of the Queen's ladies, that I have more lessons in the honourable art of housewifery.'

Francis choked with merriment. 'My mother was never at home for time enough to learn such arts herself. Nor wished to for that matter.'

'Ah, but she has servants to initiate me. Today, I believe, it is the secrets of the still room.'

'Rather you than I.'

'Yes. And that is why I need some unladylike diversion. Or I shall drown myself in a vat of lye and never be seen again.'

Francis laughed. 'If I had not known you all my life, and what a trial you can be, I would wed you myself.'

'Yes,' I pushed him off, laughing, 'we are lucky our parents have not fixed it up already. Cousins are nothing to them. Though your betrothed, Mary, is richer than I.'

'Your portion is respectable. Enough to tempt some men.'

'Then I hope I do not meet them!'

'And what do you think tempts Master Manners? Does he need a new roof on his manor and your dowry is the very thing to provide it? Or is it the desire to tame you?'

'Francis,' I teased him, 'such a worldly head on such young shoulders.'

'Love, then? The root of all evil?'

'I thought that was money.'

'Money cannot touch love for the harm it does. Why do poets lament its deadly arrows, else?'

'Francis, go!' I shook my head as I sent him off and went to look for my aunt.

I realized I knew not where in this great labyrinth of a house, the still room lay. I found it, after much searching and some help from the usher of the ewery.

My aunt was there already, wearing a plain gown, busy adding water to a glass container which bubbled on a flame. She looked up and I thought she would ask me what I made of my suitor. But my aunt knew me too well.

'Ann, welcome. We have useful work to do. Yesterday my lord husband wrenched his shoulder as he climbed from his horse. He has called for a poultice of *flos unguentorum*, the flower of ointments. Now let me see where I put the receipt.'

My aunt hunted around until the receipt fell out of *Gerard's Herbal*, newly published by the Queen's printer and causing much sensation with all its wondrous illustrations of healing herbs from belladonna to black henbane and heartmint. I wandered round the still room, intrigued in spite of myself. We had such a room at Loseley, indeed my grandmother was famous for her herbal cures, yet it was nothing compared to here. This was a marvellous place, with benches along three sides on which were ranged bottles in every size from jeroboams to tiny vials with stoppers, containing the most costly of the essences. Hanging above them, on wooden rails, were hundreds of different herbs, with still more preserved in bottles of distilled water.

The best thing about the room was the scent: faintly medicinal, yet overlaid with spice and the pungent whiff of herbs. Entering the room was at once comforting like unto breathing in the fumes of some healing posset.

Every lady who ran a large establishment, my grandmother had often told me, must know how to make the potions and medicines for her household. And for this I had to understand the basis of medical diagnosis, how God formed every one of us out of four humours—yellow bile, black bile, blood and phlegm—and when these humours became out of balance, then illness and pain surely followed.

'Ah, here it is. Help me, Ann, if you please.'

I hastened to help, grateful she seemed to be overlooking my outburst over the Court, at least for the moment.

She read the receipt out aloud. 'Flower of ointments: exceeding good against the pulling or swelling of the joints—just what we have need of—and to restore the balance of the humours. That will be excellent,' she confided, 'if it can remove a little of his black bile. The Lord Keeper is usually the calmest and fairest of men but this injury hath released all his bile and choler.' She studied the receipt once more. 'Now what need we? Rozin. Ann, you will find that on the shelves. Yellow wax, olibanum, turpentine, myrrh. The white wine we will have to find in the ewery. But what's this?' she tutted in impatience. 'Half a pound of sheep's suet? Ann, run along to the clerk of the kitchen and see if he has aught of that.'

But the clerk had none. No call for it in *his* cooking, he told me with much disdain, nasty peasant stuff.

'Shame, shame,' my aunt sighed, 'I have no more liberty to go marketing today but I will take you to the Shambles tomorrow. Tonight we must prepare for a great banquet. Your father has some good news.'

I wondered what news my father might have that would warrant such a celebration. A hint of fear made my hands shake. Surely it could not be so soon to announce my betrothal?

My aunt stole a sudden look at me, but I continued modestly packing away the poultice we had started to prepare.

I ran to my bedchamber, my thoughts jumbling in my head. Master Manners had more address than I expected but I hardly knew what manner of man he was. Whether he was kind, or Godfearing, or of a generous and loving nature? I thought back to the betrothals of my sisters, trying to remember how much choice they were given in the matter. Margaret and Bett had accepted my father's decision without demur. Only Mary had fought to be allowed her Nick. And Nick, I recognized with sadness, had turned out to be a disappointment in my father's eyes at least.

As the light began to dim Joan arrived with my candle. Smiling to herself she pulled the great curtains.

'Stay your hand awhile, Joan, I will draw them myself. I love to watch the sunset sink over the river.'

'Which gown will you wear, Mistress Ann?'

I surveyed the dresses I had brought with me from Loseley—paid for generously by my grandmother's hens. I had worn them but little since for my visit to Court my aunt had made me wear my hated white dress as punishment for my stubborn nature. I picked up my favourite, in sarcenet, the colour of old gold, and held it against myself in the glass. Outside the last rays of the sun glowed through the great windows lighting up my russet hair.

'This one.'

I washed my hands and face in rose water and stood for Joan to dress me. 'No coif, thank you, Joan. I will have my hair loose tonight.' She arranged my burnished curls about my ears with the horn comb.

'And what jewels would you like, Mistress Ann?' She held out the small coffer in which I stored my few items of jewellery.

I held up two necklaces, a thick golden chain from which hung six or seven jewelled stars, and a simple square cross embellished with four large garnets.

I knew at once the cross became me better. 'Joan, can you tie the clasp on this for me?'

Being several inches smaller than I, Joan had to reach on tiptoe, but still she was too low. So she knelt instead on the great bed and bade me lean against it.

'There.' She captured a stray curl and pushed it back behind my ear. 'I have never seen you look so lovely, mistress.'

For answer, I laughed.

Looking back, I know not why. Did I feel some strange power surging through me that I had never felt before?

I waited in my chamber until I could hear from the loud sounds in the Great Hall below that all the company were assembled. And then I took myself slowly down the grand staircase, entering the hall from the back, beside the carved wooden screen behind which the ushers scurried back and forth to the kitchens.

Around thirty ladies and gentlemen were already seated at the long table, their cloths laid across their arms or shoulders to dry their hands when the usher of the ewery brought round washing bowls between courses. The ladies vied with each other in extravagances clad in their taffeta and silk, in jewelled colours of rose and ruby all embossed with gilded thread, which caught the flare of the candles in a scene of rare magnificence. At the far end, musicians played softly on lute and tabor as the ushers brought in dish after dish piled high with capons, peacock and leg of mutton boiled with lemons.

My father saw me first and rose to bow and let me pass, and next to him a smiling Master Manners.

'Ann, you are late, you should have been led into dinner,' complained my aunt. 'Now you will have to seat yourself where you may.'

The diners began to shuffle to their feet, offering me their place. The offer I accepted, since it would cause least embarrassment, was from my cousin Francis. Sweeping up my gown over one arm I at last sat down with Francis' betrothed, Mary, on my right.

Francis leaned across to his neighbour on the other side. 'Master Donne, living at York House as you do, I assume you have already encountered my cousin, Mistress Ann More?'

Laughing eyes turned to mine and for the merest moment registered extreme shock.

Master Donne had recognized in the great lady before him the chamber maid he had tried to bed a few hours since.

Then, as smoothly as water sliding from the feathers of a swan, Master Donne recovered his composure.

'Indeed. We had a strange and fatal interview this very afternoon.'

Francis looked puzzled at this reply.

'How, fatal? John, is this one of your elaborate conceits?'

'I meant simply that I killed my chance of Mistress More approving of me.'

'How did you so lose her good opinion, then?'

'I'm afraid I mistook Mistress More for a serving maid.'

'God's blood, John!' exclaimed Gregory Downhall, one of my uncle's other secretaries, who had been listening in. 'I hope you gave her no offence.'

'That is for Mistress More herself to judge.' His glance held mine, challenging and dark. 'I treated Mistress More as I would a countess.'

For a passing moment I was tempted to smile. And yet I should not accept such conduct so lightly. Instead I rose to my feet. 'Then perhaps no woman in the land is safe. Francis, there has been a misunderstanding. I should be seated at the far end of the table near my father.'

I ignored the look of surprise from Francis and the two old dames seated opposite, who watched curiously as I gathered up my fan and took myself off to where my father sat next to the Lord Keeper and his lady.

'They say she is a tempestuous girl,' I heard one crone whisper to the other, 'and needs a husband to govern her wildness.'

Her neighbour raised her eyebrow knowingly. 'They also say she will get one soon enough, and good luck to him.'

If I had hoped for a reaction from Master Donne, I was to be disappointed. When I looked back he was already charming the gossipy grandams who took such an unwelcome interest in my future happiness.

'Come, Ann,' my father bid me, 'sit here next to Master Manners. Now how did you two young people like each other when you met? Quite a prickly thing, my Ann, eh, Richard?'

Master Manners smiled. 'Only as the rose has thorns to protect its beauty from those who do not value it.'

'Oho, quite the poet, Master Manners,' commented the Lord Keeper from his position at the head of the table. 'Watch out, John,' he raised his voice so that it could be heard at the other end, 'you have a rival here in Master Manners. Perhaps we should have a wager over who can write the most lyrical love sonnet?'

'Then certainly I should lose, my lord,' Master Donne replied with infuriating calmness, 'for my poor verses are not lyrical but harsh. For music you must seek another voice than mine.'

'It is true, Father,' the Lord Keeper's son Thomas smilingly agreed. 'In my friend John's verse the thorn would be the object, not the rose. It would pierce his mistress's finger so she bled and he would prick his own in harmony and say they were both thorns in the crown of Christ, so blessed in heavenly grace that they must join in body also . . .'

Everyone in the company laughed save Richard Manners, who looked at Master Donne through narrowed eyes, while I studied my trencher with great attention. 'Surely such ideas have a taint of blasphemy about them, do they not?' enquired Master Manners softly.

The Lord Keeper laughed, refusing to be drawn into dangerous waters. 'My son is right. John's verses are full of such images. He loves nothing more than comparing his mistress with saints and angels. It comes of having a Popish upbringing, as indeed I had myself. But John has put the whiff of incense behind him. Wisely he saw the error of his ways.' I glanced at Master Donne and saw him look briefly away. 'Neither he nor I is cut from martyr's cloth, are we, John? And you have proved your loyalty to your Queen by your bravery in the Azores.'

Master Donne looked straight ahead, though I knew there was no laughter in his tone when he made his reply. 'I confine myself to the worship of women, my lord. I find that it is safer.'

My temper fired again at this, yet the assembled company only laughed. 'Until their husbands find out! Usher! More wine for my guests,' Sir Thomas commanded. 'Fill up all glasses for we are to have a toast.'

The ushers arrived with the wine while the grooms cleared away the carcases of peacock and capon, picked clean until they looked like corpses attacked by a flock of vultures. I sat as if in stone, quaking. Would this toast concern the resolution of my future, as I feared? My father had been casting me sidelong glances during all the meal, and I wondered if the reason for his self-congratulation was about to be revealed.

As the Lord Keeper rose to his feet a dizziness took hold of me or I would have tried to run from the room, so uncertain was I of my feelings. 'My friends,' he began, refilling his goblet from the great ewer, 'a toast! News of great delight I know you will all share with me.' I held my breath, my eyes anywhere but on Master Manners. By chance they fastened on Master Donne's and there I spied an unthought-of sympathy, even a fleeting sadness, as if we waited to hear the death read out of someone dear to us.

'The announcement I have to make is from the Queen herself. It concerns my brother-in-law George More, than whom there is none more deserving. Her Majesty has decided in her great wisdom that since his father, Sir William, lives to a great age and shows no sign of joining his Redeemer,' the audience laughed greatly at that, 'she is to award a knighthood to the son while the father is still living. A signal honour for, as we all know, unlike the Earl of Essex, who dubs half his followers, a knighthood bestowed by the Queen is as common as a phoenix egg. Please raise your tankards to the future *Sir* George More!'

'Sir George More!' I echoed, with no need to feign my enthusiasm. I was not to be betrothed after all!

'Felicitations, Mistress Ann,' congratulated a voice next to me. It was Master Manners. He took my hand and kissed it, bowing low. 'I think you feared there might be some other subject for the toasting tonight.'

I glanced up. Had he read my mind so easily, then?

'I wish we were all free to make our choices where our desires allowed,' he said softly. I warmed to the man at this for it was so greatly how I felt myself. His smile held both humour and, it seemed to me, regret. 'Yet for myself at least my heart and head follow the same direction. I hope you will understand that I have to make my departure for Leicestershire tomorrow morning. I bid you goodbye, Mistress More, and hope it will not be too long until we meet again.'

I looked after him, confused.

'Why is Master Manners leaving, Father?' I enquired when my father sat down again.

'Oh, I've lost all patience with the fellow. His father is not pleased with the size of your portion and has summoned his pup back to their estate. If he thinks he can get himself the daughter of a duke or earl good luck to him, though I doubt they will settle for a paltry esquire as father-in-law. Not without coffers of coin at least.'

I watched Master Manners take his leave of my aunt and the Lord

Keeper, and saw how several ladies, one youthful and as pretty as a young dove, also monitored his slow departure. And the notion struck me that he had not fought so very hard for the privilege of soliciting my hand and heart.

Such is the frailty of woman that, despite my earlier misgiving, I felt a certain prick of disappointment.

I turned my head and found that clever, satirical gaze upon me from the distant end of the table. I did not give him the satisfaction of acknowledging it.

Instead I found that my stepmother Constance had sought me out. She was a good-looking woman of perhaps seven and thirty years of age, and yet there was a peevishness about her features, as if she felt the Almighty had never quite delivered the life to which she felt entitled.

'So, Ann, you have defied your aunt and see yourself as too good to serve even the Queen of this country?'

She gave me no chance to defend myself from her accusation before adding, in a low hissing voice, 'You ever had too much pride, and too much freedom fed it. You should have been with us at Baynard's. I would have taught you some humility. Instead your grandfather indulged you. You were ever a selfish wild girl, and this is the outcome.'

'And yet you try to find me a husband, Stepmother. If I am so woeful a case, I am surprised you care so.'

'The right husband would brook no such behaviour from you. He would teach you humility and respect.'

'And you think Master Manners would be such a husband?'

At that she simply raised her eyebrow. 'Someone must or you will bring great dishonour on your family, Ann More. I can see the seeds of it in you already.'

At that she turned from me and assumed a look of pious gentleness with which she ever cozened my father.

As was the custom we left the Great Hall after the dishes had been cleared to eat our sweetmeats in the banqueting room in one of the towers overlooking the gardens so that servants could prepare the hall for sleeping in.

We were fewer in number as the old crones had chosen their beds and the Lord Keeper, despite the lateness of the hour, had been summoned by the Council for some pressing discussions. Neither was there sign of Master Donne. Perhaps his presence as the Lord Keeper's secretary had been required at the Council meeting also.

My aunt patted the stool next to hers and I sat down, finding myself in a pool of candlelight, almost as if I were a statue in some ancient church before the idolatrous images of the saints had been stripped away.

'You look beautiful this night, niece. How did you find your Master Manners? Your stepmother has been pleading his case most eloquently.'

'He seems likeable enough.'

'No more than likeable? He is very handsome with those merry blue eyes and quantities of brown hair.'

'I did not have time to get to know his nature, Aunt. And surely that is what matters in marriage?'

'Come now, Ann! You mean that a gentleman's looks are of no importance? Times have changed, then, since I was a girl.'

'Besides, Master Manners is leaving. My portion is not sizeable enough for his father's needs, it seems.'

'And you are piqued.' She took my hand in hers. 'Yet he will be back, I am sure. Such things are but counters in the negotiation. His father will get some more rents or leases from your father than he wishes to give, that is all. And you will be with me the longer. I shall teach you to be the most proficient mistress of a great house on God's earth. Marriage is not so bad an estate, Ann. You will be busy and happy, and have a brood of children.'

I looked away in sudden shyness, and caught the eye of my cousin. As soon as my aunt moved away Francis came and sat beside me. 'Here,' he handed me a sheaf of stiffened papers, 'the verses you requested. Hide them well. I do not wish to incur the wrath of my mother for corrupting innocent souls.'

I glanced around until none was watching and placed them inside my silken sleeve.

After that each minute seemed like an eternity until I could slip away to my bedchamber.

Finally alone, I sat upon the great bed, lit by the light of my bedside candle, and opened up the scroll.

There were two poems, written out in a fair and formal hand, though whether it was Master Donne's own, or some fellow's from Lincoln's Inn, I knew not. I unscrolled the first, entitled 'To His Mistress Going to Bed'.

Come, Madam, come, all rest my powers defy;
Until I labour, I in labour lie.
The foe oft-times, having the foe in sight,
Is tired with standing, though they never fight.
Off with that girdle, like heaven's zone glistering,
But a far fairer world encompassing.
Unpin that spangled breastplate, which you wear
That th' eyes of busy fools may be stopped there;
Unlace yourself, for that harmonious chime
Tells me from you that now 'tis your bed-time.
Off with that happy busk, which I envy,
That still can be, and still can stand so nigh.
Your gown going off, such beauteous state reveals,
As when from flowery meads th' hill's shadow steals.
Off with your wiry coronet and show
The hairy diadem which on you doth grow.
Off with those shoes: and then safely tread
In this love's hallow'd temple, this soft bed.
In such white robes heaven's angels used to be
Received by men; thou, angel, bring'st with thee
A heaven like Mahomet's paradise; and though
Ill spirits walk in white, we easily know
By this these angels from an evil sprite,
They set our hairs, but these our flesh upright.
Licence my roving hands, and let them go
Behind, before, above, between, below.
O my America, my new found land,
My kingdom, safeliest when with one man manned,
My mine of precious stones, my empery;
How blessed am I in this discovering thee.
To enter in these bonds is to be free;
Then, where my hand is set my seal shall be.
Full nakedness, all joys are due to thee.

As souls unbodied, bodies unclothed must be,
To taste whole joys. Gems which you women use
Are like Atlanta's balls, cast in men's views,
That when a fool's eye lighteth on a gem
His earthly soul may covet theirs, not them.
Like pictures, or like books' gay coverings made
For laymen, are all women thus arrayed;
Themselves are mystic books, which only we
Whom their imputed grace will dignify
Must see revealed. Then since I may know,
As liberally as to a midwife show
Thyself; cast all, yea this white linen hence,
Here is no penance, much less innocence.
To teach thee, I am naked first: why then
What needst thou have more covering than a man?

I held my breath, feeling a fiery blush stain the whiteness of my maiden's cheeks. Nothing in all my life had prepared me for this moment. My sisters had jested about what happened in the marriage-bed and I had perused my grandfather's library freely, yet none suggested that the act could be as full of passion and lingering exquisite impatience as these verses did.

And yet, was there not in this verse the peremptory voice of the lord and master? The lady like a kingdom to be conquered and invaded, made subject to his pleasure?

As I read the verse again I found my temper flaring at the arrogance of the man, at his utter overweening pride.

And yet, reading on, I gasped, assailed by feelings that confused me utterly: for instead of seeming like a spy or interloper with my eye to the keyhole, I felt myself responding with a mounting arousal of my own, as if it were I who were standing in that room, as naked as she was, joyful and quivering, before his lustful scrutiny.

I flung the poem from me and reached for the second, entitled simply 'Jealousy'.

Fond woman, which wouldst have thy husband die,
And yet complain'st of his great jealousy;

If swoll'n with poison, he lay in his last bed,
His body with a sere-bark covered,
Drawing his breath, as thick and short, as can
The nimblest crocheting musician,
Ready with loathsome vomiting to spew
His soul out of one hell, into a new,
Made deaf with his poor kindred's howling cries,
Begging with few feigned tears, great legacies,
Thou wouldst not weep, but jolly, and frolic be,
As a slave, which tomorrow should be free;
Yet weep'st thou, when thou seest him hungerly
Swallow his own death, heart's-bane jealousy.
O give him many thanks, he is courteous,
That in suspecting kindly warneth us.
We must not, as we used, flout openly,
In scoffing riddles, his deformity;
Nor at his board together being sat,
With words, nor touch, scarce looks adulterate.
Nor when he swoll'n, and pampered with great fare,
Sits down, and snorts, caged in his basket chair,
Must we usurp his own bed any more,
Nor kiss and play in his house, as before.
Now I see many dangers; for that is
His realm, his castle, and his diocese.
But if, as envious men, which would revile
Their prince, or coin his gold, themselves exile
Into another country, and do it there,
We play in another house, what should we fear?
There we will scorn his household policies,
His silly plots, and pensionary spies,
As the inhabitants of Thames' right side
Do London's Mayor; or Germans, the Pope's pride.

This time there was no answering sense of arousal in me, simply fury and disgust.

I was no simpleton. I knew enough of art to know that these scenes, these pictures of libidinous assignations, might never have taken place, might even be the copies of some ancient Roman fancy. And yet in his words there was so much of directness, and of intimacy, so much caressing pleasure and such angry bile that, despite my logic, it seemed to me they must be true, and had indeed unfolded just as his words described them.

Which meant that Master John Donne was as immoral and pleasure-seeking and careless of other human beings as our first encounter had intimated.

I picked up both sheets and tore them angrily into strips, meaning to set light to them with my candle, and render them into a pyre of ashes as they deserved. I know not why, at the last moment, I stayed my hand and slipped the pieces, ragged and unreadable as they were, into the press that stored my gowns.

As I sank to my knees beside the great bed I caught sight of the sampler sewn for me by my sister Frances, with its timely reminder:

> *Virtue is the chiefest Beauty of the Mind*
> *The noblest Ornament of Womankind;*
> *Virtue's our Safeguard, our guiding Star*
> *That stirs up Reason when our Senses err.*

'Thank you, Frances,' I breathed as good sense and godliness flooded through my being, 'for embroidering me lines that would never, under any circumstances, be written by one Master John Donne.'

Chapter 6

THE NEXT MORNING my aunt sought me out to accompany her to the meat market at the Shambles to procure sheep's suet for the Lord Keeper's poultice.

'Come, Ann. This is not a task I would do myself from habit,' she explained, 'and yet it will be a good lesson for you in how to go marketing when you have a household of your own.'

It was a fine, breezy day and my aunt decided that since it was dry and the mud in the streets would not sully our gowns, it would benefit our health to walk. I was happy. There was always so much to look at in this city of two hundred thousand souls, probably the busiest city in the whole world.

We first recognized the Shambles by its stench. Dozens of butchers' shops, cheek by jowl next to the slaughterhouses that fed them, scented the air with the ripe, rotting smell of discarded animal flesh. There were two rows of butchers' shops and another down the middle, each with a large window and wide sill, two feet deep, where the lumps of meat were on display to be poked and sniffed by fussy housewives and the clerks of the gentry's kitchens. My aunt chose the cleanest of the establishments and placed her request.

'Half a pound of sheep's suet, my lady, *half a pound*?'

The butcher laughed so loud I thought he might keel over and die. He kept laughing as he weighed out the suet, a tiny mound of white measured against his bell-shaped bronze weights with their intricate hieroglyphic inscriptions. 'All this way for half a pound of suet? Can't you afford more than that, my fine ladies? The country must be going down the jakes when the gentle folks are eating half a pound of suet. Is it for dumplings, ladies?'

My aunt did not deign to reply, but I could not resist. 'No indeed. It is for a *flos unguentorum.*'

'A floss argumentorum, did you say?' The butcher mimicked the refinement of my voice and winked at his assistant. 'Then you've come to the right place!'

'*Un*guentorum,' I replied, short of temper at being laughed at. 'Flower of ointments. For a poultice.'

'Why said you not before?' The butcher started smiling instead of laughing at us, his big florid face of a sudden friendly. 'I could do with some for my sore kneecap. My grandam swore by the stuff.'

'Thank you, sir.'

My aunt was already out of the shop. 'Such forwardness! I would have him in the stocks for less. The way he addressed us as if he were our equal!'

'I thought that was just London ways.' I was getting used to London ways. How everyone talked to you in the street, advising you on where to shop for the best bargain, or how to get to the destination you required whether you asked them or no, or soliciting from you the source of your fan or the fabric of your gown, as if they were old friends. And the children! I had noticed them when we came through Southwark but there were even more here. As we walked along Cheapside we were surrounded by great gangs of them. There were far more children in London, it seemed to me, than there were adults to support them. They reminded me of swarms of bees forever hunting for a hive. And just as like to sting you.

A poor, pinched-looking child of five or six, her legs bent and her face covered in grime, ran up to us. 'Have you got a coin to spare please, mistress? Only we've eaten naught since day before yesterday.'

I reached for the purse tied to my waist and handed her a coin.

'Ann, you will only encourage them.'

'And would it be godly to let them starve when I have money in my purse I do not need?'

My aunt raised an eyebrow in exasperation at my seeming innocence. 'You have much to learn about the world, niece. More than you think.'

'I hope I will never learn so much that I turn my back on God's creatures,' I flashed. 'Why are there so many children swarming about so in the streets?'

'The pox or the plague have cut down their parents. This new law the Queen passed is to get many of them apprenticed so they might not be forever begging in the streets.'

'I hope it helps them.'

My aunt left me stood alone for a moment by the conduit opposite the Mercer's Chapel, while she went on an errand to Goldsmith's Row. I tried to ignore the customers of the Conduit Tavern, straight across the road, who were making noisy comments on the subject of my youth and appearance. Instead I stood mesmerized by the statue in the middle of the conduit.

It was an almost life-size representation of the goddess Diana, half naked, carved from alabaster, with water from the river trilling from her left breast. I remembered how Francis had told me of it, how the statue here had once been, before worshipping her was disallowed, not of Diana but the Virgin Mary.

Despite myself and the raucous crowd behind me, I could not fail to laugh at such absurdity, until a voice interrupted my thoughts.

'A sound far sweeter than the water that runs from that fair breast.'

I turned and found myself not three feet away from my uncle's secretary.

But I returned not his smile. The memory of those poems with their cynical indulgence and their casual deceits was too fresh in my memory. 'Oh, please, no sugared words. They are wasted on me, I assure you.'

'I shall stick only to vinegar then,' he said and bowed low, doffing his hat as he did so. 'But what made you smile at that poor goddess? She is more used to worship than to being laughed at.'

'Perhaps I was musing on the loss of her predecessor, the Blessed Virgin.'

He stiffened at that, his smile frozen. Such talk was probably treasonous in me, the Blessed Virgin being tainted so with Popery, and perhaps he sensed I lay some kind of trap, knowing as I did that his background was Catholic.

But in fact I spoke the truth. Having lost my own mother, I did feel a closeness to the Mother of God, whether it was dangerous to admit or no.

I was glad of the sudden frost between us, for I could not persuade myself what manner of man he was. My first impression as he talked to the amorous doves had made me warm to his humour and pleasing informality. Yet after that I had cause to see him as both dangerous and also two-faced, one who might be honourable in company, but secretly, when none observed him, would take advantage of a power-less maidservant or a weak-willed wife.

'Then perhaps you should not admit as much,' Master Donne said quietly, glancing around him, 'at least in public. You may be young and new to the city, but such talk is not tolerated. The Queen is the only Virgin we venerate now.'

I would not have him snatch the virtuous ground away from me so easily, when I knew from his verses how deceitful he might be.

'Lecture me not, Master Donne. For are you not one who holds pub-lic office and yet in private behaves in quite another manner, which behaviour you boast of in your verses?'

He had the gall to pretend he was pained. 'If you have read my verses then I am sorry indeed. I would not, for the sake of God's own wounds, have you read aught that ever I have written. I have already had cause to regret the writing of them, and have never shown them but to my closest friends.'

'Then you must number half the gold-laced gallants of Lincoln's Inn amongst your closest friends.'

I almost added that my cousin had had so little trouble in the get-ting of them that Master Donne must not guard them very close, but he might then conclude that it was I who had solicited their getting. And I blushed to admit so much.

I could see he was already wondering how it was I might have en-countered his poetry.

'I was blessed with a plentiful education, and was encouraged to read widely,' I enlightened him coldly. 'It is my pleasure to study a great range of literature, both poetry and prose.'

'Ah,' he shook his head, all seeming serious now. 'And how measured my poor verses against those others you had studied?'

My answer would have been gentler had I not had the strong suspicion he laughed at me. 'I thought their writer seemed one who would take advantage of the frailty of others.'

He flinched at that, as if I had struck him.

'Madam, you are harsh indeed. I assure you the ladies involved were more than willing to play their parts.'

I meant to ignore him then, but the low desire overtook me to show off the educated mind of which I had boasted, and that I was not the simple innocent he took me for. 'You asked me what I thought as I looked at Diana's statue.' I kept my voice distant and reproving for I was no merchant's lustful wife nor liveryman's eager daughter, hoping for some clandestine encounter while husband or father were busy in their counting houses. 'I was thinking of the irony that lies behind the alabaster image.'

I could see that disconcerted him. 'How so?'

'Here is Diana, mother naked for every urchin and shopkeeper to stare at and yet in legend poor Actaeon but glimpsed her nakedness and paid the price by being turned into a stag and eaten by his own hounds.'

I found him watching me curiously now, his head on one side under his great black hat. 'And how does a gently bred maid from the county of Surrey know of the misfortunes of poor Actaeon?'

'From reading her grandfather's Ovid. I told you my education was a curious one.'

'Translated by Kit Marlowe?' he asked with sudden interest. 'What a world he has opened up to all with that.'

And now I scored my point. 'No. I read the work in the original. My grandfather instructed me in the Latin tongue.' Godly or not, I revelled in his look of wonder.

'Mistress Ann More, you are indeed full of surprises.'

'And you, Master Donne, are as easy to read as an open book.'

I turned on my heel and walked after my aunt towards the goldsmith's shop.

'Mistress More . . .' Master Donne clearly relished having the last word yet I fully intended not to give it to him. 'I think you will find your aunt is outside that mercer's shop. She returned some moments past and has been waving at you with her kerchief.'

AFTER THAT ENCOUNTER I did not see Master Donne at the supper table or in the winding passageways of York House for many days. Either he avoided me or my uncle had sent him hence on some distant business.

Whatever the truth I resolved to think of him no more. I even came to wish that I had not asked Francis to procure me his verses, for there was that in them which brought a heat to the blood that even I recognized as ungodly. So I pushed such thoughts from my mind and made myself useful to my aunt, who had begun to soften towards me, played with the innocent little daughters of the younger Sir Thomas, and took as many walks as I could with my cousin, always an entertaining companion.

And it was with Francis, several weeks later, that I visited the Inns of Court. At my request we stopped to pray a moment in the Temple Church, with its mysterious and ancient shades all around us of the Knights Templar. Next we took ourselves to the library of Lincoln's Inn, next to the ancient hall near Chancery Lane, where Francis sought some text he wished to consult for his studies.

Ever since a small girl, sitting quiet in my grandfather's library, I have been happy in places such as this. I loved the very silence, which was not empty but broken by the gentle turning of pages or the rare contented sigh of enlightenment. In this place, with its latticed windows and scholarly calm, I felt comforted by the warm solidity of the furniture of English oak, the flicker of candlelight on yellowing parchment, the love of learning that brought men here to pursue their passions while they forgot the hour or the need for sustenance, just as my grandfather was apt to forget until I, at ten years old, shook his sleeve and pointed to the clock.

The memory made me smile.

'Is it your vaunted love of learning that makes you look so content here, Mistress More? Surely one your age would be happier at the Royal Exchange amongst the haberdashers or the vendors of pretty gewgaws than hidden among the venerable scholars of this dusty Inn?'

I started at the interruption and noticed that the gentleman seated opposite, his head hitherto buried in a great volume more than a foot high and almost as thick, was my uncle's secretary, and that his words were indeed incurring disapproval from the venerable scholars around him.

He rose and came towards me just at the moment Francis appeared from behind a great wall of books.

'John, well met. I am here to seek out a copy of Sir Thomas North, the new collection, for my studies and yet they tell me it is not here.'

'The volume of two years since? It must be here, since he is a member of this very Inn.'

Francis and I watched as Master Donne, amidst many a twitching and clucking from elderly gentlemen at the disturbance, strode off, to return moments later with a slender calfbound volume. 'I fancy the churl of an assistant was keeping it for himself. None brings the ancient world to life as North does.'

'Thank you, John. And, since I have come upon you so happily, what of Homer? Whose translation would you recommend?'

'Come, Francis,' he shook his head, the look in his eyes belying his harsh words, 'be not so slovenly. Surely you can read Homer untranslated? I am sure Mistress More does so.'

My eyes looked to his to see if he jested at my expense and found only the raising of an eyebrow to answer me, so that I knew not if he laughed at me or no.

Back out on the paved court of Lincoln's Inn it had begun to rain and my mind turned to getting home without miring my skirts in London mud. 'Why asked you Master Donne for his opinion on Homer?' I leaned on my cousin as a carrier trotted past, splashing stinking water a foot high in our direction. 'Surely my uncle would be a better judge?'

'I value his opinion. Master Donne reads as others breathe. You must not judge him so narrowly, coz, because his verses shocked you. It was you who sought them out, remember. They were not intended for eyes such as yours.' He looked at me closely. 'Aye. I warrant they moved you, too, and now you cannot forgive him for it.'

I stood up straight and released my cousin's arm, the danger being past.

'What nonsense you do speak, Francis, for one who studies Morals and Philosophy.'

'Yet Morals and Philosophy are not found just in books, sweet Ann. As I think perhaps you are discovering.'

I would never admit it, yet there was truth in his observation. I was indeed angry with Master Donne for the feelings his verse had stoked up in me, glimpses into that other hidden world of passion and arousal.

As we walked back I felt the chill of winter descending. It would not be long now until the Parliament was dissolved and the thoughts of all turned to Christmastide and the Twelfth Night celebrations, which all the country enjoyed, rich and poor. Merriment was needed to keep us going through the hard winter days.

Already I was glad of a brick to warm my feet at night, and pulled the fur cover over me to keep out the frozen wind that sometimes swept off the river. The last few winters had been truly bitter with even the Thames freezing over and people said that this year might be cold enough again for a Frost Fair, when the river froze so solid that men and horses could ride across its surface, and makeshift taverns were set up in the middle.

This night there was a full moon and I stood with Francis in the long gallery looking out at the white-rimed trees in York House gardens that stood out, bare and stark as blackened bones, against the pale beauty of the moonlight.

I was lost in contemplation of its majesty when I noticed that Mercy had appeared holding a parcel. 'This is for you, mistress.'

'From whom?' I wondered if a messenger had come from my grandmother at Loseley or my dearest Bett at Camois Court.

'I know not, mistress. The usher found it on the table near to the great front entrance with your name on the cover.'

I undid the cloth wrapper and inside found a sheaf of papers, on each of which was written a different psalm, loosely bound in a leather covering.

Francis, teasing me, reached into the wrapper and pulled out a note which he read aloud before I could stop him. 'In token of my great contrition in exposing your bright soul to the profanity of my verse I offer you in recompense these lines translated by Mary Sidney, Countess of Pembroke, a woman whose learning and wit I admire most humbly, and which when completed will be offered to the Queen.'

Francis looked at me and laughed. 'Well, Ann, here is some verse you can have no objection to on moral grounds. A translation of the psalms of David—and by a woman! Master Donne seeks to raise your mind to holy things. Perhaps you have turned him into a reformed character—though for my own part, I hope you have not!'

I grabbed the paper from him.

Yet Francis would not desist. 'And you are given them before Her Majesty! I hope you are sensible of the honour. I wonder what message John wishes to convey? That he can be godly also? Or that, despite appearances, he respects the wit and learning of a woman as well as her more earthly charms?'

I answered Francis not, for I, no more than he, was certain of Master Donne's intention. And yet I was indeed flattered that he had sought to feed my mind and not offer some pretty trifle. I saw too that it was clever in him. Perhaps Master Donne was simply skilled in the subtle art of flattery and could not resist weaving his spells even on one as young and inexperienced as I. And then I recalled my feelings on reading those other poems, how stirred I had been and how angry at him for stirring me.

That night, alone, I opened the wrappings. The folder fell open at Psalm 52 and I began to read the Countess of Pembroke's translation, directed towards that great seducer, Satan.

Tyrant, why swell'st thou thus,
Of mischief vaunting?
Since help from God to us
Is never wanting.

Lewd lies thy tongue contrives,
Loud lies it soundeth;
Sharper than sharpest knives
With lies it woundeth.

Falsehood thy wit approves,
All truth rejected:
Thy will all vices loves,
Virtue neglected.

And yet, as I read I was shocked to find a smile creep over my features and a face other than Satan's imprint itself upon my mind.

If Master Donne had intended, by sending me verses of such great virtue, to establish his own in my eyes, the scheme had gone sadly awry.

SOON AFTERWARDS THE wife of the Lord Keeper's son, Thomas, sickened with an ague and I was kept more than occupied in diverting their young daughters to think of either Master Donne's soul or my own.

As I played with the little maids I listened to all the plans for revels and masques to be held at York House over Christmas, and although I had always praised the country over the city, it was with a sigh of sadness that the day came for me to leave London to spend the Yuletide at Loseley.

Mary chose to stay in Mile End with the Throckmortons and Margaret, with child again, meant to hole up cosily in the rural peace of Peckham, leaving only a small party to mark the Saviour's birth in Surrey.

Yet the pleasure of seeing my beloved grandmother and grandfather was compensation enough. Soon I was busily occupied with giving out the seasonal dole to the poor of the parish, a thing more needy after the failure of the harvest these last years, and since the dissolution of the monasteries. I am sure the monks were as corrupt as all painted them, yet the poor people still mourned their passing in the deep days of winter, when alms and food might be all that saved them from starving in the ditches.

My grandmother, aided by the funds from her busy hens, had made me a mantle of berry red, edged with fox fur. Frances had painted me a likeness of Perkin, which made me laugh for it caught his look of blissful idleness. Grandfather had set aside a volume of his favourite poet, Chaucer, for me. And I much enjoyed the look of delight on their faces when they opened the gifts I had bought in London, purchased on my ventures into the city—a pretty birdcage with a live linnet for Frances; a gilded fan for my grandmother, which she made a great show of pretending to flirt behind; and for my grandfather some fine but strong leather gloves, perfumed with lavender.

'They will protect you from evil also, I am assured.' For his enjoyment I repeated the colourful tale told me by the glove maker who fashioned them. 'It seems that Mother Mary laid the babe's swaddling clothes upon a lavender bush to dry, and the bush gave up its scent as an offering, so that now, besides its perfume, all lavender offers the gift of holy protection.'

After that I had so little diversion at Loseley that it was a guilty relief when, as soon as the Twelve Days had passed, my aunt, who had been missing my good offices, summoned me back to York House again.

'A dull time of it we had here without your lively presence,' she greeted me with a warm embrace, my sin at declining the role at Court temporarily forgotten. 'Lawyers, lawyers and lawyers. I was adrift in a dreary sea of black. So I have decided to cheer myself with a banquet to mark your father's ennoblement. Think you that that would please him?'

I could think of few things that would please him more than a hundred people feasting in his honour—and all paid by another.

'Indeed, Aunt, I am sure it would give him great pleasure—even though he might pretend otherwise, feeling the need for a show of modesty and humility.'

'Modesty and humility? My brother? Come, Ann, wake up and throw those winter cobwebs from your mind.'

So we started to plan the banquet. My father's ennoblement was to take place at Shrovetide, another of the great celebrations, when all made merry before Lent descended on us. I was happy indeed that my grandfather and grandmother, and my sisters Margaret and Mary and Frances would all be bidden to York House to celebrate.

All but my beloved Bett, for Bett, to my great joy and happiness, had been with child for many months now and would be too close to her confinement to venture this far.

And it was to tell me of Bett that my sister Mary arrived one clear bright morning.

I jumped upon her eager for all I could gather of how my sister's condition progressed, yet there was that in Mary's face that made me run to her before she had even removed her cloak, wrapped tight around her against the February chill. 'Is all well with our sister? When does she gather her gossips around her for the birth?'

'Sir John passed by our house in Mile End yesternight, on his way to hunt with the Duke of Suffolk.'

'Did he bring news of Bett?' I asked eagerly, imagining my sweet Bett singing as she sewed her tiny nightgowns and swaddling clothes. Motherhood would suit her soft humour so much better than mine. 'How is she faring?'

Mary gave her cloak to a servant and took my hands in hers. 'Ailing, it seems,' she said gently. 'She is asking to have us about her, you especially, Ann, to help with her confinement.'

'But is it not for some weeks yet?'

'Sir John says they think six. But she longs for your company as soon as you may go there.'

My picture of the singing Bett was replaced by one of Bett feeling motherless and alone, and I resolved that, no matter what distractions might tempt me here, I should go to her as soon as ever I was able.

Childbirth, of the many trials it was woman's lot to undergo, was of all the most frightening. Our own mother had died giving birth to Frances, never having the joy of holding her babe in her arms, but speeding instead to meet her Maker. I wondered if Bett dwelt on that morbid thought in the cold dark reaches of the night when the mind refuses to be salved by warmth and peace and stalks instead by the cold shores of pain and death.

'I will ask my aunt when I may go. Will you be coming also, Mary?'

'I hope so, yet I know not.' She sighed and looked away. 'I have my own household to supervise.' It was then I noticed how unlike herself she seemed, a fainter copy of Mary rather than the woman herself, like parchment that had faded in the sun, as if her lively mind were shut up somewhere far from here.

'Is it fear for Bett that troubles you so sorely, sister?'

Mary looked at me as if she were not sure of whether to answer or no. 'Can you keep a secret, Ann?'

I knew from the fear in her voice that this was something of great matter and I nodded gravely.

'It is my husband. Or rather his debts. He play acts as if the sun shone down upon him daily and all were well. And yet I know he has gambled heavily and borrowed money and, in trying to cast off his debts, borrowed more money again.' She took my hands and pressed them so hard that the knuckles whitened. I had never seen my brave and fearless sister thus reduced. 'I came upon these papers in his closet. Ann, he has so many debts.' Her voice, so low and musical, was shrill with fear. 'And, see here, all the notes are to one gentleman, a Master Matthew Freeman of Fairby in the county of Yorkshire. What can it mean?'

'And you know not this Master Freeman?'

Mary shook her head.

'And what has Nick to say?'

'He will not talk of money. If I raise it he shouts and stamps and when I next look round he has gone.'

'Perhaps this man could be a moneylender, think you?'

At that Mary began, very softly, to weep. A sight so shocking because I had never witnessed it before, not even when our mother died. Mary had simply straightened her young back, taken Frances in her arms and proved a tower of strength, far stronger than our father, who blamed all—the Heavens, his doctor, even the infant Frances—for his terrible agonizing loss, and withdrew to his chamber. Mary, but a maid of twelve, as slender as a reed and hardly five feet tall, took charge of all. With the help of my grandmother she summoned the priest, my aunt from the Court (from where the Queen was loath to lose her) and comforted my father as best she could.

'The sum is two hundred pounds!'

I gasped at that. It was a fortune.

'And he seeks immediate payment. Ann, this gentleman from the north has written to *me* to ask if I would meet with him and discuss how we can meet my husband's obligations.'

'You? Why is he not applying to Nick direct?'

Her only answer was to sob.

'He has a letter. To a gentleman of my acquaintance. The servant who delivered it must have betrayed me to him.'

'Who is this gentleman?'

'One I turned to when my worries over Nick were too great to bear alone.'

'And what said you in this letter?'

'Things I should not have said to one who is not my husband. Now he threatens to expose me.'

'But surely Nick is the one at fault here?'

'He will turn it round so that I am the one who has sinned more greatly. I know the cast of his mind. I must retrieve the letter from this Master Freeman. And yet—oh Ann—what if Nick discovers my weakness?'

I was so truly alarmed to see Mary, strong, brave Mary, thus reduced that I made a misguided offer of my own. 'This gentleman,' I ventured, desperate to ease her burden when she had so bravely eased ours, 'would it answer if I, who have no connection to the matter, tried to seek him out?'

'It has not come to that. I still have my necklace of amethysts and emeralds. I will sell that first.'

'Oh, Mary, the necklet that belonged to our mother, Anne?'

Mary looked away but the bright sunlight caught the tear that ran down her face and made it sparkle. But not with joy.

'Better than disgrace or penury.'

'Have you nowhere else to apply to? What about our father?'

'He might help, but Constance will turn him against me. And remember, it was I who persuaded Father to let me marry Nick, I who wore him down with tales of Nick's connections and his expectations. Oh, Ann, I cannot admit that we have fallen to such a low as this, with the debtors' prison holding out desirous arms to us. I must find some other resolution.'

I did not argue with the truth of this. I wished only I had something I could give her to help. And then I remembered the little there was left from Grandmother's eggs. I found my hidden purse and held it out to her.

Mary's answer was to weep some more. 'Ann, I cannot take your pennies.'

'Please, Sister. They will be of more help to you, I want for nothing here.'

Mary smiled sadly and pushed the purse back to me. 'The truth is, my little Ann, they would be a raindrop washed away into the ocean.' She dried her eyes and looked at me askance. 'By the way, Sister, I hear from our cousin Francis that you have won a heart.'

I stopped short at that, more flustered than I wished her to see. 'If you speak of whom I think, his heart is well protected. It was more his vanity that made him notice me, I'd venture. He suspects me a blank page on which to imprint his thoughts.'

'Then he will be surprised at how many pages are writ there already. You are full of complexity and contradiction, Ann.'

We descended to the Great Chamber to find my father parading in his Court costume for the approval of his sister. For so small a man he did look fine indeed. And yet if only the cost of that fine suit could have been given to Mary, it seemed to me, all her hardship would be over.

But this prospect was as likely as a ship laden with Spanish treasure mooring at York House steps.

'What think you, ladies, of my new suit of clothes?' My father turned for us to both admire him.

I could not tell the truth, that in my present state he brought to mind a nobleman's pet monkey dressed in borrowed finery.

'Father,' I began, 'here is Mary, come to me with a message from Bett. She fears her confinement comes upon her sooner than she expected and Sir John has left her alone to go hunting. She begs for me to go to Camois as soon as ever I can to assist her.'

I dared not mention my fears for her safety in childbed after what had happened to my mother, since my father was one for hiding his hurts away under lock and key and liked not the person who tried to release them.

Today he had the look of a sulky child. 'Bett's confinement is not for some weeks yet. Besides, she will have other gossips around her than you. Sir John's mother and his sisters will already be with her. They have no need of you.' His voice took on a querulous, stubborn tone which often it did when he wished to get his own way against heavy opposition. 'There are plenty of churchmen who hold that this ritual of confinement goes on far too long. Indeed the Reverend Able quoted more than fifty relatives attending one childbed, and consuming enough sweet wine and hot spiced caudle to inebriate an army. I cannot hold with it. So many women gathered together in so small a chamber must surely bring with them a far greater chance of infection than if they stayed away!'

'I am sure you are right, Father,' I soothed. 'But Bett is all alone, Mary says, and becoming fearful, which cannot be good for the expected child, can it?'

'Giving birth is part of nature,' intoned my father, making me wish to throw a goblet of ale at him, 'accomplished every day by the beasts of the field and the commonest country wench. Bett fears too much.' I watched him, startled. Could those locks be so tightly shut that he truly did not remember the loss of his dear wife?

'I would like to go, Father, as soon as my aunt can spare me.'

'*I* cannot spare you, and there's an end to it. I wish you to come to Court for my dubbing.' His tone softened. He put his arm about my shoulders. 'And I wish you to have a new gown, so that you may shine even brighter than the other ladies. My sister will take you to buy it, will you not, Elizabeth?'

My eyes widened at the thought of a new gown but my conscience would not let me off so easily. If I held to my position, what would he do? Lock me in my chamber? Confine me to York House?

'But, Father, what if Bett really is ill?'

I could see my father was at the end of his patience with me. 'Daughter, dispute no more. You will come with your grandmother and grandfather to the Court for my ennoblement. Our family honour requires it. After that you may go to your sister.'

I almost argued further but good sense and the thought of the cinnamon-coloured satin I had seen in a shop in the new Royal Exchange stopped my mouth. What difference could a few days make?

'And afterwards, can I go to Bett the very next morn?'

'You have the persistence of a fly on a dung heap, Ann. I pity your poor husband.' He looked at me tetchily. 'If ever you have one.'

My sorrow at my father's stubbornness was assuaged by two things: the cinnamon satin and the arrival of my grandparents.

My aunt had requested they stay in my chamber and that I move while they were present to a smaller room, which I was happy to do.

The day appointed for my grandparents' arrival I waited for them by the river steps all morning in the cold February air, and almost leapt into the water with joy when at last I saw the barge the Lord Keeper had sent to meet them approaching from Southwark, carrying both my grandparents, my sister Frances, and my grandmother's gentlewoman, Prudence.

Prudence alighted first to help my grandmother climb down, whispering to me smugly as she did so, 'Stephen, the usher of the bedchamber was as mad as a speared boar that I was bidden to come instead of he, but my lady has ever had a low opinion of serving men, so here I am in London Town.'

Next came Sir William, my grandfather, and the thought struck me that though I had seen him but recently, he had suddenly grown old. When we were private I would ask my grandmother how he was faring.

'Well, Ann, let me look at you,' my grandmother instructed. She, I was grateful to see, was as brisk and as bustling and as bad-tempered as ever before.

For the occasion she had added to her usual severe black gown a double chain of silver links, fastened in the centre under her chin. This, though no doubt designed to compete with the moneyed merchants and landed aristocrats she would encounter here, had instead the effect of making her resemble the Lord Mayor of London.

'Such a tiresome journey,' she complained. 'The mud was so bad between Loseley and Guildford that we had to dismount and walk like a string of pilgrims.' I tried not to smile. My grandmother rarely if ever found anything away from Loseley to her satisfaction. I suspected that to do so would quite spoil her pleasure in life.

'Here, Ann,' she handed me a basket covered in a chequered cloth, 'I have brought you some fruit from our hothouse.'

All of a sudden the cloth moved. I screamed, thinking it haunted, and pulled it back to find my cat hidden beneath.

'You have brought Perkin!' I shouted from joy.

'He would not settle since you left. No good to man nor beast. The mice dance about in front of him and he claps his paws in time. Perhaps the London rats will restore his zest for life. You look well, Ann. I thought only country girls had pink in their cheeks but I find you blooming like a rose in the hedgerow.'

'It is her two admirers,' Mary commented with a sly look, seeming to have forgotten for the moment all her own problems in the pleasure of greeting my grandparents.

'Two?' My father looked at her searchingly, but Mary had gone to prepare a comfortable chair for my grandfather whose stiff joints troubled him sorely on long journeys.

'Ann,' my father persisted, 'what is your sister's meaning?'

'I have the very thing for Grandfather's knee.' I skipped off towards the door of the chamber. 'My aunt and I prepared it for the Lord Keeper. Grandmother will greatly approve of it. A *flos unguentorum* made of herbs mixed with sheep's suet.'

Once out in the passageway I stopped, trying to catch my own breath and silence the rush of blood that was pounding in my ears at the thought of the man Mary was describing as my other admirer.

And what a fool I would be to succumb to the lures of one whom I knew to be as great a libertine as Master John Donne.

Chapter 7

ON THE DAY my father was to be knighted, I dressed with care, though my thoughts kept straying to the inference my sister Mary had made about myself and Master Donne. Then I remembered the pressing secret she had entrusted to me and wondered in what way we might solve it and save our honour at the same time.

Mercy smiled as she helped me into my new gown of cinnamon satin, the kirtle embroidered with green strands of ivy. The habit now is for dresses to be slashed as if by a thousand knife cuts, the under layer being cloth of a different hue which is pulled through the rent to make an elaborate pattern. To me such dresses make the wearer seem laughable, like a scarecrow in the fields. Instead I favour this style with its high waist, flattened chest and delicate cobweb ruff which makes me feel as light as thistledown, though this is by no means the truth.

'Bring me my casket of jewels,' I bid Mercy. 'Today I will wear my mother's amethyst ring.'

The ring winked up at me from its case of purple leather. I slipped it onto my second finger. It was fastened, as is also the fashion, to a black silken cord which I wrapped three times round my wrist. They do say a lace from the second finger runs straight to the heart. If my mother had lived until this day, my father's new title would have made her the Lady Anne. Would she have relished the ennoblement? Or laughed at the tawdry nature of earthly glory? Yet on this day, for the first time, I wondered about the ring's value, and whether I should offer it to my sister Mary, sore though I would feel at parting with it.

'Mistress Ann,' Mercy whispered as she finished brushing my hair, her voice bringing me back to the present, 'the colour of your new gown is lovelier on you than any I have yet seen.'

'It is, is it not?' I laughed, enjoying the rare and wicked pleasure of vanity. 'Let us hope it does me some good!'

I walked into the Great Hall to search for my father and found instead a large group of black-clad gentlemen waiting there. I started to see that Master Donne was amongst their number.

The Lord Keeper, who was ever polite but rarely seemed to notice I was beyond six years old, looked startled, as if a stranger had appeared. 'Mistress Ann, you are the very picture of your sainted mother, whom I had the joy to meet at Loseley. Come, John, does our little mistress not outshine the stars this day?'

'And the moon also. She is a veritable angel of beauty.'

I knew, given my sister's implication of the other night that I should look modestly down and keep silent. Yet it angered me that Master Donne, whose mind was clear and sharp, should come up with so empty and conventional a compliment.

'Indeed?' I replied. 'Yet I have always thought angels to be dull beings, all goodness and light and standing around forever singing and waiting to do the Lord's bidding.'

'Dull?' he repeated, laughter rippling through his voice. 'Even proud Lucifer, who thought to rival Almighty God in His magnificence? Was he dull also?'

'Lucifer above all.' I looked him in the eye, recalling the psalm he had sent me. 'For anyone with so much pride as Lucifer would be interested in none but themselves.'

'Ann!' The voice that cut through Master Donne's laughter like the crack of a whip was my father's. I had not known he was standing so near me.

My father is well known for his eruptions of choler, which often come like thunder exploding in a calm blue sky. 'How can you speak in that way of heavenly matters! I hope these are not the ways you have been learning in my sister's house?'

For answer I dropped a curtsey, relieved that he was simply angry at my levity and not whom I addressed it to. When I rose back to my feet I saw that I was now taller than my father by almost two inches.

'No, Father, I have met in my aunt and uncle's home nothing but dutiful respect to God our Maker.'

'Good. Now show some respect to your earthly parent and bring me the black cloak from my chamber. It may be chill on the water.'

'I will, Father. With all my heart I would not wish you to take a chill on such a day as this. Mayhap a fur-lined coverlet would warm you the better?'

He listened to my tender tone with suspicion. 'Thank you, Ann. I am not a dotard yet.'

My aunt had come to the water's edge to wish him luck. 'Farewell, brother. Send my good wishes to Her Majesty.'

The Lord Keeper had been summoned to Greenwich on the Queen's business also and he accompanied us downriver on his barge, a wherry being too frail a craft, and the river water likely to besmirch our fine clothes.

We talked little on the journey and as we rowed eastwards I occupied myself with looking at the busy river banks where builders, like little ants, threw up houses so fast that you half expected one to have risen on the way home that had not been there on your outwards journey.

The tide was with us, and it was less than an hour before we reached the Queen's favourite palace.

We moored by the great watergate and walked up the steps through the garden and thence to a courtyard where many people crowded together, some holding petitions, all dressed in their richest outfits. Some had come to seek favours or preferments, to ask for lands to be restored, for benefices if they were clergy, or leniency if their debts threatened to engulf their manor houses. Others wanted justice of the courts.

At last it was our turn to see the Queen.

This time I knew to look out for the ladies who waited on her, asking myself what idle gossip or vicious chatter they would have to share this time. But today they were silent and looked around disdainfully. Any one of them could have helped the crowd of petitioners but none would do so except for her own reward or advancement.

The throng began to ease forward, like a jewelled sea, pulled onwards by the lure of Majesty, when I heard a whisper from one of the ladies. 'I gather *he* is going to arrive for the dubbing ceremony.'

I needed not to ask whom it was they were discussing. There was but one 'he' in this court: the dazzling and noble Earl of Essex.

As we neared the Privy Chamber I wondered if, this time, the Queen would be in a better temper. No doubt that, too, depended on her youthful admirer.

It was a scene of vast magnificence. All around us the bright colours of the courtiers' clothes were framed against even richer tapestries, their costly jewels all lit up in the flickering glow of a thousand candles. I breathed in the pungent odours of spices and pomander, always redolent of the Court to me.

'Ann!' The sound of my father's sharp voice followed by the royal fanfare woke me from my reverie. 'Remember where you are. Here comes Her Majesty!'

And there before me was Queen Elizabeth.

She looked a different woman on this occasion, regal and as dignified as a statue, her face stark under its mask of ceruse, her lips and cheeks reddened with cochineal. Her gown, not filched this time from her lady in waiting, was the finest I had ever seen, covered in sapphires and emeralds, and vast pearls sewn into the sweeping neckline, set off by more rings, necklets and gemstones than I had ever seen on any lady, her sleeves legs of mutton a whole foot wide, her ruff so large it stood up like an open fan all round her neck.

Yet it was the eyes that held you, pale and lidless, almost like those of the toads that stared up from our lily pads at Loseley, all-seeing, with the veriest touch of sinister threat. I could not banish the thought of how I would not wish to be Lady Mary Howard, nor any lady who crossed the Queen in love.

And yet, until I saw Elizabeth in her Court, with all its grandeur and her ladies round her, I knew not the meaning of the word Majesty. It draped around the Queen like a jewelled mantle and I knew that even without her finery, Elizabeth would still be a Queen.

She stopped her procession when she saw my father and lightly touched his shoulder.

'You have been diligent in my service, George More,' she smiled. 'I am told you speak more than any other in the house of Parliament, yea, and sit on more committees. I thank you for your work, and your good service to me in your county of Surrey and while I dispense the title but sparingly I know it will content my friend your father that though he still lives you also should carry the title of knight.'

Her attendants waited for her to move on yet she leaned suddenly closer to my father and spoke with a new wistfulness in her voice. 'And I well remember how, many years ago, when I was but a green girl, you would act as a messenger between myself and the Earl of Leicester.'

The Queen's hawk eyes softened at the memory of her once and greatest love.

'I did, Ma'am,' my father gently replied. 'You once sent him a diamond ring by my good offices. From your own finger.'

'So did I.' She seemed for an instant back in those heady times of her youth. 'And you rode to him through rain as heavy as the Flood and told him that his Queen would do as the weather, nothing but weep, until she saw him again.'

They stood for a moment in a bubble of the past, a time when life even for the Queen had seemed simpler and so much more full of promise.

Watching them silently I saw my father in a new light. Not the fussy, narrow man he had become, but the once gallant deliverer of passionate messages of love.

The Queen moved on with her train of ladies behind her.

'And now it is to the Earl of Essex that she sends her diamond rings,' my father murmured sadly. 'Let us hope he proves to be worthy of her.'

'Well done, *Sir* George.' The Lord Keeper, who had remained at our side, shook his hand. I suspect he understood my father well, that to some men titles were as a shifting breeze compared with godliness or honour. But to others, my father being in their number, a knighthood was a prize indeed.

As the Lord Keeper spoke the crowd around us began suddenly to part, as if for the Israelites in the Red Sea.

A noble-looking man with dark flowing hair, glowing eyes and a square-cut red beard, his clothes surprisingly disarrayed for one of his rank, strode past us.

'My Lord of Essex,' bowed the Lord Keeper.

'Good Sir Thomas!' He shook the Lord Keeper's hand warmly, his eyes lighting up with what seemed real affection and I could see what it was about this man that moved people. There was an eagerness and directness in his manner as if, when he held fast your hand, nothing else in God's universe existed save you and he.

Behind us, out of the corner of my eye, I saw that the Queen too had stopped, waiting to feel the beam of his bright sun.

And then a strange occurrence happened. He did not shine upon her. He turned instead to me. 'Tell me, who is this new star of loveliness who shines so brilliant in our dull firmament?'

'Mistress Ann More, my lord,' explained the Lord Keeper, anxiety beginning to agitate his manner. 'Daughter to Sir George More, newly knighted by Her Majesty.'

I would wager an angel that he knew she was watching, that indeed this whole performance was for her benefit, not mine. I could have been a ship's timber arrayed in cinnamon satin and he would have paid me the same extravagant compliment.

The Queen turned on her heel and I could hear the angry swish of her robes as she hastened from the chamber, her ladies scurrying behind her.

I bit my lip, and said naught, consumed with gratitude that I had escaped a place at Court, where, innocent though I might be, I would be pulled willy-nilly into the muddied waters of others' deceptions.

'Come,' my father took hold of my arm, as relieved as I that the Earl had moved on, 'let us return to York House where they await us with much feasting.'

On the barge once more, alone, I turned to him. 'Father, is it true the Earl could succeed the Queen when finally her time arrives?'

My father looked suddenly afraid and glanced behind him. 'Ann! Such talk is treason! Besides, no matter what the Earl may wish himself, there are a dozen more deserving claimants than he and the likeliest, sorry to say, since my own father assisted with her prosecution, is the son of Mary of Scots, King James of Scotland. Yet the Queen will never name her heir. She knows full well that when she does her sun will set and all will turn towards the new light in the east. Elizabeth, great Queen though she is, would be abandoned at the end. It is the way of the world.'

There was a freezing wind on the river. As we rowed away from

Greenwich the sun did indeed set, suffusing the whole of London with a red glow. On any other day this would have seemed to me a glory of nature, something to celebrate in all its burnished beauty, but after my father's speech it seemed to betoken the end of an era.

My father tucked my hand into his arm. 'So, Ann, what think you of my ennoblement? You see what an honourable tree it is you spring from? Knights going back through three generations. And word comes to me that your sister Margaret's husband Grymes will be knighted before long. Whether that young man Manners stumps up or not, we must soon think of a husband for you, a man who can match our honour with his own.'

I looked away and said nothing.

He was silent as we travelled back upriver, leaving me to my thoughts and the sound of the oarsmen rhythmically rowing. As the towers and turrets of York House approached he dropped his voice. 'There is much company near your age residing in York House is there not, Daughter? Young Francis, his betrothed, Mary, the younger Sir Thomas and also his lady?'

'Yes, Father, it is a busy house indeed.'

'Yet, Ann,' he hesitated and fixed me with his small grey eyes, which still shone as brightly as if he were a boy, instead of a man of sixty, 'there is one whose company I would fain you shun, since it befits not an innocent maiden. Master John Donne. Your uncle thinks highly of him yet I came across some verse of his being handed round the Inns of Court and laughed over by its inmates like naughty schoolboys. It seemed to be both lewd and, even worse, satirical.'

I bit my lip, hoping it was not the poem about his mistress going to bed.

'I wish your uncle had not appointed him. He has a reputation that I like not.' He shook his head. 'Women are such fragile vessels. Even the Queen's head is softened by pretty words and a handsome leg.'

'Not I, Father.' I put my chin up and faced him. 'I am no fragile vessel. Handsome legs hold no sway with me.'

He glanced sharply at me. 'You are a hard book to read, Ann.'

I looked down, heartily glad of it. Especially since I knew not myself what the pages said. Or what my future would be.

We had reached the steps.

My aunt had caused the servants to line the path from the river to the house and when we alighted from the barge they cheered.

My father pretended to be humbled by such a fanfare for his knighthood, but I saw that secretly he was much pleased.

When we had greeted the servants I saw that my grandmother also waited inside the entrance of the Great Hall.

She smiled at her son. 'Greetings, Sir George.'

'And my father, Sir William? Is he not here to share our joy?' I could hear the regret at his father's absence in my father's voice. It was as if he were once again a small boy wishing approval for the bow and arrow he had just fashioned out of twigs.

'He is suffering from an ague. His humour is a phlegmatic one, yet today he is hot and dry as if it were of red choler.' There was concern today beneath her briskness. 'Ann, there is a great garden here at York House and though you must be cold from your time on the river, I would thank you mightily for finding me some sorrel or purslane to soothe his aches. The servants are city people and would not recognize purslane if it were worth a bag of coins.'

'I will go straightway and if I can find it bring it to your chamber.'

'Thank you, child. If you cannot find it, I know none can.'

I wrapped my cloak closely around me for the wind was sharp now that the sun had sunk beneath the horizon.

Herbs, if any were to be found, would be grown in the knot garden running down to the river on the left side of the house. Often when I walked there I caught sight of the gardener and his boy, but today the hour was too advanced.

The knot garden in February was a desolate place, almost empty apart from the small walls of hedge that divided up its sections. I saw no sign of sorrel. Trying to forget the bone-chilling cold I hunted in every section for its tall leaves, like to those of the dock plant which children rubbed upon their skin when they suffered the sting of a nettle, but none had survived. I was about to give up when I spied a pale and creeping plant with thick stems that snaked along the ground. I knelt down to inspect it further and noticed a tiny parcel of black seeds, no bigger than a tooth. It was, I found, intertwined with another plant, the other with wirier stems, that crept along by its side as if they were old friends who could not be parted.

In my head I heard my grandmother warn me, as she used to on our walks together at Loseley, that this was spurge, alike to purslane—yet venomous. I broke the stem and watched the milky sap ooze out. It was spurge indeed.

I was in the act of gently disentangling the healing purslane from its traitorous friend when I heard sounds of whispered talking no more than a few feet away. Intent on my job, I decided it was like to be one of my uncle's servants come to gossip privately. If I took two steps closer I would hear them, whispered words though they were.

Tucking my precious purslane into my sleeve I tried to return to the house yet found myself trapped as the arguing pair were between myself and my destination. The only way out of the knot garden was through a narrow opening and it was from just beyond this opening that the pair were speaking. With a start I realized that, to compound my difficult situation, one of the voices belonged to Master Donne and the other to a gentlewoman of about fifty years.

'Take care, Mother.' I had never heard such cold hard anger in his voice before. 'Remember where we are. Accuse me not of betraying my religion for the sake of my ambition! And in this place too! I have studied the works of Cardinal Bellarmine and know where I stand on the greatest of truths.'

'Then why live you amongst these people, John?' the woman's voice replied, low but clear. 'They are our persecutors. They would see all Catholics hounded and outlawed, crushed beneath their heels like cockroaches. The very Lord Keeper himself!'

Realizing the import of their conversation, I wished myself anywhere but here, yet I was trapped.

I could hear his temper rising, though his voice was so low. 'I am no betrayer. I have made my peace with God and my country so that no longer must I live in a world of watchfulness and secrets, of disguises and whispered conversations such as this! And fear. Did you know how much fear, Mother, when you bade me when I was but twelve years old come with you to the Tower to see my uncle the priest, that my presence might make your disguise the more convincing? How I shrank at the iron fastenings on the door, and the stink, and the sound of moans and despair within and only felt the light of day when we left those loathsome walls?'

The quiet voice that answered him was the most distinctive I had ever heard. Low and musical, yet so deep it almost had the quality of a bell sounding the faithful to worship. And indeed I began to understand this was what it sought to do. Master Donne's mother sought to summon him back into the fold of the Romish church despite the dangers that might befall him on the rack or scaffold, and I wondered if this was what she called a mother's love.

'John, silence! It was not you who paid the final price, but your brother.' I flinched, hearing the certainty in that commanding tone. In a man that voice was heard on the brink of battlefields, leading charges. In a woman it exhorted bravery and sacrifice and hinted at cowardice and dishonour if it were not heeded. It made me think of Volumnia, whom I had read about in my grandfather's library, proud to lose her son in battle if it meant the greater glory of Rome.

'I will not be silent!' The passion in Master Donne's voice hissed into the cold evening air. 'Do you think I have not struggled, bled, lain awake at night on the cross over this? But I have come to my accommodation.'

'Your betrayal. Let us not mince words, John. This is down to your cursed ambition. You could not live quietly like so many, but sought public office and must renounce your God.'

I peered through a small hole in the ivy-covered wicket gate. John Donne's mother, a tall, handsome woman with the same dark lustrous eyes as he, stood wrapped in a heavy black cloak.

'You ever valued Henry more than I.' I could hear in the man the anguish of a child that feels itself not loved as it wished to be. 'He was your youngest, your tender plant, nourished with all your care, the only one of us all who followed the faith as you do, to the letter.'

'He was the bravest of you all. Tomorrow I return to Antwerp. I should never have been here, it is too dangerous. I bid you farewell. I doubt we will ever speak again.'

'No! No!' I wished to cry. A mother should never renounce her son. I knew what it was to lose a mother, the pain and the longing, the lack of tender affection that can never be replaced through life's long journey.

But Master Donne's mother had passed through the gate. I stayed where I stood, as still as the frozen tree I leaned against, and heard her skirts swish as she walked fast down towards the river. Despite my doubts about him, I found myself wanting to offer comfort. Yet to do so would reveal my presence, that I had silently witnessed this most dangerous of conversations. If it were suspected that Master Donne for one moment embraced the Papist cause he would lose all—livelihood, honour, acceptance in Elizabeth's society. So I kept my peace and waited as he stood, staring after her. I imagined his eyes all dark with pain.

In a few moments he took one last glance over the river in the direction she had left, exasperated, angry and yet withall faintly despairing, and strode off back towards the house so that I could at last make my escape.

Sorry for him as I might feel, it could not smother the excitement I felt at the prospect of visiting Bett tomorrow. So I ran to find my grandmother and gave her the purslane which she carried to the still room.

On the morrow, as soon as all were risen, I was to leave on my journey with my uncle's groom.

The day dawned pale, frosty and clear, good weather for riding to Camois Court, with just one stop at an inn. My grandmother had generously offered Prudence as my companion, since my sister Mary, despite her worries at what to do about Master Freeman, had gone ahead with Margaret.

Yet Prudence's sadness at having to leave London the moment when she had just arrived, and her twittering response to each sight we passed on the road, no matter how trivial, from the marvel of paving stones, to the fascination of every shop, tavern or bear pit, and the exclamation every two minutes at how polite the Lord Keeper's servants had been when I am sure these august gentlemen took her for a humble rustic, made me wish she had stayed behind.

I tried to take my mind from her chatter by thinking of Bett. As was the custom Bett had taken to her chamber some six weeks before the babe was expected. The best hangings in the house would already surround her and her favourite possessions be gathered about her. The windows would be closed fast against fresh air, universally acknowledged to be harmful at such a time as this. Instead the fires would be banked up and the chamber kept as hot as hellfire, be it sun or cold outside.

Like many a husband Sir John had made himself scarce, summoning instead the gossips Bett had requested to attend her lying-in. Some husbands harrumphed at the cost of the wines and sweetmeats, the comfits and the carraways, the marmalade and the marchpane that such occasions demanded and quite likely Sir John was among them.

Yet others were happy to pay since it meant their presence was not required. Lying-ins were the most female of rituals. I wondered who would be at Bett's side already. Sir John's mother and sisters and any other female relative who considered she had an interest. The midwife and wet nurse. My own two sisters Mary and Margaret. Frances was deemed too young to attend such occasions, a fact that made her mad with resentment.

The pleasure at the thought of seeing my beloved sister again, and hearing her hopes and dreams for the future of this babe, diverted me from the dullness of the journey.

As did Prudence.

'Look, Mistress Ann,' she cried as we passed the great pond at the edge of London. 'Swans! Is it true they belong to the Queen and only she can eat them? And that at great banquets they serve a capon stuffed with a pheasant and also a quail, as if each had swallowed the last?'

I tried to recall the few banquets I had attended but could recall no such curious extravagance as this.

'The Lord Keeper's steward says things are much improved in his lordship's house since he married your lady aunt. The last lady Egerton was somewhat lax in her housekeeping but my lady Elizabeth, your aunt, is a true manager of a great house.'

'I am sure she would be relieved to hear so.' I tried not to smile as I replied. I knew I should tell her not to listen to such tittle-tattle but this glimpse into the hidden world of servants was enticing. 'So, what else do they have to say at the steward's table, Prudence?'

She looked at me slyly, pretending to shorten the length of her reins. 'That tis time you married, Mistress Ann, and that your father should spend less time in the chamber of Parliament and more on finding you a husband who would tame your fire. The Lord Keeper's almoner saw you running across the lawn with your skirts around your ankles, and you have been marked several times walking abroad without even a gentlewoman to accompany you.'

'God's blood!' I knew not whether to laugh or be angered at such scrutiny. 'I hope that is all the gossip they enjoy at my expense.'

Prudence hesitated, blushing a fiery red.

'Not quite, mistress. They do also say your father must be a blind man, and your uncle too, to have an innocent lamb like you in the same stable as the wolf that would tear it apart.'

I sped up my horse, glancing to see if my uncle's groom was following the discourse, but, to my relief, he seemed as unmoved as a stone.

I overtook both Prudence and the groom and galloped across the greensward ahead of us, needing to feel the cool of the wind against my face. To be the object of such gossip angered me beyond enduring. My father already knew of the wolf in the stable and—innocent lamb though I might be—I was neither so weak nor so foolish as to allow myself to be torn apart by anyone, wolf or no.

As we rode southwards I spoke as little as possible, to encourage no further idle gossip. The bright day slowly died in the sky, leaving first a red glow and then blackness, broken only by the bright light of the stars. I had always loved the vastness of the night sky and missed it while in London where the presence of two hundred thousand souls, all jumbled on top of each other like bottles layered in my grandfather's storeroom, meant that it seemed neither day nor night in the way it had at Loseley.

I was tired now, my back aching from riding side-saddle so long. Yet the stars still moved me. Was there truly a fiery girdle round the earth where angels could pass unscathed, dipping their swords as they passed until they flamed brightly? And are we truly affected, as the astrologers believe, not just by the sun and the moon but by every planet shining down on those born within its ambit?

I also felt keenly the excitement at seeing Bett tomorrow and of staying at an inn tonight with only the groom and Prudence for company. This seemed a wild, outrageous thing to do for I had never been alone under such conditions of freedom before. A pity, then, to be so out of sorts with Prudence for her great gabby mouth that I took brief sustenance and went early to bed. The stiffness made me sleep at once until Prudence, so merry and tipsy after two hours downstairs with the company, knocked over the chamberpot.

With bad grace I rolled over to one side of the bed, leaving room for Prudence but offering no covers, then relented and gave her half the blankets so that in a moment she snored like one of my grandmother's Old Spot sows.

The next day on the road we saw several passers-by with black marks on their foreheads they tried to hide. It was Ash Wednesday, I remembered. Under the old religion all would be marked with a cross on the forehead while the priest reminded them 'You are dust and unto dust you shall return,' yet such Popish practices are dangerous now. I thought of Master Donne's stern mother and marvelled again that she could risk his future so by visiting York House. Had he known she would visit him there at such mortal risk? This time I shivered at this reminder of our own mortality and flicked my mare with the switch to get to my sister the sooner.

At last we were in sight of Camois Court. The house was solid and large, its brick and timbers welcoming us with the thought of warm beds and hot water and the sight of my beloved Bett. As I jumped down from my horse my heart soared within me.

Only to be dashed by the sight of my sister Margaret, all great with child, who had heard the hoofbeats and was standing alone by the great front door awaiting my arrival.

'Ann! Ann! Come quickly. Bett is calling for you!'

Inside, the house was dark and strangely quiet. There was no sense, as I had expected, of warm fires, glowing candles and the warming scent of spiced possets, of crowded chambers and female chatter and happy anticipation as at the usual lying-in. I followed Margaret up the great staircase, beneath the stern looks of generations of Mills ancestors, and halfway up I heard a single sudden cry and clutched my sister's hand.

'What ails her? The babe's not due for four weeks yet.'

Margaret looked back at me with anguished eyes. 'Maybe tis early or Bett mistook herself in her calculations. In all events, the babe is coming now.'

We ran pell-mell into Bett's chamber. In the deep gloom and the sweltering heat I could hardly see even the shadow of my sister. Instead I could make out a vast log fire, and all around the room burning pastilles which made the very air thick and hard to breathe, even for one in rude health such as I was. I began to cough.

'Is that you, Ann? Oh, thank God you are come. The midwife thinks my son can wait no longer in his eagerness to be born!'

I saw her then. Childlike and pale, her hair hanging wetly down hollowed cheeks, so different from the Bett who had left so many months before.

She began to scream again, and writhe as if her belly were full of gnawing serpents, not one small babe.

'Be still, my lady.' The midwife tried to soothe her, stroking Bett's forehead with a hand that seemed to me less than clean. Yet Bett kept screaming.

'The babe is eager to join the world.' The midwife attempted a tone that was light and gay, but I could hear the worry beneath. 'And yet he is not lying in the right position.'

'Then get a doctor!' I looked round for Margaret. 'And where is Sir John?'

'On his way back from Lincolnshire.' My sister Mary appeared from the suffocating darkness. She seemed but a shadow of her usual commanding self. 'We have sent a groom to hasten him.'

'There is no time for a doctor, my lady.' The midwife was wringing her hands and I could see the sweat running from her face into the runnel between her breasts.

'Send for one all the same! Now!'

Bett screamed again, yet this time it was the scream of an animal caught in a trap.

'Have you given her Mother's Caudle?' asked a lady of middle years, dressed in great finery but with a look of fear in her eyes, the fear I could feel spreading through the room like a canker. I recognized her as Sir John's mother, whom I had met at Bett's nuptials. 'Will it not help her keep up her strength?'

Another cry split the air.

'The eagle stone? Where is the eagle stone?' demanded Mary, ever more at home in parlour or Great Hall than sick room. 'That will help attract the babe from out of the womb, surely?'

All hunted around until a piece of rock, about four inches long and the colour of rust, was found. As it was passed to the midwife I heard it rattle and saw that it was hollow.

The stone was placed on Bett's heaving stomach yet stayed there but a second or two before she bucked again in pain.

'You must tie it on,' counselled Margaret, removing her girdle to try and attach the stone to the outer side of Bett's thigh.

'My son!' Bett seemed to be almost delirious. 'Where is my son!'

I sat next to her and took her hand. 'Pray God he will arrive soon,' I soothed, stroking her poor head. 'Midwife,' I shouted, getting ever the more desperate. 'Is there any sign of the baby's head?'

The midwife reached out a hand and felt inside Bett's private places. 'He is sideways on, my lady, like a cartload of hay that cannot fit through a twitten.'

'God's blood, woman, is there nothing you can do for my sister?'

'Yes,' she said as she made a sign of the cross, then looked round to see if we had noted the blasphemy. 'Hope and pray to our Lord and Saviour.'

'Ann,' Bett asked in a brief moment of peace, 'where is my lord? I wish him here when our son is born.'

'Soon. Soon. He will be here as soon as ever he can.'

The room was so dark and so hot that even I began to feel faint and ill and had to sharply discipline myself. It was then I noticed how overheated Bett had become, like a horseshoe glowing on the anvil. She was wearing both shift and overdress. 'A shift will be more than enough,' I insisted to the midwife. 'Help me to take off the dress at once.'

The midwife looked at me askance but agreed to assist. We had just helped Bett to her feet and removed the heavy dress, apparently worn for modesty's sake, when Bett began to scream again and this time threw herself to the ground where she knelt, with her head thrown back, howling like a dog.

'Stop her! Stop her!' cried Sir John's mother faintly. 'This is the Devil's work! She must surely be possessed by some demon.'

I was so angry I turned my back on her. 'This is no Devil's work. Do you not recall what God Almighty said in Genesis? "In sorrow shall you bring forth children." Perhaps you have forgotten the pain of childbirth, my lady?'

'Saucy girl who has not even given birth herself!'

'Ann, Ann,' Bett gasped, her eyes wide with fear and her body arched in a spasm of terrible pain. 'I cannot endure this! I cannot!'

'Can you not twist the baby round like the cowman does with the calf? I have seen him doing so at my grandfather's when the calf is stuck inside the mother.'

Five pairs of eyes watched me in horror as if I had suggested some evil ritual.

'I have done all I can, mistress, but the babe will not shift.'

Bett screamed again, and her whole body bucked as if she would surely split in two.

'Is there nothing else, for pity's sake, woman? My sister is dying of the pain.' I turned to Margaret but my gentle, kind sister stared at Bett as if she were already a ghost.

'Mary, sister, you ever know what must be done in a crisis.'

Mary reached out her hand, as if to push away the pain that stalked our sister. 'In the hall and kitchen, yes. But a laying-in is different. Childbed holds naught but fear to me.'

I saw I was alone.

'It is in God's hands now, mistress,' the midwife intoned piously, rubbing her nose with her dirty hand. 'I attended a lady yesterday whom God chose to gather, together with her babe also.'

I wanted to scream and strike her. 'Well, He is not taking my beloved Bett.'

At that Bett sat up, the pain loosening its iron hands for a moment. Her hair hung in rat's tails and her skin was as pale as chalk, yet her eyes of a sudden were fierce and clear. 'Goodwife, I care more for my son than myself. Is there no way you can save him, even if I must die in the process?'

At that she fainted away from the effort of speech.

The midwife shrugged and called me quietly to her side. 'There is only one hope.'

She opened the bag she had brought and my stomach lurched inside me as she showed me three sharp hooks. 'But, surely, those would kill both mother and baby.'

'The baby, aye. But the mother might yet survive.'

Her grudging, narrow eyes were fixed upon me knowing that this went against God's holy teaching and that only I in all this room would consider such a course.

I wished I could fall to my knees and ask His assistance, and yet I knew the ruling. The baby must be saved at the cost of the mother.

In desperation I turned to Sir John's mother. 'This manor has a farm has it not, my lady?'

She nodded as if I had lost sight of my senses.

'Then I am going myself to find your cowman.' I ran from the room and out into the darkness of the night, passing a servant on the stairs and Margaret going to the Great Hall to wait up for Sir John.

'There is no sign yet of his return?'

'None.'

I had to try three hovels at the manor gates, each so poor they were almost bare of warmth or furniture, before I found where the cowman lived. He was sitting by the fire with a small child on his knee, feeding it with sippets of bread soaked in water. A tall young man with fair hair and a ready smile.

'I am sorry to pull you from your home, but could you help with birthing a baby instead of a calf, a baby that is stuck on his side and the midwife cannot move him?'

The young man looked shaken. 'My lady, I know not . . .'

I remembered that in the purse tied round my waist was the last of my grandmother's egg money. 'I could pay a little.'

'Is it for the lord's wife, mistress? I heard she was birthing early.'

I nodded. His wife put her hand on his arm. 'Jonathan, tis a great matter. Mayhap it would be better . . .'

'To let it pass. Aye. No doubt you are right, like the cock crowed while Simon Peter thrice denied the Lord. But I cannot.'

I thanked him for his generosity, seeing what he had at stake if aught went wrong with Bett, his master's young wife, then pulled him onto the back of my own horse and we galloped up to the house. There was still no sign of its owner as we ran upstairs to the bed-chamber.

By now Bett was white as a shroud. Instead of bucking with pain she moved hardly at all.

'Can you help her, Jonathan?' I asked him.

The midwife looked at us as if we had some contagious disease. And perhaps we did. Hope.

Bett was lying on her back and, talking to her softly, as if she were indeed one of his cows, he persuaded her slowly onto her knees. 'Aye. Tis what in cattle we call a footling breech.'

'Can you turn it?'

He began to press gently up into Bett's stomach while the room fell so silent that the only sound was the crackle of the logs and Bett's panting gasps. Disapproval hung in the air like acrid smoke.

In those few moments I prayed harder than in my whole life before.

Once or twice he glanced at me again, or shrugged, biting his lip until it seemed as bloodless as a corpse's. And then I heard a cry of relief as the babe's head slipped out, then one shoulder and the other, and, with one last shuddering effort, the legs. Jonathan held the babe by its ankles and slapped it until a small mewling cry started up. 'A son, my lady.'

'This is the Devil's work,' murmured the midwife. 'Such a birth is not possible.'

'It is God's work,' I heard my own voice ring out, strong and commending though I knew not from whence it came. 'Brought about by the power of prayer, in which I trust each in this room had a part.' I slipped to my knees. 'Thank you, Lord Jesus Christ, for saving this innocent life tonight.'

And all the others said, 'Amen,' save the midwife, who shot me a look of such naked hatred that I turned my back.

'How pleased Sir John will be,' I murmured, 'to find you have given him a son and heir.'

'He will, will he not?' Bett smiled wanly back and closed her eyes. 'Stay with me, Ann.'

Though I was dog-tired with the worry and the hunt for the cowman, I tried to keep awake for my sister. Yet it was no good. Before long I too closed my eyes and slept.

In the midst of my sleep I had a strange dream where a wolf did indeed come down on a fold full of sheep and begin to tear them apart, and continued until I could wake up and stop it.

When I sat up at last, remembering where I was, I shivered a little.

Hours must have passed since I fell asleep and the chamber was cold. I roused myself and put some logs onto the fire, watching the sparks fly up and dance as I blew on the ashes.

A sudden sound from the bed made me turn and I saw that Bett had a strange look about her, and that while her hands and feet were as cold as ice, yet her forehead burned like a furnace. Not trusting to the midwife I woke the steward and sent again for the doctor while I bathed her fiery forehead with a cloth dipped in cool water.

The doctor arrived as the dawn broke on one of the clearest and most beautiful mornings I had ever seen. All around us the fields glowed as if they had been dipped in gold, mocking our misery. Mist hung high on the trees, giving the world a dreamlike vision, yet I knew we would soon enough wake up to harsh reality.

The doctor knelt at Bett's side, feeling her head and looking into her distant, faraway eyes. 'It is the childbed fever. It follows straightway from the birth. How is the babe?'

'Sleeping with the wet nurse. He thrives.'

The doctor sighed, his eyes filled with helpless sadness. 'She will be glad of that, at least. And Sir John?'

'Returning from a hunt in Lincolnshire.'

'I hope he hastes.'

My heart felt pierced by thorns. 'Is there nothing you can do?'

He shook his head. 'Naught but what you have been doing before. I will call again at midday.'

When I returned to the bed, Bett's eyes were open. 'How fares my son?'

'Well,' I smiled.

'I am glad. It is better this way, that he lives. And tell me not that I could have had another. I could not have borne the loss. Come here, Ann. Pull the curtains round the bed as we did when we were maids.'

I drew the heavy drapes until we were enclosed inside the great bed as we had been so many times before.

'Our own little world,' she whispered into the darkness. Her sigh chipped away at my poor heart. 'Sir John is a good man. Not clever or gay but a solid gentleman. He will look after our son.' She took my hand. 'First our mother, now myself. A pity the menfolk in our family live forever and the women wither on the vine.'

I wanted to protest, to say she also would live forever, but I could hear her breath starting to rattle and had heard from my grandmother what this foretold. The hand in mine gripped hard as if it were holding on to me as to life itself, then it lay still as the grave. The sob I heard was my own. My tears fell down so fast they soaked Bett's pillow. Forgetting all else I kissed her sweet brow and held her lifeless form against my breast.

Down in the Great Hall I heard a sudden commotion and ran to the top of the stairs.

Sir John stood at the foot. Around his shoulders, like the sacrifice for some cruel and ancient ritual, a white hart was slung, marked only by a small red patch where the arrow must have entered it. 'Where is Bett? How doth my lovely wife?'

Margaret appeared at my side, roused from her bed, a shawl around her shift. I looked at her helplessly then shook my head and glanced away. A sob escaped me.

'You have a son, sir. A healthy son to carry on your line.' Tears began to blind my eyes and I had to hold fast to the banister to keep from falling.

'Steward!' he called, smiling and stamping his feet against the cold as he dropped the white hart to the floor. 'Take away this beast to the pantry. And bring some wine. We need a toast to my wife and son!'

His sister had appeared now and stood silent on the landing, staring down, and Sir John's mother behind her. Slowly, as if my every step were dragged through quicksand, I made my way down the stairs, the eyes of all the others upon me for they expected me to tell Sir John the terrible news, yet my throat pained so fiercely that no words came.

Chapter 8

I SAT IN the family chapel, waiting for Bett's burial, feeling as if never would I be warm again, thinking of that cold white body which should be feeling the sharp pull of a babe at its breast, and the joy of mothering. Instead, Bett, who had run and jumped and laughed at my side, would be interred in this dark cold place, forever hidden from the light of the sun.

'The Lord giveth and the Lord taketh away,' murmured Margaret, meeting my eyes, trying to offer comfort, but at that moment I could not love and praise God.

Sir John wanted no great ceremony, no trumpets sounding dolefully nor preachers telling him that man was but here for a short time, and I was glad of it for I felt not acceptance but anger.

My father, newly arrived from London, knelt also in the chapel, hunched over as if he could hardly comprehend that such a thing could happen twice, both to his wife and to his daughter.

He stared at his hands as he knelt. Stooped, his stature was almost that of a child and I felt a sudden pang almost of maternal tenderness for him. His temper was often choleric, and he believed his authority over us should be absolute, but underneath all there was love for us in his heart.

'Father, let me lead you out.'

He climbed stiffly to his feet. 'I feel my years, Ann, like some ancient city that has been sacked and left with nothing.'

We walked slowly down the aisle to where Sir John and his mother and sisters still stood at the door.

'Goodbye, John.' My father held out his hand and Sir John took it, the picture of wordless grief, imbued with a sudden dignity he had possessed not until this moment.

I too held out my hand, but Sir John turned abruptly away and asked his mother if she needed his arm.

I stood, as shocked as if he had struck me across the cheek with his own palm.

Margaret came towards us, clucking like one of my grandmother's broody hens. 'We are leaving now and we will stop in Peckham to rest the night. My husband, Sir Thomas, has given orders for beds to be prepared.'

'Come, Ann.' Mary threaded her arm through mine. 'Our lady aunt will be missing you at York House. She has come to rely on you, to provide her with diversions. Is it true she dressed you up as a serving maid and made you walk about the streets of London?'

I nodded, my eyes still fixed upon Sir John, my heart racing with fear. Had his slight been deliberate?

'Mary,' I interrupted her chatter, 'why would Sir John not take my hand as he did Father's?'

'Come, Father.' Mary ignored my question and fell behind to walk at my father's side.

I saw him whisper something to her and made pretence of looking at some glass in the church window.

'Sir John has been listening too much to his mother,' Mary's voice was so clear I could hear her even when she tried to lower it. 'My lady Mills believes it was Ann's fault. That God was punishing her for trying to counteract His will and took her sister from us.'

Mary's words were like flax left too near a flame. They burned into me. If I had not brought in the cowman would my sister truly have survived or was this thought born just of ignorance and prejudice?

I hardly noticed the ride from Camois back to London. Even the bustle of London's multitudes did not rouse me from my pain and questioning.

The Great Hall of York House was thronged with people on our solemn return. After the still sadness of Sussex it was like opening the door of some teeming workshop, full of fevered activity and clanging sound. Black-garbed men ran hither and thither, some holding manuscripts, others papers for cases in the Star Chamber or court of Chancery. The palaces of Whitehall and Westminster, but a few moments upriver from here, were the beating heart of Queen Elizabeth's government. Even if courtiers might speculate, in hushed low voices, over who would succeed when the ageing queen died, there was no let-up in Court business.

And now, according to my father, the rebellion in Ireland was brewing up dangerously so that soon some action must be taken about the rebels. I was fortunate indeed not to be waiting on the Queen since, so gossip had it, she was in such bad sorts over Ireland that she regularly boxed her ladies' ears, made them stand waiting for hours on end and even broke the finger of one of her Ladies of the Bedchamber who did not remove her gloves quick enough for the Queen's pleasure.

My aunt was amongst those waiting in the hall and came across to me with her open arms. 'Ann, my love, my heart breaks for poor Bett, just launched on life's journey. I have lost two husbands, but no loved one of Bett's tender years. To die in childbed is the curse of our sex.'

At these words my grief, contained by an act of willpower deep within me, would be subdued no longer. 'My lady aunt, I . . .'

Bett's face swam in front of my tear-filled eyes, the same sweet face I had seen every morn on the pillow close to mine, who had been the calm to my storm, the balm to all my hurts, the sharer of all my secrets, happy or sad. And now she was gone forever, her smile never again to light up the dark corners of my life.

I sobbed so that no more words were possible. Instead I buried my face on the prickly gold thread of my aunt's gown, heedless of whomever might see me, and my aunt held me fast.

'Ann, Ann, you were the best and kindest to her. She must have thanked God for His bounty that, though she had no mother, she had a sister such as you.'

'And yet I could not help her when she needed help the most.'

'That is pride, Ann. Only God can decide such things and His ways, though hard for us to accept, are not for us to question.'

I wished that I could accept the will of God as easily as she did. Instead, in my restless mind, I questioned the ways of man, and the ignorance of midwives.

For I know not how long I clung to my aunt, she patting my hair the while, until, slowly as a tide receding, my grief subsided and I retreated from her.

She, meanwhile, wiped my face with her kerchief and straightened the hair beneath my coif.

'Now, Ann,' she smiled at me tenderly and gestured to one who was standing behind me, 'here is someone who has been waiting to see you, and who hopes you will let him share your grief.'

I felt a quick start of alarm deep inside me, confused between dream and the solid world around me, and turned to find myself looking into the earnest blue eyes of Richard Manners.

'Mistress Ann, I came as soon as I heard the terrible news about your sister.' His voice was as sober as the tolling of a bell. 'At least you can comfort yourself that she is in the loving care of our communal Father.'

'Yes, Ann,' seconded the clear, gentle voice of the Lord Keeper, 'though I know in the heart of one's grief that can seem like cold comfort.'

A few feet behind the Lord Keeper, trying to remain discreetly in the shadows, I glimpsed his secretary. There was no sign now of the flirtatious courtier; instead I saw a look of tender sympathy on his face.

I do not know what bad angel prompted me to turn towards him. 'And you, Master Donne, as a poet you must think about such things. Do you think it is the act of a just and merciful God that my sister is taken from me at so tender an age, with her whole life ahead of her?'

He paused, knowing that every eye was upon him.

'I can give no easy answer, mistress. My own three sisters and brother were also taken early from this earth and I, too, struggled to see the justice in their loss. The common answer is that pain and death are the price of our own free will as sons and daughters of Adam and Eve who ate of the Tree of Knowledge in the Garden of Eden.'

'I know the common answer, Master Donne.' I heard the harshness in my voice but I had hoped for something more enlightening from one such as him.

'Now, Ann,' my aunt interrupted. 'You cannot invite a lesson in philosophy from Master Donne and reject it thus peremptorily.'

'I am sorry, Master Donne. It is the pain that makes me sharp.'

He bowed; his eyes, though, were two black pools of sorrow. And in that instant I saw a sympathy and understanding of my plight I had not looked for in one of his reputation.

'Come, John,' my uncle took his arm, 'we have work to do in Chancery today.'

I wondered, had we been alone, if he might have said more than the usual empty offerings. And then the shock of my own thoughts engulfed me. When my own sister lay cold in her grave how could I feel warmed and comforted by one whom all had warned me against?

'Fine words from Master Donne,' Richard Manners's voice jolted me back to the present. 'Yet I did hear, when the brother he talks of died in Newgate Prison for sheltering a priest, Master Donne was not slow to profit from his brother's inheritance.'

'I hope what you say is not true of any man,' I answered with a firmness I did not feel. Master Manners's accusation brought back the conversation between Master Donne and his mother which I sorely wished I had not heard. Had his mother, when she accused him of betrayal of his religion, meant also a betrayal of his brother for his own ends?

'Come, Master Manners, you should not repeat such imputations when they may be naught but idle gossip.' My aunt softened her words with a smile. 'Now, tell us, how is your good father at home in Leicestershire? You left in such haste at his bidding when last we met.'

Master Manners laughed a gay laugh which, in the midst of our mournfulness, struck a strange note. He was a handsome man indeed when his looks were happy. 'My father!' He turned once again to me. 'He is as changeable as a weathercock. You are fortunate indeed to have a father who knows his own mind.'

I thought of my father, who knew his mind all too well and would listen to the opinions of none other.

'I will not talk of marriage at such a time as this,' continued Master Manners with a tact I could only feel grateful for. 'Suffice it to say that it was my father, never myself, who scattered thorns upon the path of my ambitions towards you, Mistress More.'

I smiled at his extravagant words.

'See, Mistress More,' there was an ill-concealed delight in his tone, 'I have made you smile. I am grateful at least for that small mercy.'

'Now, Master Manners,' my aunt shooed him away with her fan, 'it is time that Ann and I fulfilled our household obligations.'

Master Manners bowed low and I saw him watch me until my aunt and I had left the Great Hall entirely.

'I have to own,' my aunt whispered as we made our way down to the kitchens, 'I have a weakness for a handsome face, but I felt his boldness in talking thus of his intentions was too great in your present state of sadness.' She stopped and took my hand, holding me at her arm's length. 'The flowers will be blooming in the gardens before too long. And so will you. You are welcome to spend as long here with us as ever you like, it is nothing but pleasure to the Lord Keeper and myself. Yet you should think about your future, sweet Ann, and the joys that lie ahead of you in marriage.'

'And in childbed?' My grief engulfed me again at the thought of that pale ghost, so recently laid into the ground. 'Is that a joy to be devoutly wished?'

'Ann, Ann, sorrow as long as you wish. But one day, and not too long hence, you will yearn for the pleasures of hearth and home.' She looked at me slyly. 'And of the bedchamber also.'

At that I flushed as red as the rose that would soon flourish in my uncle's gardens. 'Aunt,' I took her arm and led her along the passage-way, 'I see I must keep you from the sight of too many handsome faces.'

'Now, Ann! You were ever a naughty child! Come, now, and we will instruct the clerk of the kitchen. Later on you can come with me on a visit to my lady Warwick, who also waits upon the Queen.'

After we had done with the clerk and my aunt had no need of me for a while, I tried, in my chamber, to read the story of Abelard and Heloise which I had brought with me from my grandfather's library. Yet this tale of doomed desire, where Heloise falls in love with her tutor, Peter Abelard, and gives herself to him, only to find that her brothers are so angry they forcibly remove his manhood, was hardly a distraction from my misery. 'What you need, my Ann,' I heard my grandmother's voice in my head, as she had told me so many times when I was a maid, 'is to find work for those idle hands and food for that nimble brain of yours.'

I put Abelard away in my coffer. Perhaps I should go back to Loseley. For here I was too young and too unimportant to be of use to anyone.

I knew what the visit to my lady Warwick would be. Two hours in a draughty gallery listening to more gossip of Court life, yet I went and sat and listened to not one word.

I MOURNED MY sister through the cold and fog of early springtime, the weather echoing my own loss and deadness of spirit. The sharp winds of March blew away some of my dark imaginings, yet it was not until the sun shone through with sudden brightness that I roused myself and sought diversion. It was too early to wish for courtly entertainment so I vowed at least to make myself useful and went to hunt for my aunt's gentlewoman, Joan, to see if she had tasks that needed assistance.

Joan, round as a barrel, with apple cheeks to match, the picture of a countrywoman, yet she had never taken a step outside the smoke of London, accepted my offer with a smile. 'Bored of your prayers, are you?' And then she thought better, sensing I might take it amiss when my sister was so recently taken. 'Sorry, mistress, I did not mean to lighten your loss. We were all saddened to hear of your sister. A lovely girl from what I hear.'

'Trouble yourself not, Joan. You are right about the prayers. I find it hard to thank God when I feel so angry with Him.'

'Mistress!'

'Sssh! I should not say such things, I know. What can I aid you with?'

'My mistress says she has a taste for Kentish apples, and I have heard, despite the season, there are some to be had in Borough Market, though why the mistress hath not them stored over winter at Pyrford, I know not.'

She looked at my rich dress. 'Tis Southwark, mistress, and we will be down amongst the crowds of ordinary folk. Best wear a cloak to cover up your finery.'

This time we crossed by water, hailing a wherry from the York House steps with a cry of 'Eastward Ho!' And before long we found ourselves alighting in Southwark at Paris Garden Stairs. This bank of the Thames seemed busier, if that were possible, than the other. We walked along a great row of houses, past ponds and playhouses, water-mills and smoky workshops. Outside the bear pit we heard shouting from within, yet I hated the thought of the poor beast being hounded by dogs. A cruel pastime. I peeped into a pleasure garden before Joan pulled me onwards towards the market, beyond the Great Beer house and another set of steps down to the river, whose name made me smile: Pickle Herring Stairs. A painted young woman leaned out of a window above us, calling, 'Morning, young mistresses, what brings you to this saucy part of town?'

'Tsk, Mistress Ann, look not back at her. Tis a stewhouse and well known for it. The Castle upon Hope Inn, they call it, though castle it be not, and those within are certainly not ladies, I can warrant you. Not far now to the market.'

I was in no hurry. For the first time in weeks I had forgotten my cares, wrapped up in so many diverse sights and sounds. Yet one thing penetrated my gaiety: the gangs of children I had seen before, some so young it seemed as if they had not long learned to walk, others carried in the arms of their brothers or sisters not much older themselves, all looking tired and pinched and hungry, their great hollow eyes following me as if they could see through my disguise and knew I came from a lord's house where there was so much plenty that the master's dogs ate better than they.

'Aye,' Joan commented, 'there's one crop that is always in season, more's the pity, unlike your aunt's apples. The poorer the mother the more children she brings into the world, it seems to me. I suppose the poor have few other comforts. Since the failure of the harvests they flock to London from the country villages. Oft times they abandon their children if they can't feed them, hoping for the goodwill of the parish.'

'And does the parish help them?'

'Not if it can help it. It would rather send them away like stray dogs. And this new law now, which taxes us all to build a Poor House, no one knows if that will help or hinder.'

She pulled her shawl round herself more tightly, ignoring the gaggle of ragged children that followed her, their hands outstretched.

'Shoo!' She stamped her feet and the children scattered, never speaking, like a crowd of tiny phantoms.

'Hang on to your purse, mistress. Innocence isn't always what it seems in this part of town.'

Just before Borough Market we saw a milkmaid standing in the shade of the trees, her pails hung over her shoulders, talking to a customer. I stopped a while, recognizing her face from a previous sortie with Joan. It was the young girl we had seen before, whom I gave money to, forgetting I was dressed as a servant.

She looked at me a long time, taking in the fine clothes under my cloak, wondering if her eyes deceived her, and then there burst on to the scene a great commotion.

A young boy, tall and gangling, like the heron that feeds at the pond at Loseley, yet dirty, thin and ragged, aged about twelve or thirteen years, ran around the corner and, seeing the milkmaid, clung to her as if the hangman pursued him and only she could grant him pardon.

'Sarah! Please! He's after me! He'll kill me if he catches me. I'll not stay with him, I won't!'

Out of an alley appeared a rough-looking man and I saw both Sarah and the youth cringe back. The man was ill-dressed and reeked of the alehouse. He growled like a hungry bear and made as if to knock the lad down. 'Release that boy!'

The milkmaid threw me a look so desperate and beseeching that I took a step forward and stood between the boy and the man who sought him.

'Stop!' I stood my ground fearlessly. 'Who are you and why is this boy so frightened that he clings thus to that young woman?'

'I am John Maunsley, tanner. And who might you be that places herself between me and my lawful apprentice?'

I stood on my dignity in the way I had seen my sister Mary do with troublesome servants.

'I am Mistress Ann More,' I replied in a voice as cold as the east wind that shrivels the new buds of spring. 'Daughter to Sir George More, knight and Deputy Sheriff in the Counties of Surrey and Sussex.'

'Huh,' he grunted, looking at me warily at this mention of official-dom, keeping his distance as if I might suddenly produce a warrant from my mantle. 'And what does Mistress Ann More have to do with my apprentice, Wat, who cannot even be trusted to stir the hides with-out weeping for his mother?'

'I did not weep for my mother!' the boy Wat squared up, braver now that he perceived he had a protectress. 'I have no mother, naught but my sister Sarah.' He turned to her despairingly. 'He makes me do the cruellest jobs, the ones no other will do, dipping my hands in stuff that bites and flays my skin. Look!' He held out hands that were blis-tered and flaking, running with open sores. 'And then I must stir the skins in vats of dog dirt to make them supple!'

I recoiled at this hellish vision and knew that I must do what I could to help.

'He'll soon grow accustomed,' growled the tanner. 'Skin soon hard-ens; look at mine.' He held out his own hands for inspection. 'Twenty years of tanning and hands soft as a babe's.'

'You never go near the vats, that's why!' insisted the boy, recover-ing his spirit. 'With this new law you have boys to do it for you, of nine or ten, sent by the parish, and no questions asked!'

'They get board and lodging.'

'Sleeping in your cellar with the rats to tell us stories, and mouldy bread to eat or rotting kitchen stuff you buy cheap from city kitchen maids!'

I stifled a smile at the boy's way with words. The tanner had not yet managed to crush his imagination.

'You learn a trade! That is what the law requires of me. I know my duty.' His attempt at piety disgusted me more than his cruelty, espe-cially if he believed it himself.

'Come! If you come not, I will fetch the Watch.'

'Please, mistress . . .' interceded the boy's sister. 'I knew you were kind when you gave me that coin before.' She thrust the boy towards me so I could feel his bones through his torn clothing and study the sooty mark of a bruise across his nose. I looked hard at him, taking in his thick black hair, skin so pale the veins showed blue beneath, and yet despite all there was a spark of surprising wit in his eyes.

'I would take him with me as I deliver my milk but the parish would send him back to the tanner. He is quick, mistress, and can even read the signs in the shops and market. And he has such a good heart! Take him with you, mistress, for the sake of our sainted mother, who died in childbed. Please!'

Perhaps some angel sent those words to her.

I thought at once of my sister Bett, not yet cold in her shroud, and the guilt that I carried around with me like a sack, wondering if I had served to hasten her end. Helping this boy might lighten that load.

'I will take him,' I said without stopping to think if my kindly aunt and uncle would want another servant.

'But he is my bounden apprentice, sent to me under the law!' The tanner tried to grab him back.

'How much would you have spent on this boy's board and keep for the term of his apprenticeship?'

'Ah, well,' his sharp eyes widened, 'the term of the apprenticeship is not fixed, but it would last some years. Tis till he has learned his trade, like.'

'Say five years. And I will be saving you the cost of board and lodging for him.'

Wat laughed bitterly at this.

'And I will be losing the labour he would have provided me.'

'Three angels. I will give you three gold angels, to be sent to your address tomorrow.'

'And you will make no more of it with your father, the Deputy So-and-so of Surrey?' He glanced unwillingly at Wat's injured hands.

'I will make no more of it. Come, Wat.' I held his arm and pulled him with me through the crowd that had gathered to watch our transaction.

'May I tell Sarah where I will be found?'

I looked back at the tanner, not wishing him to know of Wat's new whereabouts. 'Joan, tell Sarah quietly where her brother will be living.'

Unwillingly Joan lumbered through the crowd and whispered in Sarah's ear. The milkmaid's eyes opened in alarm at so great a change in status for her brother.

'What about my lady's apples?' grumbled Joan as we headed swiftly back towards the river. 'And what is my mistress going to say about the arrival of this lad?'

'Apples, did you say, mistress?' Wat piped up, a merry look displacing the fearfulness from his blue eyes. 'I can show you where to get good apples. The tanner's wife is with child, poor lady, can you imagine how she . . . ?' He thought better of the question. 'No. She had a craving for Orange Pippins. We were not allowed them, of course, but I was sent to find bushels of them. I can show you where to find the very best.'

He led the way down a narrow alley, which had us looking fearfully behind in case the tanner or any other malcontents lurked there to do us ill, and after several twists and turns, once narrowly avoiding the slops from an upstairs window, we found ourselves slap in the centre of Borough Market, next to a stall piled high with vegetables and fruit.

Yet there was no sign of apples.

'He keeps them under the trestle, wrapped in straw against the winter frosts,' Wat informed us.

Joan filled her basket with Orange Pippins, so well stored they held still the misty tang of autumn. As we walked back to the wherry I handed one to Wat as his reward. He looked at it with wide eyes, as if it were one of the golden apples of Hera.

'Thank you, mistress, for your great kindness.'

We were silent on the wherry crossing. Joan occasionally raised her eyebrows at me then shrugged and moved away from Wat, as if he were not an injured and oppressed child, but a plague carrier.

When we got to the steps at York House she clambered out as fast as she could, no doubt eager to reach the steward's table to gossip to the other servants about Mistress Ann's madness.

'What is this place, mistress?' Wat asked, overawed, as we walked towards the vast mansion ahead, with its towers and turrets and its three great windows looking from the Great Hall into the gardens.

'It is called York House, my uncle's home. I am sure he and my aunt will have some place for you in their household if you have no objection to hard work.'

As we walked through the gate, Wat at my back glancing behind him all the while, as if expecting a hue and cry to follow us, I found that the gardens were not empty. Two men, laughing and talking, stood at the river end, half hidden by an apple tree.

It was Master John Donne. He turned at my helter-skelter arrival. 'Good morrow, Mistress More.' He raised an eyebrow at my rough companion but said nothing, assuming, I supposed, that I would offer an explanation. 'This is my very good friend Henry Wotton.'

Master Wotton bowed deeply. He was a thickset gentleman, with lively eyes and a nimble gait that belied his frame, and a fine thick red-brown beard, which seemed to have grown in greater abundance as it left his head. 'Mistress More, a pleasure. I have long admired your uncle as a fair and honest servant of the Queen. Not so common in these days, I assure you.'

'Thank you, Master Wotton. He is a good man.'

'Master Wotton and I are old friends, and he currently is secretary to the Earl of Essex.'

I smiled without knowing I did so.

'Why smile you, Mistress More?' asked Master Wotton, intrigued.

'I heard so much at Court about the Earl and numerous ladies, I imagine his secretary would be kept very busy with love letters.'

Master Wotton laughed loudly. 'The Earl is a man of action. He believes in deeds rather than words.'

'Yes. It was the deeds the ladies talked of.' I remembered Wat, who had backed away into the garden and was hiding by the wall. I was beginning, as we approached York House, to wonder at my aunt's reception of him. And then, seeing Master Donne, a happy inspiration occurred to me.

'Master Donne, do you have a servant?'

For reasons I understood not, Master Donne and his friend both laughed out loud.

'Not at present. I would rather shake out my own doublet than pay another to do it ill. Servants, I have found, are not always worth the trouble of employing them.'

'That is because you have not met the right one. For this boy, by name of Wat—do you have another name, Wat?'

'Snaresbrook, mistress.'

'Wat Snaresbrook. Wat is urgently looking for employment and would make an excellent servant.'

Master Donne's answer was the bark of a laugh.

'You have found the wrong man, Mistress More! I have had enough of boys to last me several lifetimes! The last I employed helped himself to my best clothes and ran away with them.'

'But Wat is honest, are you not, Wat?'

'As honest as the day is long, mistress.' Wat bowed as he had seen Master Wotton do a moment back, smiling all the while. 'And mayhap the night time too in spite of all the wicked deeds that do happen then!'

'God save us from a boy who can speak so eloquently!' murmured Master Donne, shaking his head.

'Come, John, a poet cannot object to the clever use of words, surely?' smiled Master Wotton. Yet his friend shook his head.

'Mistress More, I live here in York House. If I had lodgings of my own, perhaps . . .'

'I am sure my uncle, the Lord Keeper, would have no objection if I talk to him. Wat could sleep on a pallet on your floor as Prudence oftentimes does on mine at Loseley.'

'Heigh, heigh, go not so fast, mistress . . .'

'Consider it at least. Wat could run errands for you. To the courts.'

'And the alehouse,' added Wat. 'Or the stewhouse.'

'Wat!' I scolded, turning back to Master Donne.

'The other day you asked if there was aught you could do to relieve the misery of my sister's loss.' I knew this to be blackmail but the cause was honest. 'This lad's mother died in childbirth like my sister. Taking him in seemed a kind of expiation.'

'Which you are generously passing on to me?' The words could have been cruelly said, but there was a kindness in them. 'For pity's sake, what has happened to him?' He picked up one of the boy's hands, not even flinching at the oozing sores.

'He was apprenticed to a tanner who made him put his hands into cruel and fiery liquids.'

'And this tanner, to whom he was apprenticed, might I expect a call from him demanding the return of his property?'

I bit my lip. 'Very probably. But he may be daunted to discover his charge now lives in the household of the Keeper of the Great Seal.'

'A relief. I would not wish to have dangerous liquids flung in my face by an angry tanner.'

'Never fear, sir,' Wat informed him helpfully. 'Master Maunsley is far too scared even to touch the stuff himself.'

'A relief indeed.'

'Then you will take him as your servant after all? Here, Wat, you are to have a new master,' I told him eagerly, giving Master Donne no chance to change his mind. 'Master John Donne is secretary to my uncle, as well as one of our most famous poets.'

'Come, come. I have not published a word.'

'Yet my cousin says your verse is circulated among so many, you have no need.' I turned to Wat. 'I will take the boy and have him cleaned up so his appearance is more respectable.'

'I wish you great good luck.'

Chapter 9

I LEFT WAT to wait awhile near the kitchen door while I sought out Joan to help me clean him up. I was halfway up the staircase when from downstairs in the Great Hall I heard a piercing shriek.

My aunt had discovered the presence of an urchin boy in her household and had firmly taken hold of Wat's ear and was dragging him towards the withdrawing chamber to find her husband.

'Do you know whose house you have falsely entered, boy, and who knows with what malicious intent? To steal and rob us, I fancy.'

'Please, mistress, spare me! I am not come to rob your household, but was brought here to do honest work by the young gentlewoman.'

My aunt turned to me. 'Ann? Is this true? Who is this boy and what thought you to bring him here, without applying to me first?'

'He was being ill-treated by his apprentice master, Aunt. Look, look at his wounds before you condemn me.' I took Wat's poor hands in mine and showed them to her. 'I saw it as my duty before God our Maker to try and save him, knowing that in your goodness and kindness you would yourself have done the same.'

'God's wounds! Would I so?' Her voice was harsh but yet I hoped to persuade her.

'Besides, he will not bother you. Master Donne has agreed to take him as a servant boy.'

'Has he now?' said my cousin, who had just appeared in the hall in the company of Master Manners. 'That is generous indeed. You must have been extremely persuasive, Ann, since this boy will be as much effort as reward, I wager.'

Wat who had been following this statement with rapt attention, stood up straight at this.

'He won't regret it, sir. I want the gentleman to say, "I know not how I managed before I had Wat Snaresbrook in my service."'

We all laughed at that.

'It is very generous of Master Donne,' I admitted.

'And does that not surprise you?' questioned Richard Manners. 'I have never heard of Master Donne as one who acts so selflessly. Indeed I hope you have done right in giving him the boy.'

'What mean you by that, Master Manners?'

'I heard a rumour there was trouble between Master Donne and a servant before.'

'What manner of trouble?'

He shrugged. 'I know not, but it ended in court, I fancy.'

This news alarmed me somewhat. I had thought Master Donne would prove a kindly master.

'You know a surprising deal about my stepfather's secretary, Master Manners,' Francis commented looking at him askance.

'He is a man much gossiped about. If I behaved as Master Donne does, rumour would abound about me also.'

'So you behave at all times like a good Christian gentleman?' Francis asked.

'So I would hope,' was the pious reply.

There was something in his voice that made me bristle. 'No doubt you will get your reward in Heaven.'

Penetrating blue eyes turned in my direction, pinning me to the spot. 'I had hoped to win it sooner than that.'

There was no mistaking the intention of his words. I dropped my gaze at such uncalled-for intimacy and took myself to find Joan, who had, complaining all the while, taken on the task of supervising Wat's bathing and had found him a suit of clothes in black stuff with a neat white collar that one of the serving men had grown out of. The collar was too large for his neck and I took out my scissors to make it smaller.

'Here, mistress,' Joan gently removed the garment from my hands, 'I can see you are no needlewoman.'

'No,' I laughed. 'My sister Frances was handier with a needle than I, never happier than with her Irish stitchwork. My stitchery was a despair to my grandmother. I would rather be riding out or playing with my cat than wasting time making dainty designs on silk or calico.'

'You set no store by a lady's accomplishments, then?'

'I can see that running a household has its pleasures, but I would lief be reading or riding abroad!'

'You had better have plenty of servants, then, mistress.' Joan finished sewing the collar and laid it over the jacket.

A thought occurred to me. 'Like you the life of a servant, Joan?'

Joan laughed at me and shook her head. 'You're a strange one, Mistress Ann. What kind of question is that?'

'More than you enjoy being a lady, mistress,' spoke up Wat, whom we had almost forgotten. 'You would sooner be out in the world living like a man, I'd wager.'

'Keep a civil tongue in your head, young doddypol!' Joan corrected him. 'Ignorant whelp that you are.'

'I heard tell in the alehouse of a lady who wanted to be with her lover, some rich duke, so she dressed up as his page!' Wat informed us gaily.

'I'd reckon you'd spent too many hours watching plays, my lad, if you'd only had money enough for a ticket!' Joan jerked the jacket over his head.

'Oww!'

She straightened the altered collar and reached for a wooden haircomb. 'Tell me honestly, are you lousy?'

Wat put his head on one side, considering the proposition. 'Not any more. My sister dosed the lice with warm milk and wormwood.'

'An enterprising girl, this Sarah.'

'And kind as the day is long. When my mother died, Sarah kept me and my brother and sister from being taken by the parish.'

Joan tugged the comb through his dark hair.

'Owwww!'

'Cry baby!'

Wat pushed her off. 'I am not!'

'Let us look at you.'

She turned him to face us both.

The wonder of it was that Wat Snaresbrook, cleaned up and freshly combed, looked as if he had worn a fine suit of clothes every day of his young life.

'Come, Wat. I will take you to find your new employer.'

'And I will come with you, mistress,' Joan offered to my surprise. 'There's no telling where he will be in this great honeycomb of a house.'

'Thank you, Joan,'

We found Master Donne, after much searching, in the Lord Keeper's library looking at some law book.

'Here is your boy, Master Donne, all polished up and gleaming like a new penny.'

Master Donne surveyed Wat with a smile, and then a look of sternness came over his features. 'I hope you have no taste for silk hose and velvet suits, Wat.'

Wat looked confused. 'Serge is good enough for me, sir.'

'My last boy helped himself to my best satin suit and a handful of gold lace.'

'And yet, Master Donne,' I asked, in a voice of innocent good humour, 'did not one of your own verses mock the downy-chinned gallants for going off to war in satin suits and quantities of gold lace much like those you lost?'

Francis had told me that of all Master Donne's verses this was the one he liked the most.

'Mistress More, it did,' conceded Master Donne. He looked at me askance, his eyes narrowed in amusement. 'You know a surprising deal about my poor verses it seems to me.'

'They are much talked of. This boy who ran off—what was his name?'

'Tom Danby.'

'Perhaps Tom Danby thought to save you the humiliation of donning your satin suit and looking like one of those sad gallants you describe.'

Master Donne cracked with laughter. 'What a charitable construction indeed—save that he sold the clothes he stole for five and twenty pounds in a Cheapside frippery and was seen neither hide nor hair of again! In fact, I have lately been recompensed with thirty pounds by the court of Chancery for my pains.'

I own I was glad to hear it and that the tale Master Manners reported did not stand up against him, not for my own sake, but for Wat's, for I would not wish to land him with a cruel master.

Master Donne noticed Joan standing shyly behind me and beckoned her forward.

'Mistress Joan, what a pleasure indeed.'

Joan, though all of forty years, reddened like a maiden announcing her betrothal. Surely solid Joan could not have fallen for Master Donne's silver words, as half the wives of city merchants and alehouse keepers seemed to have done?

'Speaking of Chancery, how goes your suit in the court there?'

'That is what I came to tell you, sir. We have had a judgement. Fifty pounds to be shared between us, and no more bribes under the counter, thanks to your kind involvement.'

'I am delighted to be of service. The Lord Keeper is trying to put an end to the outrageous fees demanded by every court official; they are a canker on the honour of our system.' Master Donne signalled to the boy. 'Come, Wat, I will find you some honest employment.'

'So, Joan,' I asked her in a low voice when Master Donne was called away a moment, 'what was this suit in Chancery Master Donne talked of? I thought Master Donne was the wolf waiting to pounce on the innocent lamb in your eyes.'

'Perhaps my judgement was a little harsh,' Joan admitted. 'The suit was concerning my grandfather's inheritance. Only a small cottage, but the profit of it is as much as my brothers and I are like to earn in our whole lifetimes. It was all tangled up in the law and we were being asked for fines and fees and all manner of palm-greasings to sort it out.'

'And you took the problem to Master Donne?' I was surprised at Joan taking so bold a step. 'Why went you not to the Lord Keeper or my aunt, your own employers?'

Joan twisted her hands. 'I knew not where to turn and one day Master Donne came upon me wringing out a dishcloth and weeping into the suds. I finished by telling him all and he bade me take the matter to him. And now it is all resolved in our favour.'

This new side of Master Donne as problem solver struck me deeply.

For one brief moment I wondered if I might confide in him my sister Mary's difficulties with Master Freeman, for as Joan had endorsed there was that about him that made me feel he could be trusted. But what if I were wrong, and he gossiped of her indiscretion in the Parliament or Inns of Court? No, however tempting it was to share the burden of my worries, I must keep them to myself.

'Mistress More,' he interrupted my troubled thoughts. 'I have often meant these last weeks to ask you of your lost sister, and to say that I was sorry to have given you so ill an answer when you were so angered at losing her. I do indeed know how great such pain can be.'

'Because of your own brother?'

He stared suddenly at my face, startled.

'How know you of my brother?'

Swiftly, before I had the chance to snatch back the words, I answered him, 'I overheard you talking of him to your mother.'

'My *mother*?' I saw at once how vulnerable this revelation rendered him and how shaken he was to hear me say it.

'Master Donne, I never meant to speak, and the secret of her presence is safe with me, I promise you.'

I saw how for one instant he thought to deny her visit, then shrugged instead and sighed, while I rushed on.

'I wished but to say this: your mother now seems lost to you but it is not so. My own died when I was but a maid of four, and I well know the anguish of such feelings. Yet my mother has returned, in thought and memory.' Involuntarily I touched the locket round my neck. 'And your mother also will return to you.'

'I trust you are right.' Yet there was a chill in his voice as if I had opened some private door which he wished to be kept shut.

'I am, Master Donne, I know it.'

'You have an understanding of matters beyond your years, Mistress More.'

'I know there is a sadness at the heart of things that not even God our Maker warms with His grace.'

'Indeed there is, yet not many see that truth and dare live with its cruel sentence.'

'I am one who can.'

At that he held my gaze with such intentness that we two seemed for one instant held together by a silken thread before it was broken and the noisy, rushing world of York House enveloped us once more.

I turned away to seek out Joan, noticing that all around us my uncle's servants were running back and forth carrying the best platters of silver and pewter, jugs of ale and of flowers. And the thought occurred to me that the ceremony for tonight's meal was far greater than the usual.

'Who dines with my uncle this night that so much silver is to be laid on for them?' I asked. 'Not Her Majesty or surely I would have heard of it?'

'Not the Queen, no. Another great lady. The Countess of Straven. I have bidden Mercy to come and help to dress you. The other ladies of the house are putting on all their finery.'

Although I pretended lack of interest, my curiosity was yet excited by a guest who was being treated with so much show and ritual.

'What is she like, this Countess of Straven? A venerable dame like my aunt? An acquaintance of hers perhaps from her days at Court?'

'Not she.' Joan shook out my gown of leaf-green taffeta. 'She is a distant cousin of my lord's, whom your uncle knows and honours.' She cast a sly glance in my direction. 'She comes with quite a reputation by all accounts.'

'And with a convenient earl for a husband,' snorted Mercy, who had appeared with a pitcher of water to share in the excitement of my preparations. 'He never ventures from their country estate, so I heard Thomas the steward say. On account of his speech is strange. His words do trip so over each other, says Thomas, that it takes a se'enight for him to finish a sentence.'

'She must be a patient woman.'

'It suits her well enough. She leads her own life, lucky lady, and her husband is content to let her, so Thomas says, since she brought him ten thousand pounds and the manor of Bell Episcopi.'

'Ten thousand pounds!' I whistled. 'A royal fortune!'

Even the Queen had not such wealth in her coffers, nor nothing like.

'Yet she be most unwomanly in her deportment,' Mercy whispered, 'for they do say she spends more time in her closet with her books than managing her household.'

I, who told myself I cared nothing for her other attributes, found I minded very much to hear of this paragon's great learning. 'And this educated Countess,' I asked, 'is she a sober-looking lady, Mercy?'

'Thomas welcomed her an hour past, Mistress Ann, with the yeoman of the horse and the gentlemen ushers.' She smiled at me wickedly. 'Thomas says she is as beauteous as the morning star.'

Mercy and Joan curtsied and excused themselves to accomplish other tasks, while I stole one last glance in the glass. I bit my lips to make them redder and rubbed each cheek till they glowed like russet apples. I wished my bodies had been pulled tighter to show off my budding breasts to better advantage, but to ask for Mercy's help in doing so would only have made her smile and recount the tale to the other servants that Mistress Ann was feeling the Devil's pinch of jealousy.

And then I remembered all of a sudden my sweet Bett, not cold in the ground, and felt ashamed of my unworthy thoughts. 'Dear God, who is our Saviour, forgive me,' I quickly prayed. And added as an afterthought: 'Yet make this Countess not too learned nor too lovely.'

Perhaps to punish me, God did not answer my prayer for the Countess was indeed both educated and beautiful to boot.

I joined my aunt and uncle and their assembled guests in the long gallery overlooking the busy thoroughfare of London's river.

'Good eve, Mistress Ann.' Joseph, my uncle's yeoman of the ewery, bowed and handed me a cup of lemon mead. 'Just brewed this week, and still warm, for your pleasure.'

I sniffed the pale golden liquid, fragrant with honey and ginger. The strong scent of lemons and rosemary transported me on the instant back to our hothouse at Loseley in early evening time when the scents are strongest.

'Thank you, yeoman,' said a clear, ringing voice which, though soft, would carry through a crowd of costermongers, 'I will try your mead. At home we make it with our own honey, but here in the city you must be forced to purchase yours. I must send my lady Egerton some of our combs as a thank-you token.'

I turned slowly, not wishing her to know that I had heard this gracious offer, and beheld one of the loveliest women it had been my misfortune ever to encounter. Taller than I, yet with the narrowness and straightness of a young tree, her pale skin glowing like the polished pearls on my mother's necklace, her hair the colour of a newly minted brass coin. And such eyes, how I hated those eyes, so bright and brimming with knowledge and assurance, and the satisfaction that none could rival the wit and comeliness of Isabella, Countess of Straven.

One small item gave me satisfaction: with hair the colour of brass I would not have worn a gown of scarlet red with an underskirt of pale white plush. It put me in mind of the childish game I used to play with red and white counters.

But the gentlemen seemed to have missed this minor slip in judgement. The group stood all agog, watching the newcomer's arrival as dazzled as if the sun had appeared in the midst of night to outshine the subtle silver beauty of the moon.

And the most dazzled of all was Master John Donne.

The Countess bestowed her warmest smile in his direction.

'Master Donne,' gone was the meddling voice of the housewife beekeeper, and in its stead the creamy charm of the courtesan, 'it is too long since last I saw you. You are still writing your verses, I trust, for there is none to touch you. Not Master Jonson, nor Kit Marlowe, nor even Master Shakespeare.'

I waited for him to deny such outrageousness or at least smile at the extravagance of her assertion. But I underestimated the power of flattery when it came from the lips of a subtle and beautiful woman.

I drank down my mead angrily and awaited his reply.

Joseph appeared at my elbow with the jug of mead and began to refill my goblet. 'Young mistress,' he whispered into my ear as he poured the golden liquid, 'beware of the treachery that hides beneath the sweetness. It is stronger than it seems.'

I laughed and drank it back. The treachery beneath the sweetness seemed an apt description of more than mead this night.

When we sat down, counting all the busy household together with the visitor and her train, there were almost thirty around the great wooden dining table.

The Countess was seated in the place of honour near to my aunt and uncle. Two places down, sat Master Donne.

I found myself a few feet away, amidst my uncle's dull advisors, near enough to overhear snatches of their discourse but too distant to follow every word.

All down the long table the best candles threw a warm glow onto the assembled faces. My aunt had used double the usual quantity in their guest's honour, I noticed.

'And your husband, my lady, the good Earl, how fares he?' enquired my uncle.

'Burying himself in the country.' I could tell from her tone she, like Master Donne, had no affection for rural pursuits. 'Hunting deer and writing me dull letters of how he manages the estate and how fares each and every yeoman and peasant, which I answer extremely shortly.'

At that, all laughed heartily. 'Yet you write verse yourself, do you not, your ladyship?' prompted Henry Wotton, Master Donne's good friend.

The Countess smiled with gentle modesty, which made me hate her the more. Any moment and she would simperingly agree to read us some.

'A few tinkering words. But nothing to match the marvels of Master Donne. "The Flea" was a small miracle, so clever and so full of wit.' She turned towards him. 'Yet tell me, Master Donne, where came so much distrust of my own sex? Why believe you so that women are fickle creatures who can never feel the fires of passion or the strength of love as men can?'

I listened intently at this, though pretending to study my plate, yet it was his friend who replied.

'It is not the fault of women that they cannot love as men do, my lady,' smiled Henry Wotton, all admiration of her great intellect ringing in his voice. 'For women must choose hearth and home over the dictates of the heart.'

'Yet surely, sir, women have loved as greatly as men?' the Countess challenged. 'What of Cleopatra, or Helen, or the lady Heloise? Did she not love Abelard, her teacher then her lover, even after her family had deprived him of his manhood?'

My aunt looked across at me, shocked at such unsuitable discourse in front of one as young as I. Yet I knew the tale of Abelard and Heloise as well as they since I had often read it in my grandfather's library.

'Come, Ann.' My aunt hustled me to my feet, fearing more unsuitable conversation, and led me quickly off towards the seclusion of the long gallery, casting a look of severe disapproval at the Countess of Straven as we passed her.

I thought of trying to resist, yet knew such a reaction would be viewed by all as unmaidenly. And if I stayed in that room longer I would betray my anger that he, who one day could show himself a man of moral depth, could just as soon play lapdog to a brazen beauty who used him to proclaim her wit and belittle her husband.

'I must apologize for that young woman's conduct,' my aunt murmured, closing the door of the gallery behind us. 'Her father is an old friend of the Lord Keeper or we would not ask her hither.'

I longed to say that in my opinion the story of Abelard and the lady Heloise was not scandalous but one of true tenderness and enduring passion, but choler tied my tongue.

'I must return to the table. I shall speak to that young woman later.'

A rustle of silks told us we were no longer alone.

We turned to find the Countess herself standing but a few feet behind us, and, holding open the door to the gallery, none other than Master Donne. 'My lady, there is no need. I have come to beg pardon for my stupid indiscretion.' The Countess curtsied before us with all the apparent modesty of a maid at her first communion. 'Innocence must always be protected.' She looked slyly up at her companion. 'Is that not so, Master Donne?'

'I am glad you have remembered that at last,' my aunt said tartly. 'And now I must return to my other guests.'

'Fear not, Mistress More,' the Countess said softly once my aunt had gone. 'You are safe with us. We will not corrupt you further, will we, Master Donne?'

There was so much of complicity and of seduction in her tone that my eyes darted swiftly to his, and found that he looked not at me, but, like the fly caught in a silken spider's web, his attention was all fixed upon his companion.

'You wished to answer back, did you not, Mistress More, when your aunt removed you from my scurrilous presence?'

I kept my peace, refusing to play her games.

'Just as well your father will find you a husband soon who will help you hold your tongue. Women who speak out—apart from the Queen—are not encouraged in our society, are they, Master Donne?'

Again that look passed between them of dangerous complicity. I hated him then: that this very night I had risked so much by talking of his mother, and he had seemed grateful of my understanding, yet now, but hours later, made himself a lapdog to the lady Isabella, who thought herself so learned and so lovely.

I knew that I should remain silent, but the sight of that painted face, so confident of its own power, infuriated me beyond endurance.

'Indeed, my lady, when I have a husband of my own,' I kept my expression meek and my eyes downcast as I turned to leave them in the gallery, 'I trust he will be as generous and accommodating as your own.'

Chapter 10

THE SUN WAS higher than usual when I awoke next morning, and I lay for a moment longer watching the beams steal through my curtains and thinking of my rudeness to the Countess of Straven. Was it simply her overweening confidence that fired me so with anger, or Master Donne behaving like some pet dog that longed to be petted by those slim white fingers? Despite his reputation as a libertine, my own encounters with him had begun to make me see him as a man of wit and discrimination, and yet, in front of my lady's charms, all tumbled like the walls of Jericho at Joshua's trumpet.

I had no more time to dwell upon the fragrant charms of my lady Straven, due to the unexpected arrival of my sister Mary.

I had not yet arisen from my bed when Mary appeared in my chamber, pale as a wraith, urging me to sit up and talk to her. Mary was usually the neatest of dressers, not willing even to venture abroad if her shoe is scuffed, or her dress has a mark on it the size of a flea bite. I have seen her shout at her tire-woman if her ruff is not freshly poked and pinned to her curtain every morning of the week, even Sundays. Yet today her hair was lose and unkempt and I could see the sign of last night's meat upon her collar.

'Ann, Ann, wake up. I have need of your counsel.'

I sat up abruptly, shaking the hair from my face and rubbing the sleep out of the corner of my eyes. 'Mary! What is it? Not Father?'

'No, no. Father is at his lodgings in Charing Cross, no doubt eating a hearty breakfast, ready as ever to bore all in the Parliament with the regulation of watermen or the outrageous cost of kerseymere.'

I smiled but the stricken look in Mary's eyes stopped me and I climbed from my bed.

'Mary, sister, what is it that brings you?' I pulled a gown from my press and hastily began to dress, not bothering to call Joan or Mercy to help me.

'Our debts are worse.' She sank down onto the edge of the bed and hid her face in her hands.

'And can you truly apply to none for help? Could you not make suit to Nick's brother-in-law, Sir Walter Ralegh? His adventurings must surely have made him one of the richest men in the kingdom? He could surely assist you in your current difficulties?'

My sister shook her head. 'I am sad to say he is out of favour. He pines to be on the Council yet is ever excluded. And he has spent all he made on foreign expeditions and his house in the country.'

'And your necklace? The one our mother left to you?'

Mary bit her lip so hard that, to my shock, I saw a pinprick of blood appear. She turned her face away. 'Sold already.'

'Oh, Mary. And what of this gentleman to whom you are so sorely encumbered?'

'I have had communication from him again.' She threw a letter down onto the bed beside me. The paper was thick and costly and the heavy red seal, adorned with rampant lions and castles, spoke of wealth and luxury. 'Matthew Freeman, *Esquire*,' she spat the title as if no man deserved it less, 'says he saw me once and has not forgotten my grace and beauty. If I wished to meet with him alone he would consider ways to absolve us of our embarrassment and my small indiscretion.'

'You cannot mean . . . ?'

Mary looked at me, her eyes narrowing and her voice as hard as the clang of the hammer on the anvil. 'There is only one currency I know of where such debts can be settled in private and without money.'

'When does he bid you meet him?'

'Tomorrow afternoon. At an establishment called the Castle upon Hope Inn.' She smiled bitterly. 'I would wager an angel it will not be a royal castle.'

'But I know it! Our aunt's woman, Joan, showed it to me when we were walking in Southwark. Mary,' I tried to take her hand but she pulled it from me, 'according to Joan it is a bawdy house.'

'I did not imagine it was a place of religious devotion.'

'Your husband, Nick, surely he would never countenance such a transaction?'

Mary grabbed my hands and held them so tight she almost crumbled my bones. 'Nick must never know aught of this. He would either die or kill me if he had the merest suspicion of any such action.'

'Mary, I beg you not to follow this rash course. There must be other ways of avoiding disaster.'

'There are. I have examined them all. This is my last resort.'

'You are the kindest of women,' I forced her to look me in the eye, 'and the bravest. Yet surely it cannot be worth this?'

'No, Ann,' Mary replied as if her determination had been sharpened like a knife on the whetstone. 'I am neither kind nor brave. But I refuse to lose all that I have and forfeit my children's inheritance because of my husband's fondness for gambling and a stupid letter I should never have written.'

'So you are going to meet this man tomorrow?'

'I am. I came today for two reasons.' Her clear green eyes seemed strangely calm now that her mind was made up. 'First, that once I had made the announcement to you, I would have to go on the morrow. Second, I may jump fences at the gallop and never think twice of my safety but I thought one close to me should know of my venturing alone into Southwark to see him.'

I saw that beneath her calm Mary was frightened indeed. 'I am glad you trusted me. But I beg you, do not follow this road. Surely it would be better to importune Father? He is a rich man after all.'

'And let him see the weakness of the man I have chosen? Never!' She held me briefly against her heart. 'Men risk blood and death in battle. Lying on a feather bed, no matter with what distasteful company, can hardly compare with that. I will not lose an eye or a limb in this combat.'

'You might lose a soul,' I wanted to say, but kept my peace. Besides, I had not yet conceded that it must come to this. I needed to think if any other way were open to us.

After Mary left I slipped quietly down the back staircase to the gardens beneath. I needed a moment alone to think before my aunt called me to my tasks.

All around the weather mocked my unhappiness with its perfect beauty. Every bird in London seemed to be singing his heart out under warm May skies of heavenly blue. Without noticing where my steps led me, I followed a path towards the river.

Whom could I apply to, I asked myself, for wisdom and wise counsel? My aunt had been so kind to me, I wondered if she could be trusted? The bitter truth struck me of a sudden that it was to Mary herself, certain, brave Mary, that in times of trial I would most often turn, and now she was applying to me, and I had not been able to save her.

Bett, too, was lost to me; could I bear disaster to befall another of my sisters?

'Mistress More . . . ?' A quiet voice broke into my thoughts.

I turned to find Master Donne standing but a few feet away. I put up my chin, waiting for him to make some jest about the rudeness last night to my lady Straven.

Instead his voice held only gentle concern. 'Is aught distressing you? Forgive me for intruding but it seemed to me you stared towards the river like one seeking its watery embrace.'

The kindness in his voice took me aback and again I felt a temptation to explain the whole to him, and seek his advice. Yet the display last night with the Countess had rocked my judgement in him. Perhaps his soul was not the shining beacon I had begun to think it. 'Not I. I was listening to the birds sing and thinking of Loseley where I grew up. The birdsong there is louder than anywhere I have ever heard it.'

'Louder even than the cooing of amorous London doves?'

I blushed at this reference to our first meeting and changed the subject lest he see me blush further.

'Tell me, Master Donne, how is Wat faring?'

Master Donne's answer was a laugh. 'He is a fast learner, I grant you. Already he knows at what time I want my morning beer, the way my clothes are to be hung or folded, and he has found his way round the palace of Whitehall faster than a dog hunts out a juicy bone.' His eyes sought my face. 'Do you enjoy the country so much better than the Court, then, Mistress More, that you pine so for its birdsong?'

'I do. And you? Do country pleasures appeal to you, Master Donne?'

'Alas, no. I am a Londoner born and bred. To me the cry of the costermonger is far lovelier than the call of the cuckoo.'

Despite my worries I laughed at that.

'That is better. Yet your merry brown eyes still seem clouded. Are you sure there is nothing for which I could offer my humble services?'

This time the temptation to unburden myself was too strong and I would certainly have confided in him had not from the far end of the garden a vision appeared in palest cream satin, worked with golden threads, her long hair loose about her shoulders like some Grecian goddess.

The Countess of Straven had come to claim her due.

And already my companion's tender concern was fixing itself elsewhere.

'Master Donne,' her voice, so steely in command, now tinkled like the brook in the mead at Loseley, 'I am glad to find you here. I seek a classical allusion for the poem I am engaged in writing. It tells the story of two maids vying with each other in love.' To my surprise, she looked at me slyly. 'One is far nobler than the other, and loves with a pure bright fire. The other, knowing she is not worthy, stoops to tactics that are ignoble and underhand to trick him into loving her. What think you of the notion of Atalanta's balls?'

I had meant to say farewell and leave them to their versifying, but there was that in the Countess's manner that brought out the sinful Eve in me.

'Why not the Judgement of Paris?' I suggested, my voice as cloying as sugared almonds in a sweet bag. 'For I have often found that even good men are blinded by beauty into choices they later discover to be mistaken.'

I took my leave before the Countess thought up a rejoinder or had time to conclude to whom I might be alluding.

But Master Donne, who had followed my thinking entirely, watched me depart with the smallest ghost of a smile.

THAT NIGHT I slept not at all but twisted and turned like a soul in torment. As the sun rose over the misty reaches of the Thames I had my answer.

I would go myself and visit Master Freeman in her stead.

I knew the risk this would mean to my reputation, how my reluctance to go to Court would be as nothing compared to this if I were discovered. A young woman's reputation was as important as her portion or her parentage. And yet it seemed to me my very innocence would be a protection. Yet, dared I risk all this for my sister?

The memory of Mary, ever brave and resourceful, reduced so low and desperate persuaded me. Despite her foolishness I could not see my sister lose all.

And yet, how would it be accomplished?

And then I remembered what Wat had once told me, about the high-born lady passing herself off as her lover's page. I had heard tell, also, of a wild young woman who rode about the country dressed in a gentleman's clothing and who had once had the audacity to hold up a noble coach on the Hertford road.

And yet, what if I were caught and unmasked? Women might pass themselves off as men in Master Shakespeare's plays, yet these same women were played by boys while real women would never dare go on a stage.

I turned to my coffer, to hold in my hand my mother's amethyst ring. Beneath it, wrapped in cloth, was a lock of Bett's brown hair. I touched it against the chill of my cheek. Yes! I would do this for Mary, who had done so much for me.

And so I summoned Wat.

I had done him a good turn, and I knew he was both loyal and grateful, and if applied to he would not let me down.

I found him playing jacks with another boy in a closet not far from the kitchens. 'Wat!' I called to him softly. 'I have need of your help. Come with me, quick.'

He shrugged to his friend and followed me through the winding corridors of York House. 'Do you have a spare set of clothes, Wat?'

'Aye, my Sunday best. Bought especially for me by my master.'

'Lend me them. You shall have them back by evening.'

'Why, mistress, what need have you of a groom's clothes?'

'I have a task to do that requires me to wear men's garb.'

'What is this task, mistress?' he enquired, concern clouding his shrewd blue eyes.

'Never you mind. Just remember the favours I have done you and keep your counsel.'

As slow as a snail, Wat trailed miserably off, returning with a neat pile of clothing. 'I thought you might need this also.' He handed over, in addition, a long black cloak.

'Thank you.' I took the cloak gratefully. 'Now, off you go and I will return your belongings later.'

'Take care, mistress,' were his final words as he ran back to find his jack-playing friend.

'I will, Wat,' I said, trying to convince myself that the task ahead was not as daunting as I feared.

I pulled my bodies so tight that my breasts were rendered as flat as a board, then drew on the white lawn shirt, plain black doublet and hose, and finished all with a plain cotton ruff. Then I tied up my hair with a shoelace and stuffed it into a large black hat I had discreetly lifted from the row outside the wardrobe. Later, one of my uncle's advisors would find himself hatless as he went to see some great minister of state and wonder if he was losing his memory.

One quick glance in the glass on the great landing told me that if I kept my head down and tried not to speak I would pass muster. Willing myself not to look behind me after every step, I scuttled down through the endless passageways of York House until I reached the river. Here I turned left until I came to the nearest public stairs, so that I would not be remarked, and put out my hand for a wherry.

Yet before I could shout 'Oars!' a figure emerged from the shadows and grabbed me bodily by the arm.

It was Master Donne, his eyes blazing with fury.

'What lunatic charade is this?' he demanded. An approaching wherryman watched us, then pulled his hat down and rowed away, not wanting to be involved in trouble with his betters. 'Wat has come to me with some tale of your borrowing his clothes. And here I find you wearing them, alone, and bound for Southwark or some such wild place. Have you lost your senses entirely?'

He marched me away from the river. 'Speak! Before I throw you into the Thames and be damned to you!'

I stiffened mutinously. 'I can swim.'

He ignored this rebellion. 'What were you dreaming of?'

My instinct was to bluff. What matter was our private business to him? Then, cold and frightened, suddenly fearful of my face being known, my stout heart faltered and I told him all. 'My sister is in trouble. Her husband has been gambling and a certain gentleman has acquired his notes of debt and a letter she foolishly sent to another gentleman, which fell into the hands of this Master Freeman. He promised to return them all to her if she met him alone. I elected to go in her stead. He means no harm to me.'

'He does not need to, for you harm yourself!' He half dragged me down an alley between York House and the Strand, which was mercifully empty. 'And where had you undertaken to meet this Master Freeman, pray?'

I turned my head, unwilling to divulge.

'Where?' He pushed me roughly against the wall.

'The Castle upon Hope Inn.'

'God's nails! You were going to a stewhouse! You might as well parade naked in Whitehall, for none would believe your innocence after that!'

'Thank you, Master Donne.' I tried to wrench myself out of his grip. 'Yet I do not remember asking your assistance in this matter.'

'And you will get none! How did you imagine, when you faced this Master Freeman, that you would persuade him to release your sister's husband from his debts?'

'By threatening to expose him for the corrupt man he is!'

Master Donne laughed and shook his head. 'I had thought you a gentlewoman of unusual sense. Especially for your years. Did you think it would be brave to sacrifice yourself for your sister? A Joan of Arc at Orleans? You are not brave, but criminally foolish!' Master Donne's eyes were still dark with fury as he looked into mine. 'What crazy madness makes you think you can don a boy's clothing and go down alone among thieves and ruffians and argue with a greater villain than any of them! He might have slain you or . . .'

'Or worse? Forced me to pay my sister's price?' I knew he was right, that I should be thanking him, but there was that in his tone which summoned up my blood.

'Yes. Even by going there, if it were known abroad, or gossiped about in jest, your good name would be blemished forever and your word dismissed—how much good would that have done your sister?' I made no answer so he turned me round to face him. 'And thought you of the risks others must take to help you? Wat, who could be dismissed for lending his clothes. And I, too, who risk my position and my rank if I go not now this moment and betray you to the Lord Keeper, for he would expect no less of me? You are happy enough to visit stewhouses and threaten the safety of others for your own ends, I see . . .'

I pulled my wrist out of his grasp, as angry now as he was. 'There speaks one who dallies with the wife of an absent earl! And seduces the wives of good and honest men then sets his victories to verse! From such a one should I take my moral counsel?'

'Madam, you overstate my talents.' His eyes sparked with anger at my accusation. 'What I write in my verse is not for such as you—unless you are so desirous to read of the promptings of the flesh that you bid your cousin secretly acquire it for you . . .'

I gasped. 'Rein in your vanity, sir . . . Or, tell me, was it to quell such lascivious promptings that you sent me the psalms of David? That I might chastise myself with good works, and lo, even good works translated by a lady? Thought you then to set me a good example? Though it be not one that you choose yourself to follow?'

'Mistress More, I am a man . . .'

'Yet man is cast in the image of God, is he not? Has he not the gift of Godlike reason, that he might not be rendered passion's slave?' I knew that perhaps I went too far, yet I was incensed beyond resisting. 'If what you write in your verse be true, you seem to creep like a thief from ladies' chambers, stealing their virtue and taking much pleasure in the deception.'

I saw that I had struck a blow and might have regretted this high speech had he not quickly answered me.

'Mistress More, the ladies I consort with do so willingly, I assure you. And it would be better if you had the humility to admit the danger, instead of disputing with me as to which of us is in the wrong.'

I fell silent for a moment at that, humbled. 'Master Donne, does it indeed behove you to tell my aunt and uncle of this day's work?'

The eyes that had glittered with anger softened a little. 'I think not. I concede that some might say it was brave of you to take so outrageous a risk to save your sister.'

'Or foolhardy,' I admitted in a voice that was barely audible.

But Master Donne was contemplating an error of judgement of his own. 'Since you eavesdropped upon my conversation with my mother you know that my own brother Henry also acted unwisely, or bravely according to his lights. He gave shelter to a fleeing priest and brought down upon himself the full weight of the law. When he was cast into Newgate, some whispered that I was not busy enough on his behalf, that I wished not to risk the implication of Popery for the sake of my own advancement.'

'Perhaps you had more sense.'

He looked out across the darkened river and I had to bend to catch his words. 'Or not enough courage. He died there of a sudden plague.' He turned to me once more. 'And even when he was dead, there were those who pointed out that I profited from his share of our inheritance.'

'People are not kind.'

'No. So I will not betray you to the Lord Keeper. Yet I lay down one condition.'

'Which I may guess.'

'There is a difference between men and women.'

'Yes.' There was the smallest smile in my voice as I replied. 'This is a matter I have perceived.'

'You must stop such japes as this and act the part of a modest young woman.'

'Modest! Even if that word sentences me to a life of housewifery and endless stitchwork?'

He laughed at that. 'And if the housewifery and stitchwork were for your own husband and household? Would that not be a task worth undertaking?'

'That would depend on the husband.'

He raised my hood up over my head and for one instant I thought he might touch my lips with his. And wretch that I am I longed for the feel of his mouth on mine. Yet he did not do so. 'Keep your cloak pulled up and slip in by the kitchen passageway. Go!' He thrust me roughly and I all but stumbled as I crept along, hugging the wall, glad of the shadows and yet all the while chafing my anger to keep it warm. How dared he behave in so high-handed a manner?

I had almost regained the small door in the side of the wall leading to York House when I stopped short, winded, as if I had been hit by a lance to the stomach in the tiltyard. For coming towards me down the narrow alley was a young gentleman, finely clad, whistling an off-key tune as he walked.

It was Master Manners.

I tried to turn and run back towards the river, but it was too late.

'Mistress Ann More, by God's wounds!' he shouted, dashing all my hopes that he might not have recognized me in a boy's apparel. 'By all the saints, what do you do abroad alone, and dressed in such clothing?'

Fear coursed through me that he had seen Master Donne or would guess the nature of my excursion. I prayed to the Mother of God to give me inspiration. And she, in her kindness and mercy, blessed me with an answer.

'Master Manners, you startled me!' The face I turned to him was all innocent surprise. 'Can I let you into my secret? You will not betray me to my aunt or uncle?'

'Mistress More, I can make no such promise . . .' Master Manners began sternly.

'I have been visiting the brother and sisters of our new servant boy, Wat. He came to me with a story of such sadness that they lacked a mother or father, and their sister Sarah prayed each day to the Almighty that He might grant them an education and give them a chance to rise from the low tide of their birth.'

Master Manners listened, disbelief printed upon his brow.

'But why should that make you dress as a boy and travel alone into the city?'

'To protect my maidenly innocence from comment and stares. I have travelled to Southwark to visit them.'

'To Southwark? Alone?'

'Master Manners we have a Queen upon the throne who has ruled us as well as a man for almost forty years. I think I am fit to travel across three miles of London without needing to call the Watch.'

'You should not be the judge of that, Mistress More,' was his angry response. 'It is for your olders and betters to make such rulings. Or your husband if you had one.'

I put up my chin at that.

'Not all would be as sympathetic to your venture as you might like. They might think you had been to visit a lover or engage in some hoydenish behaviour.'

'Master Manners,' I said, my voice as sugared as the lemon mead we drank two nights past, 'could you think me guilty of hoydenish behaviour when I was about the Lord's work? I have undertaken to teach these children their letters. What use is there for the plentiful education God has bestowed upon me, unless I can use it to better the path of others less fortunate than myself? Tell my aunt if you must, but I would rather do it in my own time and you would endear yourself greatly to me if you forbore.'

I did not wait for an answer. I could see him watching me, his face a picture of confused suspicion. I angered him in some manner he could not find the name for.

It was a dangerous game, for I could see in his face that it only made him want me in his power the more.

Back in my chamber, thankfully observed by no groom or tirewoman on my return, I stripped off my boy's attire and hid it beneath my pillow.

Then, dressed only in my shift, I sank to my knees at the foot of the bed and wept in anger, in frustration and in fear.

Chapter 11

'THERE YOU ARE, mistress!' Mercy greeted me just as I fastened up the final hook on my woman's apparel. 'Your aunt sent me to find you betimes, and I searched high and low, yet not hide nor hair of you could I discover. And the mystery is, no gown seemed to have been taken from your press or coffer.'

'I was wearing an old dress brought from the country. I am sorry, Mercy. I must have dawdled in the garden reading my prayer book.'

'For five long hours?' she enquired with the veriest trace of insolence. 'Your soul must surely be saved after that, mistress.'

Without knowing it, I found myself smiling at the debate I would have had with Master Donne on this topic. Could prayer and good works help save a soul, as some believed, or were the chosen few truly elected by God before even they were born, and no amount of dipping into prayer books or good deeds could alter their predestined fate?

'I need to speak with Wat about a pressing matter that concerns his family. Please bring him hither.'

Mercy trudged off with a grudging look to seek out Wat, leaving me alone with my thoughts.

For once Wat looked as meek as a lamb when he made his entrance to my chamber. He waited till Mercy had unwillingly left, for she wished to hear more of these strange happenings, before he spoke. His bright eyes, often times so full of mischief and of fun, and intelligent withal, were clouded by anxiety at my probable reaction. 'I am sorry, Mistress Ann, for so betraying you to Master Donne. I saw you making for a wherry, dressed in my clothes. I could not let you trespass on the wilder shores of Southwark alone and unprotected.'

'As a matter of fact,' I replied sternly, 'I am well able to protect myself.' His young face looked so rebuked that I added: 'Yet thank you for your care of me.'

He bowed low and doffed his hat, for all the world like his master or a Court gallant, and despite my anger I could not but laugh to see him grown so noble.

'You saved me from the tanner, mistress. See, look at my hands.' He held out both palms for my inspection. They were pink and soft. 'Joan gave me the wool grease from her cousin's ewe to rub into them.'

I smiled at how fierce Joan had kept this kindness to herself. Wat's merry soul seemed to bring out the gentleness in us all.

He was about to take his leave.

'Wat, one thing. Your brother and sister.'

'Yes, mistress.'

'Is it true your sister Sarah can no longer care for them?'

The narrow face looked suddenly older, as if borne in on by cares he knew not how to manage. 'She is sick, mistress, struck down with the sweats.'

I nodded. The sweats were a terrible affliction, often striking the young and strong and sometimes carrying them off within a day.

I reached for my purse with the few pennies I still had left. 'Go to the apothecary and see if there is aught that can help her. Then let us see if we can find shelter for them here.'

Now I had only the small task of persuading my aunt to give her approval.

I remembered that the next day we were to go to Greenwich to hear my uncle's chaplain preach a sermon. I would try and persuade my aunt then. I wondered if the Queen would attend, since sermons could be as popular as plays or masques when they were delivered by an eloquent and interesting thinker, though secretly the churchgoers enjoyed assessing each other's finery as much as listening to the topic of the worthy discourse.

I found myself wondering, on the morrow, as I dressed myself carefully, if Master Donne had a mind to listen to preachers. I would bet an angel coin he preferred to do the things preachers condemned, than to sit and hear the condemning. But we would see.

Before I had finished dressing my sister Mary burst into my chamber, her smile as wide as if one close to her had recovered after a long illness. 'Ann, Ann, I am come here with the greatest speed. Master Freeman has returned Nick's notes not an hour ago and will harry us no more! You can hardly picture with what relief I greeted the letter when it arrived at our house this morning. And Nick! He was so amazed he fell to his knees to thank the Almighty God there and then for our deliverance.'

I was filled with confusion at this revelation. Why should Master Freeman have changed his mind and freed my sister and her husband from their obligations so suddenly?

'Sister, I am indeed glad for you! And now you must make the most of Nick's repentance and ensure that he does not waste his money on gambling again.'

'Indeed.' She put her arm around me, and we both stood silent, overwhelmed by relief that we were safe and neither of us ruined, looking out over the bustling thoroughfare of the Thames, where small wherries wended their way through big cargo boats loaded with building materials for the city's expansion, and the painted and canopied barges of the nobility.

'And your letter is returned as well?' I demanded of her.

She flushed at that, as if already she had tried to put it from her thoughts.

'Mind that you take no such risk again. Know you what caused this sudden freak of mercifulness in Master Freeman?'

She shrugged as if she cared not a jot how it had come about, now that the burden had been lifted from her shoulders. 'Francis has gone to make discreet enquiries. I had to let him into my confidence. He is our cousin after all.'

We took ourselves to the withdrawing chamber where my aunt sat sipping sugared wine, listening to sweet music sung by four pretty youths.

'Ann! Keep away from the Lord Keeper! He is in such a choler! And all because he needed Master Donne by his side this morning for some business of the Privy Council's and he was nowhere to be found.

He shouts of his secretary being a man of straw and even refused my chamomile infusion to soothe his temper!'

A sudden premonition assailed me, that made me flush with shame and guilt. From the corner of my eye I noticed my cousin slipping into the room, and indicating with a shake of the head that Mary and I should extricate ourselves and follow him.

'Francis!' His mother suddenly noticed him. 'You also have been absent. Where have you been visiting this morning?'

Francis bowed deeply and kissed her hand. 'Hawking, Mother, across the river in Peckham.'

He patted the elaborate headdress on the top of his mother's head and followed us both from the chamber.

'Well, Mary, you and Nick have Master Donne to thank for your relief. It seems he threatened this Freeman with the full apparatus of the Lord Keeper's stately power to make him release Nick's debts.'

'*Master Donne?*' my sister parroted in horrified tones. 'What knows he of our private matters?' She turned to me.

'I told him. He apprehended me trying to cross the river to try and beard Master Freeman myself.'

'Ann! You would not!'

Master Donne's words of criticism rang in my ears. How I had not thought of those whose honour and livelihood I implicated in my scheme. And now it seemed he had taken that risk upon himself.

'Indeed,' mused Francis, 'it was a generous act.'

'Yet Nick and I are barely acquainted with Master Donne,' Mary protested. 'Why should he risk so much to help us?'

Francis shrugged, his eyes on mine. 'You are slow for an educated wench, Mary. It was not you and Nick he risked his good name for . . .'

My breath quickened as if I had run all the way from York House to the river bank. Had he acted simply out of generosity or was there indeed, as Francis implied, another motive altogether in his mind? To take such a risk as this implied a depth of soul I had not expected in him. And now I found an answering emotion in my breast.

'I must return to my mother,' Francis bowed his farewell. 'Already she wonders what takes place between we three.'

Slowly Mary turned to me. 'Yet beware, Ann, remember his reputation.'

'Is this the act of a dangerous libertine?' I demanded, fired up at her ingratitude. 'He has risked his rank and livelihood for us. If the man chose to dispute his authority he would have been ruined as much as you or Nick!'

'Master Donne!' Mary repeated, dropping her arm from mine. 'So now he too knows about our shameful situation! Ann, I could wish you had not involved him in our affairs when he is nothing to us.'

'Without Master Donne's intervention your affairs would be in a sorrier state by far,' I answered, tart as vinegar. 'It is not Master Donne who should be called to account but your own dear Nick! Was it not somewhat late for him to fall to his knees? Should he not have considered the shame and risk to your credit and his family's fortunes before this?'

Mary looked away. 'Master Donne has turned your head with his poetry and his dark gaze. Oh yes, I joked not when I said you had two admirers. I have seen the looks he casts at you when none observe him. If he were nobler or richer, and knew our father would not send him off with a flea in his ear, he would be seeking a betrothal himself!'

'Mary, desist,' I answered hotly, astonished and confused by her suggestion and my own reaction to it. 'I will listen no more to this! Master Donne acted from nothing save generosity. I happen to know he loves a woman whose estate is far higher than my own.'

'Then he is an arrant fool, unless he means simply to bed her. And if you talk of Isabella Straven, then her husband would find no complaint, for it seems the Earl wishes not to bed her himself or he would keep her on a closer rein!'

She left me alone at that, my thoughts swirling, and the beauty of the day and my sense of relief at Master Freeman's forgoing their debts overshadowed by her disturbing accusations.

I stopped, leaning out over the wide waters of the river, my hands gripping the stone balustrade. Surely she was mistaken that Master Donne had cast me longing looks?

I glanced back to where I had first espied him, watching the love-lorn pigeons and, remembering his lips on mine, felt a sudden spurt of flame deep within me. And yet, even if I did come to question my old condemnation of him, no love between us would ever be permitted. The sooner I accepted it the better. And yet, whether I denied it or not, this generosity towards my sister had moved me deeply. And like a bird that flies to its nest, I knew where my own heart would wing its way if ever it were released unfettered into the bright blue day.

BEFORE WE SET off for Greenwich I sought out my aunt in her closet where Mercy said she had withdrawn to do some spiritual reading. Yet the haste with which she hid the book when I entered made me wonder if it were so spiritual after all. She caught my enquiring glance and revealed, tucked into her missal among the psalms, a copy of *The Faerie Queene*. 'You have caught me out, niece, for I should be saying my prayers.' Yet her face was smiling the while. 'You have enlivened my quiet life with your presence, Ann.'

I laughed at this since my aunt's life is as quiet as the life of the captain of some great ship or the commander of a vast army.

'I never had a daughter and only since you came to visit have I known what I missed.'

'I will happily be your daughter. Yet whether you will want me as such, I know not, when you hear my request. Though it is indeed God's work I sincerely do believe.'

'Why does my heart sink like a wise woman on a ducking stool at those words from you, my Ann?'

I could not help but smile. 'Perhaps because I am forever teasing you with some new outlandish scheme.'

'And what is your newest, pray?'

'To give shelter to Wat's young brother and sister and perhaps find them some worthier employment.'

To my surprise my aunt did not pour scorn upon my supplication, but rather considered it. 'Your uncle's chaplain urges me to do more good works and, truth to tell, I do not have the taste for it, going amongst the poor and scabrous, washing the feet of beggars.'

I tried not to smile at the idea of my aunt, always so richly and elegantly robed, her hair carefully knotted round a jewelled headdress, who hated even to get mud on her velvet shoes, getting within a league of a beggar.

'Ask Joan if she can find them some tasks to fulfil around the household. Yet keep them away from the Lord Keeper. He has enough to concern him. The Queen cannot decide whom to send in command of the Irish war and she is angry with all around her. Your uncle tries to advise and gets the sharp edge of the blade for his troubles.'

I did as I was bid, yet the troublesome question of Ireland soon overtook us all. At York House the talk was of nothing but the Irish rebellion and the scandalous tale that the Earl of Essex, angry with the Queen at not being given command, had drawn his sword on his sovereign then stamped off, angry as a stuck pig, to his estate in Wanstead.

My uncle much admired the Earl and sought to persuade him to return and take his place in the Council. But my lord Essex was too proud to do it. Instead he scandalized the Court by writing back asking my uncle the treasonous question: Could not princes err? And subjects be wronged?

There was so much fear in the air that I forgot, when next I saw Master Donne, the circumstances of our last meeting. We had foregathered in the Great Hall before the evening meal and both Master Donne and, to my surprise, Richard Manners were amongst our number.

'Will there be war, then, with Ireland?' I asked Master Donne, knowing how close he was to my uncle and the great affairs of State and that his friend Henry Wotton, standing beside him, was secretary to my lord Essex.

'I fear there will,' Master Wotton replied. 'We are having too many reports of the estates of English settlers burned and ravaged.'

'And will you be going, Master Donne,' Master Manners asked, I suspected hopefully, 'since you have so distinguished a record in Cadiz and the Islands?'

'My soldiering days are past,' Master Donne replied. 'I will leave it to the younger men,' he gestured towards the Lord Keeper's handsome son Thomas, who sat next to his wife and three small daughters, the smallest of whom came hardly up to his knee.

Thomas picked her up and pretended to ride her up and down, making the clicking sound of a pony. 'Shall Papa be a soldier, Dorothy?' he asked her. 'And ride a fine horse into battle, to fight for the Queen?'

The child nodded, not understanding what she was consenting to, poor mite.

'The battlefields of Ireland are no place for fine horses,' commented his father grimly. 'They would disappear into the bogs and you with them. It is a curse that we must fight the Irish rebels, yet so it must be

along the passageway and found myself outside the door of the chamber where Master Donne took his rest.

Glancing quickly behind me, I pushed it open. I had never crossed its threshold before and knew that if my aunt discovered I had done so, I would be in deep disgrace.

The chamber gave little away. It was no den of wickedness as I might have pictured it, with sweat-soaked linen tossed and tangled from nightly battles. Indeed, it was extreme neat in its appearance, with its pillows piled uniformly, its coverlets smoothed, and, standing in one corner, his boots all ranged in descending order, which it made me smile to see. I wondered where he wrote his verse since there were neither quills nor parchment to hand, and no commonplace book open and waiting for inspiration. Perhaps he carried his verses within him. Indeed there was little sign of the man in the chamber at all, save to the left side of the bed, on the wall a little higher than my head.

It was a portrait of Master Donne, dark and shadowy, his grey eyes looking to one side, his lips full and red as a woman's. I stared at it, trying to decipher the measure of the man. Was he one who could love a woman truly, with tender passion? Or would he, like the amorous bird he watched at our first meeting, ever be hopping to the next branch in search of newer nests?

I studied the picture closer and saw that there was a rabbit's foot tucked into his sleeve for a good-luck charm, and that the picture was inscribed with the words 'Illumina Tenebras Nostras Domina.' *Lighten our darkness, Lady.* I knew from my prayer book the words echoed the third collect of evening, yet surely here they were addressed not to the mother of God but to some gentlewoman he supposed he loved to distraction. Had he given the portrait to her and she returned it when their passion died?

And then, a sound made me turn, my breath so fast I thought that I might faint.

Chapter 12

NOT TWO PACES behind me, a sardonic smile lighting up his eyes, stood the original of the painting.

'Master Donne, I . . .' For the first occasion in my life I stumbled for words. '. . . I came to thank you for your great kindness shown to my sister and my brother-in-law . . .'

'It was not your sister or your brother-in-law I sought to help,' was his simple reply.

'You took a great risk. Not one I ought to have asked of you. Thank you.'

'Perhaps now you will steer your brother-in-law clear of his pernicious habits. You seem to me to be a straightforward young woman,' he smiled faintly, 'perhaps too straightforward for your own good, who has no difficulty speaking her own mind. There is a clearness of purpose in you that he is bound to respect, for even I am humbled by it. Tell him straight what risks he leads others into.'

'I will.'

'Besides I have reasons of my own to be grateful to you.'

My breath quickened to hear that. Was he about to admit I had rescued him from the lures of depravity?

'Wat.'

'*Wat?*' I was so startled I repeated his name.

'My servant. A boy of thirteen. Dark hair. Blue eyes. Somewhat given to cheek.'

'I know who Wat is.'

'I feared he might be a burden and have found him instead an object of delight. He has greatly increased my standing among my peers. Indeed some have tried to lure him to their service, others content themselves with copying his dress and manners.'

'I see.'

His smile widened. 'Thought you that there were other reasons I should be grateful to you? Useful criticism of my verse, perhaps? Maidenly ideas on how I might improve my morals? I am very grateful for both, I assure you.'

'I am sure you do not need such from one so young and inexperienced as I.' I tried to keep the annoyance from my voice for I feared he toyed with me, as a cat does with a mouse.

Despite his tender words to Master Wotton, he had clearly seen the rashness in acting on them. Perhaps he had even recovered his equilibrium.

And then, when I was least expecting it, he took my hand in his.

Quietly, gently, he overturned the palm and kissed the tender flesh so that, without warning, I quaked throughout my whole being as if some deep volcano had erupted within me like unto distant Vesuvius.

I know not what might have happened after, whether all my maid's modesty could have quenched the fire that suddenly raged through all my senses.

Yet I was not to discover, for the door of his chamber opened and Wat stood there, his look telling of the dog that fears its master's displeasure, and informed Master Donne that he was needed on the instant by the Lord Keeper.

At that I gathered my skirts over my arm, looking at neither Master Donne nor Wat, and ran towards the great staircase and from thence back into the hall where, to my great agitation, Master Manners stood lounging against the oaken table. At sight of him my face flamed up, and as he looked at me his eyes narrowed.

'Good even, Master Manners.' I held my head high and told myself to be calm, that he possessed not the powers of the Devil to see the sin in our hearts. I asked the first question of him that flew into my head. 'Have you seen my father for I must needs talk with him?'

He bowed low. 'No, Mistress More, I have not had sight of Sir

George this day. Perhaps like all in Parliament and Council he concerns himself with the crisis in Ireland.'

'Yes, yes you are right. I will find a boy to take a message to him there.'

'If it would please you, I would take such a message myself,' he offered, staring into my eyes with so penetrating a gaze that I had to look away.

'No, no. I am making too much of a trifle. I will speak with him later.'

As I left the hall I felt his eyes follow me and hoped with all my heart that Master Donne chose not this moment to make his appearance.

Thankfully he did not.

'Ann, Ann,' my aunt's voice was as welcome as the angels' from heaven, 'the very one I need to help me brew a remedy on the morrow for Thomas the steward's palsy. What was that herb my lady mother bade you find in the gardens?'

The next morning as I heated up the herbs for the healing brew, my mind pondered on quite another and far more perplexing fire. What was the explanation of my deep confusion? Was it but the promptings of the flesh, so unknown to me before now? In the words of my sister's sampler, were my senses erring and leading my reason astray?

'Ann! Take care!'

My aunt's advice could be against a far greater threat than any she suspected.

I found the brew had boiled over the top of the phial and scalded my fingers.

'Silly wench!' my aunt berated me. 'Here am I come to cure the sickness of my steward and my niece adds her injury to his!' She made me dip my fingers in cold water.

'I am sorry, Aunt. Here, the brew is finished now.'

My aunt took the phial from me and sniffed it, which made her cough heartily. 'Excellent,' she pronounced. 'I find with many ailments the fouler the draught, the sooner a cure is affected. With a foul potion, I fancy the sufferer remarks the treatment more and so feels the benefit.'

She poured the mixture into smaller phials and added a stopper to each, as I tried to be helpful and dutiful and think not of my present difficulty, at which point our purposes were interrupted by the arrival of her servant Mercy.

'Mistress Ann! A pair of ragged children have arrived asking for you and the steward is all for sending them away. He asked me if I knew aught of their arrival.' Mercy sniffed her disapproval. 'I said that knowing yourself, mistress, a troop of one-legged vagrants or a pack of stray dogs might have been bidden to sup with us.'

'Thank you, Mercy,' I answered her loftily. 'I shall come and talk to Thomas myself.' I picked a phial from the still-room rack where my aunt had been ranging them, adorning each with one of her beautiful labels, written in her own hand, illustrated with plants and leaves in green and gold leaf, works of art in themselves. 'And I shall give him this to ease all the suffering I cause him.'

'Ann, Ann.' My aunt shook her head as I skipped from the still room. 'Remember to tell Thomas they are not to annoy him or they will be sent away forthwith.'

'Yes, Aunt.'

I found the two, a boy of about ten and one small maid, quaking under the towering gaze of my uncle's steward, who was a huge man near six feet tall, dressed from head to toe in black like some giant crow. They both stood staring up at the gilded ceiling and the statues, as if wondering whether they found themselves at the gates of Heaven or of Hell.

'Welcome.' I dipped down to my knees. 'Now you must each tell me your names.'

'I be Stephen,' announced the boy. 'And this is my sister Hope.'

'Hope,' I took the maid's small hand in mine, 'what a very excellent name to be sure.'

'The midwife gave it to me,' Hope announced with a touch of pride. 'She said that with my mother dying I was like to need it.'

Behind us, Thomas grunted.

I heard no more of the children for the rest of the day, and deemed it safer not to ask. I was sure, if there was a problem I would soon be called on to solve it.

Instead I fulfilled my other duties, walking in the garden, down by the river, to take some air and stock up my aunt's store of herbal remedies. Here I spent a busy hour amongst the agrimony and the feverwort, admiring the flowers of the deadly nightshade and picking the clary sage and a bunch of cinquefoil which my grandmother swore was the best remedy she knew against the night sweats. I wondered then about Wat's sister Sarah, and whether there was aught I could do to help her fever. At that the thought of Bett came into my mind and how I had not been able to aid her for all my learning about herbs and potions.

Before I knew it, the supper bell sounded and I ran up and threw on the nearest gown, hardly thinking how I looked, my hair all blown about, my cheeks whipped into colour by the sharp evening wind. My uncle was just beginning grace when I arrived and I saw with mixed emotions that my father sat at his left hand and the Countess of Straven on his right.

I sensed, rather than saw, the presence of Master Donne, and willed myself to look not in his direction, lest the memory of that encounter, and the fires it stoked, made me give away more than I intended. My eyes strayed in the other direction and found those of Master Manners regarding me intently. He reached out and found a wild strand of my hair that had escaped from the wire of my headdress.

'Have you ridden abroad today, Mistress More?' To my great confusion he added, 'What think you, Master Donne, is not Mistress More's colour as fresh as if she had hunted the hart all afternoon long?' What had he noticed passing between we two that made him thus question Master Donne?

'I cannot answer, Master Manners, for I hunt not,' was his calm reply.

'Then you miss much. Hunting adds spice to life as cinnamon does to a hot codling.'

'Yet it is too dangerous for my taste,' replied Master Donne. 'And the outcome over-bloody.'

'Yet does not danger make us feel alive, think you not?'

'Do you hunt a great deal, Master Manners?' I asked, to fill the deep trench of silence that suddenly surrounded us.

'I do.' His eyes fixed onto mine. 'And always on horses that I have broken myself, the wilder the better.'

His meaning was so clear that I had to look away.

'My lady Straven,' I enquired swiftly, 'do you hunt also?'

'Whenever I may. I have found that hunting is the second best pastime I have yet discovered.'

At this all the table laughed heartily and my aunt, ever the diplomat, swiftly returned the talk to modesty by praising the Queen's prowess on horseback and how she could stay all day in the saddle and jump fences greater than those of all her courtiers.

As the repast unfolded, I fell silent until I sensed the eyes of all upon me and saw that my lady Straven had asked me a question.

'Is it true,' she repeated, 'as the Lord Keeper's steward informed me, that you have picked up brats from the gutter and given them a home?'

'Until their sister is recovered, yes,' I replied as calm as I could. 'Their brother Wat is the new servant to Master Donne and is doing very well, is he not?'

'Excellent well,' replied Master Donne with a bow. 'He is a thousand times better than my last boy, though he was of gentler breeding. Mistress More has an excellent eye.'

I thought of how it was not my excellent eye but my guilt at my own good luck that had made me rescue Wat the day he came careering into me, and, in truth, I welcomed not having his brother and sister foisted upon us also.

'I hear you are given to rash acts, Mistress More,' the Countess commented, 'which later you may come to regret.'

My gaze darted anxiously to Master Donne at that, wondering if he had vouchsafed my secret over our encounter upstairs or, worse still, the episode in Southwark.

Yet his gaze was steady, looking staunchly forward, giving naught away.

I breathed again that there were to be no more eruptions tonight; but my relief came too soon, I realized, when I heard the next words from my father.

'I have had the ill fortune to come across one of your satires, Master Donne,' he announced, pulling from his sleeve a piece of parchment from which he began to read aloud to the company in a disparaging voice.

'Shall I, none's slave, of high-born or raised men
Fear frowns? And my mistress Truth, betray thee
To the huffing braggart, puffed nobility?'

'So, Master Donne,' demanded my father, his colour rising, 'am I one of these "raised men" that you speak of so scathingly in your verses? Or mayhap you do me greater honour and I am among the number of your "puffed nobility"?'

Master Donne bowed. 'Sir George, I thought not of you, nor any hard-working member of Parliament when I penned those words but rather the idle courtier or the scheming Court official.'

'Yet though you despise so many of us, you have a goodly notion of your own consequence, I warrant, since Truth chooses only to be *your* mistress.'

I could hear the cold fury in my father's voice and knew that in his eyes Master Donne, poet and scholar, trusted employee of the Lord Keeper though he might be, was nothing but a jumped-up servant and a troublesome meddler in the ways of his betters. And his witty verses, esteemed and valued by his contemporaries, were to my father merely harsh, discordant and, worst of all, critical of the current social order. To stoke up his ire still further I feared he suspected a dangerous quickening of interest in me.

I longed to say my piece at this criticism, to cry, 'Father, you are wrong! It is the canker of corruption Master Donne seeks to root out not to pull down honest nobility!' And yet I knew to challenge the authority of my father thus, and express opinions that were the prerogative of men in front of this great assembly, would do naught but damage to myself and to Master Donne himself. So I stayed silent.

'I wish that Truth were indeed my mistress . . .' Master Donne began.

'Truth! You know naught of truth in your seditious verses!' ranted back my father. 'The bishops wish to burn all satires such as yours and I support them with my whole heart! If it were myself I would burn them into ashes to stop them from poisoning godfearing people's minds!'

My eyes flew to Master Donne's, silently apologizing.

Hoping to clear the air, my aunt suggested we adjourn to the chamber in the tower and leave the servants to their clearing. But first she requested that I fetch another phial of medicine, this time for her ailing husband.

I was but halfway down the great passageway, all around me bustling servants carrying wine and ale, and bearing trays of sweetmeats towards the withdrawing room in the tower when I heard a voice call to me.

It was the Countess of Straven.

'Mistress More, stay one moment.' To my surprise, she took my hand and led me to an alcove behind the statue of Julius Caesar. With our great hooped dresses there was hardly room for us both and she had to list towards me like a ship in a storm to speak privately.

Yet when I heard her words I wished myself a hundred miles away. 'I see it writ upon your face that you are smitten by Master Donne. I have noted how you follow his every word, as if he were your tutor and you the aptest of his pupils. You yearn to defend him when your father goes to the attack like a lioness does her mate. And who can blame you? He is a man of great address, with a fine mind to boot.' She dropped her voice still further so that I had almost to strain to hear. 'Yet, Mistress More, think awhile. Your father plainly hates him and will never consent that you should be his wife. What would you then, his mistress?'

I gasped as if she had slapped me hard across the face. How dare this painted insolent Countess imagine I was victim to the libertine charms of Master Donne?

And then, like to the door opening on a dungeon, out swept the forces of truth, swords drawn, and I had to ask myself if she was right. Did I indeed feel for him as she implied?

She laughed fruitily. 'I am sure he would oblige in making you his mistress, since he has obliged many others.'

And now I turned angrily away, fighting back the itch to run my nails down the white skin of her exposed neck.

'I see I have offended your innocent nature, but consider for one moment.' Her voice, though quietly spoken, was now full of persuasive candour. 'Let us imagine that Master Donne burns for you also, that he is so afire for Mistress Ann More that, for her, he will risk everything, advancement, reputation, all. And since your father continues refusing to sanction your union you decide to wed clandestinely? And what would be the outcome of that? The ruin of your good name and his future. Open your eyes, Ann, and see the truth. Master Donne is not for you. Marry Master Manners and have a dozen blue-eyed offspring.'

In that moment I hated the Countess of Straven with a bright white flame. The words she spoke were no more than the truth, but why did she choose to speak them? Did she want him to herself? Or merely to brook no competition from so green a one as I?

I had no more time to ponder the answer since I saw my father had come and stood behind me, his face, which was commonly the colour of whey, as red as an angry boil, his eyes shining with righteous anger. And I wondered how much of the private conversation between the Countess and I he had overheard.

'Father, I . . .' My thought was to try and stem the tide of his anger.

'Ann, I have heard enough from you since you first came to stay in this house. You ignore your family's wishes for you at the Court. You resist even the Queen's good offices. The company you keep in London is not what I would wish for you. For your own protection you will leave tomorrow for Loseley. Your aunt is happy to excuse you and I will send a message to your grandparents that you arrive on the morrow.'

'Please, Father . . .' I attempted, assaying to put my hand on his arm.

'No, Ann.' He shook it off as if I were a leper begging for alms at Cripplegate. 'You have had more freedom than a young woman should, and this is the result. You will go tomorrow.'

As I turned sadly towards my chamber, I saw a smile upon the lovely face of Isabella Straven.

'Good luck, my lady,' I said so softly she had to lean forward to hear me. 'The field is yours now, I wish you joy of it. Though I hope your husband reads no verses or he may learn of your indiscretion sooner than you hope.'

The Countess raised a haughty brow. 'My husband reads not poetry. His interests lie in animal husbandry.'

Our eyes locked. 'Then mayhap some well-meaning soul should encourage him to.'

My aunt came to my chamber that night as I undid my hair.

'Ann, my child,' she reached out a hand and stroked my face, 'I wish you went not from me thus. Yet your father is right, you must learn to do what others counsel and remember you are a weak and gentle woman.'

'Are *you* a weak and gentle woman, Aunt? Is Her Majesty? Or indeed the Countess of Straven?'

'For shame, Ann, you can hardly compare yourself with our sovereign. And if we are not as weak as others would have us, we learn to hide it, and so also must you.'

'Why must I?'

'It is the way of the world. It may seem heavy to you, yet a common wench who spoke out as you do might have found she wore a scold's bridle.'

I shuddered at the thought of such inhumanity, that a woman who argued could be thus reduced by cruel metal clamping her tongue.

'Ann, Ann,' my aunt was ever a busy, brusque lady, and yet the tenderness in her voice made all my anger melt away like the snows in March, 'while you are at Loseley you must think on your future and learn to accept it humbly.'

'My father would have had me married betimes had not Master Manners's father proved so stubborn in negotiation on the matter of my jointure.'

'Then he will find you another suitor.'

I bowed my head and began to undo my bodies.

When I had finished my aunt lifted them gently over my head.

'Ann,' she hung the bodies on the hook by my press, 'the other suitor your father will find...' Her eyes briefly held mine. 'It will never be Master Donne.'

I dropped my gaze and silently untied my skirts from their farthingale. Was I so obvious a book that all thought they could read me?

'Goodnight, niece. Remember, you are young and beauteous and you have a fine mind.'

'A drawback, it seems, for aught I can tell. Unless I learn to hide it.'

'Ahead lies your whole future, husband, babes, a fine house of your own to manage.'

'I know, Aunt, and I thank you for your care and love of me.'

She opened her arms at that and I ran into them, my tears dampening the brocade of her gown, and felt the nearest thing to a mother's love I was ever like to feel.

'Francis will come with you to Loseley in the morning. He is journeying to our house at Pyrford to hunt the hart with your brother Robert.'

I smiled at the thought of seeing Robert, who shared the same Poynings' looks as I did, unruly auburn hair and eyes the colour of the chestnut. My father had brought Robert up in his own image, yet my brother had a spirit and a zest that even my father had not managed entirely to quash.

I had half packed the few belongings I intended to take when I recalled the fate of Stephen and Hope, whom I had agreed to care for until Sarah recovered. Dared I take them with me to Loseley?

To foist two uninvited orphans upon my grandparents was just the kind of hoydenish and unthought-of behaviour Master Manners had charged me with.

I would do it.

I sent for Wat to get them word. They should be ready next morn by ten of the clock. How I would transport them I would consider before the morning.

London was swathed in thick darkness, like a cloak had been thrown over the city, save for the little pricks of light betokening link boys out with torches or lanterns, when I heard a gentle rap on my chamber door.

It was Wat. His face was wan with tiredness and I regretted that I had added to his burden of long hours, yet there was a spark of adventure in his eyes at his siblings' unexpected treat.

'When I tell them, mistress, they will be in high excitement. Will you be gone long from the city?'

'As long as my father's anger lasts. A week? A month? With my father's tempests it is hard to foretell. Get to your pallet soon, Wat, and good night to you.'

I tried to sleep by reminding myself of the pleasure at seeing all at Loseley again, yet a sense of loss at what was to be left behind kept opening my eyes. Was it my aunt's love I would regret leaving or Master Donne's sharp wit? And yet, I reminded myself, though he might glimpse the mind and soul in me, he was not above wanting to mould them to his own desires. I thought then of the swords crossed when we met in the streets of London, or the words exchanged among the passageways of York House, and knew that I would miss exceeding much the cut and thrust of our new friendship.

Outside the bellman rang his bell and called, 'Two of the clock and a fine clear night!' His every cry reminded me how much I had come to love the city and how quiet it would be on the morrow with no sound but the sighing of the pines, and the lonely bark of the fox in the woods beyond our park.

I know not what time it was before I fell asleep, but it seemed not a moment before Mercy shook me awake with the news that the Lord Keeper, sorry for my untimely departure, had called for his coach to carry me to Surrey and that it stood waiting for me outside, with four fine grey horses.

I dressed with all haste, not waiting to break my fast, and threw a cloak over my travelling dress.

My heart beat as I wondered who would come to bid me farewell but, apart from my aunt and Mercy, only my lady Straven was assembled in the Great Hall.

'Thank my uncle for his great kindness to me, Aunt.' I kissed my aunt on her proffered cheek. 'I shall travel to Loseley in fine style. Goodbye Lady Straven.'

Isabella Straven smiled her catlike smile. 'Mistress More, I trust the country air will calm your restless spirits.'

I curtsied and said nothing lest my words would give too much away.

Wat, with his keen wit, had stowed the children discreetly in the coach and bid them sit still and be quiet.

'Farewell, Mistress More, I hope your noble grandfather will permit me to visit you.' Master Manners had slipped quietly from the hall and was making a low bow, so that his black hat brushed the very cobbles of the street.

'I am sure he will, though we lead an extremely quiet life at Loseley.'

I could not help but glance round me yet there was no sign of Master Donne. So much for his vaunted interest in me. I supposed he had business of State with my uncle in the Chancery or at Whitehall. I wondered what it would be like to be a man, to have a part in politics, to consider important judgements even on war or peace. Greater considerations than saying farewell to one troublesome girl.

Master Manners watched me, his keen blue eyes missing nothing. 'Is there aught you are expecting? Another person of whom you wish to take your leave?'

'No, no,' I lied. 'I had hoped for the arrival of a bolt of cloth for my grandmother, that is all.'

He bowed again. 'I would be honoured to bring it to you.'

Waving one last time to my aunt, I climbed into the coach and my uncle's coachman cracked his whip to begin the jolting journey.

At that, little Hope could contain herself no more and climbed onto the seat to look out of the window.

'God's blood!' I heard my lady Straven exclaim. 'Is that a child in the coach with Mistress More?'

And my aunt replying in fainter accents, 'My lady, I find where my niece is concerned it is wiser not to ask too many questions.'

Chapter 13

AS THE FAMILIAR grey stone of my family home appeared I knew that I had never returned to it with greater confusion. It had always been my haven and yet now I left London with a wrench. I had not visited it since the death of my sister and once again I felt her loss keenly. And this time I had other great concerns of my own. Was I giving my heart to one who would not treasure it but break it? Did becoming a woman always bring such pain?

'Is this the place, mistress?' whispered Hope, who had slept for most of the journey as if the coach were not the jolting, cold and uncomfortable conveyance it seemed to me, but the height of comfort and convenience, which to her perhaps it was.

I asked myself if the welcome I received, bringing two urchin children, would be as warm as I hoped. My grandfather, though not as narrow and settled in his ways as my father, was a busy man who yet valued his peace and quiet. And my grandmother might be as brave as Boadicea in her appearance yet she always did as my grandfather bid her in the end.

Thus it was that I told the children to be silent and sit quietly hidden in the coach while I laid the ground for their arrival.

'Ann! Beloved grandchild!' My grandfather William was the first to spy the coach and come out into the wide, sweeping pathway to greet it. I quickly opened the door, before the coachman had the chance to do it for me, thus revealing its occupants. 'Without your presence, this place hath been quiet as the tomb.' He clasped me fondly. 'Your grandmother does nothing but carp—the food is too salty, the servants slothful, her leg pains her. And your sister Frances! That child is so often on her knees it astounds me the pew has not worn quite through. And her good works! She is up at dawn and on with her pattens even before the household rises, and out to the henhouse to fetch eggs for the poor which your grandmother has ever collected for herself. Lately she has begun to take the servants to task for not showing enough diligence in joining her. Your grandmother is at her wits' end.'

'Poor Frances, she will make some gentleman the ideal wife!'

'Aye. And her servants' life a misery! Let me look at you, child.' He stared intently into my face. 'Grieve you still for your sister?'

I hung my head. 'It is like the soldier's tale of losing a limb—how it hurts the more though it is there no longer. I cannot believe the world goes on, the seasons change, the sun comes up, when she is not here to see them.'

'My own sweet Ann, I miss her also.' He folded me into his embrace. Since I was a maid it had been the safest place in all the world, to be within his arms.

And then he started back with shock, and I turned to find Hope, no longer able to contain her curiosity, had pulled back the curtain so that her small face was peering out. 'Ann! Who is that child sitting in the coach?'

'Ah.' I breathed in deeply. 'That is Hope, Grandfather, and her brother Stephen. I have undertaken, as a work ordained by God, to teach them their letters, that they may have a better start in life and can later find some gainful employment.'

My grandfather's eyes narrowed and his voice lost some of its welcoming note. 'What right have you to do such a thing, Ann? Have we not enough vagrants' children of our own to deal with in the county?'

'They are not vagrants! They have a sister who is for the moment ill. They will return to her when she has recovered her rude health.'

'Surely the parish, not you, should be their guardian in such things.'

'The parish would split them asunder and send them to different masters. There are so many children in London, Grandfather, whom no one cares for or wants even to feed or clothe. They are like vermin, plagues of locusts to be swatted away. These children have spirit and wit. They are as sponges of the sea, or flowers of the desert, eager for every mouthful of knowledge or learning. You, who love learning, would not turn them away, surely?'

'Ann,' his tone was harsher than I had looked for, and his smile had set like the sun, leaving sudden darkness, 'there are ways and means in which the world works. The Mores have been given much—because they earned it. They were loyal and hard-working in their service to the Crown. Yet we come from a certain stock. And that stock is the base of England's greatness. To try and raise the poor beyond their expectations will be like shaking the walls of the temple. Dangerous and foolhardy.' He looked at the children, who peered fearfully out of the coach, hearing voices raised. 'I am not content with this arrangement, and it was wrong in you to foist it upon me.'

I yearned for him to smile, as he often did after he had cause to discipline me, but this day there was none.

Brusque as a tax collector, he turned away. 'You had best find somewhere amongst the servants' chambers for these children until we arrange their return.'

'Ann! Ann! You are come at last!' My sister Frances came tripping out over the great stone threshold, holding up her heavy embroidered skirts to save them from the mud. Like all children we had worn such clothes, those of adults in miniature, since we were babes, but only Frances had relished it. Frances, my sister Mary often pronounced, was born a woman not a child. She looked in astonishment at Stephen and Hope. 'But who are the ragged children in your company?' She shied away as if they stank or were verminous, which, I suppose, they may have been.

'Frances,' I put my arm about her small waist, 'you are a God-fearing girl, are you not?'

'I would hope if my Saviour asked me to do his bidding I would not shirk it.'

'Excellent. I believe Almighty God has bidden us to help these children come closer unto Him through knowledge.'

Frances looked at them with sudden zeal, as if a vision had bidden her to ease their path to godliness. 'Then I will do my duty to help them.'

The great oaken front door was thrown open again for the arrival of my grandmother, with Prudence in her wake. My sister Frances, sensing she had been the unwilling victim of one of my unsuitable devices, was determined to have the last word. 'Come, Grandmother,' she smiled with saintly sweetness, 'here is Ann come back from London—and still no sign of a husband!'

My grandmother, on sight of the two children, was near as angry as my grandfather. 'Ann, Ann, we have enough mouths to feed in this great house already. Had you not thought that your goodness and generosity might bring hard work and inconvenience to others?'

I felt a little shame at this for there was truth in it.

'You are right.' I held out my hand to Hope, who clung to it desperately. 'Perhaps my grandfather is right that they must return to London and their sister.'

My grandmother clapped her hands. 'For now, at least we can feed and clothe them. Prudence take these brats off to the kitchens, and before he says there is naught for them, remind the clerk there remains both beef and venison in the pantry and a honey cake I had put aside to take to Goody Frobisher. Since she knows naught of it she is not like to miss the treat.'

Prudence looked as if she would protest but Hope, with an instinct born of hunger and self-preservation, held her hand out and it would have been a soul of iron that could have resisted taking it.

That night I shared my bed again with Frances, though I would have given all my earthly hopes and goods to share it once more with my sweet Bett.

Outside our window the silence was so deep it was as if a sudden fall of snow had surrounded us. I saw that, without remarking it, I had become accustomed to the nightly noises of a great city, and found I missed the sound of bells and raucous laughter as men tumbled out of the alehouse, the bellman calling the hour, the rumble of barrels on cobble, the clank of shop signs in the wind from the river and, yes, Master Donne's cry of the costermonger. In the darkness I grinned at that.

'What makes you smile so slyly?' asked my sister who, it seemed, had amongst her other powers, that of seeing through night. 'Mary says your Master Manners has not yet persuaded his father to offer the settlement for you that Father is asking.'

'Frances,' I corrected piously, 'talk not so crudely as if I were some lump of beef to be haggled over in the Shambles marketplace.'

My sister turned and pulled up the covers.

'We are all lumps of beef, sister, yet some of us are pure bred and worth the more. I hope my price is not so high as yours, that I moulder on the slab as you are doing.'

In the morning I broke my fast with my sister and grandmother, nursing a heavy heart. I knew Wat could not care for his brother and sister and without my help their future would be uncertain indeed. I found an unlikely ally in Frances, who announced that until they returned to London they could help with the hens. My grandmother might be too stubborn to admit it, she whispered, but keeping the management of the hens solely to herself was taking its toll.

As luck would have it, my grandfather was too busy with the business of the County to notice. He had passed many of his duties on to my father, such as muster commissioner in charge of raising reluctant men for the Irish war, yet he did what he could while my father sat in London at the Parliament.

'None wishes to go to Ireland,' he grumbled. 'There is no chance of treasure or glory as in the Spanish ventures, only cold and hunger and the fear of death in a land of barbarous Papists.'

I wrapped up well, for though it was warm there had been a night-frost, and went to see how Hope fared with the hens. Being a Londoner born and bred, she might scream at the mere sight of them.

Yet there was a stillness about the child, born perhaps of lurking under tables and in shadows, never wishing to attract attention, that the hens took to. I prayed that she dropped no eggs, nor failed to lock up the henhouse so the fox came in and ravished all.

'These hens are my friends also,' I confided, holding out some corn for the silly straggle-legged bantam who was my grandmother's best layer. 'They have helped to pay for my grand London gowns.'

'Come, Ann,' my grandmother corrected me sternly. 'If the child stays, she works. And where, may I ask in God's name, is the boy got to?'

Stephen had been set to cleaning pewter with horse-tails from the garden by the clerk of the kitchen which he did silently and with enough diligence to satisfy the clerk, without so much that he would cause resentment to the scullion, who might fear his job being threatened by too obvious an industry. Stephen, I noted, had the same watchful look about him as the girl. I saw how he jumped when the usher of the ewery clanked down a great metal urn onto the stone of the kitchen floor.

Both children, it seemed, had a talent for survival, blending quietly in. Wat had been luckier, for Master Donne seemed to value his humour and amusing tongue.

No firm decision as to the children's staying seemed to be made, yet the horses were sent back to London and the two allocated a place for taking their meals at the kitchen and scullery table next to Sampson Ashley, the coachman's man, John Haite, groom of the stranger's horse, Marfidy Snipt, deputy cook, and Soloman the bird catcher.

I kept my peace and helped in the house and still room. The following week my grandmother sent me off to the attic to hunt out some lost receipt for bisket bread, and there, under dust and spider's webs, I came upon the hornbooks with which our grandfather had instructed us in our letters when we were little children.

These were just as I remembered them, with the lessons written on parchment tacked onto wooden paddles, an illustrated alphabet, a list of vowels and consonants, together with the first ten numbers and a copy of the Lord's Prayer, which I had learned by rote as had every child in dame or petty school.

Each paddle, just as I recalled it, was fitted with a leather thong that we might tie it to our belts and not face caning for its loss.

My sister Frances, with her pious nature, had revelled in being taught her alphabet through scenes from Scripture with 'A for Adam's fall, B for Boaz, C for Christ crucified, D for the Deluge . . . J for Job who feels the rod, yet blesses God.' The rest of us preferred Apple, Ball and Cat.

I carried them down together with the receipt and showed them to my grandmother, who laughed at their reappearance. She even made no objection when I asked to give the children some instruction.

So I filled my days at Loseley with playing teacher, being careful that they also did their tasks in the kitchen and the henhouse.

One morning, when the sun shone and the birds sang so loud we could no longer stay indoors, we walked from Loseley's great park to the meadows beyond.

Stephen found a small brook and, as boys do, began to dam the stream. Hope chattered happily alone, whispering to imaginary friends and I, without knowing it, fell asleep in the long grass under a tree.

And there I had the strangest dream.

I was lying in the great childhood bed I shared with Bett, the curtains pulled around us, as we often drew them, creating our own private universe. Outside the sun shone, and on the window sill a lazy bee drummed restlessly. And yet, all was not well. Some great threat I understood not had come down upon me, filling me with black terror so that I felt myself tumbling down and down towards eternal darkness. Yet at the very moment of darkest fear a hand reached out and pulled me back towards the light and of a sudden I knew the greatest peace and contentment I have ever known, as a soul might feel on the Day of Judgement as it wings its way to certain paradise. I turned to Bett to find that it was not she who lay beside me but a face I could not see.

And then I awoke to find there was indeed a figure standing over me, dressed in fine London clothes, the face hidden by the shining of the sun, and it was so like to my dream that I gasped.

'Mistress More, I came upon you in a private moment, forgive me.'

Still quaking I scrambled to my feet.

'Master Donne,' I shook my head as if I knew not whether I waked or slept, 'am I dreaming still or are you standing here in Loseley?'

'I am indeed.'

'I thought you were some blessed being. A good angel who had bargained for my black soul.'

He laughed at my words. 'I have rarely been called that.' Yet he saw I trembled still and his voice became serious. 'Your soul is not black I am sure.'

'No.' I shook my head again, suddenly shy at speaking of things so strange and intimate. 'I had not thought so but the dream seemed real enough. And frightening.'

'Dreams are the release of the unquiet spirit. I have seen it amongst men in war. Yet is yours so unquiet?'

I glanced at him, wondering. Young girls of my estate did not talk of things so deep, but of accomplishments and household skills. To betray a troubled soul such as I had would be held against me by most. And yet I would hazard that Master Donne would not judge me harshly. He too was an outsider, as I often felt myself—though not by virtue of my upbringing and family, but because I seemed always to be at odds with others' expectations.

'My sister's death weighs upon me still. I tried to help her and she died withal.' I had spoken of this to none before. 'The midwife laid the blame at my door.'

'You did your best while others dared not. It is in your nature. I have seen it.' He smiled gently, remembering Master Freeman. 'Even when it may be wiser sometimes to temper it.'

I hung my head. 'I wish it were not.'

'No, Mistress More.' There was sudden passion in his voice. 'Your soul shines out of you, let none destroy it! Think not of this midwife. Midwives fear to be blamed themselves at such times. Your sister had the sacrament at the end?'

I nodded.

'Life on this earth is uncertain. We can none of us ask for more.'

I closed my eyes and silently said, 'Amen', feeling lighter in my spirit than I ever had since that dark day. When I opened them Master Donne was watching me. 'Yet what brings you here so unexpectedly?' I asked.

'Some business of your aunt's at nearby Pyrford. Her tenants dispute a boundary and your aunt would have it settled speedily.'

He saw the children playing in the stream. 'Wat's siblings? They have a look of him.'

I nodded. 'I have undertaken to teach them their letters.'

'You are generous indeed.'

I decided to confess the truth. 'Master Donne, I needed some occupation.'

He smiled at me, much amused at my candour. 'Yet I thought the call of the countryside had you in its thrall? Have you not had your cuckoo to charm you?'

'Spoken like a true city dweller. Tis too late in the year for the cuckoo, she has long laid her eggs in the nests of other birds, where they have hatched and, truth to tell, may have devoured the chicks of any rivals for their sustenance.'

He laughed at that. 'At least in London we do not devour each other's offspring.'

'You will not persuade country people of that. The fact is, I have been given an education and yet a lady of Loseley has not much call to use it.'

'Have you not access to your grandfather's library?'

'Indeed. Yet I have perused it.'

'Not all, surely?'

I shrugged. 'The Hebrew defeats me, it is true, and the writings of the schoolmen wear me out with their logic. I cannot share the concerns of Seneca . . .'

Master Donne was shaking his head. 'I am sure he would be much disappointed. If you have exhausted your grandfather's library, I could recommend some other works, of literature perhaps?'

'Not *The Faerie Queene*!'

'I can see your taste runs not to the lyrical, then?'

'The earthier charms of Chaucer hold more appeal for me. Save for the tale of Patient Griselda. Tell me, Master Donne, would any man wish for a wife such as she, who allows her lord to mistreat her at every turn, even to the point of turning her from their home and taking away her sweet babes, and still she gives him her full obedience?'

'You do not find her the pattern for every good Christian lady?' His face was serious and yet, underneath, I suspected a hidden smile.

'Master Donne, I do not. And neither, I surmise, do you, having witnessed the pattern of Christian ladies I have seen in your company.'

He laughed at that, yet made no attempt to deny it and I wondered, with a bitter twist of my heart, how many women he had enjoyed to gain so notorious a reputation.

'Yet, tell me, how fare all at York House? I yearn for news.'

His face took on a sterner complexion. 'All the talk now is of war. The Earl of Essex must go to Ireland and quell the rebels there, and young Sir Thomas, the Lord Keeper's son, is all afire to go with him.'

I thought of his wife and three sweet daughters and hoped God would protect him. A sudden fear took hold and I asked, perhaps too urgently, 'And what of yourself, will you be accompanying him?'

His eyes held mine, searching, as if asking himself how much I might care about his safety, and why.

I looked away, studying the long-haired brown cattle in a distant meadow as if they could tell me whether Master Donne, whom—I saw now—I both desired and admired would value my love like a precious goblet wrought of delicate glass or dash it carelessly to the ground.

He answered at last. 'I saw enough of war and death in Spain, of soldiers ablaze or drowning in their own ships. My friend Henry Wotton goes as my lord of Essex's secretary so I shall hear enough of its progress. And your uncle has need of me in Chancery. Will you soon be returning, or has your father other plans?'

I glanced at him, overwhelmed with unaccustomed modesty, suspecting that the plans he referred to were those concerning Master Manners and my father's desire for a betrothal.

To cover my confusion I turned away, shaking out the grass from my skirts and calling to Stephen and Hope. 'I neglect my duties. I am sure my grandparents would wish to offer you some refreshment.'

At that his features clouded over as when rain chases away sunshine. 'Thank you, no. I must continue my journey. I was a fair way to my destination when I saw the Loseley milestone and thought to pay you my respects.'

He turned and left us then, standing in a pool of sunlight. And the thought occurred to me, with a secret smile of triumph, that the road to Pyrford stops some miles before Loseley.

We watched until he found his horse and climbed into the saddle. As he rode off I thought how much I had missed the wit and spirit of our exchanges, and had come to look forward to them without even knowing it.

My grandmother stood at the great front door, arms folded like a goodwife, and waited for our return.

'Did I see a gentleman riding towards the turnpike, Ann? Who was it who creeps about our parkland unannounced?'

'No one of importance, Grandmother.' Some instinct bade me take little Hope firmly by the hand in case she spoke the truth. 'Naught but a traveller who had lost his way and sought the road to Pyrford.'

'Pyrford! Then he is plentifully adrift. Pyrford is a good few miles north of here.'

I smiled again. 'Indeed it is, Grandmother, I cannot think how the traveller made such an unfortunate mistake.'

OUR LESSONS WENT apace.

Stephen showed an unlooked-for talent at his letters, and Hope learned quickly to recite the Lord's Prayer. Yet it had to be said that ever since Master Donne's departure, our days here—only a score of miles, yet several planets away from the noisy draw of London—hung heavier than before.

So it was with extreme delight that I greeted the sudden arrival of my sister Mary as she rode up, magnificent in her red frogged robe, feathered hat, and smart new leather gloves in softest burgundy kid. I wondered, with my new knowledge of her husband's finances, just how the gloves had been paid for and hoped they did not signal that Nick's new-found prudence was at an end.

'Mary!' I called, my heart leaping at the sight of my sister, her slender body so quick and full of joy for life. Mary, it often seemed to me, was like the sleek panther I had once seen down at the docks in London, imported from the distant Indies, ever tugging at her lead to be allowed off into some wild and dangerous adventure. And I could not but love her for it.

We embraced and walked through the Great Hall, nodding to the servants, who smiled at the sight of bold Mary, then once out of their sight we ran up the broad staircase as if we were children once again.

'How fare Nick and your babes?'

'All well. Though Nick is as grumpy as a bear at our new economies, and worse at giving up his cocking and bowling, yet his loss is my lads' gain, since now it pleases him to play at croquet with them, and toss quoits. And instead of Nick spending his nights in the tavern or playhouse he spends them playing at Glecko with his lady wife!'

Would that this vision of domestic bliss continued.

'Since Master Freeman kindly absolved him of his debts, my lord and master has been trying his best to please me.'

A secret smile came upon her face at the memory of her husband's efforts. 'Indeed,' my sister looked suddenly coy, 'since we must stay at home instead of being ever abroad we have found new diversions to entertain us.' She tapped her stomach.

'Mary! Are you with child again? I thought you wished not to be a brood mare for the Throckmortons?'

She laughed, acknowledging my teasing tone. 'Aye, but this time there was pleasure in the getting of it.'

'Good, then there will be no distractions from other quarters.' She looked modestly away as if she knew not what my words implied.

'And this time I long for a daughter.' She looked at me narrowly. 'And you, Ann, do you not also look to such pleasures? What of your Master Manners? If he wanted you truly could he not have talked his father into compromise by now?'

'His father is a close old man, from all I hear, who ever lives in fear of being cheated.'

'And our father is not one to open his palm either. He visits, by the way, in two days hence and wanted me to tell you. He seemed big with news so perhaps the mean old man has capitulated after all.'

I stared out of the window at this unwelcome intimation.

'And your Master Donne has been kicking up a dust. Putting salt on the tails of all the clerks at Chancery, demanding receipts and accounts for every last transaction. I dined at York House three nights since and heard our uncle praise him for his good works. "Master Donne,"' she put on a deep, gruff voice so like unto our uncle's that I laughed out loud, '"work thus hard, and behave so honourably, and you will rise far in my service."'

'I am glad for his sake.'

'Yet Nick says he has also made himself some enemies in the doing of it. Though that boy of his watches out for him like Cerberus.'

I felt grateful for that. 'How is Wat?'

'The boy goes everywhere with him. His master has taken to dressing him in clothes like unto his own, so that they are as hidden dolls that open unto a smaller version of the same! It is much laughed about, though not unkindly, and several masters have started to do the same!'

I laughed at this, surprised Master Donne would want to start such a fashion. 'And what of Wat's education?'

'He has caused a stir there too. For I hear that if Wat stays with him three years he has promised to send him to the grammar school at Highgate.'

'That is kind indeed.' I was truly moved at how different Wat's life would be after so much learning. And at Master Donne's generosity in giving it to him.

'There are those who say it sets a bad example to other servants, that they might expect the same.'

'And a good example to their masters!' I replied with spirit.

'Wat bade me give you a message. That his sister Sarah is recovered from her sweats.'

I thanked God for it.

Mary looked at me silently, her head cocked to one side, considering.

'What? What is it, sister? Spit it out!'

'I wondered if I should betray the other piece of scandalous London gossip. Shall I?'

I nodded.

'That my lady Straven has been so much abroad with your Master Donne that her husband hath finally got wind of it and comes to London to face her.'

Her words burned into me, as corrosive as the fluids that had ravaged Wat's hands, idle gossip though they might be. Had Master Donne a cruel or deluded nature that he could paddle in my palm and visit me at Loseley while climbing into the Countess of Straven's bed the while?

That night, before I went upstairs to my sleep, I picked up Hope and sat with her upon my knee, watching the darkening sky and thinking of the babe in my sister's belly. And I found myself wishing with such strong force that I would have a babe of my own to love and cherish, that a tear came to my eyes and fell upon her fair head. If I but agreed, and his father relented a little, I would be married to Richard Manners and live in Leicestershire, with a brood of my own before long.

Why then, did I still feel so reluctant to accept him?

'Weep not, Mistress Ann,' came Hope's soft reply. 'God will give you what you pray for, for you are a good kind lady.'

At that I kissed her head and said, 'Amen to that.'

If only I could be sure what it was I did pray for.

When, after two days, I heard a great commotion of horses and dogs barking, servants running as if the Queen herself were approaching in her coach of state, I knew my father had arrived.

For a gentleman that likes to save his money, my father also loves to stand on ceremony. Chiefly he arrives at this by borrowing his coaches and horses and making many demands on other people's servants. In this case, those of my grandfather.

I could hear him shouting orders to John Haite, groom of the stranger's horse, and Henry, my grandfather's steward, and even Moses Petley, the under farrier, to shoe one of his horses instantly, as if Loseley were already his own, and yet my grandfather still very much alive.

When my father had taken off his dusty cloak, and made good use of my grandfather's ewery to wash his hands and face, and ordered beef and ale, he besought my grandmother to call us all to the withdrawing chamber.

As I walked slowly down the staircase I looked into my heart. What would I say if his announcement was that Master Manners's father had relented at last and he and I were indeed to be wed?

My father was in great good humour, clapping each on the back, and proffering advice to all and sundry, whether they wanted it or no.

'Mother, be seated there,' he fussed, while my grandmother told him roundly that she had not suffered the pangs of childbed to have him tell her where she might rest her bones in her own home.

Mary caught my eye. She was no longer in my father's power and, with an easy-going husband, could make choices of her own. How I envied that freedom in her, even though she had not always used it wisely.

At last we were all in position, with sufficient victuals to satisfy even my father's taste. 'I have called all here to make an announcement.' He glanced quickly at myself, yet I looked modestly down. 'I bring the happy news of a betrothal.'

At that my heart pounded in my chest like galloping hoofbeats, and the blood in my veins seemed to course with the force of a river in spate.

'Between my daughter . . .' He stopped until all eyes were fixed upon me, waiting for the announcement of my betrothal. 'Frances . . .'

There was a gasp throughout the chamber.

'And one Sir John Oglander of Nunwell in the Isle of Wight, a good and honourable gentleman.'

'Then I will be My Lady!' Frances danced around the chamber, her saintliness seeming to desert her in her hour of triumph. 'And I will be betrothed before my sister Ann!'

'Yet that is not the custom,' pointed out my grandfather, his eyes seeking mine in tender reassurance, 'while your elder sister remains unspoken for.'

'Tosh to custom,' insisted my father testily. 'I have had enough of the Manners and their shilly-shallying.' He held up his goblet of ale. 'To the future Lady Oglander of Nunwell.'

We raised our glasses to join in the toast.

Mary's gaze sought mine, hers all soft with sympathy. She did not need to say the words out loud that all were thinking—that my twelve-year-old sister was now officially betrothed before I was.

To me, the relief was great enough to make my toasting genuine.

Yet my joy for Frances soon wore thin.

Frances unbetrothed was trial enough, but Frances betrothed would have tried the patience of Job. She begged from the cook and clerk of the kitchen receipts for all their favourite dishes, dogged my grand-mother's footsteps in the still room to learn medicinal remedies, and drove Prudence to distraction by eternal questions concerning the effective laundering of linens. She even wrote to our sister Margaret to enquire on the management of nursemaids. Pushed to her limit, my grandmother finally cried, 'Enough, Frances! You are but twelve years old. You will not marry this unlucky gentleman for four more years, so now go back to sewing your samplers!'

Loseley, a little dull before Frances' great announcement, became such a place of purgatory that after several days I was forced to apply to my father and ask if I might return once more to York House. 'Now that young Sir Thomas has gone to war in Ireland, I could be of great assistance to his wife with their three young daughters,' I importuned him, remembering that Master Donne had told me of his departure. 'And to my aunt, your sister, also.'

My father, all attired to go out hunting the hart with my brother Robert, looked at me narrowly. 'No, Ann, you will not go back to York

House. And how knew you of Sir Thomas's departure? He went but three days ago and in some secrecy.'

Mary's eyes were on me also, as my cheeks fired guiltily and I fiddled with my girdle trying to find an answer that would satisfy his blade-sharp mind. A Herculean task since, though we had comings and goings of tradesmen and petitioners here, and guests who turned up unbidden if the inns were full, none who had such information had passed through Loseley in the last few days.

'Well?' I could see why my father was effective in the countless committees he sat on in the house of Parliament, dangling his fish on the hook till it gasped for breath.

Mary, seeing my difficulty, came at last to my rescue. 'I told her, Father. Nick had it from his brother-in-law Sir Walter, who has estates in Ireland. Indeed why could not Ann come and stay with us? Now that I am with child I would welcome her presence to soothe my brow and brew that tisane of herbs she has learned to make from our grandmother. She could help me with your two lively grandsons.'

'Have you not nursemaids to do such things for you?'

'None who can read stories and tell tales like Ann. They would love nothing more than a visit from their aunt. She could ride with me when I return to town and stay a day with Margaret on the way, since Margaret is with child also.'

'And I provide the horse, I venture?'

'I am sure my grandfather could spare a horse for a day.'

Finally it was agreed, to my great delight, that I might return with Mary. Frances was in a pet that she should lose the person she was triumphing over, but forgave me at last when, with the greatest strength of will I could muster, I gave her my hearty congratulations on her betrothal.

'Worry not, Ann,' was the reply which made me wish to hit her with the horsehair brush we used to beat the laundry, 'it will be your turn soon.'

As I packed up the clothes in my chamber, Mary came to help. She held up my green necklet in the glass, admiring herself, and how it matched her eyes, when an unwelcome thought occurred to her.

'If I told you not about young Sir Thomas going to Ireland, how did you know?'

I gathered my chemises from the coffer and folded them briskly. 'Master Donne informed me.'

'Master Donne! And when saw you Master Donne?'

'He paid me a visit.' I moved her from her perch to find my best wool stockings. 'Look not so. He was on his way to Pyrford on some business of our aunt's at her estate there and broke his journey here.'

'If he travels to Pyrford by way of Loseley, I would not like to be his fellow traveller. And did my grandparents welcome him here?'

'He had not the time for such niceties. His business at Pyrford was pressing.'

'And so you entertained him alone?'

'I entertained him not at all. We exchanged words in the meadow, that is all.'

'Ann, Ann,' her voice was harsher now, 'this is not some lyric verse where nymphs and shepherds laze in bosky groves. This is a dangerous game you play. What does Master Donne here, wooing you, and in secret, when I have seen him in the company of my lady Straven and no doubt others besides?'

Anger burned through me at that, hot and searing, yet I would not show it to my sister. 'I wonder how he finds the time, since you say he works for my uncle from dawn to midnight.'

'Ann, jest not. If it were known, your good name would be lost entirely.'

'And my plan to visit a bawdy house to deal with your Master Freeman,' I asked, much angered at her hypocrisy, 'was that not a risk to my good name also?'

Mary's face paled as if her morning sickness had come upon her. 'God's blood, Ann, do I not know it? It was wicked in me to enmesh you in our difficulties, for which I am heartily sorry.'

'Then say no more about this. I came to no harm in the end.'

'Unless Master Donne has spread the rumour of your interview. We will find out soon enough when we go home to London. Our house is far enough from my uncle and aunt's at least. Yet, Ann,' a thought struck her which should have been mine, 'what about the brats? We cannot take them with us; my husband's generosity, though wide enough, would not stretch so far.'

Guilt overtook me that I could so easily forget about these souls whom I had transported here and I went straight away to seek them out and see what would be best for all. Hope was in the scullery with Prudence, to whom she seemed attached by an invisible string, following the maid round in all her tasks. Yet Hope, with her sunny smile so like her brother's, had befriended all in the house. Stephen was a different matter. Like a pilgrim on a Lenten fast, he seemed afflicted with a permanent hunger, and greatly annoyed the clerk of the kitchen by filching sippets left soaking for a marrow pudding.

'Have you seen the boy Stephen?' I asked the clerk.

'Your grandfather gave him a job, mistress. Sorting out his books in his library.'

I went to look for Stephen and indeed found him in the library dusting books while my grandfather sat at the table working at his papers.

All seemed to be progressing well enough, yet at my sudden entrance Stephen took fright and dropped one of my grandfather's precious tomes.

'God's nails, boy, take care!' my grandfather shouted. 'Ann, why you would wish these clumsy unlettered children upon us, I know not!'

Stephen who had seemed to be enjoying his task, looked stricken and stood with his hands hanging by his sides, the book face down upon the floor untouched.

I picked the volume up and led him to a place next to the great fire where I sat him down out of harm's way. There was a piece of old parchment on the floor and I picked him out a small piece of half-burned charcoal and handed it to him. 'Draw a picture while I talk to my grandfather and we will venture abroad in the park after.'

I forgot about the boy and went back to discuss my plans for London with my grandfather, who sat in his favourite chair, the skull from the portrait by Lucas de Heere sitting on his desk as if it were a paperweight.

When, five minutes later, I made to go I saw that Stephen had used his time to sketch my grandfather.

I took the parchment from him, and studied it. Rough and untutored though it was, it had captured something of my grandfather in its strokes, the melding of stern and soft, the forked white beard and most of all the clear alertness of the eyes that seemed to belong to a much younger man.

'Grandfather,' I said softly, not wishing to disturb his writing again, 'Mary says she cannot give board to the children . . .' I breathed in deeply before asking him this favour.

'You wish to leave them here like parcels to be passed around in a game?'

'Well, I . . .' God gave me inspiration.

'See, Grandfather,' I held out the rough sketch to him, 'mark the likeness Stephen has drawn of you. He has caught your soul and put it down on the page.'

'Now, Ann, utter not blasphemy in my house.'

'No blasphemy, it is the truth.' I turned to the scared-looking boy. 'Would you sell it to me, Stephen? To take to London as a reminder of my grandfather?'

Before he had the chance to answer we were both startled by the guffaw of laughter from the sketch's subject.

'He has caught me indeed.' He held the sketch up against the picture on the wall. 'Take it not with you, Ann, we will put it next to my portrait by Master de Heere.'

I watched, astounded, as my grandfather tucked the parchment in behind his likeness captured by one of the greatest Court painters of the day. Though indeed, Stephen's was merely a rough childish sketch next to the work of a great master. My grandfather surveyed them both and began to laugh again. 'That fellow made me hold the pose for hours on end and this child studied me for but a moment. Stephen, I like your drawing the better of the two!' He turned to me. 'You may leave the children here, at least for the moment.'

Next day we journeyed back to London, breaking our travels at my sister Margaret's house at Peckham, a quiet hamlet in the parish of Camberwell, a few miles from the Queen's palace at Greenwich.

My sister Margaret never ceased to sing the praises of her cherished Peckham, its deep groves, its green lanes and flowery meadows—and all but five miles from the stews of London! To most, Peckham was known just as the last stopping place for Kentish drovers bringing their beasts into market, and the site of the famous fair, declared by King John after killing a stag on its southern slopes. My brother-in-law

Thomas also cited the fame of its tavern, the Rosemary Bush, where the landlord rang a bell whenever a new cask of ale was tapped, that all the good people in the vicinity might come and sup it.

Margaret's house, which Thomas's parents had built, was of good solid brick. It was not large, as Mary ever liked to point out, but it stood, square and firm, between the twin manors of Camberwell Friern and Camberwell Buckingham.

Margaret's husband liked his English oak, and each room throughout all the house, save the dining hall, was wainscoted, and decorated with painted coats of arms. Mary whispered that Thomas put himself forward with these, since his family was but one remove from the yeomanry, yet I listened not. The dining hall itself boasted a fine long table made of polished ship's timbers, with open cupboard shelves loaded with pewter platters, yet the eye was drawn at once to the end wall, the whole of which was adorned with a great tapestry illustrating Susannah and the Elders.

We sat patiently in the hall waiting for Margaret's children to be brought down by their nurse, a scheme Mary thought scandalous, since her own brood stayed firmly by her side, when Margaret and Thomas were called momentarily away. Of a sudden Mary pointed to the wall and began to giggle. 'How like is one of those lustful elders to our good brother-in-law Thomas?'

I glanced at the tapestry and started to laugh also, for Mary was right. One of the ancients illustrated there—indeed the one with particularly bulged eyes and lecherous expression, did exactly resemble Margaret's husband.

'Mayhap he quarrelled with the embroiderers over payment and this was their way of settling the score!' suggested Mary, still smiling when Margaret and her husband came back into the hall.

'What laugh you at, sisters?' demanded Margaret and, when she got no answer, shrugged and asked us were not her babes the most beautiful, the most talented, the sweetest babes in all of Christendom?

After that Thomas went about his business leaving my two sisters to talk of being with child, Mary saying she hoped the time would fly and she would not grow as big as a cow on our grandfather's farm. Margaret, that happy lady, vowed she would stay with child forever if she could, and made me touch the hardness of her stomach.

'Feel! Is it not like to the swelling of a hazelnut in autumn?'

'Margaret says she loves to be with child,' Mary teased, 'yet tells us not the truth of why that is.'

'And what is the truth, pray?' Margaret asked with a peevish shrug.

'That when you are breeding your husband keeps to his chamber and troubles you not for three-quarters of a year and, if you are lucky, another quarter until you are churched afterwards!'

'Yet he does not,' Margaret simpered, taking us by surprise. 'Indeed he comes to my chamber almost up until the day of the birthing.'

I have rarely seen my worldly sister Mary so full of shock.

At that we all fell to laughing and Mary, to Margaret's raised eyebrows, asked if it were not too early to call for some ale.

After two merry days we journeyed onwards again to Mary's house in Mile End, but a few miles away as the crow flies, yet as different from Peckham as fine manchet bread is to a coarse country loaf.

Mile End is on the north bank of the river. Although it is sited beyond the walls of the city of London, yet it is near enough to share the bustle and sense the beating of that great city's ceaseless heart.

All along the north of the Thames we pass docks and shipyards and when I breathe deeply I can smell the scent of spice newly brought from the East Indies and stored in riverside warehouses.

And once we arrive, I see the two houses are as different as two houses could be. Where Margaret's rule demanded peace and order, Mary's was a realm of colour and of chaos.

Mary's husband being brother-in-law to Sir Walter Ralegh, Mary had benefited from a small part of that gentleman's exotic spoils. Their wedding gift had been bales of vermilion and cerise silks, divers jewelled candlesticks, and cushions embroidered with elephants and peacocks. Everywhere there were flowers, not growing but dried, in shades of blue or purple, and the scent! In every room of the house Mary had placed a bowl of petals and spices like unto the smell of a pomander, which regularly she dosed with oil. And, most strange and wondrous of all, were her Turkey carpets, woven in hues of brick red and cobalt blue. Where others would hang these precious items on the wall or lay them over a table for some great occasion, Mary placed them on the floor where all could walk on them!

The life here also was like none other I had known. Mary rose late and so did all her servants. I wondered if the freshest goods had been already bought by the time her cook sauntered down to the market. And Mary's guests! There seemed a stream of them longer than the river Thames. From noon till nightfall the bell would ring and some arrived without ringing, appearing like a gilded mist, all dressed as grandly as if for Court, yet draped themselves about her furniture calling for spiced wine and pomegranates.

And in the midst her children played, while their nursemaids snored or, for aught I knew, drank the spiced wine along with the guests.

And then, just as they had come, they would go again, all in a crowd, to the playhouse, or the bear baiting, or to bowl skittles. Once they even took themselves to hear a sermon, another fashionable pursuit, and smiled and whispered all through it. And if ever Mary, being with child, was too tired, they would still beg Nick to come with them, so that he cast sorrowful eyes at his wife until she, weak with him though she could be as strong as steel with others, said, 'Go, go!'

And thus the weeks passed, pleasurable at first, yet I soon bored of all this indolence and worried—though Mary did not—about who would pay for it.

Yet I was not to be bored for long for Mary announced, her eyes gleaming with sudden delight, that we were bidden by my cousin Francis to a costumed feast, and that the feast was to take place at York House.

I turned away, knowing that at my aunt and uncle's house I would encounter Master Donne, and, remembering the Countess of Straven's accusation, felt naught but confusion at how I would feel when I did.

Chapter 14

MY SISTER MARY roused herself from her indolence and spent the next days laughing and chattering like a parakeet, as she planned her costume for the feast. Always daring, she chose Venus, goddess of love. I trusted this boded not badly for Nick, Venus being not famed for her fidelity. Margaret, who had come to stay since Peckham was judged too far to return to after the festivity, was ever practical and wished not to spend kind Thomas's money on wasteful fripperies. She was to make her costume with her own needle. No doubt had Frances been amongst us she would have opted for the garb of a long-dead saint, and forged her own manacles.

'What character are you intending, sister?' Margaret asked me as she sewed leaves onto a sash of gold silk.

I shook my head. I had had an idea yet it meant borrowing the attire from another and I wished to make sure she would lend it to me.

Next day I sent a message for Wat, who had told me that his sister Sarah was blessedly recovered from the sweats, and asked if she might visit me, which she did that very day.

'Mistress More!' Sarah's eyes shone with gratitude at what she saw as my kindness to her brother and sister. I felt ashamed at that since, to tell the truth, my generosity to the younger two had been grudging at first, and I had wished not to undertake their care.

'And are you truly recovered yourself?' I asked.

'I am.'

She readily agreed to my suggestion and indeed laughed and promised to lend me all that I needed.

The day of the feast I was ready before my sisters and waited for them outside which they found passing strange until at last they saw the reason. I was dressed in a milkmaid's costume, borrowed from Sarah, with a bonnet tied all up with ribbon, and across my shoulders a yoke and all draped in summer greenery, and two pails. I even had a little churn of milk adorned with flowers to fill my buckets when we reached our destination.

'How lovely you look, Ann!' Margaret shook her head. 'You even have roses in your cheeks like a true country maiden.'

The roses came from the discreet use of madder root but I accepted the compliment.

We travelled to York House by water, passing the busy docks on the north bank and the green orchards of Bermondsey House on the south side, once an abbey, now the home, Mary said, of the Earl of Sussex.

We were greeted by my genial cousin, dressed as Pan in beard and goat legs and holding a reed pipe, as we disembarked and climbed the York House stairs. Francis had loved feasts ever since we were children together.

'Cousins, ho! What three beauties! Mary, you would dim the stars in the sky with your loveliness, and dressed as Venus! No man will be safe from your darts today!' He turned to Margaret, ignoring the obvious swell of her increasing stomach. 'And what vision of nature's bounties you offer, cousin Margaret.' Finally his laughing eyes alighted upon me. 'A milkmaid! The perfect costume to display your sweet country innocence! A quality not much encountered in these naughty times.'

'And you, Francis,' Mary teased. 'I had not known you had such hairy legs!'

He threw back his head and laughed. 'I smell like a goat also. John Egerton has ejected the contents of his dinner upon me after too much wine!'

We sisters exchanged glances at that. It was going to be a lively occasion, it seemed.

'There is to be a masque, I hear,' Mary announced, looking at me. 'The Countess of Straven plans to surprise us all.'

'Indeed,' I replied, refusing to catch Mary's eye. 'Let us hope it is not Salome with the seven veils. Francis, take my sisters in. I must fill my pails from this churn first.'

'Real milk? I knew not you had this taste for the theatrical, Ann. Perhaps you will be the one who surprises us.'

While the others entered, I filled my pails, my hands shaking with sudden weakness at how Master Donne would greet me.

At last, my pails filled, I raised my chin and followed the guests into the Great Hall, passing my uncle dressed as Julius Caesar in conversation with my father, in the costume of King Cnut. How like my father to think himself a man wishing to hold back the tides of time!

Once inside I dipped a cup into my milk and called out, 'Lords and ladies, try my milk! Fresh from the cow this very morn!'

My cry was met with silence followed by shouts of humorous appreciation as the guests milled forward to sample my wares.

But none amongst them was Master Donne.

And then I spied him.

For the occasion he had chosen the attire of a privateer from the Indies, with scarf tied round his black hair and short sword tucked in his belt.

And yet I had to smile. For he looked neither fierce nor barbaric. The brutal attire served but to bring out his gentleness. The whiteness of his skin, the tender wisps of his moustache, and the long slender fingers that rested on his belt spoke not of privateering but of the scholar dressed in pirate's clothing.

I had thought to venture forth and offer him my milk when the ranks of guests suddenly parted and a vision appeared, robed in Grecian attire, cut so low that her full breasts were plainly visible, her hair hidden by a long fair wig, and bare arms decked with golden armlets.

Isabella, Countess of Straven, had come modestly to the feast attired as Helen of Troy. And then her hand was suddenly upon his arm, and her bewitching smile would indeed have launched a thousand ships. Her eyes, as they rested on him, caressed as clearly as if the two lay down upon a couch together.

And I, who had never known the fires of love, nor the prick of lovers' jealousy, longed to throw my pail and drench them in the milk of my outraged innocence.

I was saved from any such unseemly act by Master Manners, who had noted me amongst the crowd and now came towards me, dressed in pastoral attire, with a wooden crook in his hand.

'Master Manners,' I said, a little too loudly, my face still flushed with anger, not thinking what I spoke but that I must remove myself. 'Are you indeed a shepherd?' I held out my hand for him to shake. 'Corydon perhaps?'

At that he laughed and the couple I wished to avoid turned towards us. 'Not Corydon, mistress. I know you are both fair and learned yet you have not read your Eclogues diligently. As I remember Corydon loved a boy but it is no boy, I assure you, who is the object of this shepherd's affections.'

At this witty rejoinder all about us laughed. Master Donne threw me a look which might have been sympathy or pity, yet the gleam in the Countess's eye at my ignorance being thus exposed was obvious to all.

'Come, mistress,' Master Manners took my hand, 'let us go to dine. A shepherd and his milkmaid, who could desire a more fitting couple than that?'

And indeed, to my even greater embarrassment, the other guests near about us began to clap as he took my hand in his and led me eagerly away.

Though my heart seethed with hurt and indignation there was much to divert me here, for this was the grandest occasion I had ever witnessed outside the Court. All the long table in the hall was decked with boughs of ivy, on which real jewels had been laid, and silken knots of ribbon. In the centre a vast cascade of dark liquid poured from tier to tier like a true waterfall. To my amazement it was made not of water but of wine! Indeed I was surprised at such magnificence in my uncle's house and wondered how Francis had persuaded him.

I looked down the table to see where Master Donne and his Helen were seated, yet there seemed no sign of them.

In each room musicians played and youths sang madrigals about shepherds and their dear loves. Listening to their words, Master Manners bade me dance with him. Next to us my sister Mary made sheep's eyes at her Nick, as if he were the only gentleman in all this wide world, and I smiled at them, hoping that long might it last.

'You are a pretty pair, Ann,' Mary whispered as we turned in the dance, 'just as God would have ordained.' I knew at once what she intended by this inference, that Master Manners was my equal, nearer in age and in rank than any jumped-up ironmonger's son.

I pretended not to catch her meaning.

When we returned to the table the food had been spread out, and many forgot they were dressed as gods and goddesses as they fell to tearing it apart.

Afterwards, while the sweetmeats were being laid, there was a sudden clap and on a dais at the end of the table a curtain parted, revealing a rocky mountain made of sharp and dangerous peaks.

In the centre of the mountain the assembly gasped to see the Countess of Straven, now dressed as a virgin, her long hair about her shoulders, her hands crossed in prayer. Beneath her, pawing at the mountain, were two ravening beasts, one bearing the legend Lust, the other Licentiousness, and above the tableau a painted sign read 'Purity Triumphing Over Trial and Temptation'.

'It must fain be the first time,' I heard one guest murmur to his neighbour and I slipped quietly away, not wanting to feed the Countess's vanity with my applause.

'Mistress More!'

At the far end of the hall, a passage led towards the pantry and beyond that the kitchens. He stood, half in shadow, the candlelight catching the silver of his sword, beckoning me towards the entrance.

I followed, anger burning up in me.

I had thought him a deep well and yet he had proved both shallow and faithless.

'Well, Master Donne, will not my lady Straven's nose be quite put of joint that you are not there to applaud her triumph?'

He took my wrist and pulled me further into the shadows.

'That is not worthy of you who is so generous of spirit.'

'Even generous spirits may be wounded to see those whom they admire behave ignobly. The lovely Isabella has a husband after all.'

'Who cares only for her wealth, and naught for her happiness.'

'I see. So she must console herself elsewhere.'

'As it happens I have counselled her many times to return to him.'

'Generous to a fault. Then you would have the chance—how was it you put it in your verse?—"to kiss and play in his house".'

He still held my wrist and now twisted it so hard it pained me. 'You have indeed a poor judgement of me. I would never do so.'

'Honour amongst adulterers? I am touched.'

His eyes scanned mine. 'I am not proud of the life I have lived before I met you. I have known many women, it is true, and may pay the price with eternal damnation. Yet there is one sin I would not commit: I would not abuse the honour of the innocent.'

'Forgive me if I do not commiserate with you.' At last I wrested my wrist from his grasp. It had blue marks which tomorrow I would have to hide. 'For the evidence seems to me to be otherwise!'

My cheeks flamed as I made my way back through the crowded hall, overwhelmed by a tide of anger and confusion. It seemed that I might wish and pray to feel nothing for Master Donne, yet despite all he had the power as no other man on earth did to move me.

WITH THE NEW babe in her belly Mary began to grow in size before my eyes.

Much of the cause for this was her sudden taste for sweetmeats. Mary, lean as a whippet and used to chiding our weighty sister Margaret, was now forever sending me to bother the cook with requests for butter fritters, creamapple pie and feberry fool. Once, when the cook barked back that my lady had eaten her out of almonds, I was sent out myself to find her dumplings from a cookshop.

And yet so much consumption seemed never to diminish her prodigious energy. She called all the time for friends to come and play at cards, read her poetry, and even to perform playlets to distract her from the great boredom and dislike she professed at being in whelp.

Sometimes I was shocked at the behaviour of their circle. They seemed a shallow crowd, prone to gossip and to garrulousness, lying around sipping Mary's sack from the moment she had risen from her bed, ever criticizing others for their idleness yet never seeming to do any useful thing themselves.

Once, back from an excursion to find candied fruits, Mary's fad for this week, I came across a pair fumbling at each other's clothing in the dry food pantry. And when I entered all they did was laugh and show not a shred of shame.

And then came the terrible news that carefree young Sir Thomas, elder son of the Lord Keeper and father of the three small girls it had been my role sometimes to care for, had died of wounds sustained fighting the Irish.

Knowing the terrible blow this would be to my uncle I went with all speed to York House to offer him my sympathy. As I alighted at the river stairs I wondered if I might see Master Donne, whose friend Sir Thomas had been. I wished, if I saw him, to offer him also my sympathy, all thoughts of the encounter the other night forgotten now that Death had laid his icy fingers upon us.

I found my uncle pale and sorrowing, yet busying himself still with the business of State.

'My dear son Thomas is to be buried tomorrow with all honours at Chester Cathedral.' His honest eyes held mine a brief moment and I saw in them the depths of his pain. 'I wish to go and sorrow for him, yet Her Majesty says she is loath to lose me even for so short a time.'

I nodded, wondering at the price Queen Elizabeth exacted from her true and loyal servants.

'His brother John has gone to Chester and Master Donne and others are representing me.'

'I am sure they will serve your honour well,' I replied sadly and embraced his young wife, who, it seemed shockingly, was not to go to his funeral either, it not being thought a womanly thing.

As I left that sad house for the frivolous cheer of my sister's, I saw a new guest arriving. The Countess of Straven.

'You waste your time,' I almost said. 'He is already gone.' Instead I lifted my head and smiled and asked how her husband did and that I heard he had come to London at last.

At that she looked at me narrowly. 'You are out of date, Mistress More. He has returned to the country, not finding London to his taste. Yet here *you* are again, and still without a husband.'

'Yet when I do find one, I intend to love and honour him and not spend my life a hundred miles apart.'

'Such innocence, Mistress More. A hundred miles is an excellent distance between husband and wife, as I am sure you will yet discover.'

With all her lovely face, and imagined experience, I believed her not. If I was allowed to have the husband of my choice, I would not spend my life a hundred miles apart but hold him fast within the circle of my arms.

When I regained my sister's house at Mile End she was in a pettish mood, moving from chair to couch, now staring out of the window, then pacing like a caged bear.

Her husband was at his wits' end with her.

'Here,' he thrust a parchment into her hands, 'perhaps this will amuse you. A saucy verse penned by your uncle's secretary. It is doing the rounds of the Inns of Court. Not for ladies' eyes, so I knew you would wish to see it.'

He chucked her chin affectionately, to cut the edge of his words.

Mary opened the paper. 'It is called "The Flea". Not the fittest of subjects for poetry.' Clearing her throat she read the verse aloud.

> *'Mark but this flea, and mark in this,*
> *How little that which thou deny'st me is;*
> *It sucked me first, and now sucks thee,*
> *And in this flea, our two bloods mingled be;*
> *Thou know'st that this cannot be said*
> *A sin, or shame, or loss of maidenhead,*
> *Yet this enjoys before it woo,*
> *And pampered swells with one blood made of two,*
> *And this, alas, is more than we would do.*
>
> *Oh stay, three lives in one flea spare,*
> *Where we almost, nay, more than married are.*
> *This flea is you and I, and this*
> *Our marriage bed, and marriage temple is;*
> *Though parents grudge, and you, we'are met,*
> *And cloistered in these living walls of jet.*
> *Though use make you apt to kill me,*
> *Let not to this, self murder added be,*
> *And sacrilege, three sins in killing three.*
>
> *Cruel and sudden, hast thou since*
> *Purpled thy nail, in blood of innocence?*
> *In what could this flea guilty be,*

Except in that drop which it sucked from thee?
Yet thou triumph'st, and say'st that thou
Find'st not thyself, nor me the weaker now;
'Tis true, then learn how false fears be;
Just so much honour, when thou yield'st to me,
Will waste, as this flea's death took life from thee.'

As she finished reading my sister started to laugh so much she had to drink a sip of ale to quiet herself. 'I must admit, he is a witty fellow your Master Donne. I wonder if he wrote it to woo the lovely Isabella.'

I twitched the paper from her. 'He is not *my* Master Donne. And the lovely Isabella has no maidenhead to protect. Unless her husband is even more incompetent than he seems.'

Yet the truth was, I was stirred more than I chose to admit by the lines I had heard, witty and polished on the surface yet with the veiled hint of mastery beneath.

For there was that in me which might, despite the strictures of God and family, be tempted to surrender my own maidenhead to a laughing, dark-eyed suitor.

Yet I covered such thoughts by pretending scorn and anger so that I stamped from the room, imagining the smiles on the faces of my sister and her husband as I ran to my chamber and threw the parchment on the floor, my face flushed with anger mixed with unmaidenly desires.

AFTER THE DEATH of young Sir Thomas we had some calm days until the news that shook us all. The Earl of Essex, returning suddenly from the wars in Ireland, which were going very ill, had burst into the Queen's bedchamber at Nonsuch Palace. She, without wig or make-up and wearing only her nightgown and with none of the lengthy preparations that readied Her Majesty to face the world, might have had him killed for less. The Court held its breath. Yet the Queen was surprisingly tender and sent him kindly away.

Yet when he returned she was much changed and so angry that he had without her permission concluded a treaty, that she declared he must be imprisoned at her pleasure. And to my uncle's great discomfort York House was selected as the Earl's place of his detainment.

And so, and at his own expense, my uncle the Lord Keeper had an unexpected and unwelcome guest. Rumour even held it that Master Donne and others must give up their lodgings to make room for the Earl and all his train.

In the weeks that succeeded I saw no more of Master Donne, yet we heard much of life at my aunt and uncle's house. The Earl of Essex, hitherto a good friend to the Lord Keeper, was now driving him to desperation by his melancholic fits. For the good of the country my uncle wished him to make his peace with the Queen, yet the Earl seemed to be declining faster than the sun upon St Lucy's Day, the shortest of all the year.

Indeed, the Earl's decline was so violent and extreme that one night it was thought that the fever he had taken would cause his untimely end. The Queen was told and, by cover of darkness, she came secretly to visit York House in the royal barge, to bid her last farewell.

After that he rallied. And as his melancholy lessened yet a sorrier rumour came to us in Mile End that my aunt herself was stricken by illness.

'Tis likely to be naught,' my sister counselled, 'perhaps my lord Essex's appropriation of her house has brought her spirits lower still.'

I resolved that the next day, while my sister lay abed as she often did after the midday meal, I would seek more news of my aunt's ailment.

It was a cold afternoon, the balmy days of October, with their golden glory, had now vanished and we were well through the month of November. Last week had been the Queen's Accession Day feast, one of the greatest in all the year, with tilting and masques and all manner of celebration. I wondered if the Queen missed her Earl and whether this time his sin was too great to forgive, being about not the peccadilloes of love but the defence of her realm. Was life at her Court, now functioning smooth again, too quiet without her gentle knight who, though so many years her junior, made her ache with pain as often as thrill with pleasure? Perhaps at well past sixty years any feeling was better than none? Or yet again, she might be bored of such tiring games as his, forever dallying with her ladies, or sulking at slights to his honour.

When I arrived by water at York House it was quieter than I had ever known it, despite the presence of the Earl of Essex. My uncle had been called to an urgent meeting of the Privy Council and had taken many of his advisors and secretaries with him. The Earl of Essex himself seemed wrapped in melancholy and glid around like a wraith outside in the gardens all day long, clad in old clothes.

When I asked the groom of the Great Chamber to see my aunt I found it was Joan, her tire-woman, who came to greet me.

'Joan, good day to you,' I wished her, remembering the outings she and I had shared around this fair city. Indeed I had to hide a smile at the memory of her tutoring in the art of bedmaking, and how it ended in so strange and fatal an encounter.

'My sister heard a tale of your mistress suffering some illness. How is she today and is there aught I could do to help her?'

'My lady is in her chamber resting. I think it better she is left alone.' Without more words she turned swiftly for the door.

'Joan, Joan . . .' I knew the woman well and this day it seemed there was something in her manner I knew not, a refusal to meet my eyes, the way she moved, as fast and silent as a rat scuttling from the broom. 'What manner of illness is it?'

'A fever. She talks of chills and cramps as if she had stood all night in the rain. Her head aches somewhat.'

It was unfortunate that my aunt was herself the one who dosed others, so that when the finger fell upon her, there was none to aid her.

'Have you talked to the apothecary? What has the Lord Keeper to say of her condition?'

'She wishes not to bother the Lord Keeper. He grieves still for his son and my lady wants not to add to his burden.'

I could understand this, and yet it worried me.

'Tell her I will return tomorrow and bring some of the orange pippins that delight her so.'

Still not catching my eye, Joan curtsied. 'I will, Mistress Ann.'

I made a small detour on my route homewards. Before taking to the water I stopped at the church of St Bride's, hard by Fleet Steet, and slipped in before evening prayers. When I was a small child it was still possible, if you were discreet, to light a candle to symbolize some wish or intercession. Now such things were frowned upon as the trappings of dangerous Popery. Instead I offered up a prayer for my aunt's health to be restored.

A lively gathering was wending its rowdy way through Mary's house when I arrived, settling now in this chamber, now in that. Darkness had fallen and the candles and torches were lit, casting a coloured glow on the assembled gathering in all their finery as if they were Italian princelings or the young nobility of some Spanish court.

'How was my lady aunt?' Mary enquired, yet I could see her mind was on filling goblets from a gilded tray for her chattering guests.

'I did not see her. Joan, her waiting woman, said she was resting in her chamber.'

'And a good thing too,' Mary nodded. 'A lady needs to have her rest from care and labour lest her household take too much advantage of her.'

I tried not to smile, since Mary's life did not seem so very full of care and labour.

'I will go again tomorrow. I wish our lady grandmother were close by, with all her knowledge of plants and their good properties.'

'Come, Ann, you make too much. Join us in a glass of sack, and after perhaps you could read to Francis and to Nicholas? They have been asking for you this last half-hour. I can tell my headache begins to come apace.'

I forwent the sack and took pleasure in reading to the children. They were quiet, contented infants who seemed to find Mary's unwifely ways as normal as if all households were conducted with the laxity of Mary's. Had she consigned them to their nurses and seen them not for days on end, as befell many children, they would have found that strange behaviour indeed.

Next morning I awoke before the rest, and went downstairs in my night attire. I shook my head that it was almost eight and the fires not yet lit, while in most houses they would have blazed since five, and shivered in the chill air that seeped under the garden door. Outside all was covered in a thick hoar frost, white almost as snow, in the walled garden. I opened the door and ventured out to pick some ivy strands, rich with purple berries, and a handful of Christmas roses to fashion a winter nosegay for my aunt. As I reached for a bough of holly, bright with berries, of a sudden I heard a loud knocking at the front door and turned so swiftly I caught myself upon the bush and tore my flesh so that blood began to gush, marking the white linen of my nightgown with a stain of brightest red.

And yet no servant opened the door. So I, my hand still dripping from the wound, opened it myself to find Joan, her skirts all muddy from the London streets, standing upon the doorstep.

'Mistress Ann, it is your lady aunt. She is taken worse and the Lord Keeper nowhere to be found. Perhaps he is with the Queen. She told me to bother none, that she would rally soon.' Joan looked distraught, indeed near to weeping, and wrung her hands incessantly. 'I knew not who to turn to, mistress, and Mercy and I remembered you, and that you love her well, and she you.'

I took her in and stood her in the withdrawing room, next the Great Chamber, while I went to dress myself. I could see her look around in wonder at so exotic a dwelling place, and yet none from the household up and busy.

Fumbling at the hooks of my bodies I cursed at having to dress in so elaborate a selection of clothing without even Prudence to help hook me up, and yet at last I was dressed and ready. I bound up my hand with a napkin from the press by the kitchen, hoping it was clean, though in this house that was by no means certain, and went to wake my sister.

No knock roused her so I gently opened the door of her chamber.

She and Nick lay in the great bed, wound together like a plait of hair, Mary's nightgown discarded on the floor beside them.

I tried to avert my gaze but, against my will, found it drawn back like iron to a lodestone. Yet it was not Mary and her husband I pictured there, with bodies so entwined, but myself and quite another.

Shocked at my own imaginings, I roused my sister from her sleep. 'Mary,' I shook her gently. 'It is our aunt. Joan is below and says she is much the worse.'

Mary's eyes opened at last and she struggled to sit up, hampered by the mountain of her growing belly. 'And you go to her?' Becoming aware of her nakedness, she reached for her nightgown. 'Must I also?'

'No, no, you are with child. I will send you a message of how I find her.'

Mary lay back against her sleeping husband, fitting her gourd-like body along his like two spoons in a drawer. 'Then I will doze a little more,' she murmured sleepily.

Joan stood waiting in the withdrawing room, her cloak held tight about her as if she did not want to be contaminated by this strange, and possibly godless household.

I gathered up the nosegay I had picked for my aunt and flung my own cloak over my gown, putting on my pattens the while, for it would be deep in mud outside once the frost melted.

As we made our way through the noisy, bustling streets down towards the river, to hail a wherry to take us to York House, I looked back at Mary's house, a sleeping island amidst the busy clatter and clanging of Mile End. It seemed my lot in life to ever be the one who took action.

On the way I made Joan tell me my aunt's list of ailments, as carefully as she could remember, when each started and for how long.

Three days since, I learned, she had a fever, and complained of chills and back pain. Her arms and legs ached like to a sudden fit of winter illness. This day, when Joan pulled back her curtains, she shouted out loud that Joan was trying to kill her.

'She asked for a bowl and then spewed greatly into it, still telling me to trouble none with her infirmity, yet I worried for her weakness and sought out the Lord Keeper. Finding him not, I came to look for you.'

After this we stayed silent until the familiar shape of York House hove into view. Then with a failing heart I ran up the great staircase knowing not what I might find awaiting me.

All was quiet in my aunt's chamber and, following Joan's advice, I pulled the curtains back to let in only a crack of sunlight. Yet even this dim ray made my aunt cry out afresh.

'We must call a physician straight away, and find the Lord Keeper whether he is with the Queen or no. Indeed, the Queen may send her own physician, knowing the love she bears my aunt.'

I closed the curtains once more, knowing all light is bad for illness, and sat beside my aunt, making her drink a cordial of elderflower whenever she would accept it.

Around midday she murmured to me that she would sit up, and to my great joy I was able to arrange her against a bank of cushions and even to open the curtains an inch so that by the time her husband came, his tall frame aquiver with worry at the message he had received, she was greatly better.

'Now, now, husband,' she weakly joked, 'what brings you in so much haste from the State's business?'

He took her hand in is, his pale eyes softening. 'Something of greater moment than either Queen or courthouse.'

She smiled and shook her head at such nonsense. 'Beware such treasonous utterances, man, even the walls have ears.'

The physician came not half an hour later and pronounced the worst to be over.

At that I sat beside her and she took my wounded hand in hers. 'What ails you, Ann, that you wear this bloodstained napkin?'

'A prick from the holly tree, no more. I was surprised how much I bled.'

A shadow crossed her face at that. 'Like unto the wound from the crown of thorns on our Saviour's head before he died upon the cross.'

'No, no,' I laughed to cheer her from such sad thoughts, 'more like the merry boughs we pick to adorn the house at Christmas time.'

'They are the same, Ann, the very same.'

I read to her a little after that, until she slept. And then I slept myself and found when I awoke that darkness had fallen.

I smoothed the covers of the bed, and folded back the sheet, exposing the tender whiteness of her long, pale arm.

I lifted her hand to hold it for a moment in my own, and saw a sight that made me gasp with fear.

A flat red rash covered the inside of her palm.

At that I fell to my knees and prayed to the very Saviour of whose death for us she had this day reminded me.

'Our Lord, which art in Heaven,' I interceded, 'let not this be the mark of the smallpox upon my dearest aunt's hand.'

Chapter 15

JOAN SAW IT next, but said naught, only looked me in the eye then lowered her gaze and kept her distance. Mercy, always a chatterbox would not be so discreet.

The worst was summoning the Lord Keeper, happy as a lark in springtime since the doctor's visit, and showing him the dreadful evidence.

At first he would not believe there was aught to worry over. Yet I made him call back the physician, insisting that I had heard my grandmother talk of such a rash, and what it led to.

The physician pursed his lips and shook his head and said it might yet turn out to be the chicken pox. 'If the rash spreads to her breasts and belly and spares her face and legs, then God be praised.'

Yet, as I had feared, it was her breast and belly that were spared. The rash spread instead to her feet and legs, and upwards, breaking our hearts as it did, to her face and mouth. On the third day the rash became raised bumps. And on the fourth these turned to hard-centred pustules filled with a thick, opaque fluid, leaving no shred of doubt as to their deadly nature.

My cousin Francis, almost as thin and stricken as his mother, begged her to let him stay. Yet she would not relent. He was the future, all their hopes resting in him, and he must be gone to Pyrford and to safety.

'You must be gone also, Ann,' my uncle told me, his honest face pale as a wraith's. 'Go with Francis, or else you risk the same contagion.'

'But who will care for her if we leave?' I asked, for Mercy had not been near her door in days and even Joan, who claimed to love her, would not enter the room but left all that was called for beside the door.

'I will,' said my uncle softly.

I held fast to his hand, knowing that, although his love was great, his stricken state made him of little use to my aunt in her private needs. And the Queen, with her memory of the smallpox still fresh in her mind although it had struck her years before, would never countenance it. Then, when all had left her, my aunt would be tended by a hired servant who made a living from such tasks, and whose face she would never have seen before.

Young though I was, and my thirst for living great, I could not abandon her.

My uncle would hear nothing of it at first, yet God gave me the words and at last he agreed to my insistent persuasion.

Joan found me one of the servant's pallets and placed it where I bid her, next the bed. As she left she made the forbidden sign of the cross. In our extremes, many turn to the old faith. That night as I lay at my aunt's bedside it seemed all slept throughout that great house save my beloved aunt, who writhed and mumbled as she travelled on her terrible journey alone.

And as I listened, cold and fearful, the words of Psalm 91, often read aloud by my grandfather during evening prayers at Loseley, came to me as if straight from Heaven.

> *Thou shalt not be afraid for any terror by night:*
> *Nor for the arrow that flieth by day:*
> *Nor for that pestilence that walketh in darkness:*
> *Nor for the sickness that destroyeth in the noonday.*
> *A thousand shall fall beside thee*
> *And ten thousand at thy right hand:*
> *But it shall not come nigh thee.*

As the words rang in my ears, I wished with all my being that I was safe back at Loseley, in the comforting arms of my grandparents. Yet I knew in the deepest reaches of my conscience that my place was here.

My own mother had been taken from me. My aunt, lying in her sickness next to me, had been all the mother I had known and I could not forsake her.

May God protect me.

The word of my aunt's illness spread faster than the fuse on a barrel of gunpowder, so that soon all London knew of it. The Earl of Essex, billeted in the far corner of the house, kept his distance and walked no more in the wintry gardens for fear of catching the infection.

When, to my surprise, the Countess of Straven called to pay her respects I had to revise my opinion of that lady for it was brave in her to venture here to this place where contagion stalked amongst the fine furniture and gilded statuary.

I had been called down to greet her myself, for in that stricken house there was none other left to receive her.

I offered her cakes and small beer in the long gallery that gave onto the river. 'I thank you, my lady, for coming to York House when most would keep away.'

'Why,' she asked, her silks rustling as she laughed, 'is the Lord Keeper fallen so out of favour with the Queen?'

'Her Majesty loves him still. I meant my aunt's most dread condition.'

The change wrought upon that lovely face when she at last understood me, was worthy of a bitter comedy. Her skin, creamy and blooming as money and good food could make it, paled into sudden greyness. And I saw the truth: she had been out of town, away from wagging tongues, and had known nothing of our new affliction.

Faster than the wink of an eye from a painted doxy, she was gone.

I gathered my gown over my arm and turned towards the stairs, stopping at the sight of Master Donne hastening in my direction. 'Mistress More,' his face was haggard, older and more careworn than I had ever seen it, the laughing dazzle of the poet and gallant eclipsed by concern and dark presentiment. 'I have heard the news of your good aunt and come to give you my greatest sympathy.'

'Thank you, Master Donne. I thought my lady Straven had come to offer her sympathy also,' I could not keep a little of the bitter amusement from my voice, 'yet it seems she knew naught of our misfortune and has hurried homewards as if this were a plague house.'

'Has she indeed?' He was in the grip of such strong emotion that my irony was lost on him. Instead he took my hand in his, holding it so tight that my fingers pained me. 'And so ought you, Mistress More. Go back to your sister in Mile End or better still to Loseley.'

'Master Donne,' I drew my hand away, holding myself as high and straight as I could, my newness of purpose giving me strength, 'your brother who died in Newgate, stricken and alone? Would you not have nursed him if you could?'

Master Donne's haunted eyes slid away from mine, and his shoulders hung in sudden shame. 'Mistress More,' he hesitated, his voice jagged with long-nurtured pain, 'as Jesus is our Saviour, I know not the answer.'

I was grateful for his honesty, that he tried not to fob me off with easy untruth. 'Such things are different for all, yet I know this is a task I cannot shirk, nor want to either. It is my gift to her who loved me.'

'Yet is it a gift she wishes to receive?' The words seemed wrenched from him. 'Your beauty, Ann? Or your sweet young life, if the smallpox claims you?'

He had not called me Ann before.

'I was never beautiful. And surely beauty counts not so much in the face of love or death?'

He hung his head, and then, reaching into his own soul, looked into my eyes, seeking strength there.

We were alone in the hall, the bustling servants quietened by calamity. I reached out to him and he held fast my hand against his heart. 'May God protect you, sweetest Ann.'

'Amen to that.' I loosened his handgrasp and walked slowly up the stairs knowing, as he did, that for good or ill this contagion would change our lives forever.

By cruel irony, my aunt's affliction had come upon her at Christmas time, when all around us was joyful celebration. As the days passed, from my seat at the side of her great bed I could hear merry revellers tipping out of taverns in the Strand, the tolling of seasonal bells; and even, when I ventured briefly abroad, I could smell the scent of Christmas pies and cakes baking in the cookshops.

At York House all was quiet. My aunt, when she had been well, loved to deck every mantel with swags of holly and draped great swathes of ivy over doors and staircases and the minstrels' gallery. Each room had scented pomanders and musicians playing festive tunes upon the lute or tabor.

In memory of those happier times I fetched an orange from the kitchen and a bundle of cloves. Sitting by her bedside I stuck a hundred cloves into the orange and bound it up with the red ribbon I had bought to tie a gift for Mary.

'See, Aunt, do you remember that when I was a maid you taught me how to make these oranges for keepsakes and Christmas gifts?'

In the darkened chamber my aunt stirred and held out a hand, so that I put the orange into it and she held it to her nose.

'Ann, I cannot see, open the drapes a little.' Her voice, used so little of late, creaked like a rusty gate.

I walked to the window looking out over the great river and drew back the heavy curtains an inch or two, grateful to bring some daylight into that dark, oppressive room where pastilles burned to combat the sickly smell of disease. The windows were firmly closed and the fire blazing, as was the custom in any time of illness.

I turned back to my aunt and struggled not to gasp in horror at the sight before me. The rash on her face had spread, dissolving all her features in a mass of oozing pustules.

I fell to my knees beside her, and as I did, caught the putrid smell of the pus that leaked from her myriad lesions.

'My lady aunt, are you in great pain?' I longed to reach for her hand.

She seemed to sense this and waved me back from the bed. 'No more than our Saviour on the cross.'

A peal of joyful bells rang of a sudden through the room.

'What day is this?' she asked.

Time had slid quietly by in our curtained-off world and I could not answer her.

There was a soft knock on the door and my uncle the Lord Keeper entered. 'It is Christmas morn and I have brought the barley cream you favour so,' he told her tenderly, not seeming even to notice the catastrophe her face had become. He put the drink on the table next to the bed and began to lift her up against her cushions, for all the world as if she were a lovely young girl on the morning of her marriage. He sat himself in the chair I had vacated. 'I am come to celebrate the birth of Our Lord with you and to thank Him for the times of great content He has given us.'

He held the drink to her lips and she took a tiny sip.

'Light the candles, Ann,' he requested. 'That we may feel the warmth of their happy glow.'

At that I left them to be private together and went downstairs to see how the household kept its Christmas without us.

The table in the Great Hall could have seated forty people. My aunt was famous for her hospitality and the pleasure she took in entertaining others. Once, when I was a child, we spent Christmas at her home in Pyrford. She had laid the festive table to echo her knot garden, all with borders, paths and edges made from foods of riotous colour, with more than twenty dishes of capon, partridge, pheasant and roast beef, finished with gilded marchpanes and sweetmeats shaped like flowers and diamonds, crowned by a cake moulded into the shape of Pyrford Place itself, complete with its gables and weathervane.

Today all was silent. Guests, servants, all had gone elsewhere to celebrate the twelve days of Christmas and left York House ringing with its own emptiness.

My aunt's dread journey ended on Monday, the twentieth of January, in the year of 1600.

It was at that moment when the night seems endless and there is yet no sign of light in the sky. She had slipped down the bed so that her feet touched its very posts. I arose from my pallet and saw that she was curled almost into a ball, her hair, which she had once so loved, covering the battleground of her dear face. And she breathed no longer.

I knew I should be glad. Her pain had ended. She was at peace after so much suffering. And yet I was not glad. At first I felt but a deadening akin to jarring your knee against a chair or table, and then pain seared through me, like the branding of a hot knife against tender flesh, burning and stinking and agonizing. Pain is no beautiful purifying thing. It is ugly and cruel. It takes, giving nothing in return but hopelessness and loss.

At last I left my aunt in the presence of her grieving husband and of Francis, her son, summoned from Pyrford at the last, and ran helter-skelter up the stairs towards my chamber.

On the darkened landing a figure stepped out of the shadows and barred my path. It was Master Donne, who had not abandoned the household as had so many others but returned here out of loyalty to my uncle. It seemed as if his eyes had at last been opened to the Countess. 'Ann, my sweet Ann, I am sorely sorry for your trouble, and wished to tell you that you are ever in my thoughts and prayers.'

'Prayers!' I had not known how sharp with fury my voice would sound. 'Too late for that! I cannot thank God for taking from me all those whom I have loved. Mother. Aunt. Sister. All lost. Shall I yet thank Almighty God for His generosity and loving kindness?'

At the other end of the passage a door opened and I pulled Master Donne silently into my chamber, caring not a shred in my loss and anger of what might be made of it.

'Tell me, Master Donne, believe you in the rewards of everlasting life? Are we truly to be judged and sit forever at the right hand of the Father?'

Master Donne smiled gently. 'Is not that the privilege of the risen Christ?'

Heretic though I might be, I had rarely felt so angry in all my life until this moment. 'I care no more for Heaven, nor its promise of eternal happiness. It is this life, here in this earthly paradise, that I yearn for, that it should be lived, and enjoyed with all our senses, that we should look around us at its wonder.' I turned away and stared across the endless greyness of the river and then back towards him. 'Can you, a poet and scholar, persuade me that the rewards of Heaven are so much greater than the pleasures of this Earth?'

His face had lost its teasing humour and those haunting eyes looked into mine, as if into a window on my soul. And then he spoke, so soft I could hardly hear him. 'I want, with my whole heart, to believe that I will one day be ravished into God's loving arms and held there for all eternity. Yet, in the very depths of my soul, sweet Ann, I fear with all my sins I shall be left to perish on the shore.'

'And what of woman's arms?' I raised up my eyes until they were fixed upon his own. 'Do you not long to be ravished into a woman's hold, and stay there, forever, in the circle of her loving arms?'

'Were they your arms, I would gladly forget the world and all its lures.'

I stepped towards him rashly, my eyes afire, overwhelmed by the desire to obliterate myself in him, to lose this terrible numbness and, callous though it seemed, to feel alive and breathing in the midst of death.

For one fleeting moment he caught my fire and I felt the crushing delight of his embrace.

Then he seemed to shake himself. 'Ann, Ann, sweet Ann. My body and my soul are at your disposal. Yet I am not so lost to the world as to forget your innocence, above all at such a time as this.'

'An apt time indeed you have chosen for this sudden saintliness.' I stroked his face, and ran my finger over his full woman's lips which yet had such masculine persuasive force. 'Then hold me as you would a child for I am sorely in need of tender comfort.'

I could see the struggle that took place within him before he reached out and held me safe against his chest.

And there I stayed, my breathing stilled almost to holy silence, feeling peace such as I had last felt only in my grandfather's study, while around us the shadows fell and the silence enveloped us.

In this world of tears we were left alone. At his dear wife's death the wound of my uncle's grief, not yet healed from the loss of his oldest son but five months since, opened again. Darkness overcame him, the Lord Keeper would see no one, and refused to leave his chamber, no matter how august the summoner. Messages came from the Privy Council demanding his attendance, from the Star Chamber and the court of Chancery, yet my uncle heeded none of them.

For seven blissful days, Master Donne and I were readmitted to that garden of delight lost so long ago by our first father and mother. And, like Adam and Eve before the first stain of sin sullied their lives and ours forever, we gloried in the grandeur of our innocence.

It was strange, for though I longed for the touch of his skin on mine, there was yet a release in simple affection, the succour such as a mother gives a babe.

At first I was so needy that I slept.

It was as if I had imbibed some opiate that dulled my senses yet calmed the soul. And each time I awoke I saw him seated next to me on bed or chair, and knew I was safe to sleep again.

When I awoke at last refreshed he told me that the sun had set twice on my slumbers. I sat up hungrier than ever I could remember.

'Where can we find food at such an hour?'

'At the cookshop across the road, behind the Strand.' He shook his head at the length of my requests, and returned with my groaning order of rabbit pie, pastry coffins crammed with cold meats, pears and warm almond cakes. 'Your grief hath not quite killed your appetite, I fancy,' he remarked.

For answer I threw a slice of good cold beef at him, which he caught in his mouth, and made me laugh until I choked and must be patted on the back. And then guilt overwhelmed me at smiling so when my aunt lay still and my uncle grieved, yet I knew her own words would be that life must go on.

And go on it did in our small paradise.

The next day I washed his hair, tenderly, in lukewarm water I fetched myself from the kitchen, and dried on an old shift, watching it spring into soft black curls he said would make him the envy of every maid from Cheapside to Chancery Lane.

He told me of his mother, Elizabeth, that stern lady whom he yet loved much, of his sister Anne, and lost brother Henry, and three young sisters besides who died in childhood.

'What of your father?' I asked, as we sat upon the bed watching the sun sink once more.

'He was taken from us when I was but four years old, the best father any boy had. I remember him still, his kindness, that he always kept the managing of me to himself, and would allow no servant to discipline me.' He turned his face away and I saw, with great surprise, for I had thought it was only I who mourned a parent's loss so long, that the wound of his father's loss still caused him pain.

'We are alike, then,' I told him gently, 'whom you think so different in estate. We each lost the softer parent who would have nurtured and protected us.' I raised his hand to my lips, surprised that he quivered as gently as the breeze through a summer tree at my touch. 'We are twin souls, you and I.'

'Indeed?' He smiled, and yet there was bitterness in it. 'The man of eight and twenty, beyond his youth, a writer of rags of verse whose reputation is already tarnished, beholden to others for his fortune?

And a maid upon whom the bloom of youth still glows like the rising sun, hopeful and eager, who must wed a man of her own rank?'

I heard his litany of our two selves and saw, like a sudden shaft of light in a darkened cell, that despite the risk and danger our love might bring, he was the only one who could set me free. 'And yet,' I said firmly, 'without you I am bereft. My rectitude needs your impudence, my straightforward soul your clever refracted ways. You are the prism through which I see the world in all its wonder and complexity.'

'And in you I see a shining light, a certainty I find not in myself. Your true heart begets a holy thirst in me to make myself a better man.'

'I would not that you became *too* good, and lose the very thing that woke my slumbering senses.'

He reached for me then, his mouth seeking mine, his breath hot upon my neck, his hands exploring, yielding to the softness of my breasts until I thought I might die of my desire.

And then he groaned and tore himself away. 'If we go down this road there will be no stopping place.' He marched over to the window and stared down at the wide river below.

I straightened my clothes and followed him. 'Life will go on whatever we two choose to do.'

'Ann, we must not. I have loved many in my youth, yet none who offered me their innocence.'

I smiled, weaving my body close to his, as the woodbine winds around the ivy. 'Yet in "The Flea" you wooed the lady for her maidenhead.'

'It was naught but a pretty verse designed to bring a smile to wearied courtiers.'

I saw that I would not persuade him from his course. 'If I may not have your body, then I shall require at least the fruits of your mind, since my cousin Francis admires it so. Will you share your thoughts of Ovid and Catullus?'

He kissed my hand fondly. 'Ovid will lead us both astray. We will read the works of Petrarch and his Laura, and confine our joys to the realms of ideal love.'

And so we sat and read the works of Homer and of Petrarch, I playing the pupil and he the teacher, to our mutual comfort and delight, hidden away from the public gaze, yet knowing our time was running swiftly out.

Only Mercy noticed our continued absence. 'Beware, mistress,' she whispered one day as I fetched bread and beer, 'this morning the Queen has sent a message to my master commanding him to return to his duties. Public service must be preferred over private passions, she decrees.'

At hearing this I fired up with anger at Her Majesty's response to the death of one she called her 'sweet apple'. Yet I also knew that Mercy's words were intended as a warning and that our peaceful interlude, overlooked and interfered with by none, would soon be at an end.

'Be grateful, my sweet Ann,' he kissed me softly upon the eyelids, 'for we will ever remember these few days with joy and wonder.'

I turned away to hide the dampness of my eyes. For there was that in his voice which spoke of endings, where my own heart sang of a beginning.

The funeral was held with quiet dignity two days after, my poor aunt buried in a lead coffin for the sake of her contagion. The Queen, perhaps repenting, offered that it should take place at the palace of Whitehall. Yet my uncle—in a deliberate provocation that made all at York House hold our breath—answered that since private passions must not take precedence over public service, he would grieve alone.

We wondered if he would end up in the Tower for such insolence but Her Majesty accepted it, and even granted his further wish that the Earl of Essex, my uncle's prisoner as well as his pensioner here at York House for four long months, should return to his own home and let my uncle grieve in his.

My father came for the funeral, bringing my sisters Mary and Margaret. Yet Grandfather, whom I knew would long to say farewell to his beloved daughter, was prevented making the journey by an ague, my grandmother staying at Loseley to minister to him.

Master Donne also stayed away, not wishing to intrude upon family misery, but detained me a moment on the morning of the requiem.

'I long to share your sadness as well as your joy. Yet for me to come to so small a gathering might attract the notice of others.' He raised my hand swiftly to his lips.

The new tenderness that passed between us must have shone from my face, for my sister Mary, waiting at the great front door, spoke of it at once.

'Shame on you, Ann, to look so at our aunt's departure from this life. Master Donne must have been weaving spells indeed to make you act so unbecomingly.'

'I know not what you mean,' was my reply.

'Ann, I know that look, I have seen it before on ladies who have put passion before reason. If this goes on it will bring you nothing but shame and ruin. You must think at least of your family, of our father's position.'

'You wrong me, sister.' I raised my chin proudly. 'Naught but common human sympathy has passed between myself and Master Donne.'

My sister shrugged. 'From the look in both your eyes, human sympathy must be a dangerous commodity indeed.'

The small party waiting to go to the burial stood outside. My father, wrapped in furs against the cold, my cousin Francis, his eyes red-rimmed with grief at the loss of his mother, and next to him his betrothed, named Mary also. Margaret stood a pace apart with her solemn-faced husband, Thomas, and of course the Lord Keeper.

And behind all stood Master Manners, his face turned towards us as if listening intently to our murmured discourse.

We made our way sadly to the graveside, the minister reminding us to thank God that my aunt was now delivered from the miseries of this sinful world.

'Earth to earth,' he intoned, throwing a handful of soil into the gaping hole where my aunt's coffin had been lowered, 'ashes to ashes, dust to dust, in sure and certain hope of the Resurrection into eternal life to come.'

The snow began to fall as we stood mourning, adding its soft tears to my own, numbing my flesh until it felt as dead as my soul. Why did all I loved have to die untimely?

By the time the prayers ended hardly an hour had passed and yet the snow had settled thick upon the ground, leaving all of London muffled and quiet, its noisy engine stilled, as if out of respect for my aunt's sad passing. Beneath its covering of snowfall the city hid its dirty clothes and glowed and dazzled with such whiteness it seemed almost a miracle.

My father laid his hand on the Lord Keeper's shoulder. 'It is a sign that her departed soul is received into Heaven.'

Then he embraced his nephew. 'Pyrford is yours now, Francis, and I hope we will see you there.'

The shock he delivered to me was one I should have looked for, but had not. 'And what of you, Ann?' my father asked. 'You must go home to Loseley since there is no more need for you to bother the Lord Keeper with an extra mouth to feed now that your aunt has gone.'

These words sounded as a scaffold being built, each nail going straight into my heart.

For my father spoke the unwelcome truth. With my aunt's passing there was no rhyme or reason for me to stay on living at York House, or even in London.

Save one.

'She can come again to Mile End,' Mary offered. And giving me a speaking look, added, 'I will guard her like a jailer.'

'Why should you need to guard her at all, Mistress Throckmorton?' We turned to find the shrewd and measuring gaze of Master Manners upon us once more.

Mary, who can jump side-saddle over six-foot fences without flinching, faltered at this. 'My sister Ann,' she answered him, regaining confidence, 'is prone to rash and impetuous conduct—the acquisition of small boys, of whole families indeed, berating cruel masters, dressing in boy's clothing . . .'

'Indeed,' he regarded me narrowly, 'these sound more the actions of a hoyden or a playactor than a high-born lady.'

'Ann is prone to forget, in the heat of the moment, that she *is* a high-born lady.'

'Then she needs someone to remind her.'

Though his face was smiling and handsome there was that in his voice that made me shiver, and not from the snow that fell steadily upon my shoulders either.

'I would be happy for you to visit my father's house in Leicester-shire,' he announced, 'so that you might see for yourself my birth-right.'

'It has forty rooms,' whispered Mary.

'And a dining pavilion besides,' added Margaret. I could see that my sisters had been gossiping together and planned some new campaign.

I kissed my father and returned to my chamber, my soul as heavy as the lead coffin it had taken six strong men to carry to her graveside.

That night I passed a note to Wat, bidding him ask his master to visit me as soon as ever he could.

My whole being leapt like a hart on a spring morning when I heard his knock on my chamber door.

'I must say goodbye. I am to go back again to Mile End with my sister.'

Despite my sorrow he seemed relieved. 'Better than banishment to Loseley. Mile End is not so far. You may still visit us at York House from there.'

'Yet we will have no time to read and talk together as we have done this last week. There will be no more meeting of true plain hearts.'

'And what of bodies, Ann?' he burst out suddenly, as if he could no longer contain himself. 'Are we never to express our love through the flesh also?'

Remembering how I had tried to take him to bed, and he had out of conscience refused me, the words of another of his poems came to me. '"Or else a great prince in prison lies"?'

He shook his head. 'Know you that verse of mine also?'

I laughed and quoted further: '"Love's mysteries in souls do grow, But yet the body is his book."'

At that he pulled me against him and held me there, the tautness of his body pressed against mine, and the fire inside me flamed bright enough to burn down all York House and both our futures with it.

When at last he let me go, all I cared for was that we found a way to cast our futures in the same mould.

'I am not yet betrothed to Master Manners. No legal contract exists between us. Why do we not go together to my father and beseech him, in the name of love, to let us wed? He has a fiery temper but he is not a cruel man.'

Even as I spoke I knew my words to be like mist over the Tyburn gibbet, dissolving in the morning sunshine to show the brutal truth beneath.

'Ann, my Ann, the love we feel is seen by such as he as a sickness, a danger, a very threat to all that he believes in. He will accept me only if he sees that I am fit for you. If we go now he will accuse me of taking advantage of your innocence. Though I would wish it else with my last breath, it is best that we stand blameless of his charges.'

'Yet if we go not to plead our case to my father,' I protested, 'he may wed me to Master Manners whether I agree or no.'

'Then I must haste and prove to the Lord Keeper that I am worthy of advancement. That should he but rear me up and set me out, I shall indeed be worthy of your father's trust and your love.'

'Amen to that.'

And so we knelt by the side of the great bed which had been our secret garden and our golden refuge and joined our hands together. Had there been a crucifix as there would once have been above each bed before the great changes, I would have looked to it. Instead I bowed my head. 'We will be together, you and I, if it be God's will, and so I swear.'

'You are nearer to God than I,' he answered, his eyes still cloudy with desire. 'For I would have us be together were it God's will or not, even if it cost me my immortal soul.'

My eyes held his, soft with my new-found love. 'Then let us hope the price will be cheaper than that.'

AS THE WORLD of York House came back to life after its week-long sleep of grief, I sadly embraced my uncle, my cousin Francis and his betrothed, and went to live again with my sister Mary, whose great belly was growing vaster by the moment.

From there my sister made it her greatest project that I should be too busy or too bone-tired to clap eyes on Master Donne. She ever wanted this book or that medicine, or a cordial from this apothecary or a tonic from that herbalist, and all the while sent her servants along under strict instruction to keep me in their sight and him from it. I felt almost a prisoner in my sister's home. And yet, slowly as if each minute were an hour, the weeks and months began to pass.

The sole saviour of my sanity was Wat, whose existence they all forgot. And Wat loved me with so great a devotion for saving both himself and his siblings, that he would do aught that I asked him or even lie that I had said nothing.

And it was he who told me with what industry Master Donne was keeping his word to raise himself in the Lord Keeper's eyes. No more frequenting plays, or visiting ladies, or writing verses, as his master was wont to do. Now, said Wat, Master Donne did naught but harry the six clerks who between them administered all the cases at the court of Chancery; question the Examiners who demanded money from petitioners to take their statements and make sure they did not overcharge; and haggle endlessly with the Clerks of the Sub-poena Office and the Clerks of the Petty Bag, all in the cause of the Lord Keeper's reforms. On one occasion, Wat recounted, he even took issue with the Royal Chafewax for demanding extra payment to heat the wax to have a document sealed!

I could see this was a dangerous business, for those who lost out on their bribes and overcharging would not take it happily.

My uncle, it seemed, was burying his grief by redoubling his efforts to root out petty corruption, and Master Donne was proving an able accomplice.

Yet though I applauded my love's good intentions, I sorrowed in the fact that it seemed he was now too occupied to write or visit me. My only consolation was that, as he intended, his endeavours would advance him with my uncle and, in that way, lead to more chance of acceptance by my father. Yet his absence pained me sorely. And my sister did her best to turn the knife in my wound.

'Perhaps it is not all work and no play with Master Donne, as you so generously imagine,' my sister told me slyly one afternoon as she lay upon her daybed, her belly so great it brought to mind a seethed egg perched upon a sippet of bread. 'For I hear Isabella Straven is up to her tricks once more. The Earl, her husband, has fallen from his horse and instead of tending him as a wife should, my lady has come to London to seek her diversion.'

I had to feel that Mary told me for my protection yet she did not need to relish the revelation so.

And still this silence.

My confidence, at first as bright as the evening star, began daily to wane. While my sister whispered that I was but another conquest of a corrupted soul, I refused to listen to her.

One day I caught my reflection in Mary's costly new looking glass, so much prized and eagerly sought by the fashionable, and saw the saddened look that was in my eyes, not long since so merry and over-flowing with my love.

And yet I would not believe such. I had seen the tenderness re-flected in his eyes, had felt the gentle touch of love upon my skin as well as the raging fires of passion that we had been forced to damp down with the needs of present practicality.

I would keep my faith.

And keep it I needed to, as the days passed, for I was sorely tried by so long a silence.

'The truth is,' my sister told me baldly, as she came upon me staring sadly down the street in the direction of the city, 'he has thought better of your arrangement. He knows he could have you at the flick of the dice and now he thinks of his own advancement, how it would be dangerous indeed in him to break his master's trust, and go creeping through cor-ridors to slake his lust upon the great man's innocent niece. Indeed he wonders how he could ever have been so foolish and is no doubt grateful that all has ended without discovery.' She looked narrowly at me, hold-ing on to my shoulders, gripping them so hard there would be a bruise tomorrow, while my heart shrivelled like an oyster doused in lemon. 'Wake up, sister, from this dream! Our father will never consent to such a union.' She scanned my face intently. 'There has been no unwanted legacy? You have had your flowers this month as usual?'

'Mary, stop!' I felt my face flame up at her scrutiny. 'I have no cause to look to my flowers. Hard though you may find it to believe, we com-mitted no sin of the flesh.'

'In *deed* perhaps, but in thought you did.'

'Aye . . . well, in thought. But in deed . . .' I smiled suddenly, remem-bering his verse, 'his prince remained in prison.'

Mary threw back her head and laughed so loud her belly wobbled like an apple jelly. 'The best place for it. Tell him to keep it there.'

Would that I had the chance. But his silence was breeding the beginnings of doubt in me.

As we stood, Mary and I, regarding each other suspiciously, there was a knock upon the door. I knew I should wait for her steward or groom but I wished to get away from her condemning looks. So I opened the door myself to find Wat standing there upon the doorstep, smiling as if it were the final day of Lent.

'Mistress Ann, I have a letter from my master.' I could see that he shared my relief.

'Hah!' said Mary, who had waddled down the stairs behind me. 'No doubt it will be as I said. How he is sorry not to have honoured your worthy trust in him, yet sees he must extricate himself from a relation that must in the end dishonour you.' She glanced at Wat, seeing that she had been indiscreet in front of him. 'You, boy, get you hence. We want none of you nor your sly master neither!'

Yet the parchment I cradled in my hands said none of this. I leaned against the door, shutting out the chill early spring air, in which, despite the heavy months of winter, new life was starting again to bud and blossom, like my heart.

Both from relief and the desire to show my sister she was wrong, I held it up and began to read aloud the lines he had written me. 'Shush, sister. It is a verse entitled "The Good Morrow".

> *'I wonder by my troth, what thou, and I*
> *Did, till we loved? Were we not weaned till then,*
> *But sucked on country pleasures, childishly?*
> *Or snorted we in the seven sleepers' den?*
> *'Twas so; but this, all pleasures fancies be.*
> *If ever any beauty I did see,*
> *Which I desired, and got, 'twas but a dream of thee.*
>
> *And now good morrow to our waking souls,*
> *Which watch not one another out of fear;*
> *For love, all love of other sights controls,*
> *And makes one little room, an everywhere.*
> *Let sea-discoverers to new worlds have gone,*

Let maps to others, worlds on worlds have shown,
Let us possess one world, each hath one, and is one.

My face in thine eye, thine in mine appears,
And true plain hearts do in the faces rest,
Where can we find two better hemispheres
Without sharp north, without declining west?
Whatever dies, was not mixed equally;
If our two loves be one, or, thou and I
Love so alike, that none do slacken, none can die.'

'Pretty words indeed,' snorted my sister, gathering her skirts over her arm, 'but I wonder how many others he has desired and got, and if he loves them still. And whether my lady Straven is amongst their gathering?'

Yet I doubted him no longer, for I knew that the verse rang as true as the purest bells tolling out over London. The words held within them a happy optimism, a fresh sense of hope and mutual cherishing that I had never before detected in his verses. These were words written and dedicated to someone who was truly and deeply loved.

And the thought I valued most of all was that amidst the world we both inhabited of Court manners, cheapened ways and false declarations, he had likened we two unto 'true plain hearts' just as I had done.

I thought of my grandparents, whose true plain hearts had beat together for so long, and I knew that there would be safe land ahead for he and I, no matter what wild dangerous waters stood between us now.

'Ann, Ann,' Mary pressed me, 'think you that all this talk of love will soften the heart of our father? He who married Constance for her inheritance and has even now betrothed our sister Frances, who is but twelve years old, to a man she has never met?'

I stopped my ears at that, for I would not let her spoil my new-found contentment. 'Master Donne has not cast me aside, as you suggest, for the advancement of his career, nor is he amusing himself with my lady Straven, but working all the hours God gives to further his reputation and make himself the worthier in the eyes of our uncle, that he may yet win my father's consent to our eventual union.'

'You dream, my sister, for it is only in the world of dreams that you will find such an outcome. Our father dislikes your lover for a fist of reasons—his lack of present fortune, his religion, his reputation—and if these were not obstacle enough, he finds Master Donne uneasy company, for your beloved poet is too clever by half for the tastes of a country gentleman.'

'And was not your Nick clever also?'

'Aye, but he was rich, or so my father thought, and of extreme good family. Besides, my father is disappointed in Nick, and would rather he had the staunch virtues of Thomas, Margaret's worthy husband, or poor Sir John Mill, Bett's dullard squire, who knows not his Chaucer from his chamberpot. And one thing yet which you seem to understand not.'

'What is that?'

'Our father's pride. He sees it as his right to choose your husband for himself, for such is a father's power to do.'

I tucked the verses into my gown, where I could keep them fast. No matter that Mary cavilled and cautioned me, my true plain heart was singing like a bird.

Not many days after my mind was distracted from Master Donne, not from lack of faith but by my concern for Mary. Until this moment she had been well and busy yet now her peach-like bloom faded and she took sick and feverish.

With Bett's loss brought fresh to my mind by grief for my aunt, I put Mary tenderly to bed or made her rest by the fireside. After two careful weeks of guarding her like the most tender flower she began to rally and I could breathe once more.

One benefit was that, with worries of her own, Mary's eagle eye was no longer upon me and I took good advantage of it to call Wat and send a message through him to Master Donne.

I marvelled, watching Wat in all his finery walk up Mary's path; he seemed so graceful and self-assured, a gentleman in miniature, that it was hard to imagine his life at the tanner's.

'Have you heard, mistress?' he greeted me. 'About the uproar at York House? I am glad my master and I live there no longer.'

'Why, Wat, is something there amiss?'

'It is the Lord Keeper, mistress. He is preparing to marry again, to the Countess of Derby, widow of some great earl. And all the servants fear for their positions, for Lady Alice brings forty of her own.'

I shook my head in disbelief, a great pain clouding my head at such a dreadful revelation. 'Wat, your news cannot be true! It is but a few months since my beloved aunt was laid to rest! And the Lord Keeper's grief was deeper than a bottomless well.'

Wat shrugged sadly. 'Aye. Well he has managed to fill it up again. They are to be wed quietly at York House come November next, yet the lady seems already to be in command of the household.'

I was so angered with my uncle that I yearned to share it with one who would understand. My sister Mary would shrug in that worldly way of hers, tell me not to play the country innocent, and how it proved, if aught did, that marriage was a practical arrangement.

'Wat,' I whispered, looking behind me that none could overhear. 'Tell your master I would speak with him. I will come tomorrow, to his new lodgings. Near to the Savoy Hospital said you?'

Wat looked dubious. He might have been a street boy but he had learned fast that well-born ladies did not visit single gentlemen alone in their lodgings.

'Yet, mistress, think you . . . ?'

'The direction, Wat,' I pressed him.

'He lodges with a Master Haines.'

'I will be there at five of the clock.'

Wat took himself unhappily away.

After he had left I stared out over Mary's garden with its statues of nymphs, their arms outstretched towards some hidden lover, and I envied them. Yet their Arcadia had never existed beyond the minds of the sculptors who created them. To visit Master Donne was to risk much, perhaps all. I might care naught for the world's opinion, yet my family of necessity cared greatly. To them my reputation was every-thing. And yet, I had risked it for my sister, perhaps unwisely; surely I deserved to take the risk when my own happiness might be lost at the turn of fortune's dice?

Dared I go? What if I were seen? And yet this loneliness I felt, this sense of wandering sadly in the desert overwhelmed me. There was but one other I had met in my short life who understood it, to whose soul I felt my own joined by an invisible thread.

On the morrow I dressed discreetly, covering my face with a vizor, and told Mary's groom that I went to find a soothing herbal remedy that would hasten his mistress's recovery. The man seemed relieved that this time he had not to accompany me. In any other house than that my sojourning out alone would be remarked on, yet Mary's household was as lax as she was.

By my bad luck there were no empty wherries to be found and I needs must share with a stranger, and still pay double since we rowed against the tide.

Yet at least he was not a talkative stranger and made no mention of the curious sight of a gentlewoman alone, and even harrumphed at each new line of talk the wherryman attempted to beguile us with.

I found the lodging easily enough and tapped gently on his door. Before even I had time to push it open, his arms enfolded me, and I melted into them, my heart locked against his.

'Ann, my Ann, how I have yearned for your sweet presence all these days.'

'And I yours. Yet I came to find if it is indeed true that the Lord Keeper consoles himself with thoughts of a new wife. I cannot believe that he plans to wed again?'

At that he smiled sadly. 'It is true enough. And yet the lady, though beauteous and noble, is most headstrong and wilful, used entirely to her own way, so that I fear for his future peace.'

'Then may it serve him right!' I could not gainsay the strength of my passion. 'Indeed I would my aunt's soul should come and haunt him for I am much mistaken in my uncle's character! I saw how deep seemed his grief, and now he fills his bed once more.'

'More like his table than his bed. Men like their comforts and great men most of all.'

'Are men indeed so fickle? I thought that was woman's fault? Did you not swear in your verse that "Nowhere lives a woman true and fair"?'

He laughed at that. 'That was before I met you.'

He took my hand, serious again. 'I see that you are truly hurt by this news of the Lord Keeper's.'

'He loved my aunt true, I am sure of it, and nursed her in her extremity. Yet it seems as if that counted for naught. He has buried her and will wed again but a short time later.'

'It is the way of the world.'

'Just as it is the way of the world that I must wed the man my father chooses for me whether I would or not?'

He flinched as if I had struck him, for he knew the truth of my words.

'Say not that, Ann.'

A knock on the door silenced us. It was Master Haines, his landlord, delivering a message.

'I must leave,' he sighed. 'I am bidden to attend my lord at the Privy Council, late though it is.'

I stood up and readied myself for my return.

'You have an air of mystery with your vizor on,' he teased me. 'Like some great courtesan on an assignation.'

I placed my finger on his lips. 'Enough. I must also be gone. Wait you here awhile, until I am at the street's end.'

'Such mystery and subterfuge,' he smiled.

'I wish they were not needful.'

And saying that, I took myself quietly from his chambers and out into the darkened street. From the shadow a link boy, no more than eight years old, offered me a light to guide me and I accepted. He led me down the dark and winding alleys from the old hospital of the Savoy, now rented out as accommodation to the gentry, past the bright doorways of taverns and alehouses, and the dingy rat-infested tenements of the poor, towards the lights of the thoroughfare beyond. Once in the Strand, I felt my pounding heart slow down with the familiar sight of shops and buildings.

'Where to now, mistress?' asked the link boy, holding up his lantern to my face.

'The river, if you please.'

'Ann?' a voice, stiff with anger and shock enquired behind me. 'Is that truly you, Ann?'

My whole being froze as if I had heard the judgement of God Almighty on all my sins.

It was my father, Sir George More, standing not two feet beyond the light of the link boy's lantern.

Chapter 16

MY FIRST THOUGHT, since a vizor covered my face, was to wonder if I could dissemble and pretend he had mistook me for some other lady?

Yet this was my father, my own flesh and blood, and he would be bound to know me. So obvious a lie might serve to turn a misdemeanour into a hanging case.

Instead I assayed a smaller dishonesty. 'Father, what do you do here?'

'How dare you question me thus?' His face was white with fury. 'Why in God's name are you abroad and with not even a groom to escort you? Have you lost your senses entirely?'

I searched desperately for what lie to tell him. 'There were no grooms to spare nor any servingmen. I would never have ventured out alone were it not so needful. Knew you that Mary has been taken bad?' This was true yet guilt assailed me in making more of it than was truly justified. 'I have hunted high and low this day for the remedy that might help her and the babe.' I prayed Mary would forgive me for a lie that could too easily become a truth.

'Two miles from her home, by cover of darkness?' If he had travelled here by coach I think he would have hit me and bundled me into it. 'God's thorns, is there no apothecary in Mile End that could serve?' His small eyes fixed on mine like unto the beam of a lighthouse, yet far more threatening. 'And what of Mary's husband? Why could he not find this remedy? Gaming again? Or busy at some playhouse?'

Behind us a man began to step out of the shadows and I prayed with all my being it would not be he.

As my father turned to look at him, the figure disappeared into the night, the boy's lantern catching only a froth of lace and the shape of a black hat, common enough garb in London.

Yet I knew his identity at once and quaked in fear. For I guessed how deep would be my father's fury had he recognized the stranger.

My father stood a moment, looking after him, while I held my breath. Had he, after all, known the man for Master Donne?

At last he spoke. 'My own groom will accompany you back to Mile End while I consider a fitting punishment for this behaviour.'

In my relief I curtsied. He had not guessed my secret.

'Thank you, Father. Indeed I will not venture abroad again unaccompanied.'

He nodded curtly as I began to hasten away, eager for the London night with all its sinners and vagabonds, since I was but another, to swallow me up.

'Daughter?'

'Yes, Father?'

The blow fell like the thud of the axe.

'You are grown too wilful and careless of your maiden state and your sister is too lax to guard you. Tomorrow you go home to Loseley. I will send a message to my father tonight.'

'But Mary? The babe? Her confinement is but three weeks off . . .'

'Then she will suffer it without you.' I had rarely heard such bitter harshness in his words before.

'Father, I beg. Remember Bett . . .'

'Mary has her sister Margaret not five miles hence. If needs be your grandmother can ride up to aid her.'

I knew I should say no more, that of all things my father hated to be brooked in his instructions, and yet I needed to know with my whole soul what he had seen.

'Why, Father? Why do you banish me to Loseley?'

His slight body stiffened. 'It is not seemly for you to wander the streets of London like some common drab who struts her wares.'

I pulled in my breath sharply at the cruelty of his words.

'Go now, Ann. Unless you would I kept you under lock and key.'

This time as I climbed aboard a boat for Mile End the steady beat of the wherryman's oars tolled out only the sentence of my banishment.

'Ann! Ann, thank God Almighty!' My sister Mary fell upon me before even I turned the lock. 'Where have you been for so many hours? I have told Nick he may not go to the Rose Theatre but must comb the streets for you!'

In my despair I had not even thought what reason I might give her for my disappearance. Yet I had not the heart to lie. 'I met our father. I told him I looked for a remedy for your fever.'

'Where is it, then?' She raised a mocking eyebrow, knowing I had no such thing. 'I take it our father did not believe you. Did he see who you met?'

I shook my head, too tired and heartsore to deny it.

'All's well then?'

'If banishment to Loseley is well. I may even be kept from your confinement.'

At that, she pulled my head onto her now ample chest, stroked the springy curls of my chestnut hair. 'Ann, sweet sister, heed. I know this punishment breaks your heart. I too felt the promptings of illicit love, and it was a stronger, headier draught than any I had ever tasted.'

'For whom?' I asked, for I had forgotten there had been any other for my sister before Nick. 'The gentleman to whom you wrote the letter?'

She nodded. 'Ann, I know your heart breaks, but mayhap it is because the truth is painful. You know in your true soul that Master Donne is not for you, that our father would never accept him as a suitor for your hand. Go home. Forget your dangerous poet and think of Richard Manners. He is a handsome man, of reasonable wealth and more to come when his father dies. You will live in easeful luxury and have a row of tow-haired children whom you will love and they love you in return, far more than any man will.'

'And what of you, Mary? Took you your own counsel? Or did you follow your own heart?'

Mary heaved a sigh. And I had to admit there was a whole ocean of regret in it. 'Yet did I the right thing? Where is he now, but out cocking and at plays again while the servants lack their pay?' Her spirited face at once looked careworn. 'I am no great example, sister, of the road to happiness.'

'Oh, Mary.' A sob escaped me, even though I wished with all my heart to be brave. 'I will miss your childbed.'

She stroked my face. 'Think of your own, Ann. Marry Richard Manners and you could be cradling your own babe a year hence.'

She smiled, thinking she was winning me over to this thought. Yet Mary knew not my deepest secret: that I had given my heart to one who had no manor of his own, nor titled father, nor any expectations but of his own wit or pen.

Next morning I wrote a message to Master Donne and bribed my sister's groom to take it to him, then packed up my belongings and mounted the horse my father had already sent from Loseley.

Unlike my arrival in London, full of anticipation and delight, this was a journey of despair, every hoofbeat reminding me of all I left behind me.

I had not even had the chance to say farewell, for my sister watched me now. Whereas before she had been almost kind to me, she was now of my father's party.

My only consolation was the joy on the face of the child Hope when I rode up the long avenue towards Loseley. She sat atop a pillar like to a small stone angel, and waved both arms to me, before jumping a full five feet to the ground and running towards my mount.

I leaned down and pulled her up onto the saddle where we rode the last few yards together. Her brother Stephen was in the yard, clutching one of my grandmother's chickens.

'She broke her leg escaping from a fox that killed all the others. I made this splint for her,' he told me proudly. He showed me the small length of wood attached to the chicken's leg. I had to hide my smile at so comical a sight. 'Now she can run if the fox returns.'

I wondered how he had persuaded my grandmother of such a course when, if I knew that practical lady, she would have sentenced the chicken straight to the pot.

Not two minutes later my grandmother herself appeared, yet I did not ask her, for her face was sterner than I had ever seen it.

'Well, Ann,' she shooed the children off to their appointed tasks, 'I hear you are in deep disgrace. Trolling the streets at night, alone and

some weeks and I was able to enjoy the summer. Except that there was still not one word to me from Master Donne.

I reminded myself of all the reasons why this might be: his industry, the difficulty of getting word to me, even his fears that it would anger my father to the detriment of our future chances. Yet I still yearned and looked up each time a messenger came to the great oak door.

One glad day in August a messenger did indeed come, to tell us that Mary's babe had been born and that they both did well. I looked up hopefully at that but my hopes were soon dashed. My father would not relent an inch: there were to be no visits to my sister, babe or no babe.

So Frances and I had to content ourselves with sewing tiny night-dresses. Of course Frances' was far superior to my own, but—oh!—the love I poured into every stitch!

At last the day came when Master Manners was due to come for his official visit. I tried to act as if it was of no importance, yet even the children knew and hung around the stableyard when his grand coach drew up one late September morning.

At my father's insistence I was dressed all in white like some sacrificial virgin. He himself was not yet here since he had been delayed by some business in London.

'Master Manners.' I dropped him a curtsey, looking down modestly.

Yet there was something about the expression in his eyes today that forced me to glance up. It was the look of one who has hunted long and hard and whose quarry is finally in his sights.

'Good morning, Mistress More. I have looked forward for many months to the moment when our fathers might finally come to an agreement.' He kissed my hand.

Behind us Hope giggled with one of the maids.

Master Manners had dressed in all his finery. He was a handsome man, I had to admit, with his thick brown hair and blue eyes like the haze on some distant hill, and his fresh complexion. For one who spent much time in London he had the beam of ruddy health upon him.

My grandparents made great state of him at supper, seating him at my right hand, with my grandmother next to him on the other side. My father had been detained by some important act of Parliament and would not be here until tomorrow.

And still there was no word from Master Donne to comfort me and keep my faith alive. That night, lying in bed, I took out the verses he had sent to me so long ago.

Yet this night they worked not their usual magic.

It had been six months since last I had word from him. How long could I fan the faltering flame of my love? Once again, in the dark throes of midnight, I asked myself if I had indeed been led astray, and had given my heart to a man who valued it not.

I was woken by the usual commotion that attends my father when he arrives. A clamour of grooms, whinnying horses, my father shouting, all the stir of a small man who likes to stand on consequence.

My brain began to hunt feverishly for ways out, as if I were in the maze of some great garden, which I could by ingenuity and resource—like Ariadne using her thread—find my way through, and emerge safe and sound the other side.

I dressed slowly, never having less reason to want to look my best, dragging a comb through my unruly hair, wishing myself in any corner of God's earth, save here.

I had barely finished when Frances, happy as a cork bobbing on a turquoise sea, informed me that my father required my presence in the withdrawing room.

I had ever found this a forbidding room, in thrall to its great white chimney piece carved from one single piece of chalk, its columns, its huge figures and ugly evil faces peeping out from it to ward off bad spirits. It was never more daunting than it was today.

My father and Master Manners stood in front of a huge fire, whose logs spat and hissed.

I was about to enter when I saw that they were quarrelling loudly about some matter, and instinct told me to stop on the threshold to listen.

'I heard talk in London which troubled me greatly,' Master Manners asserted.

'What talk is that?'

'About your daughter and the Lord Keeper's Secretary.'

I stopped short and hung back, my stomach lurching.

'What idle gossip is this? I am surprised, Master Manners, that you listen to such empty chatter.'

'Except that it was from a certain gentleman, an intimate of the secretary's, and he had it direct from Master Donne.'

At that my throat tightened over, and I ground my nails into my palms so hard I near drew blood.

'And what is this gossip you speak of?'

'That he and your daughter have been intimate, and on one more than one occasion.'

My father held fast to the back of a chair as if he might fall else. 'God's wounds, man, it is a wicked lie!'

'Know you also what the wags are whispering about her in the Inns of Court?'

I felt as if I had wandered with no warning into some strange and brutal nightmare.

'That where one has broke the ice,' accused Master Manners, 'others may have followed.'

I longed to rush in and strike him for his foul imputation. In agony I waited for my father to defend me, and insist that he leave our house forthwith.

Yet my father did not do so. Instead, without a word in my defence, he returned to the negotiation.

'In the light of this unfortunate disclosure I will increase her portion. You may tell your father he may have the five hundred pounds so dear to his heart. On one condition. The betrothal must happen soon. My daughter is impetuous and until this contract is agreed, God Almighty knows what she might do.'

I hesitated, tempted to run away and throw myself upon the cold ground to weep. For there was a terrible truth that shone through the stain blackening my good name.

Master Manners had heard of our liaison and the man who told him had had it direct from Master Donne! Had he indeed implied in some boastful manner that I had given him my maidenhead?

And yet, how feeble was I to believe this slur? Had I not offered it to him myself and he refused me, on grounds of my innocence? Why, then, would he gossip to others of my unchastity?

'Father,' I stepped out of the shadows, startling both the speakers into silence, 'why defend you not your daughter's honour? Does not the Bible say virtuous women have a price above rubies? And yet instead of protesting my virtue you bargain with Master Manners, putting up the price for my alleged incontinence!'

My father mumbled some half-cooked words of apology.

'Take heed, Father. Think you so little of me? I have been intimate with no man. My maidenhead is as pure and intact as the day I was born.'

I could hardly add that I had offered it myself to Master Donne and that he, out of honour, had rejected it.

And yet, though I would never admit it, my righteous anger was built on shaky ground. For how knew Master Manners of our involvement at all, unless Master Donne had indeed spoken of it to another? Could it be that I was deadly wrong in my assessment of his character and he had duped me after all, as he had others before me, into surrendering him my heart and, worse still, my soul, simply to fan the flames of his vanity?

'Ann,' my father rallied, 'this matter is between Master Manners and myself and concerns you not.'

'Concerns me not?' I could hardly credit my ears. 'When you talk of my dishonour and how it raises the price you must pay him for my portion?'

'Come, Master Manners,' my father told him, man to man, 'we will continue our discussion in my father's library.'

They stayed within for two more hours, sending only for refreshment to keep up the strength of their negotiation, and with each hour that passed another sliver of my heart snapped off like an icicle in winter.

If only I had word, a scribbled note, even a message that I was truly loved, I could keep up my resistance. Yet there was nothing. Nothing save the thought, which I could not quite exclude nor stamp out, that Master Donne had indeed boasted of our liaison, turning it by reverse alchemy from the pure gold of love into the cheap dross of bawdy tavern talk.

Frances, forgetting her pious manners, got wind that more than the usual marriage discussions were taking place. She stopped the servant and took in the tray of cakes and ale herself.

'Your honour is worth an extra fifty pounds, it seems,' she disclosed, laying down the empty tray, 'plus some good arable land and, you will laugh at this, a dozen rams. It seems your lord-to-be sees himself a sheep farmer.'

Noticing how this hurt me sorely, she relented. 'Come, Ann, Richard Manners is a goodly-looking man. Not like Bett's great oaf, or Margaret's solid Thomas, and maybe better than my John Oglander whom as yet I have not even met, though my father says we are going to visit him presently. We are but women. We must be obedient and respect our father's choice.'

'Mary did not do so. Nick was of her own choosing.'

'And much success he has garnered. I have heard Father often complain to Grandfather that Nick is as much use as a barren womb to a king's consort.'

Behind us the door began to open and we jumped up. My father and Master Manners came out, nodding and shaking hands. Now all it seemed for me to be truly betrothed was his father's final agreement of the new terms. And since these were greatly more favourable due to my sullied character, he would hardly refuse.

Tonight I would pray to God for that old gentleman, his father, to continue in his prevarication, since it was all that came between myself and a loveless union.

And what would his family make of me, a young woman whose good name had to be bargained over? I could picture his mother, proud and disdainful, treating me like some servant girl who had lost her reputation and was kept only on sufferance until she committed some small sin and could be turned out onto the streets.

'Master Manners leaves now, Ann,' my father commanded, 'show him out to the stables.'

There were servants and grooms aplenty to do this task, so I knew my father wanted a sign that I would be a dutiful daughter at last.

Yet I could not talk to him. I could not smile and ease the passage of this future marriage. When we reached the stables I curtsied and began to take my leave.

But now he had his agreement, Master Manners was as cheerful as a chirping robin.

'Come, Mistress Ann,' he said, smiling the while, all sign of the sneering accuser gone, 'let us be friends, since we will be more than that before long. Think on this, if your Master Donne truly loved or respected you, would he tell others of that friendship, knowing how much damage it might do to your good name?'

I tried to turn away at that, so close was it to my own imaginings.

'I am sorry for my harsh words.' There was humility in his voice I had not looked for. 'I am a jealous man, who guards most preciously that which is his own.'

He seemed to think that I should praise him for his covetous nature and be flattered that he was jealous of my honour.

He took my hand and raised it to his lips.

'Yet I am not yours, Master Manners. And were I your wife, I would not be your possession. Souls belong only to God.'

He laughed bitterly at that. 'And what of bodies, Mistress Ann? To whom do they belong?'

I turned away, my face flaming. There was a hunger in his eyes which made me shrink back.

And then, like a knife that flashes and is put back in its sheath, the look was gone and Master Manners was all friendliness once more.

'Farewell, Mistress Ann, I must now depart to see my father. Yet I believe I will see you very soon.'

I bowed my head, relieved that he left so speedily.

Yet I had not long to dwell on my relief for my father, booted and spurred for his ride back to Baynard's, appeared in the courtyard beside me, his grey eyes forbidding in a face the colour of soured milk.

'See you now what a low, slanderous, sneaking man is Master Donne? He boasts and brandishes your good name about the town as if you were some Cheapside drab willing to give herself to all in exchange for a pint of ale!'

'Father, I . . .'

'Defend him not! Has Master Manners departed? The sooner he talks to that stubborn father of his the better. If Philip Manners hadn't been so diligent in rooting out recusants, he'd still be a yeoman tilling his turnips, yet he behaves as if he were doing *us* the favour.' He called for his horse. Despite his tiny stature, my father ever insisted on a mount fit for a king, which made him look not impressive, as he intended, but like to a toy soldier on the back of a giant steed.

'Goodbye, Father.'

My father simply spurred on his horse. 'Tell your sister we go to the

Isle of Wight to meet with her John Oglander. She should make herself ready three days hence. As should you. I wish you may see how a dutiful daughter behaves at the celebration of her betrothal.' He looked at me narrowly. 'Master Manners comes also. It is time you learned to treat him as your future husband.'

That night I hid my tears in my pillow. The twenty-five miles between here and London had never seemed so deep and desolate a divide.

Chapter 17

IT WAS MORE than forty miles from Loseley to Portsmouth from whence we sailed to the Isle of Wight and in autumn, as now, the journey was longer. With the days so brief we needs must break our journey and stay somewhere on the road. My grandfather said this should be at the great house of Cowdray with his friends the Montagues. Yet my father would have none of it.

Last time he did so, old lady Montague had him bring her a whey of cheese, which stank out the coach, and when he was seated next to her at supper she lectured him for an hour or more on the licentiousness of the Court then shocked him with tales of her failing health and how she had recently suffered 'a sore and extraordinary evacuation both downward and upward', which put him off his capon with gooseberry sauce.

'I would ride through the night or pay a dozen sovereigns not to spend the night under that old witch's roof,' was his final word.

So that night we stayed at the inn in Midhurst, where my father said we would be well fed, and not have to pay dearly for our accommodation in cheese and chatter.

To my surprise, Master Manners did not once mention the slurs against my character and instead did all he could to make himself agreeable to me, forever offering me cushions and asking if I was warm enough in the coach or would like a fur cloak to cover my feet. At each stop he handed me out and ran in to make sure I was first at the fireside. Frances smiled and said she hoped her John would be half as attentive.

Yet I was still holding out and keeping my faith so I listened to his sallies but said little. He took this silence with surprising patience yet that afternoon, while I gazed out of the window, of a sudden he grabbed my hand and swore, 'God's teeth, madam, how can you think of Master Donne when all London knows he sports with the Countess of Straven? Is that an honest valuation of your love?'

When I answered not, he shrugged and said no more.

Yet my heart felt as if it had been pierced by a poisoned arrow.

At four of the afternoon we arrived at Portsmouth, which was a town of narrow streets all at right angles to the High Street, its houses but two storeys high, with warehouses right amidst the dwellings, and full of forts and soldiers. Not so many years ago, my father told us, there was a great fear here of invasion by the Spanish Armada. We had been told it was a pleasant place, though it fared better in war than in peace.

'Certainly it has many alehouses and wine taverns,' my father said, disapproval writ across his face, for he often spoke in Parliament against the proliferation of such places, especially for the poor. 'I hope they are respectably managed or I will raise the matter with the High Steward.'

While we looked on he put his nose inside a noisome tavern where sailors mixed with dubious-looking women. Even before he spoke the landlord recognized the arrival of authority. 'Please, your honour,' insisted the man, bowing low, 'I have paid one shilling and six pence to the Clerk of the Peace and another shilling to the Justice's Clerk for my licence. I run a decent house with no soldiers nor recusants allowed.'

Master Manners laughed. 'You wonder who the fellow's custom is, then. There must be recusants aplenty. My father says that Portsmouth has ever been the chief escape route for priests and for Papists.'

'Indeed? And what has your father to say about my new offer on the settlement for my daughter, more to the point?'

'He considers your new offer now.' He looked across to me in apology. 'I would that he committed himself as much as you have, sir. I have good reason to wish it, do I not?'

'Yes. I suppose you do.' Then he turned to me. 'By all that's sacred, Ann, look happier! Here is a young man who wishes to marry you when many would turn away!'

'Must I thank him then,' I flashed angrily, 'for his great kindness to me?'

'Be careful, Ann, or Master Manners will think you need the scold's bridle when you are wed.' He wrapped his cloak round him, and to the great relief of the anxious alehouse keeper, headed for the docks. 'I go to see what time our boat will be ready for the island crossing. Frances, come with me.'

We walked back through the muddy streets towards our coach. Master Manners opened the door with a flourish and handed me in. 'Your father is wrong, Mistress Ann. I would never do such a thing. Indeed it was your lively mind that drew me to you. If you would trust me, we could share much together of love and contentment.' His face became serious. 'I would that you had not overheard my negotiation with your father or the crude words I used the other day. Truth to tell, I was angry on your behalf, that he who professed to care for you would so brutally betray your good name and that even now he frolics in London while you sigh for him here.'

'I sigh for no man,' I riposted angrily.

'I wish you would sigh for me.' Before I knew what he intended he had slipped down onto one knee inside the coach, taken my foot in his hand and kissed it.

My astonishment was so great I knew not what to do.

'You could trample on my heart with these small feet,' he mused.

'I have no desire to trample on hearts. Consider the mess it would entail.'

To my surprise he began to laugh and I found my lips curving in unison.

'There,' he coaxed, 'I almost teased a smile from you.'

It was early evening when we took to sea and the Solent so choppy that I felt not at all well and yearned to arrive again on dry land. Frances, of course, found her sea legs at once.

The short journey was drawing towards its close and we all stood ready to disembark. A sudden squall appeared from out at sea, hitting us sideways, and to my great terror I loosed my grip and began to be swept across the deck until a firm hand grabbed my arm and steadied me.

'Thank you, Master Manners,' I breathed, my teeth chattering.

'Here, have my cloak. I would not wish to sacrifice you to the sea.'

His blue eyes widened. 'Think of all the pleasures we would miss if you became Neptune's bride.'

I flushed at the implication of his words and stared shorewards.

My sister's future husband, Sir John, awaited us on the cold quayside when we finally negotiated the harbour mouth. I have rarely been more grateful to see dry land. He stood, waving and jumping so he almost dropped the nosegay of bright blooms he carried in his hand. He was not a handsome man, yet he had so much exuberance he put me in mind of a setter dog my grandfather once owned, who could never be trained, and yet whom, despite his stern warnings in public, my grandfather secretly loved. Had Sir John Oglander a tail he would now be wagging it.

Sir John was of middle height, aged about twenty, with what looked a tendency to plumpness, but his face was so eager and welcoming it took all attention away from any other deficiencies he might have.

As he helped us out of the boat his gaze alighted first upon me, a questioning look in his face, as if he wondered if I were his betrothed. Yet the uncertainty lasted no more than a moment for Frances, her piety forgotten, pushed past me demanding, 'Are you Sir John? I am your wife-to-be, Frances.'

He bowed, looking somewhat taken aback by her youthfulness, though surely he must have known her age, yet he covered it by handing her the flowers. 'Welcome to the Isle of Wight. I hope you will find it a veritable paradise, as I do.'

Frances simpered at that. 'Anywhere containing you, Sir John, would be a veritable paradise.'

Master Manners exchanged a mocking smile with me at these extravagant words, and I laughed behind my fan, deciding that the couple would be well matched.

And so it seemed, though Sir John adopted the manner with my sister more of the jovial uncle than the intended husband, which brought out Frances' best side.

'My house at Nunwell is not too long a ride from here.' He summoned the horses his grooms were holding. 'I would have brought the coach but the roads are rutted and full of mud.'

I was grateful for the chance to ride, for I had not been on horseback for a while and loved the freedom of it. As I rode my coif slipped back and I felt the wind whipping at my hair.

'So,' Master Manners came to ride alongside me, 'what think you of your sister's betrothed?'

'He seems a kind man. I think they will be content together—unless he lets Frances get the better of him.'

'And you, Mistress Ann, what do you look for in a husband?'

The question threw me into confusion. Master Manners's eyes were upon me, questioning and assessing, yet teasingly so.

'Kindness. Respect. A sense perhaps of adventure.'

'You ask much. And what would you give him. Obedience? Deferring to him in all things?' He laughed at that, but gently. 'I think the man for you must be one who relishes the chase.'

Before I had the time or wit to answer he jumped a wall and galloped off, hallooing the while. And what must I do, being one that acts before they think, but jump the wall after him and race up the hill until we halted on the summit and looked down upon the others.

And then his mount was alongside mine, so close that I could smell its sweat. 'There are other adventures in life besides upon a horse,' he said softly and spurred his horse on to join the others.

A few miles outside the village of Nunwell we spied Sir John's ancestral home, a pleasant brick house of three storeys built round a central buttress with a wing stretching out each side. Its long windows had a grace and elegance I warmed to immediately. Indeed, much though I loved Loseley for its stern grey beauty, Nunwell had a welcoming look to it as if it might stretch out its wings and embrace you. It was of a manageable size also.

For a fleeting moment I envied my little sister her amiable husband and her cosy house, and even more the straightforwardness of her situation when my own was so difficult and byzantine.

While Sir John showed the others proudly round his grounds, I felt the need of air again to calm my alarm, and stepped beyond the garden from where there was a fair view across the Solent.

'My father's house is thrice the size of this,' murmured a voice at my elbow and I found Master Manners had followed me out. 'He is a great age already and will not long grace this earth.'

'Master Manners,' I chided gently, 'you would not wish your father dead before his time?'

'And there is a great park around it, not piddling gardens such as these.'

'I like the gardens here. They are on a human scale, and could be tended without too much care and effort.'

'If you wish for piddling gardens, Mistress More,' Master Manners bowed extravagantly, 'then piddling gardens you shall have.'

'You are very persuasive, sir.'

'Am I?' He raised my hand suddenly to his lips. 'Indeed I hope so.'

Voices interrupted us. It was our host and his betrothed approaching together with my father, who smiled upon them both as if in appreciation of a bargain well struck. 'I intend to give you twenty pounds a year, my dear, for your apparel and all your necessaries,' Sir John explained to my entranced sister. 'I am not a rich man, and yet I keep a better table than any other on the island. You shall have salmon and musk-melon and any other things that delight your heart.' He turned to Master Manners. 'Like you London, sir? For myself I hate it. Nothing but dice and whores—pardoning your presence, mistresses—and they have brought many a man to beggary.'

'Have they indeed?' Master Manners answered with pretended seriousness. 'I try to spend my time on learning and religion.'

'Do you, sir? Then God has smiled on you. If they are ever to go to London, young men need a vocation, some modest calling, think you not? Or they reckon themselves too gentle and high for honest work.'

'I cannot say that honest work has much appealed to me.'

'That is because you are a gentleman, sir. My point entirely.'

'Do you not want our sons to be gentlemen?' Frances enquired, scandalized.

'Certainly. Yet gentlemen who have a profession.'

'Is that not a contradiction in terms?' asked Master Manners.

'I agree with Sir John,' seconded my father. 'Too many young men spend their inheritance trying to win favour with friends.'

'Ten pounds will do more for you than most men's love, I always say,' Sir John pronounced just as supper was announced.

'I think your father, Sir George, has met a man after his own stamp,' confided Master Manners as he led me to the parlour chamber.

The meal we were served was an excellent one of pigeon followed by swine's flesh and roast mutton, finished with a cheese from Sir John's own cows. He then took us on a tour inside his house, pointing out to my great amusement the very bed they would sleep in—not to mention the excellency of its feather mattress—and assuring my sister she would have her own gentlewoman to meet her every need. Yet I liked him much.

'You are fortunate indeed, Frances,' I whispered to her later. 'Sir John is a good man, I believe.'

'I know,' Frances replied, glowing with glee. 'I am going to be a happy woman.' She smiled at me angelically. 'Above all in that feather bed!'

'Frances!'

'Well, it is my betrothal we celebrate. I do know what happens in the marriage bed, sister. Remember Bett and her Sir John?'

We both held each other a moment at that, remembering how soon it was afterwards that Bett had left this world. 'Though I think my Sir John will prove a better bargain than hers did. You know, Ann . . .' she put her arm round my waist, 'you could have as happy a home and hearth as I will.'

'With Master Manners, you mean?'

'Who else could give you what he offers, *and* make your family happy? Ponder on it, Ann.'

'Have you been enlisted by our father in this cause?'

'No, sister,' she replied, all seriousness and concern, 'it is because I wish you to share the happy prospects I look forward to. Besides, you cannot truly consider going against our father's will. Such a thing is not possible. Even bold and fearless Mary did not do so.'

We were called outside at that. Sir John wished to show Frances his henhouse before inviting us to sit down to a game of Glecko.

By the time we left three days later I could picture the years of great content unfolding for Sir John and my lady Frances and the many children who would no doubt fill up this happy home. She would be the best housewife a husband could dream of, and he an amiable, loving husband, who would chide her continually to make small economies, then spoil it all by purchasing some great gift for her of jewels or silver whenever he had to go away.

I sighed as I packed up my bag, and gave Sir John a great kiss that took him by surprise as we stood outside in the chill of the morning waiting to leave.

'I hate this damned weather,' complained my father. 'Already I have the flux and fear I shall suffer it worse on our way back to Lose-ley.'

Despite the cold and wet the return crossing was far pleasanter, the sea being as calm and grey as a stagnant pond. Even so I greeted the sight of dry land with relief.

Portsmouth town was even fuller with soldiers than when we passed through on our way out. 'The townspeople complain roundly about being billeted with them,' my father admitted. 'And in time of war it is far worse.'

I thought suddenly of the expeditions to Cadiz and the Islands, when Master Donne had been a soldier, and how he had written so vividly in his verse of all the smart young gentlemen, dressed in their gold lace and feathers, signing up as voluntaries to protect their Queen and make their fortunes, only to find that war was nasty and brutal before returning, shocked and impoverished, their lace torn, their feathers drooping and deep in debt.

'What find you in all this uncouth soldiery to make you smile?' asked Master Manners.

'I had not known that I did so.'

He raised his brows, a look of suspicion clouding his handsome features. 'Come, I have promised your father we will visit the apothecary to find him some relief from the flux he suffers. I spied an apothecary's sign behind the town near to St Mary's Chapel.'

'That is kind of you. Yet surely I should be the one to find it.'

'If you think so. I will wait outside. You ought to take a care with all this soldiery abroad.'

The apothecary listened to my request politely and reached behind him towards the shelves lined with jars and urns. To my surprise, instead of opening any of these he broke off a lump of charcoal and selected one of the mortars sitting on his counter. With a brass pestle he ground the charcoal into powder. 'He must take this infusion twice a day. It may taste like the Devil's own concoction but it will answer the problem better than chamomile or peppermint. Even better than chewing ginger, though all these remedies will answer in their way.'

I thanked him.

At the inn my father had taken to his bed and was glad of the charcoal, though suspicious of its newness. Frances, still beaming at her good luck in the marriage prospects, had elected to stay and sit with him, ministering to any needs.

I stowed my cloak in my chamber to find that Master Manners had ordered supper and awaited me in our own private dining room. The food and wine were all laid out invitingly.

'I told the innkeeper we would need no boy to serve us since it seems they are short-handed.'

'That is kind of you,' and yet I wondered why he felt the need to point it out.

Silence fell between us. I refused the wine he proffered yet Master Manners drank it steadily, rarely letting his goblet touch the table, until the ewer emptied and there came a dangerous glitter in his eyes.

Growing concerned at his wild look, I got to my feet and began to bid him good night, saying that I was tired and needed to sleep.

'Aye,' he slurred. 'To lie in bed and think of Master Donne.' Uttering the name seemed like lighting the fuse on a barrel of gunpowder. 'Master Donne again! Always Master Donne!' And suddenly he was upon me as if the barrel had exploded. 'All the time in London you avoided my company,' harshly he forced me back against the wainscoting, 'yet you seemed ready enough for the company of Master Donne!'

I felt his leg pushing between mine and one hand roughly fondle my breast and I wanted to scream out, but his other hand covered my mouth. 'Yet despite all the rumours you claim still to have your maidenhead.' He held me fast, with his hand under my chin pressing roughly against my neck so that I could hardly breathe. 'If that be so, the pleasure of your deflowering belongs to me. For only then can we see if you tell God's honest truth or lie like a Deptford whore.'

As I struggled for my life and honour I felt his breath coming fast, and saw his eyes glazing in cruel anticipation and that he meant to have me there and then, standing up like some cheap doxy. In my fear and panic I looked for some implement to ward him off, but there was none.

I tried to scratch his face yet this made him smile the more as if my very resistance increased his enjoyment in the taking of me. At last I managed to cry out for help.

'What mischief takes place in here?' The innkeeper's voice rang out and I thanked the Almighty as Master Manners slackened his hold.

'We are well, thank you, landlord,' he sneered, beginning to whistle as if he had been simply surprised in a lovers' tryst.

The innkeeper looked suspiciously from Master Manners to myself. 'Need you any assistance, mistress?'

'I would welcome your company to walk with me upstairs to find my father.'

'Indeed. And does the Watch need summoning, think you?'

If I summoned the Watch I knew my father would never forgive me. I knew he cared for me, yet he cared for our family's reputation more. 'No, no, I will find my father. He is but a few steps hence.'

'Too far to come when you might need him,' shrugged the innkeeper. 'You'd best come now and I can take you myself.'

As I made ready to follow him, Master Manners grabbed my arm. 'Time enough yet,' he whispered thickly. 'There will not always be strangers to interrupt us.' He flicked my cheek with his finger as if all that passed between us had been mere playful joshing. 'Especially when we are wed.'

And my blood froze the while.

My sullied reputation might make some men turn away from me; yet with Master Manners it seemed to stoke up his desire for mastery over me the more.

'Ann! Ann!' called out my father querulously. 'Where have you been all these minutes? Come sit with me. Frances falls asleep or fidgets.'

'Father,' I requested urgently, 'can we not ride to Loseley tonight?'

'Foolish girl, we would break our necks in the dark. Besides I have the flux and am weak as a kitten.'

'Then I will sit up in your chair, Father, and make sure you have all that you need for your affliction. Frances can seek her bed.'

Frances shrugged and picked up her Irish stitchwork. 'I would be glad.'

If my father thought it strange to have me wish to stay in his room he said naught about it.

As I sat next to the bed, the cheerful sounds of the inn retreated and the silence of night wrapped me in its cold embrace and I longed with my soul and my blood and my heart for Master Donne and for London.

Chapter 18

THROUGH THE LONG night I asked myself what I must do. Should I tell my father of Richard Manners's treatment of me?

I had thought he would object to my sitting in a chair in his chamber yet he did not. Perhaps there were moments even in his life when he drew comfort from the presence of another.

By dawn I had decided.

Already the nights were growing short so that the darkness came earlier and lasted longer in the morning. Yuletide would soon be upon us again.

I stoked up the fire and pulled my shawl tighter round my shoulders, waiting for him to waken.

It was after nine of the clock when he did so, and time we were on the road. I was grateful that the next night we stayed with friends and not at another inn.

I shook him gently. 'Father, wake up. I have laid your clothes out to warm by the fire.' I sat down on his great bed, hesitating. He seemed even smaller than usual, half hidden in its downy embrace. 'There is something I must say to you, which I have thought about all the long night. After we were left alone last night Master Manners tried to dishonour me.'

'Now, Ann,' my father sat up impatiently, 'what nonsense is this? How could he have done so when you were in a busy inn with so many coming and going?'

I paused at that, knowing what an unlikely tale it sounded. 'I know. I thought myself safe in his company here for the same reason.'

'Why, had you cause to doubt him?'

'There have been moments when he looked strangely at me, and tried to press his attentions on me before.'

'Enough!' His voice was cold and as sharp as a chisel. 'What is this farrago? You are fortunate, Ann, that Master Manners ignores this gossip of you and Master Donne and considers you at all.'

'In exchange for demanding a greater portion!'

'Be silent! If his father agrees to the settlement you will marry Master Manners as immediately as it can be arranged. And for my part tomorrow would not be too soon. You have caused me a great deal of trouble, Ann, with your pert manner and your extravagant ideas of your due. First you will not even take your place at Court. Then you entangle yourself with a man of no fortune and bad reputation. And now you accuse Master Manners of dishonouring you. You have dishonoured yourself. And I will not allow you to bring down the rest of our family. I wish to hear no more of this matter. Go now and ready yourself for the journey. We leave within the hour. Go!'

I turned and ran towards my chamber. In my deepest soul I had known this was how my father would respond.

I listened out for Master Manners's voice before descending and greeting the news with the greatest relief that he had gone ahead on horseback.

We left Frances to chatter for us all on the journey back to Loseley, a challenge she rose to with no encouragement. Sir John was the perfect pattern of a man, not even Adam could come near him, Nunwell House was lovelier than all the Queen's palaces rolled into one, the view from the knot garden rivalled any she had heard of in Italy, and even Sir John's hens outcrowed Chanticleer.

Her chatter filled the great divide between my father and myself. He stared out of the window, avoiding my eye, while I wrapped up in the fur of my cloak, and pushed up ever deeper into the furthest corner of the coach. Even when we were thrown together by the infernal jolting he treated me as if I were some distant stranger, and I used every ounce of my strength to keep back the tears which I would choke on rather than show him.

As the familiar grey outline of Loseley came into view, my sister leaned towards me one last time. 'Tell me, Ann, are you not, in even the smallest portion, jealous?'

'Yes, Frances, indeed I am.'

It was not the answer she had expected, and her smile widened with delight.

Yet I did not add the reason, that she was lucky to want what was within her grasp. An amiable man who loved his land and his animals, and would love her also.

There might be no clashing of cymbals as true souls met, such as I had heard for one brief moment before they were silenced forever. Yet perhaps such things were no more than a painful chimera, a will-o'-the-wisp that leads travellers to their death on fog-filled moors.

Yes, Frances was fortunate indeed.

My admission of envy seemed to cause her inordinate delight.

I had one consolation at least. Mary was coming to stay and would be bringing with her the babe. She might oppose my feelings but at least she knew of their existence, which gave me a comfort of sorts.

Mary's babe, a fine boy, had eyes the colour of tar and a head of black hair as thick as his father's. 'A relief that he has the stamp of the Throckmortons so deep upon him,' I could not resist whispering to Mary, who in return kicked me so hard it bruised my shin.

Margaret had come also and both were bursting with London gossip which they exchanged with me as we laughed together in my bedchamber. How the Lord Keeper's new wife Alice, Countess of Derby, was causing yet more havoc with her wilful ways and had even married her daughter to John, the Lord Keeper's remaining son, apparently without her husband's consent.

I sat up at that, wondering how it could come about that a marriage could thus take place without consent and not be challenged.

And I could not help but wonder how the upheaval affected Master Donne and whether it might engulf him also.

Mary, with the sharpest wit of any of my sisters, read my mind. 'Master Donne has his hands full trying to keep the peace between them and to persuade his employer that the Countess married him not just to have his skills and position on her side in her many lawsuits, but out of affection also.'

'It sounds a weighty task.'

'She has brought forty servants and it is costing him, so he complains, £650 a year to house and pay them all. And of course her servants want to have the mastery over his.'

I was sorry to hear it, thinking of the kindness of Joan and Mercy, and Thomas the steward. I wondered if even Wat had been affected, though no doubt he lived with Master Donne in his lodgings.

'And my lord Essex is still in deep disgrace,' Mary confided, greatly enjoying her role as the purveyor of bad news. 'The Queen did not renew his monopoly of sweet wines and he faces utter ruin.'

Margaret, not one to often gossip, leaned in towards the fire, her voice a whisper as though even here, twenty-five miles from the Court, the Queen's spies would be listening, 'My Thomas says the Earl will foment sedition now he is deprived of his generous income. He wished me to come here that I might be away from London, fearing there might be some great uprising there.'

'Surely Thomas fears unnecessarily?' My thoughts were suddenly for the safety of Master Donne. 'Does the Earl have so great a following?'

'He believes he can call on the support of the trained bands in the city. They think him a hero still, or so he supposes. They are unhappy that the Queen still names no successor. Bad for business, Thomas says, and creates an instability.'

The image of Queen Elizabeth, her wig awry, in that borrowed dress from Lady Mary Howard, so short her stockinged feet stuck out like a scarecrow's, came into my mind. She had seemed an old woman even then.

'Nick says Essex is no threat,' Mary disagreed. 'Except to himself. He will lose his head on Tower Hill if he minds not what he does.'

I shivered at that thought. Would the Queen ever take such action against the man she had loved for so many years, though he was thirty years her junior?

Mary caught something in my face, some sadness or inattention to London gossip. 'And how fare you? Has the handsome Master Manners yet melted your heart?'

At that I could contain myself no longer and I told my sisters how

Master Manners had tried to dishonour me, and that our father would pay no mind to the indignity I had suffered.

Margaret could hardly credit it but Mary, more used to the ways of men, not only believed my word but flared up with anger. 'I will go and see Father now. How dare he tell you to hold your peace? Sees he not that a man who acts so before a marriage will be crueller afterwards? For marriage does not change men, believe me, it gives them licence to act in any way they desire.' She took my hand. 'Come, we will go together.'

We looked for my father all over. My grandfather thought he might be in the library. 'For he has been making use of it often enough. Between ourselves, I think he finds Constance something of a scold and is spending many hours here.'

There was no sign, neither in nor out. Then Mary thought she heard the babe cry and went back up to discover. To my surprise she was nursing him herself. I was about to follow when I noticed a pile of my father's belongings on a table next to the window seat where I had whiled away so many childish hours reading. Mostly these were documents and leases, papers for his work as justice and as sheriff. Yet beneath the undermost book I spied a parchment, sealed and folded over, as letters are. It was addressed to me.

My breath raced and I almost dizzied as I pulled the letter gently out. For I would know that hand anywhere in the world. It was the same that had penned the verses my cousin Francis had stolen for me.

As I tore it open, my pulse pounding like a hammer in my head, I wondered whom my father had bribed not to give me the letter. Were there others I had not received?

At that I looked around the room yet there were no useful hidden drawers or places of easy concealment. Gently, since they were my grandfather's most prized possessions I began to lift the books from the shelves, to search behind.

Yet there was naught there.

Until the last shelf of all. Appropriately, beyond a battered calf skin-bound copy of Ovid's *Amores*, I found a pile of three or four more letters.

And each of them addressed in the same hand.

He had not forgotten me for the Countess of Straven after all.

With quickening breath I hid the letters in the sleeve of my gown and hurried thence up the great oak stairs towards my chamber, where I broke the seal of the first and laid it upon my bed.

My sweetest lady,

It is three months since last we met and your silence chills my heart. I am like the bleak landscape of winter, with no hope of spring until I hear from your own hand that I am not entirely forgot. I have told myself all the reasons that have stayed your hand from picking up a quill and it has brought no more comfort than a condemned prisoner finds who sees his chamber swept and made clean and yet is still in prison. You have all liberty with me, all authority over me, for you are my destiny.

J. Donne

I sank down onto the covers, the joy in my heart like to a wild bird, long caged and at last released to sing its heart out in the lofty trees.

He had not betrayed me. Nor had he used me. His love, passionate yet perplexed, wholehearted yet haunted by my sudden silence, was as deep and profound as my own.

I was indeed his destiny. And he mine.

And now all I could think of was to get some message to him for I knew with utter blinding certainty that I could not now marry Master Manners, no matter what consequences might flow from my refusal.

All this I poured into my letter back to him. A sudden fear beset me that as in his own verse my silence might have made him think that 'nowhere lived a woman true and fair' and he might have sought consolation elsewhere.

Yet in that same moment I knew I wronged him.

And also I saw that a letter was not enough, I must go and see him myself, even though my father still looked at me narrowly after my complaints over Master Manners. I knew my father wanted me married as soon as he could and would be watching me as a buzzard does a shrew.

So, quietly, discreetly, I laid my plans. London was still dangerous and my father would not let me stay with Mary. Nor, with its new mistress, was there a place for me at York House.

Utter darkness began to descend upon me, and then, almost as I succumbed to it, I saw a distant chink of light. I would have to make myself so useful to my father that when next he went to the city he would agree to take me with him.

I would begin my plan that very night. Yet, if he were not to be suspicious of me I must put my cherished letters back where I had found them.

This I did with the greatest misery, wishing with all my heart to keep them close to me, to give me strength.

I would have to carry the contents in my heart.

I raised the last letter to my lips and could not stop the tears falling, smudging his life-giving words.

Afterward, when I had hold of my emotions, I went to look for my father, carrying a posset of spiced ale.

'Here, Father.' I set it down next to him in the library as I used to do with my grandfather. 'It is late and you have been working a long time on that great sheaf of papers.' Indeed, lately he had been spending more time at Loseley, both to escape Constance and to begin the business of relieving my grandfather of duties that he was beginning to find too arduous. It was hard to believe that Grandfather was nearing eighty and still Sheriff of Sussex and Surrey.

'What is this trick, Ann?' My father looked up suspiciously. 'You have never been so careful of my health before?'

'It seemed to me that you looked tired, that is all.'

To my surprise he took hold of my hand. 'Ann, when I seem harsh, it is but for your own good.' His eyes fixed on mine with a rare sympathy. 'You have a keen mind that likes to question, yet man is most content when he follows God's holy ordinance and does what is decreed that he should do.'

I almost replied that it was not God who decreed I must marry Master Manners but himself. Perhaps he thought both were the same.

I kept my eyes meekly downward. 'I have watched this burden of State business grow on you, Father, and would like to use my keen mind to aid you. You seem always to have so much to peruse as commissioner and justice and member of Parliament and yet I know you do not like to trust such affairs to a secretary.' I knew the real reason my father employed no secretary—as the Lord Keeper employed Master Donne and others—was because he wished to avoid the expense, though it were one he could well afford. 'If you thought me apt enough, perhaps I might read your petitions and divide the wheat from the chaff, so that you could devote your time to the issues closest to your heart?'

He said naught, and yet I knew this to be a good thing. If he adopted my suggestion it would have to be as though the idea came not from myself but him.

'Good night, Father.'

And so, over the coming weeks, slowly and surely, I took on the role of my father's secretary and amanuensis. And without seeming to have agreed to the process, my share of his load grew subtly greater.

To be honest, it was a role I relished. It both took my mind away from its burden of misery and proved of more interest than I would have guessed. And soon I vow no lady in the realm, save Her Majesty, and possibly not even she, knew more about the evils of horse stealing, the production of kerseymere, the prosecution of recusants, and—my father's favourite topic—the ungodly expansion of alehouses.

I think my grandmother, ever sharp-eyed, guessed there was another motive behind my sudden dutiful manner, yet did no more than raise an eyebrow and said naught. She had often been the quietest of my family where Master Manners was concerned.

With every day that passed I began to think my plan would work, and that if Master Manners's father had not yet given his agreement by the time my father returned to London, he might yet take me with him.

And then something happened I had never counted on in the joyful expectation of my young life.

I fell ill.

At first my head ached and the joints of my limbs pained me so that I could not stand. My throat raged and I had such a thirst upon me that nothing could quench it.

On the sixth day a rash appeared. My grandmother, with fear in her eyes, called a physician and I heard again those words, like nails banging into my coffin, that all depended on where the lesions spread to.

And I knew then the truth that hid in their eyes.

They feared I had the same dread pestilence that had carried away my beloved aunt.

Chapter 19

I TRIED WITH all my heart to keep it out, yet fear possessed my soul.

Would I die before I even had lived? Or feel my face dissolve in pain and agony as my aunt's had? Or would I survive, to be marked like Queen Elizabeth's devoted lady, with such disfigurement I would forever need a veil?

My grandmother nursed me, telling all that she had lived a good long life and God would choose to do with her as He saw fit.

As I remembered when a like fate befell my aunt, the house beneath me was struck suddenly silent, the servants talking only in hushed tones, and the very horses seeming to have cloth on their hooves.

On the seventh day the lesions spread thickly upon my belly and breasts, yet spared my legs.

By the ninth they had formed into scabs and begun to fall off, though all the while new ones formed.

And then I wept out of joy for I knew that I had escaped my aunt's fate and had been blessed not with smallpox but with the chicken pox.

I was no thing of beauty, scabbed and suppurating, yet I would not die nor have to hide away forever, for which I thanked Almighty God. And in some mysterious way the relief I felt served to harden my resolve.

That night my grandmother ended her lonely vigil at my bedside and the house breathed again.

Dawn had but lightened the sky for a few moments on the morning that followed when I heard a footstep beyond the curtains of my bed. I sat up, thinking my grandmother had come to see if I would take another sip of her brew of chamomile.

'Mistress Ann!' A familiar voice, low and shaking with fear at its own temerity, whispered through the heaviness of the hangings that surrounded my great bed.

I pulled them back, forgetting the ravages of my skin with its still weeping lesions.

'Wat!'

'Mistress Ann, your beauteous face!'

He fell to his knees and buried his own in the stiff worked coverlet.

I laughed at that, a rusty incongruous sound. 'Worry not, Wat. Such beauty as I had will be restored to me. That is, if I do not scratch these damned itching scabs! I am ashamed to say it is naught but chicken pox!'

'Then thank God for it!' Wat regained some of his wonted happy looks. 'My master has been on his knees since he heard the word of your affliction. He wished to come himself but his friend Sir Henry persuaded him that to risk your father's wrath and your good name would hardly help his case. So he sends a message by myself of his deep concern.'

'Are you then of less value to the world than Master Donne?' Now that I knew I was not to die or be disfigured I could afford to tease a little, especially since Wat had become so very much the gentleman.

Wat grinned. 'He did not believe your father would let him enter, while I had an excuse to visit on account of my brother and sister, that was all.'

'You have not asked after them.'

'No. They flourish, I imagine.'

'Made of sterner stuff than I, and can better withstand infection?'

'Mistress Ann,' Wat's happy eyes clouded over, 'I meant no such thing.'

'I tease, Wat. And how is your master?'

'He has suffered much since you left. First no word from you to his letters, and my lady Straven lost no time in talking of your Master Manners and what a handsome substantial man he was, and bound to win your approval and how your betrothal was soon to be announced. Hard on that the news came that you were stricken with the smallpox, like your aunt before you.'

'How did he come to hear of my affliction?'

I was surprised that word should have reached him in London.

'A message came for Master Donne with a serving woman. Prudence, I think was her name.'

I started at that. How would Prudence have known to seek out Master Donne?

My grandmother! In the extremes of her concern she must have sent word to Master Donne, fearing a burial was more like to happen than a bridal.

'I have written a letter to your master and would be grateful if you would give it to him.' I handed Wat the sealed paper.

'It would be a pleasure to see his face light up in these dark days. The Lord Keeper does naught but carp about his new wife and she screams at him, and my master is caught in the middle. It has not been an easy time.' His smile was sweet in its shyness. 'Above all, without you. He often recalls the time you had alone together and the happy meetings that occasioned when you were living at York House.'

This put me in mind of Master Manners and his vile gossip. 'I hope he has been reminiscing of his time with me to none but you.'

'Mistress, he would never do so.' His young frame stiffened with offence. 'He talks to me only because I know and love you also.'

My heart was touched at that.

'Thank you, Wat. And now, take the letter and hide it carefully.'

He nodded and hid the letter inside his doublet next to his heart, looking so young and serious as I imagine Sir Lancelot must once have done when first he encountered Guinevere.

Yet I was no Guinevere, covered as I was in dozens of weeping lesions. What token of my love and faith could I send his master? As I leaned forward a scab fell from a pustule on my face.

Struck by a thought that amused me, I picked it up and wrapped it in a piece of crumpled silk. 'Tell him my grandmother says if he puts it next to his skin it will protect him.'

I smiled at the revulsion on Wat's young face. 'The Turks do it with lesions even of the smallpox, according to my lady grandmother.'

The gown I had worn before I fell ill was hanging on a hook near the bed and next to the gown my girdle on which were tied my fan, gloves and a small pair of scissors. I reached for them and cut a lock from my auburn hair.

'Give him this also. I know his taste for saints and angels and such mysteries. Tell him it is a relic, to remind him of Saint Ann, who by some miracle is not dead as she had feared, but living and filled with a joyous longing to see him.' I laughed then with relief, and delight, and the sheer pleasure of being alive. 'And tell him he may write a verse on the subject of her deliverance. Now, go. Confide to no one you have come to see me but are visiting Stephen and Hope and bring them good wishes from your sister Sarah. Go!'

Wat saluted me, then grinned. 'Knowing Master Donne he is as like to write about the scab as about the lock of hair.'

'Let him write of both! Now that I know I am not to die I shall opt not just for life but for immortality through Master Donne's verses.'

'Dream not of that, mistress.' Wat shrugged. 'My master says his verses will be forgot in five minutes' time.'

I laughed again. 'Tell him to be not so bleak. I am sure they will last for ten.'

As I climbed from my bed and reached for my smock it struck me that I had heard not one word from my suitor, Master Manners, since I had sickened. Like my lady Straven, Master Manners, it seemed, kept a safe distance between himself and all contagion. So much for the vows he would have us say binding us to one another in sickness and in health.

It was a few more days before the last of the lesions disappeared and I felt ready to face the world. The illness, though unpleasant, was as nothing compared to my fears of it, and my escape had rendered me doubly eager to fight for my own happiness. I knew my father was a lost cause and so I approached my grandmother, aware that she had sent a message to Master Donne telling him of my illness. Yet to my great pain she too proved obdurate.

She was supervising the washing and spoke to me gruffly, as if the wash were more important than my trifling concerns for my future.

'The reason I sent word to Master Donne was that I thought you had the smallpox, and he would want to say farewell. I intended not to bring you together in this life but the next.'

'Please, Grandmother,' I dropped my voice to a whisper, 'it is in this life that I wish to be at his side.'

'Nonsense!' She banged the clothes paddle against the barrel of washing. 'He is not for you! Of all the men you could choose to marry he is the one your father dislikes the most! I should never even have sent him a message. I will hear no more of it. Go!'

I caught Prudence's eye and she shrugged in powerless sympathy.

No doubt even Prudence had more say in her choice of husband than I did.

I turned away hopelessly, feeling I had lost my last ally.

I had no choice but to try one last desperate option: persuading my grandfather to change his mind and support me. I knew that, after all Master Donne's hard work in pursuing reforms in Chancery, the Lord Keeper at least might speak up in my cause, since he stood higher in his employer's estimation than ever.

I had seen little enough of my grandfather lately with my illness and being so caught up with helping my father over his claims from the glassmakers, his disputes over enclosures and the pleas for repair to the Queen's highway.

I was about to broach the matter with him in his library when I overheard him talking to my father on a subject that interested me greatly: the secret marriage contracted between Walter Aston and one Mistress Anne Barnes, which had scandalized London not so long ago. At the time I had not been so eager to know it since it had naught to do with me. Yet now I saw its relevance for the real cause of scandal had been that Walter Aston was underage and heir to a vast fortune while Mistress Barnes had nothing. And they had married without his guardian's consent. The fact that his guardian was the Lord Chief Justice of England had made it all the more daring.

Seeing the parallels to our own situation—though my fortune was but a fraction of Walter Aston's—I listened closely to the conversation. And then wished that I had not.

'So what was the outcome for the foolhardy pair?' enquired my father.

'Mistress Barnes was despatched to the Fleet Prison for a twelve-month,' announced my grandfather with the earnest tones of rectitude satisfied. 'And all the witnesses sent to the Clink. The marriage itself was laid aside as void and invalid.'

'Just as it should be.' My father noticed my presence. 'Well, Ann, why are you lurking in the shadows? What want you?'

'You make it sound as if there were never any question the marriage should be laid aside, Father. What if this Mistress Barnes was no fortune hunter but loved her Walter Aston with her whole heart and longed with her whole soul to be his wife and cared not a single groat for his inheritance?'

They both laughed at my innocence before my father answered me testily, 'It would make no odds. His marriage was the concern of his family, not her. Ann, I weary of this matter for I know well the direction of your thought.'

I ought to have contained myself, I knew, and if I were not careful would undo the good work of the last weeks, yet my anger was such that I could silence myself no longer. 'So for the good of the Mores you would marry me to a man of bad character who has tried to violate my innocence, yet all is well if it benefits my family and your dynasty?'.

At that, my father struck me with his hand across my face.

'Silence! It is you who are the violated one, whose sullied reputation cost me dear in this negotiation. And not by him but another! Aye! And maybe others yet. For as Master Manners said, where one has broke the ice . . .'

'George, enough . . .' my grandfather interrupted, holding down my father's arm against him striking again, though he could hurt me no more with violence than with his words. 'She is but two days recovered from the chicken pox.'

'Lucky for her it were not the French pox, for it seems as if she has done enough to deserve it!' The colour in his face was livid red as if he might any moment fall down with a choleric palsy. 'This disobedience has gone on long enough! You will go now to your chamber, and there you will stay without food or sustenance until you cease all this unseemly talk and obey my will.'

My fury at his injustice knew no bounds. For had I not protested my innocence and he chosen not to credit it? 'Why not hide me away on a high mountain?' My voice was as cold and hard as his now, for I would not play a woman's tricks and weep and throw myself upon his fatherly mercy. If he had such. 'Or enclose me in a metal belt to protect me against my own incontinence?'

At that I strode from the room, leaving my grandfather to watch with sadness the strangers my father and I had become over this marriage negotiation.

For my part I was more frightened than I had disclosed. My father was a proud man, proud enough to make me truly suffer. In centuries before he might have walled me up in some small airless coffin-cell, ignoring the sound of my last desperate scratching pleas. Those barbaric times might be past, yet he had power to wound me still.

If I allowed him it.

In the days that followed I found out how good a jailer my father would have made, allowing me naught but sippets of stale bread and small beer.

None were allowed to visit me, neither my grandmother, nor my sister Frances, who was no longer able to share my bed during my rebellion and now slept on a pallet in my grandmother's chamber. Not even Prudence. I was permitted no books and my father informed all the servants to watch out for letters and messages. When I demanded how I should then spend my time, he answered, 'Think about your position. And pray.'

A whole week passed and then another. I began to know how it would be as a prisoner in the Tower, though none yet used the rack upon me.

In the parkland outside I could see the sun shining on the green meadows, hear a lark piping high in the sky, and smell the scents of blossoms and wild roses in the hedgerows. All seemed sent to torture me.

This was, I knew only too well, a battle of wills between us and my father had no doubt as to who would win.

The only way I could see, powerless as I was, to win my release was to show myself stronger than he was. And the only manner in which I could do this was to take no more food.

Yet to do such an act was a terrible sin both of pride and of disobedience, and, carried to its extreme, even of self-murder. Strong though I might be, I quaked at so great a risk of my soul's damnation. And did I, even if I could quiet my conscience, have the courage to carry it through? Did God indeed expect me to behave like Master Chaucer's story of Patient Griselda and take any blows my destined husband chose to inflict? For having had one dread glimpse of his hungry eyes I knew after our marriage I could expect no mercy from Richard Manners.

Even though God may have tested Job to the limit, I could not believe He would ordain such cruel profanity and declare it sanctified by marriage.

In the end I drew strength in seeing my denial of food not as sin but as a manner of sacrament. I would offer up my suffering to God our Father in the hope He would have true mercy upon me.

And so, the very next day, after I had prayed, I ceased to eat even the sippets of bread my father had allowed me.

I knew what his response would be, and indeed it was. 'She will soon come round when hunger gripes her belly.'

Yet love feeds a woman better than bread or water, and although I was frightened and the pains in my belly were indeed sharp as knives, I kept to my path.

My father caused the servants to bake almond cakes and leave them outside my door so that the smell haunted my every waking moment and drove me near to distraction. Yet I kept the faith even as I became daily weaker.

I did not want to die. And yet there was a delight in denial, and in the pure white light of moral certainty, for I knew that I was right, that I should not have to wed such a one as Master Manners in the name of our familial ambitions.

And then my sisters visited, each turning the great key in the lock, and sent to try and turn my rebellious mind also. First Frances bearing texts from the Bible. And Margaret, her belly greater than ever, bearing sweetmeats. Last of all, came Mary.

She gasped at my drawn-in cheeks and the dullness of my once-bright eyes. 'Ann, you must stop this crazed action now. Even marriage to a man you love not would be preferable to death!'

I pulled myself up in the chair where I had been resting, though each bodily action was growing daily more difficult and my bones ached constantly. 'No, Mary. I will not do it. I would rather perish else. I have had time here to think and that is my decision.'

She wrapped me in a fur cloak, for I was cold all the time, even though the sun shone outside, and every day the flowers bloomed, just as I faded. Indeed, I took a strange satisfaction at my life ebbing just as nature's blazed in glory.

The day came when I wondered if it would be my last.

Already I felt the lure of the Almighty's outstretched arms, waiting to fold me into His, for I would listen to none who told me I would surely face damnation.

Suddenly there was a great ruction below, with voices raised and doors opening and banging, as if an army had swept through the house.

With the small steps of an old woman I shuffled across the rush mats and opened my chamber door, now left unlocked.

Below, in the great passageway, my father stood, eyes blazing, his small frame as tense as if he stood up in the teeth of some great storm.

And that storm was my grandfather.

'This is my house,' my grandfather was shouting, 'and I will see no more of this madness! Already she has lost her beauty and the bloom of young womanhood. Would you see the child dead and buried in her grave before you relent?' His voice rose even further in his fury. 'Must we dress her in a shroud instead of a bridal gown?'

Yet my father remained unmoved, his voice as cold as frozen rock. 'She flouts my authority. And that of God Almighty who ordains in His commandments that a child must obey her father and mother. In this defiant act she challenges the very order of things, can you not see that, Father?'

'I see that I have put up with your pride and your unbending stubbornness these fifty years,' my grandfather accused, 'yet I will put up with them no longer. She shall not marry the man if she would rather die than do so!'

'Then you would let her win! And put a daughter's wish over her father's proper direction?'

'Ann is no flibbertigibbet. Young though she is in years, yet she is a wise and learned woman who I myself have raised and nurtured!'

'Wise enough to throw her good name to the wind and consort with a libertine who trumpets their liaison all round town! Long may you be proud of your teaching!'

'George, she is near to death. Is this the end you wish for your beloved daughter?'

My father's small body seemed suddenly a husk in the wind of my grandfather's disapproval. 'Then I wash my hands of her. I will release Master Manners from any negotiations. Do with her as you will.'

Upstairs, holding on to the door of my chamber, I felt like a condemned man freed from the scaffold and suddenly I fainted away.

When I came back to consciousness it was to see the stern face of my grandmother leaning over me. 'Ann, child. We thought that Jesus was to be your bridegroom. Praise to Him that you have come back to us.' She gestured to Prudence who stood behind us bearing a bowl of broth and some thin pieces of manchet bread. 'Your father has gone back to Baynard's. He leaves you now into our care and releases you from the marriage negotiations.'

I raised a feeble smile at that. 'I heard. He washes his hands of me.' I sipped my broth carefully, each mouthful paining me to swallow and yet the relief was such that each tasted like ambrosia.

'Will he then let me marry whom I wish?'

'He leaves all now to your grandfather.'

I closed my eyes, overcome with blessed relief.

Tomorrow I would begin to plan my future, the first step being to persuade my grandfather of the virtues of one Master John Donne.

Despite my weakened state that night I slept as does a babe in arms, fed with tenderness and cradled by a mother's love.

The sun shone brighter on the morrow than I had ever seen it. The gardens were new-minted as on the earth's first morning, every flower sparkling with drops of dew, each bird singing with full-throated happiness. I sat on a bench in the knot garden, the generous rays shining down upon me, and wrote my missive to Master Donne.

He must, as soon as the Lord Keeper could spare him, put on his finest clothes, polish his most eloquent phrases, and make his way to Loseley, where I would soften the path for him to speak to my grandfather.

Gradually over the next days, my strength came back to me. My face was gaunt and angular, still marked by the shadows of pain, yet it would soon return to health with the help of my new contentment.

And for the first time happiness seemed a true possibility. My grandfather was no easy touch, yet he knew of my good sense, and had seen the strength of my determination. That night I knelt and prayed to our Heavenly Father. 'Dear Lord God of all things visible and invisible, grant my prayer. That I will spend my life in your service and devotion and in the company of the man whom I love. Amen.'

On the morrow Wat appeared with a note from his master. He would arrive after the court of Chancery had finished its business, by early evening at the latest.

I dressed with as much speed as I could, and ran downstairs to find my grandfather.

My grandmother was busy in the henhouse, and the servants stowing away the remains of the morning bread and beer when I looked for him in the hall.

He was outside, the steward informed me, taking in the sunshine before the crowds of claimants and petitioners streamed in to seek his judgements.

I filled a tankard of small beer to carry to him, just as I had done so often as a child, and bore it carefully out into the gardens.

At first I found him not, then at last espied him as he sat in an old wooden chair under the apple tree, his head nodded down on his chest, his face hidden by his black hat. As I walked towards him I felt such love, that he, who knew me best of all, had had faith in my discernment. Faith I would repay by a life spent in love and devotion, and in blessing and thanking my Maker, who might finally grant me the desire of my heart.

I began to shake him gently, then, putting down the tankard, with more insistence and then at last with mounting panic. It took me many a long moment before I realized the dreadful truth.

He would not be meeting and negotiating my marriage with Master Donne.

For my beloved grandfather was dead.

Chapter 20

WITH MY GRANDFATHER'S death, I collapsed into darkness.

My grandfather had been my protector and my teacher and the figure I loved more than my own father. Now that he was taken from me all the strength, the determination, the willpower that had driven me through the days of my father's opposition abandoned me and I felt overwhelmed by despair.

Death is part of life, that had always been my grandfather's message and who knew it better than I? And yet now, while the summer days blazed outside, a dark mist clouded my mind. I felt imprisoned behind thick walls, even though they might be of my own making. My body, weakened by my fasting, slowed into inaction so that the slightest movement seemed beyond my capacities. It was as if another occupied my mind and possessed my soul.

I knew I must try to shake off this sickness. My grandmother's loss was greater than mine and she bore it with her usual strength, simply redoubling her busyness, ever active, never allowing herself to sit lest his loss overtake her. The only stillness she allowed herself was in prayer.

All my family came for my grandfather's burial, and each in turn tried to cheer me or goad me from my despondency, yet none could penetrate the curtain of black that surrounded me. Mary brought her child, now taking its first faltering steps. Margaret sat Perkin upon my lap, to no avail. I turned my back on life and sat long hours with my grandfather's portrait, wishing I too could slough off the painful coil of my existence.

Only Hope could penetrate my gloom and she came and sat at my feet, reading to me in her halting fluted tones, like some small bird chirping in winter into the high bright empty skies.

My grandmother brought me tisanes of herbs, eyebright, nettle and St John's Wort, long famed for treating maladies of the mind. Yet even her patience grew thin.

As the summer passed into the chill of late September all were going about their duties, save I. The house was bustling and busy for my father was now to take over his long-awaited inheritance. Soon the place would no longer be the haven of my childhood, but the focus of my father's ambitions to show the world how imposing he could make it.

One diamond-bright blue day when I sat staring out at the garden, my grandmother swept into the chamber, her face stonier than I had ever seen it.

To my great surprise she took me by both hands and pulled me bodily from my chair. 'Close your eyes,' she instructed me harshly. Had it been other than my own grandmother I would have been truly affrighted. As it was I pulled myself up with great reluctance.

'Trust me.' My grandmother spoke in a voice so low I could hardly decipher her words, and then I knew that her harshness came not from anger but from fear at what she suggested.

'I have the healing power. I have had it since I was a girl, though I kept uncommon quiet about it.' She smiled bitterly. 'Such things are not often understood and the owner can end up on the ducking stool or with her heels singed at the stake if she vaunts it too much abroad, the more when she is a crone as I am. I've seen it time and time again. People take the benefit then turn on the giver. Now, granddaughter, open your eyes and look at me.'

Despite the lowness of her voice there was that in her tone that would have made sovereigns do her bidding. She stood up close to me, her eyes on a level with mine. Then she placed her hands upon my shoulders and there was such lightness yet firmness in her touch that an involuntary sigh of comfort escaped me.

'Ann More, young though you be, you are a rare woman. Sharp. Strong. Full of light. I have seen many ladies in my time, yet few of your stamp. With your grandfather's death your light went out. Darkness flooded through you, your soul felt in chains. I will strike those chains.' She hit my wrist with the side of her hand and I could swear I heard the sound of metal clanging. I looked at her, bone-cold panic freezing me to the spot.

'Ann,' she spoke even softer now, so that I had to lean forward to catch her words. 'The chains. They were not made of iron, but of fear. There is no need for that fear. You think your father has treated you cruelly, yet he did what he thought right. I have persuaded him that this was not so. He goes back to London to sit at the Parliament next week. He will take you with him and you may assist him as you did before. You will never wed Richard Manners. Now shrug off this darkness and embrace the light.'

I shut my eyes and behind my closed lids felt the room fill with blinding rays. And I knew that she was right, the light had been there all the while yet I had but lost it from my sight.

'Thank you, Grandmother.' I held her to me, feeling the hard starch of her ruff cut into my cheek as I embraced her, yet I cared not a jot.

'What you do with your freedom is none of my concern,' I remembered then how she had secretly sent Prudence when she thought me so ill, 'but I will tell you this much: your father will never agree to a marriage he considers beneath him. There will come a time, Ann, when you will have to take your future into your own hands.' She turned me to look at her, at that unsmiling face with its great hawk nose and stern jawline, its dark brown eyes that bored into mine. 'Yet, remember, if you make the choice you long for, you may be choosing a life of hardship, exclusion, perhaps of poverty . . .'

'And contentment.'

'Hardship and contentment are not usual bedfellows.'

'Then I will make them so.'

'You are a strange girl, Ann.'

I took her hands in mine. 'Thank you for giving me a chance.'

'How could any of us stop you? I doubted not that you would starve yourself even unto death. Now, dress yourself and thank your Redeemer for letting you live.'

'I will.' I raised her hands and kissed her roughened fingers—my grandmother had never acted the fine lady. 'And you also.'

And then I dressed, choosing a gown of yellow under an orange kirtle, for I felt the sudden desire for the warm colours of the sun, and I combed my hair and pinched my cheeks and went downstairs for the first time in many, many days to find my grandmother and Frances in the withdrawing room, commanding the servants in the task of packing up goods, for my father was planning soon to claim his inheritance, while my grandmother moved to a dower house not far away.

'When comes my father to take occupation?'

'He and Constance come today. I am moving to the old manor. Frances stays.'

I took a long walk round the beloved house knowing it would never be as I remembered it. I loved it, in all its solid simplicity; it was a part of old England, the best part too. The portraits on the walls stared down at me: my grandfather, now restored to his proper place, my grandmother, the boy king Edward VI, the ill-fated Anne Boleyn.

Frances said my father planned a picture gallery to put them in, and a riding school also and a new chapel so God would not feel left out of all this magnificence.

By afternoon all was abustle with the arrival of my father and his wife, Constance, any moment expected.

The servants had all gathered anxiously to greet him, from the steward down to the humblest groom. There was a sense of tension in the air, for none knew what the future would hold, never mind they had worked here all their lives in my grandfather's devoted service.

And they were right in their anxiety. No sooner had I arrived in the Great Hall than I heard Constance's voice ring petulantly out. 'We have fifty liveried servants of our own at Baynard's, so I know not what work we will have for all of these. And our own steward to boot.'

Along with Frances and our grandmother, I curtsied dutifully as my stepmother took possession of our childhood home, though the feeling in my heart was as black as night.

Constance was a plump woman who had become so stout I doubted she could climb on a horse. And if ever she mounted my father she must surely smother him.

She accepted our curtsies as if she were Queen Elizabeth herself. A kinder lady would have told my lady grandmother, who was nearing eighty, that standing in line to greet her was unnecessary in one of her advanced years, yet she did not. And when we stood up again she whispered loudly to my father, 'I had forgot. At least Frances is a credit to you.'

Frances smiled proudly, until I kicked her.

Even before the servants had been dismissed I could see Constance look around the room, planning how she would improve it. How this must have seemed to our grandmother, who had lived at Loseley all her married days and filled it with her treasures, I know not for she bore it with great dignity. Yet, as Constance swept from the room to tour the house, quill and parchment in hand, I heard a small sigh escape her.

'You will soon be safe in your jointure house,' I murmured.

'Ann, be not so ungenerous,' corrected Frances. 'Our stepmother has many worthy qualities.'

My grandmother and I smiled. When Frances left on some errand my grandmother leaned into my ear. 'You are fortunate to be going to London. There will be changes enough here.'

At last the moment came of my release. We would leave for London within the hour.

As I packed up my baskets and trunk I decided to speak to Constance about Stephen and Hope, and how I would answer for their treatment if aught befell them.

'How can you answer for them when five minutes since you ran about half-mad like some demented creature from Bedlam?' Constance demanded, laughing scornfully. 'How can even you take care of yourself? And who will wed you now that you have refused Master Manners? Not your scandalous poet. We have seen the last of him.'

I turned on my heel that she would not see the pain in my eyes.

Frances tried to follow, eager to tell me aught, yet Constance called her back.

Yet despite all, my spirits could not be kept down for long. I was going to London, not York House it was true, now that the new Countess was its mistress, but a stone's throw away at the lodgings my father had taken in Charing Cross.

And but ten minutes on foot from Master Donne's lodging.

My grandfather's groom broke into my thoughts with the news that our coach was ready and waiting outside and my father installed in it.

'We will miss your lively presence, mistress,' the man said and though he smiled I could see the fear shining through about his future here.

'Not so lively lately.'

'Aye, it has been a sad time.'

He took my basket and carried it from the dark back entrance out into the sunlight where the coach stood waiting.

I took one last glance round my family home, no longer a place of peace and protection, and prepared to follow him.

'Goodbye, child!' My grandmother had followed me out. 'Go to London, and good luck to you!' I clung to her, conscious that the future awaiting me was uncertain and difficult. And yet for the first time in many weeks I felt an unfamiliar emotion.

Hope.

Chapter 21

YET I HAD to keep this feeling hidden from my father. The journey to London passed in bitter silence on his part, as if he no longer had a daughter.

His humour I found to be matched by a city that was quieter and surlier also. More taxes were being squeezed from the populace for the Irish war, and a new commander chosen, yet the war dragged on apace. The Earl of Essex, so long the Queen's delight, had met a sombre end on Tower Hill as my sister's husband had predicted, so far gone in vanity and treason that even the Queen could not save him. I wondered what the lady Mary Howard thought of that.

The lodgings my father had bidden in Charing Cross were surprisingly spacious given my father's closed fist. They comprised ten rooms, with several bedchambers, dining chamber, withdrawing room and space for cook and servants and a small garden. The views were of naught but other buildings, so near across the alley that I could reach out and shake the hand of my opposite neighbour. Each chamber was large and clean enough, yet had gloomy walls adorned with tapestries that had seen better days, each having acquired a faint greenish hue that cast a depressing light on all the occupants, as if viewed through a murky pond, and this did little to raise our sombre mood.

My father had brought baskets of petitions and submissions sent to him as member of Parliament, commissioner and justice and I began to try and make myself as useful to him here as I had at Loseley.

This was not easy as he was as cold and forbidding as a mountain crag in wintertime. Even, on one occasion, he withdrew his arm from the chair where it leaned lest I touch it as I bent to pick a paper from the floor.

All the same I worked steadily through, summing up each petition for his greater ease, using up four good swan's quills, until my eyes ached and the fingers of my hand cried out from writing, and all the while I wondered how soon I might get word of my arrival to Master Donne.

I sat in the withdrawing chamber, a good ashwood fire burning next to me, for the weather had turned cold, contemplating the great pile I had just perused—I had read enough of disputed leases and boundary arguments than ever I wished to know in my whole life—when my father's groom announced the arrival of both my sisters.

'Ann,' demanded Mary, her eyes aglow and her fresh complexion making her more lovely than I had seen her for many months, 'why hide you away here with these dusty documents? It is a fine afternoon abroad, too good for sitting here in the gloom like the bent-up clerk to some fusty apothecary.'

'I wonder what brings this new sparkle to your eye,' I replied. 'Mayhap it is your child, overwhelming you with motherly love?'

'Hah!' was all the answer Mary would give.

'I try to win over our father's good opinion. He agreed only to my coming for the sake of my grandmother's persuasion and speaks to me as if I were some distant stranger. I fear he forgives me not one jot for the routing of Master Manners.'

'We have news that will pique your interest, sweet sister,' Mary revealed, enjoying being the possessor of new gossip.

'And what is that?' I stoked up the fire and called to my father's groom to bring us spiced ale and the cook's small cakes made with almonds and raisins of the sun. Even in my saddened state the scent of warmed ale, so redolent of cloves and cinnamon, could not fail to cheer me.

'Your Master Donne is made member of Parliament for Brackley in the county of Northamptonshire.'

'But how is this?' A member of Parliament was a role of some standing and I had heard no rumour that such a thing were likely for one in Master Donne's position.

'It seems that Frances, daughter to the Countess of Derby, the Lord Keeper's new wife, brought the manor of Brackley as part of her inheritance,' my sister Margaret explained. 'And the Lord Keeper, deeming it useful to have a man sitting in the Parliament, has chosen your Master Donne to fill the post.'

A flame of joy rose in me. Perhaps this honour would make my father see in how much esteem Master Donne was held by his employer and cause a crack, no matter how small, in the granite of his great opposition.

'Mary's husband, Nick, is sitting also.' Margaret, undoing the laces of her stomacher for greater comfort as she attacked the cakes, changed the subject swiftly from Master Donne. 'And my Thomas also.'

'And our cousin Francis comes to represent the borough of Pyrford.'

I laughed at the idea of Francis forgoing hunting with his pack of staghounds, or indeed my brother-in-law Nick sacrificing his plays and cocking for the cause of sitting in Parliament, yet I was glad all the same. For these others were all gentlemen of rank if not—in Nick's case at least—of current fortune.

Now I had sufficient cause to send a message congratulating Master Donne and none could cavil at its propriety.

The sound of horses whinnying below alerted us to the arrival in our narrow street of a grand coach.

'I wonder who that might be? Perhaps a visitor for our father.'

Yet it was my sister Mary who jumped up first, a complicit look in her fine brown eyes, and even before the groom arrived to announce an arrival she was on her feet down the stairs, leaving Margaret and me to stare after her.

Startled at such behaviour, we ran to the window and there, down in the cobbled street below, we saw a gentleman, attired in pale blue silk and a profusion of gold lace, hold the door to his coach open for our sister to climb inside.

Margaret gasped and bit her lip. For the gentleman was fine indeed. Yet he in no way resembled Mary's lawfully wedded husband.

'What in the name of the Redeemer is the matter with this family of ours?' Margaret demanded. 'Three generations of knights, yet Mary risks her marriage with I know not what conduct, and you, the apple of our grandfather's eye, make yourself the object of tavern gossip for every tradesman to bandy about over their tankard of ale!'

Though the room was hot my heart chilled and my palms felt as cold as ice at her words. Had she, as well as Master Manners, heard ill rumours about me?

'I have done nothing to merit such talk, Margaret! What is this rumour you have heard?'

Margaret shook her plump shoulders impatiently. 'Oh, naught yet. But I am sure it is but a matter of time before the name of More is bandied abroad. And not to praise it! I leave now, back to my hearth and home, from which I have no desire nor need to wander!'

My father returned soon after, a little warmer towards me for the argument I had written for him had won praise from several members he respected. 'It seems I have an unrivalled grasp of the matter of multiple benefices,' he told me without even a word of recognition that the words he uttered had been not his but my own.

And yet, I cared not. At least he spoke to me again.

'Daughter, had you time to consider the matter of the committees I speak at tomorrow?' he enquired. My father, already one of the most vociferous members in the Parliament, seemed to speak yet more often since he had my assistance to inform him.

'Indeed, Father, here are some words I have prepared.' I handed over several close-written pages on such diverse questions as wandering vagrants, the operation of the Poor Law and the state of the Queen's highway in the three counties of Sussex, Surrey and Kent.

I did not mention that with a singing yet fearful heart I had also drafted a letter of congratulation to one John Donne Esquire, a title he could newly claim as member of Parliament, which I intended, when my father was busy with his many committees, to deliver on the morrow myself.

In my excitement and trepidation I slept hardly at all that night yet rose in time to bid farewell to my father before he took himself to his parliamentary business. To my delight he even offered me an excuse.

'I wonder, Ann, since there is no sitting tomorrow at the House, if you might deliver these plums sent by your grandmother from Loseley to your sister Mary? I would send them with a groom but my mother ever wishes for news of how the babe fares and I am never able to supply the details she craves.'

Neither, from what I had seen of her manner towards her babe, would Mary.

'Indeed, Father, it would be a pleasure.'

All the more since I might return, now that my father had given me the opportunity, by way of Master Donne's lodgings near the old Savoy Hospital.

My father placed his hat on his head, preparing to leave. 'And Ann . . .'

'Yes, Father?'

'I am grateful for the trouble you take with my parliamentary business.'

A wave of emotion, unlooked for and powerful, swept through me. It was rare in my father ever to acknowledge gratitude.

'I am glad to be of service to you in the Queen's business, Father.'

He nodded.

He had not mentioned Master Manners nor my disgrace for several days now. Perhaps my father had seen that, even unwed, I had my uses.

The sight of the plums gave me a sudden leap of joy at all things beautiful. Green and yellow, some speckled and carmine red, others dusky purple, and all clouded with a gentle mist as if breathed on by Pomona, goddess of all growing things, they nestled invitingly in their basket.

Were such thoughts of goddesses heresy, I wondered, smiling at the reminder of he who would share my appreciation of the question. As I went to pick the basket up I spied one plum less beauteous than the rest, with a dark line of imperfection running through, and went to throw it out, then stayed my hand. Why should all things be without stain, and did not this one blemished plum taste as ripe and delicious as the rest?

My father's groom accompanied me on the wherry to Mile End. He was a quiet man and I was able to enjoy the bustle and excitement of the most crowded waterway in Christendom, knowing that later I might see one whom I had missed for too long. Smiling to myself I

held up the hem of my gown that it would not be wet by the river water and listened to the constant ringing of churchbells, the clang of
hammers from the countless workshops and the cries of the wherry-
men from the thousands of tiny craft who kept the city moving. And I
saw that I had come to love these sounds as much as the calm of the
country for they reminded me of one to whom the London air smelled
sweeter than any hedge of dog rose and wild woodruff.

I wondered if Mary would yet be up or, as was her wont, dallying
languorously in her shift, an embroidered wrap about her shoulders,
as she tried out which hair arrangement suited best.

And, indeed, her tire-woman announced that her mistress was still
abed. 'Shall I wake her, and you wait in the withdrawing room, mistress? There is a fire just lit.'

I should, I suppose, be grateful for such small mercies that the fires
were lit at all and yet a flame so recently begun would give no more
than a breath of heat, while my sister's chamber was ever warm and
redolent of spice and mine, with its pungent pomanders and gilded
candlesticks.

I would go up and surprise her. And then a memory of the sight of
Nick and she upon the bed flooded into my mind and I asked the
woman if the master was with her also.

The woman's shake of shoulder and raising of eyebrow told me all.
The master had not visited his wife's room lately.

To my surprise Mary was up and clad in a new gown, richly worked
in red flowers upon a background of blue. She stood in front of her
looking glass, her hair loose, and she tried—strangely since there was
neither maid nor tire-woman present to aid her—with difficulty to fas-
ten a necklace around her neck which I had never seen before.

When I entered she speedily unhooked it and placed it on her table
next to her jewelled hairbrush, her cheeks blushing redder than the
roses of her dress.

'Ann! I thought not to see you soon! Has aught befallen our grandmother?' Mary, I knew, worried that after the demise of our grandfather, she would follow him soon afterwards. But our grandmother was
of sterner stuff.

'She fares well and sends you these plums from Loseley.' I handed her the basket which she barely glanced at before stowing them atop a nearby coffer.

'That is a pretty trinket.' I pointed to the necklace. 'A gift from Nick, perhaps?'

She started guiltily at that and turned to reach for a velvet cloak that lay upon her great canopied bed. 'Do you not find it cold today? Surely you have not journeyed to me from Charing Cross in that light cloak?'

'I have indeed. And it is a glorious day abroad. You should venture out yourself. And now I must depart for I have other errands for my father.'

'He has forgiven you then for your intransigence?'

'He finds I have my uses.'

She looked at me narrowly. 'And what are these errands, and where do they take you? To York House, perhaps, to meet a certain dark-eyed gentleman?'

I flushed, not knowing I was so transparent.

'Sister, must I counsel you once more against an unwise act? Not just for your own sake, for any ruin it might bring you, but for us all?'

For answer I lifted the pretty trinket from her table and held it up, studying its green stones as they dazzled in the light of her candle, dangerous and alluring. 'Might I not offer the same advice to you, sister?'

Silence filled the room, apart from the flickering of the fire in the grate and the snuffled breathing of Mary's pug, which snored on a velvet cushion at the fireside like the pet of some imperial ruler.

Mary shrugged and sat down at her looking glass. 'I am married, with a husband I can manage. The truth is not the same for you.'

'I know it, Mary. I will be careful.'

She reached up and took my hand. 'You risked much for me, sister.'

'Then squander not my efforts.'

Outside Mary's house I sent the groom on an errand of his own. I saw he wished to argue, perhaps fearing for his job if my father found I had been out unaccompanied, but I cast him so haughty a look that he dared not cavil but went off on his way.

At last, alone, I climbed down the stairs towards the river and found that I must hold the railing. Though it was a fine day, my limbs were shivering.

For two miles up the river my fate awaited me.

As the great Thames ebbed and flowed beneath me, so did my courage. Could I, the descendant of three knights, truly go and offer my innocence without the protection of God's holy matrimony?

'Frye Lane or the Savoy stairs, mistress?' The wherryman broke into my anguished musings.

The former would be quieter and less noticed by the crowds that ever milled near to the old Savoy Hospital.

'Frye Lane, wherryman.' He helped me out of the boat and onto the slippery river steps, watching me curiously the while, wondering no doubt what a young gentlewoman did abroad with no attendant. I thought of telling him some story of my groom being taken ill, but why should I lie to a simple boatman?

There was none but myself in Frye Lane and I hurried unseen down the narrow alley towards my destination.

Master Donne's lodging was found at the back of the great building, a row of black and white timbered dwellings hard by an arch which led towards the thoroughfares of the Strand end of Fleet Street.

Once outside I stopped to pray to the Blessed Virgin, even though I knew that the path I stepped down was a sinful one.

'Are you lost, my lady?' a voice behind me asked.

'Not "my lady" . . .' I turned to find Master Donne's landlord not two feet away from me, and spoke on, my voice as brisk and certain as one who knew what she was about and needed no assistance. 'Mistress will do well enough. I have a commission for Master Donne.'

'Indeed,' he bowed. 'A popular man with the ladies, Master Donne.' He smiled unctuously. 'All with commissions like yourself, no doubt.'

'Is he within?'

'Indeed, he is in company with a gentleman.'

As if in endorsement of this I heard a crack of laughter, loud and bawdy, the kind that is shared between men enjoying a joke that concerns a woman.

Coming out of the door, still clapping his visitor upon the back, Master Donne, clad in hose and undershirt, caught sight of me.

The manner of his face was hard to read. I would place it somewhere between delight and devastation.

'Mistress More . . . my sweetest Ann . . .' The words were out before he had the sense or wit to censor them.

His guest smiled and raised an eyebrow as if my name were not unfamiliar to him.

For once Master Donne seemed at a loss for words. 'My friend here, Master Davies, is just leaving.'

The gentleman endorsed this with a wink so lascivious I wondered if it had been he who spread the rumours that had come to the ears of Richard Manners.

It was no auspicious start to our encounter.

'Mistress More has come to you with a commission,' chimed in Master Haines. The insinuation in his voice was unmistakable.

'I am glad to get it.' Master Donne made himself suddenly businesslike, offering to take my gloves and cloak. 'Can I offer cakes and spiced wine while we talk of it?'

He ushered me towards his chamber, casting a nervous glance at Master Haines the while.

Once inside his door the storm broke.

'Mistress More . . . Ann . . .' he demanded roughly, 'what thought you in coming here today, all unannounced, in broad daylight without even a vizor to conceal your features, and to speak thus openly with my landlord? He is a not a man of great discretion. I fear your good name will now be trampled underfoot.'

At that my temper cracked like a bolt of lightning across a summer sky.

'My good name! You dare to speak of my good name when Master Manners told my father of your boasts that there had been relations between us! Which you had vouchsafed to some gimcrack friend— perhaps the winking Master Davies!'

My anger would not now be held back but gushed like water through holes in a broken dam. 'Know you the pretty question Master Manners asked of our precious, God-spared time together?'

Master Donne shook his head.

'That we lay together, you and I, and where one had broke the ice then perhaps others may have followed!'

'Mistress More, Ann, this is wicked calumny! You know yourself no such relations took place! Indeed, in spite of extreme temptation, I respected your innocence above my own desires!'

'True. Yet you would not be the first man to increase his credit by exaggerating such matters in private to his friends.'

Master Donne shook his head, as if seeing something clearly for the first time. 'I am touched by the good opinion you clearly hold of me, mistress.'

I felt a pang of guilt, but how had Master Manners heard such things if not through loose talk from Master Donne's own lips?

Yet I was not finished. 'And know you what my dear father said in reply to defend his cherished daughter's honour? Naught! Not even one slippery, hand-wringing attempt at my defence. Indeed, he raised the value of my portion to five hundred pounds to cover the embarrassment.'

'Ann, sweet . . .'

'I am not your sweet Ann!'

Until coming here, in my deepest soul I had not believed he had bandied our intimacy about the town, yet that odious wink from his friend had undone all my trust and certainty.

I gathered up my gloves and cloak and put them on. 'I will go now. My visit today was as you say naught but a mistake and an invitation to yet more scandal. Clearly to quash it we must end our friendship here. If I leave now I can be home before my father returns from the Parliament. We need not extend the embarrassment of pretending we have more to say.'

'No, Mistress Ann, wait. I will go first and explain to Master Haines some justification for your visit, a poem for your sister's bridal in the Isle of Wight perhaps.' Speedily he began to pull on a doublet.'

At the mention of the Isle of Wight the memory returned, as cold as icy seawater, of what took place that day, leaving me numb. I was left alone in his chamber, my dreams unravelling, my great design in pieces at my feet.

I glanced round one last time at the chamber, as neat and orderly as it had been at York House. On the coffer next to the bed I spied a scrap of fur, and saw it was the rabbit's foot he held up in his portrait.

So Master Donne still hoped his luck would turn.

Yet mine own had all run out.

In his haste to leave he had thrown down his undershirt upon the bed. A sudden impulse, I know not from where, bade me pick it up and hold the fine white lawn, still heated from his body's warmth, against my cheek.

And there I stayed, breathing in the faint musk male scent of his sweat until I heard a rustling sound behind and turned to find its owner standing watching me.

I caught my breath and pushed the shirt behind my back, my face flaming, as he walked towards me and reached behind, removing the shirt from my feeble grasp.

'Had you need of a handkerchief to mop your brow, I could have easily supplied it,' and then his mouth sought mine and I cleaved my body shamelessly to his, making no more pretence to cover my emotions.

An Elizabethan lady is no easy ship to board and he laughed and swore in equal measure as he struggled with the hooks and laces of my heavy garments.

My kirtle, sleeves and jewelled stomacher were set aside until all that remained was the folds of linen slipping from my shoulders to expose the tender buds beneath. I closed my eyes as at last he released each rounded breast from its upholstered prison and kissed it, soft and slow.

"'Come, Madam . . .'" His eyes teased as he quoted from the verse he knew had stirred me so long ago, and held out his hand to draw me towards the private world of his great curtained bed.

I shivered, remembering the lines he had left unsaid:

> *Licence my roving hands, and let them go*
> *Behind, before, above, between, below.*

And how I had secretly longed for it to be my body beneath those exploring hands.

And now it would be so.

And yet, before we made that fateful journey, he stopped and took my hands in his.

'At last we have found each other, you and I. So many false trails and long searches yet after this naught else will ever count with us, not riches, nor high opinion, nor preferment. They all will be as dross is to gold compared with this.'

And now he knelt before me and my linens slithered to the floor, leaving me as naked as was Eve in the Garden of Eden.

And yet I felt no shame. Naught but joy as he stroked the softness of my skin, and skimmed his lips across the contours of my body, moving ever downwards.

I breathed in sharp, fear fighting pleasure, to sense his tongue, as gentle as the beat of butterfly wings, and yet so strange and unfamiliar I knew not what I might expect, running down the softness of my belly until by infinite degrees it reached its destination.

Then such a wild explosion overtook me that I shook and cried out with joy. And I knew that he was right. From this moment on I would care for naught—not family, nor future, faith, nor stain of sin. Only for him and for the love we bore one another.

Afterwards, our bodies spent, we lay together and were silent, listening to one another's breathing, in the fading light of afternoon, as if drawn into but one soul.

And yet a shadow of something lingered in his grave expression.

'Is that sadness I see in your eyes?'

He kissed the palm of my hand. 'Every creature is sad after making love.'

'Aha,' I teased him merrily, recognizing his Latin reference and glowing at my own knowledge. 'Yet surely there is another thought you have forgot? Every creature is sad after making love—save women and roosters.'

He shook his head in true delight. 'Mistress Ann More praise be that you exist. For you are indeed a miracle.'

'So,' I asked him boldly as we lay in our private paradise, 'am I indeed, your new-found land, as in your scandalous verse? Or did that honour go to another lady before me?'

'No, Ann,' his harsh tone took me by surprise, 'you are not my America. That description was of another gentlewoman.'

I struggled to sit up, shocked at the seeming cruelty of his words.

'I wish I could deny that there have been others before you, yet on pain of my soul's damnation there will be none after.' He raised my hand to his lips. 'You are my north and south, my rising east and sharp declining west. You are my lodestone and my compass, the fixed centre of my universe. After this we two will never part. We must take on your father, the Lord Keeper, all.'

He knelt up suddenly upon the bed as if he were in church, and pulled me with him. 'When you and I most lovingly tie that knot, naught will ever sever it. Not sickness, nor cruel fortune, nor even shades of death itself. And I, once wed to you, will marry none other my whole life long. Wilt thou also plight me thy troth?'

In that small, darkened space it seemed to me the sacrament quietly entered in.

'I do so plight it.'

And saying no more we let our bodies celebrate the joy of this our blessed union, then fell asleep, folded lovingly in one another's arms.

It was late afternoon when we awoke, roused by the strange sound of a bird on the window sill, scratching as if it wished to come inside the room. It was a ring-necked dove and, despite the season and the lack of a mate, it puffed up its blue-green neck as if it too sought the pleasures we had so lately known. I smiled at the memory of that other bird, seen so long ago, the day that first I ever saw him.

And then in the midst of all our delight I remembered Master Manners and our encounter in Portsmouth.

'Ann, Ann, what ails you? You look as if you had seen a ghost.'

'I have.' I turned back to the bed. 'Let us hope it is not an evil spirit sent to haunt us.'

He was out of bed, and dressing, full of energy, like a taper which was waning and is given new air. 'None can touch us now. Our love will protect us more than burnished armour.' He held me fast, stroking the hair away from my face. 'Doubt not, my Ann. If we love truly, who can harm us?'

I hesitated, not wishing to burst the fragile bubble of our delight, but knew I must.

'Master Manners might. I am not contracted to him, nor ever have been, not even by promise nor by handfasting, which some accept as binding. Thank the heavens his father was so demanding that the marriage negotiations were never sealed, yet he will do what harm he can.' I ceased for an instant, for it grieved me to continue. 'Some time ago I went to the Isle of Wight to see my sister Frances celebrate her betrothal there. Master Manners came with us. My father had a notion I would look with greater favour on him if we had more acquaintance. We came back through Portsmouth and there Master Manners, driven I think by jealousy of you, attempted to dishonour me.'

'Ann!' His face was a mask of fury. 'Why did you not tell me? I would have found him out wherever he was! If he hurt but one hair of your head . . .'

'He did not. I cannot vouch for what might have happened but we were interrupted by the innkeeper. John, he is a cruel man. He will try to harm you if he can. And us also.'

He took my hands in his and held them to his chest. 'Then we must wed with all haste, before he can find a means to stop us. On the morrow I will search for a chapel where we may be married without delay, and for one who is prepared to marry us.'

The sudden furrow in his brow told me that this might prove a hard task, that some might shy away from marrying a woman as young as I, and in secret, without a father's consent and no banns read out. Though many married far younger than I, it was with the endorsement of their parents, not in secret with neither present.

Even I trembled at the magnitude of our intended action.

And then his face cleared, like the sun emerging from dark clouds on a distant peak. 'My friend Christopher Brooke! His brother Samuel is in holy orders. He might perform the office for us.'

He ran to his desk and found paper, and dashed off a note, turning it over to write the direction on the other side, then impressing the melted wax with his seal of a sheaf of snakes, the one I recognized from letters I had received myself.

I looked at the letter in his hand, my breath coming faster. All our hope, that we would in truth spend our whole life together, was sealed by that small mark of melted wax.

He saw the fear that had crept into my eyes.

'Come, Ann.' He took my hand and kissed it fondly. 'Take heart. Where is that young girl who chased away the rat? Who rides on horseback as if she were the wind itself? And would have taken on Master Freeman in a bawdy house had I not stopped her?'

I breathed in, willing myself to have the courage needed to carry through this marriage that would outrage convention, and my family and friends also—not for my age, for I was now almost seventeen, but for the absence of my father's consent—all for the sake of love for this man.

I stood up straight, my eyes fixing upon his.

'She is here, and she is ready to brave all.'

Yet when it was time to leave I looked down fearfully into the alley below, in case my father had already heard of our scheme and come to stop it. There was naught but darkness beckoning and I ran as fast as I could to find a wherry to take me the short distance back to Charing Cross.

My father was deep in his papers when I returned.

I stood on the threshold of his closet fearfully. Surely there must be aught in my eyes, some sign of love, or loss of maidenhead, or of the soaring heights of ecstasy I had so recently known.

And yet his interest was not in me but in another pressing matter: the state of repair of the Queen's highway.

'Ann,' he looked up for a brief moment, 'how was your sister? Were your grandmother's plums to her liking?'

I could not but smile for the dizzy charms of love and of rebellion were in me. 'She was happy indeed. The plums were beauteous and delicious. She devoured them all and wrung the last drop of sweetness out of each. They were the best plums ever picked since Eden's harvest.'

He looked at me curiously at that. 'And you, Ann, are you quite well yourself? You seem light-headed. A fever perhaps?'

'Never better, Father. I have asked Mary to bring us back the basket as soon as she can.' The truth was I wanted Mary to return the basket for I could not keep my secret to myself but must share it, if only with one, and Mary was the only possible confidante.

'The basket?' He looked puzzled. 'But it is a worthless thing made of reeds from the river . . .'

'No indeed, Father, it is one my grandmother treasures. I have oft heard her admire it.'

He shook his head. 'Women are strange creatures. I had hoped you might help with this reading. I have much to do.'

'Then I will do it now, Father.'

As I sat down in the carved and gilded chair opposite, with its golden lion's claw feet, my father smiled at me.

I had to look away, my heart shrivelling up with guilt and regret. All the years he had rarely noticed my presence on this earth, or been angry at my insubordination, and now he chose this moment, when I was so close to breaking free of his yoke, to soften towards me and offer me the love I had so long yearned for.

Yet there came a time when a woman must choose between father and husband.

And I would choose husband.

I managed to send a message to Mary, but was not sure if she would come. Mary could be provokingly lazy and also provokingly selfish. Perhaps she might think I wished to rebuke her again.

I slept not a moment that night for my whole being felt like a vibrating harp, whose strings were made to sing by everything that touched them. I knew I could not tell those I loved of my plans—Father, Margaret, my grandmother, even my cousin Francis who had shared so much with me over the years. Indeed of all I loved Mary was the only one who was so deep in mire herself that I could share my secret.

I found myself fixed to a spot by the window nearest to the courtyard beneath that I might see all who approached.

'Ann, what do you do?' asked my father. 'You have stood there this half-hour. I wish you would look through these papers on monopolies. There are many in the Parliament who are angered with Her Majesty for handing out monopolies like sweetmeats. It seems to them that everything in the world is now subject to a monopoly from Malmsey wine to salt and all for the benefit of her favourites and at a cost to the rest.'

'Certainly I will, Father.' A roan mare clopped into the courtyard below, ridden by a vizored lady in a lean red habit, an egret's feather nodding from her jaunty velvet hat, a small child seated before her on the saddle. 'Look, Father. Mary is below with little Nick.'

My father glanced out of the window. 'I see no sign of the precious basket you wish for so fervently.'

'No doubt she sends it with a servant.'

'Then why did she bother to come herself?'

I ignored his logic and skipped down the stairs to greet them.

Inside the small dark hallway I hugged her to me while my father's groom took Nick by the hand to carry him off to the kitchen where the cook fed him titbits she saved for him in a china crock.

I pulled Mary into the small withdrawing room, my heart beating louder than the bell of St Clement Dane's. 'Sister, we have cast the dice. He looks for a minister to marry us.'

Mary neither smiled nor held me to her but simply shrugged as if I were a lost cause, a hopeless case in which there was no merit in wasting her breath.

Instead we sat and supped macaroons dipped in mead, talking stiffly of the progress of Margaret's babe and where Mary planned to pass the twelve days of Christmas this year.

At last she stood up to go. 'I am sorry, Ann, but I have another call to make.' Seeing the fineness of her dress I could hazard where.

'Goodbye, sister. Be careful.'

A beat of silence passed before she answered me. 'I might say the same to you. My husband has made me suffer much, he has gambled away all our contentment and security. Why should he not suffer one tenth of what I have borne so bravely and without complaining?'

'The world is not the same for women as for men, Mary.'

'Aye. And there is one law for the rich and another for the rest. You are about to cross that line, Ann. Think of that before you make your final choice.'

'Mary, wealth means naught to me, you know me well enough to know that fact.'

Mary shrugged. 'That is because you have always possessed it. You have never had to worry about paying for fine spun wool, or lively chestnut mares. You have travelled by coach and in the Lord Keeper's barge. You know nothing of poverty or cramped circumstances or chafing at how to feed hungry mouths.'

I could not deny her good sense, yet I was nothing daunted. I was young and full of energy after all. 'Sister, you are right. Yet love will make me strong.'

'Love! God's blood! Love makes us weak, not strong. Goodbye, Ann.'

She rang a bell and little Nick appeared clutching a hot codling wrapped in cloth. 'Goodbye, Mary.'

Behind her, her small son held on to his codling in one hand and the bottom of her hem with the other, his big dark eyes reminding me suddenly of his father. 'Remember, Mary, you have much to lose. More, I think, even than I.'

'What a pair we are.' She shook her head, smiling sadly. 'God be thanked for Margaret and Frances.'

'We are cut from different cloth, you and I.'

'Aye, and I would not change silk for linen. They say silk is strong as well as fine.' She took Nick by the hand and began to go down the stairs.

'Aye,' I called after her, 'yet linen lasts the longer.'

I READ THROUGH all the submissions sent to my father on the unpopular subject of monopolies. At first these had been a way for the Queen to give an advantage to those she favoured, granting them the income on all from salt to playing cards, but as she awarded more and more, some as honours and others sold to raise revenues for her wars, it seemed as if the air we breathed was subject to a monopoly. And now the Queen found herself in a new situation where Parliament dared oppose her and was suggesting a bill to challenge the free hand she had shown. Even those who had been her staunch supporters wanted to take Her Majesty to task over them.

And tomorrow a committee of the Parliament met to decide what line to take in its submission.

For once my father, a natural moderate who greatly disliked any change, witnessed by the fashions he wore from forty years before, was fired up to join the charge. 'Monopolies are an eating, filthy disease which I have ever detested with all my heart,' he insisted, 'and I intend to tell Her Majesty so.'

Opposition was not a concept Queen Elizabeth was accustomed to. The picture of my lady Mary Howard and how she fared when she crossed the Queen in love, flooded into my memory, followed by the Earl of Essex facing his execution one fine day on Tower Hill.

So, gently, quietly, as if I made only the smallest suggestion, I counselled my father in how to make his case and keep his head. 'Leave the hot-heads to say their piece then thank Her Majesty humbly for deigning to listen to your case. Remember whose daughter she is, after all.' For neither the Queen nor her father Great Harry brooked being told how to run their own kingdoms.

I was glad of this diversion since there was still no word on the progress of our marriage plans. I knew not whether my father followed my suggestion until he returned from Whitehall on the morrow dazzled by the wonder of Queen Elizabeth.

'She received us all in the Presence Chamber and we fell to our knees as she entered,' he recounted, his eyes still shining with tears. 'Her great Majesty told us that there is no jewel, be it never of so rich a price, which she sets before the jewel of her love for us, her subjects. Ann, she has promised to revoke many of the worst monopolies. I did as you bid and thanked her humbly and she smiled especially upon me and said my father and I had ever been wise counsellors, and our like not to be found among the younger men!'

I listened in wonder that the Queen, so old now, having outlived all her advisors and her allies, capable as I had seen myself of such strange behaviour, could still so move her subjects that they wept from gratitude for her love.

That was power indeed.

'I am going to bid members of the Parliament to a feast in celebration of this—and, Ann, you shall be my hostess!'

'Congratulations, Father, you are a wise counsellor indeed!'

I dropped a curtsey as if he were of royal blood himself. Most fathers would smile and think it an endearing joke, yet not mine. I could see how pleased he was by the gesture, taking it as a mark of fitting filial respect at last.

'You are a good child, Ann, when you put your mind to it, and a credit to the Mores.'

I wondered what word he would use to describe me had he known where I had so recently passed my afternoon.

In the bed of one John Donne.

I made up my mind to be as useful and as dutiful as I could during this time while all the while I planned my escape. 'A mug of small beer for you, Father, or would you rather something stronger?' His response was to sneeze and I took this as excuse to order him a hot bath to be drawn in front of his chamber fire and afterwards an early night with a brick in his bed and a warming drink of spiced ale to aid his slumbers.

The prescription worked as does a charm.

The following night we threw a feast for twenty members of Parliament, Mary's Nick and Margaret's Thomas, both members in their own right, amongst them. And since he was now a member also, my father deigned to send a message bidding Master Donne.

Before the feast of swan and roasted peacock, trout pasties and smothered rabbit, I prettily poured wine—a custom my father favoured over having an usher do it. I somehow found a word and a smile for all our guests while all the time looking out for only one.

Skulking in a corner I came across my brother-in-law.

'Some wine, Nick? Why hide you away from all the company?'

When I put down the wine flask he grabbed it and refilled his goblet to the rim. 'It is quiet at our house now you've deserted us, Ann,' he told me. Then, suddenly, with no explanation for the change of mood, his eyes narrowed giving his handsome face a wolf-like look which made me worry for Mary's sake. 'All that your sister owns is mine,' he said in a voice sharpened on the whetstone of bitterness and suspicion. 'Perhaps she should remember that.' He looked at me again. 'And mayhap you should remind her.'

The threat in his voice was ugly and corrosive, leaving no hint of the usual charming courtier.

I turned away, repulsed and a little frightened. Women were so entirely in the hands of their menfolk. If Nick threw off my sister, what would become of her? And what would my father do if he found out my plans? Beat me? Incarcerate me properly this time, with Constance as jailer? A role she would much enjoy no doubt.

And then I saw Master Donne arriving with the Lord Keeper and our eyes locked for the barest of moments before I made myself busy pouring out more wine.

The Lord Keeper had brought his new wife, Alice.

'Ah, Ann,' my uncle greeted me, 'how fresh and lovely you do look in that green gown. Like a breath of spring in all this garish pageantry of approaching Yuletide.'

I curtsied in return, noting that his wife Alice was looking sour-faced in the richest of ruby reds, laced with gold and enough jewels to outdo the monarch. Perhaps my uncle had had to pay for them. She was handsome indeed, if you like your ships laden with showy treasure, yet her beauty was marred by a deep line of dissatisfaction on either side of her cochineal-hued mouth.

'Thank you, Uncle.'

The Countess Alice surveyed the peacock all laid out upon the table, its tail feathers fanning out in magnificent display.

'Exotic indeed!'

'Yes, my lady,' I smiled in agreement. 'Like a feast given by Queen Cleopatra!'

Alice looked at me curiously, then laughed out loud. 'I had heard of your learning, Mistress More. I hear your father thinks it has done you nothing but ill and wishes he had not paid for it.' She glanced frostily at her husband and added in tone that spoke of the bedroom. 'Lucky Cleopatra, eh, to be beloved by an Antony?'

My uncle stiffened at the deliberate insult, and I saw how bad things were between them.

I curtsied again and moved off, wishing to remove myself from their ire and anxious to exchange a word, no matter how brief, with Master Donne.

At last I glimpsed him standing in an alcove off the main hall. I raised my hand to greet him, then saw he was engaged in a serious discourse with another gentleman.

'Who is that conversing with Master Donne?' I asked of the Lord Keeper.

'His good friend Sir Henry Goodyer.'

I put down my jug of wine and fought my way through the crowd towards them. Yet Master Donne's words stopped my progress.

'Henry, please,' he begged, his voice an urgent whisper, 'be a witness for us. There are not so many we can trust to do this.'

'I am sensible of the honour, yet how can I when you know I am in opposition to this marriage? It will be the end of you, John, of all your hopes and aspirations.'

'No, friend.' His voice rang with such hope and certainty that my heart glowed. 'It will be the fulfilment of them.'

He saw me then and his eyes held mine, alight with the fire of love. Fearing if I stayed I would give myself away I turned back into the busy throng.

After this I saw him not until the evening's end as I helped our guests to find their mantles and their cloaks.

'My friend Samuel has agreed to help us,' whispered Master Donne. 'Next I must approach the Savoy Chapel. It is but a few minutes from my lodgings and I have heard the incumbent is an easy-going man. For a fee.'

'Then God speed us both.'

Chapter 22

AFTER THAT NIGHT'S encounter I neither saw nor heard from Master Donne in two weeks. Yet I worried not, so deep was my certainty in our great love.

November was now over and almost a week of December passed. Soon the Parliament would disband and I knew my father intended to return at once to Loseley, where he was eager to review all his great new building works.

Could it be that all agreed with Sir Henry Goodyer and none would be prepared to help us?

The thought almost caused my courage to fail and I had to hold fast to my bedpost not to faint away. What if I had given myself, body and soul, and now we could not wed after all? A knock on my chamber door brought me back to my senses. Prudence, sent by my grandmother to keep watch on me, stood on the landing, arms crossed, regarding me with a sullen eye. 'The boy Wat is below, mistress, and asks to speak with you privately. I have sent him to the small withdrawing room.'

Wat waited at one end, cap in hand. Prudence gave him a swift look of appraisal, and I saw with a shock that Wat was no longer a child but had become a handsome youth, manly enough to draw admiring female glances. As I approached he drew out a letter, sealed with the familiar red stamp. 'From my master. He bids you read it in private that I may take him back your reply by return.'

My heart jumped in my chest and beat as strong as the great bellows by the fire at Loseley.

In my haste I almost tore the parchment as I opened it, my breath racing and my palms beginning to sweat.

The incumbent of the Savoy Chapel had agreed to wed us. We were to be married the day after tomorrow, hard by his lodgings. His friend Samuel Brooke, who was in holy orders, had agreed to do the office, and Samuel's brother Christopher would give me away.

A tear sprang into my eye at the thought of the ceremony being so small and secret. If ever I had thought of my marriage as a child, it was with my father leading me to the altar, handing me into the care of my new husband.

I brushed it angrily away. This marriage of ours might be a flouting of convention but it would also break the rule that gave the bride no say nor choice with whom she spent all the days of her life.

For I had chosen for myself. And he was the one man I desired above all others.

Ever resourceful, Wat had come equipped with quill and ink.

I wrote but few words of reply: *I will be ready. May God bless our union.*

The strange thought struck me that tomorrow would be my last day as a maid.

Much as I longed for the marriage to take place, I could not banish a mournful sadness that I would have neither mother nor father, not even a sister present at the most important day of my young life.

'Stay, Wat . . .' A thought occurred to me. 'Can you take a letter to my sister Mary?'

The next day it was hard to escape from Prudence's watchful eye. I wished to try on different gowns, and assay my hair in a way fitting for a bridal, yet there she was, ever present, as if she guessed and durst not let me out of her sight.

In the end I told her I needed herbs for my father in the small garden and managed to slip away unnoticed.

There had been a sudden flurry of snow in the night, leaving a day that was cold and shining clear. Little grew in the garden now, yet I found enough for my needs and, making sure no eyes spied on me, fashioned for myself a circlet of ivy, its berries black and glossy, and wound it with the last few leaves of vivid green alchemilla. Perhaps a hellebore in purple or palest pink would complete my headdress, but I could find none in the garden.

I leaned upon a stone urn, overcome at the memory of Bett's wedding, with its feasting and bawdy merrymaking, and how different my own would be. And yet, what had the future held for Bett? A cloddish husband and a cold early death.

As I turned back towards the house a bright patch of colour caught my eye. Hidden amongst the dead wood and dried-out sweet briar was one single red rose, in bud still, as if miraculously defying all the laws of nature, waiting for this one day to bloom its last.

'Thank you, Bett,' I breathed, breaking the stem. 'This will be my special gift from you.'

That night I slept with the rose, steeped in water, at my bedside, riven by feelings of longing and of fear. At my father's lodgings all had seemed as on any other day. He had spoken of committees, and of a message he had received from Constance about delays by the stone-masons, and how they blamed the carpenters for not being ready, and how the carpenters in turn blamed them back.

He seemed not like a man who fears his daughter is about to tie the knot in a secret and forbidden marriage.

Before I climbed into my bed I knelt beside it as I had as a child and sought the succour of the Almighty.

'Dear Lord, who knowest all things, and so knowest the depth and the truth of my love, I am sorry to deceive my father in this. Help me to show him that I act out of love, which must be a blessed gift of God, and will be a loving wife, and, if I am so blessed, a loving and diligent mother. Amen.'

In the morning I sent Prudence away and dressed myself alone, shaking off regret that I had no attendants, nor chattering sisters, no singing or laughing or shared bridal cup of spiced wine to warm the chills of the day.

The gown I had chosen was the one my uncle had praised, a young fresh green, the shade of new shoots when they unfurl their delicate first leaves. My kirtle was of copper, reflecting the glints of my hair and the warm brown of my eyes that Father had once, in happier days, likened to the colour of chestnut.

Would he ever forgive me for this day's work?

All was now ready. I reached for the circlet of flowers and slipped it inside my sleeve so none could see it. I could hardly venture abroad on some imagined errand with flowers in my hair. At last I put on my mother's necklace, covered my finery with a black cloak, and was ready.

To my relief my father's servants were busy about their work when I descended the narrow staircase. Save one.

Prudence stood in the shadows near the great street door, holding it open for me. As I passed she pressed a package into my hand saying, 'Good luck, Mistress Ann,' before running back towards the kitchens.

Today I took no wherry, not wishing to dampen my dress, but turned right towards the criss-cross of alleyways that led from our lodgings in Charing Cross towards the site of the Savoy Hospital, built by John of Gaunt and now lodgings for the rich, and, but a stone's throw away, the Chapel.

Once round the corner, out of sight of the house, I undid the wrappings of my package and had to catch my breath. Prudence had given me a small nosegay made of Christmas roses all tied with green ribbon.

The kind of posy that would be carried by a bride.

I found the chapel and, as I had been bidden, sought out the back entrance. A pale wintry sun shone down upon me as I picked my way past frost-rimed tombstones in the churchyard. Indeed, with the silence and the emptiness I tried to stop myself thinking more of burials than of marriages.

I found myself, to my great astonishment, entering the chapel beyond the altar instead of at the back, as if suddenly on a stage.

A small knot of people turned to stare at me, one, in priest's attire, whom I took to be Samuel Brooke, smiled and shook my hand. All were clothed in an air not of celebration but of anxiety.

The chapel was much larger than it appeared from outside, lit by a single great candle in the nave, but otherwise lost in shadow. From out of the darkness stepped my bridegroom, clad in black velvet, a froth of gold lace at his neck.

'Ann, my sweetest love, I can scarce believe this day has come at last.' He took my hand and kissed it.

'Nor I,' I whispered, fear and love overwhelming me in equal measures.

Behind us appeared a greasy old verger with butter stains on his collar, rubbing his hands and peering into the gloom. No doubt he was getting a fat fee for allowing the marriage to take place here. The chapel, it seemed, was within a liberty and not subject to the canon laws as other churches, which led to a profitable industry for such as he. 'Who is officiating here?'

'I am.' Samuel Brooke stepped forward.

'Then you'd best get a move on. There's another party coming after you. Secret marriages are as popular as Twelfth Night masques these days.'

I tried not to shudder at the word 'secret', for it sounded so furtive.

'Let us hope the bridegroom's old enough to sign his name this time.' The verger laughed at his own joke. 'Pardon me. I'll leave you to your offices, then. Prayer book's on the altar.'

'I have no need of the prayer book,' Samuel told him curtly, trying to add some fitting solemnity to the occasion. 'I am familiar with the marriage liturgy.'

'God bless you. There's just the small question of payment.'

The bridegroom took a package from his velvet pocket and handed it over.

Noting my discomfiture, he reached across and touched my hand.

'Come, Christopher, you are to give the bride away.'

At that we took up our positions. To my surprise I saw John's reluctant friend Sir Henry Goodyer at a nearby pew, so silent a witness I had hardly noticed him, and another friend whose name I knew not at all.

Together we gathered near the altar, all wishing that the ceremony would be completed before any authority intervened.

A sudden gust behind made us draw in our breath as one and look around, full of fear, to see who it was who had barged so unceremoniously into the chapel—my father perhaps, or Master Manners—and whether their intention was to stop the marriage before it had even begun.

Chapter 23

YET IT WAS neither my father nor Master Manners but a woman, her face hidden by the folds of a black cloak.

As she walked towards the altar she threw back the hood and I saw that it was my sister Mary clad in her blazing-red riding habit, dressed for all the world as if she were upon the hunting field, and in my joy and relief I almost laughed out loud.

'I told them I went out this morning to hunt the hart,' she explained to the universal stares of the assembled group. 'Or would you rather I had said I was bound for my sister's secret marriage?'

I turned and ran down the aisle to embrace her, tears coursing down my face that I had at least one member of my family to share the most precious and holy day of my life with me.

'No, sister, we would not. Yet in the house of God it is the custom to leave your riding crop at the door.'

'Are we *now* all assembled?' the Reverend Samuel Brooke demanded. I could see he was more nervous yet and wished to proceed as soon as possible. 'No more surprise guests expected?'

I exchanged a look with my sister. 'I trust not, no.'

'Then let us begin. Dearly beloved friends, we are gathered to-gether here in the sight of God, and in the face of this congregation to join together this man . . .' he gestured towards John, who smiled, holding my gaze tenderly with his own, 'and this woman in holy Mat-rimony.'

Behind us the silence echoed, empty of music or singing, or the excited murmuring of guests. Samuel Brooke intoned the familiar words of the marriage service, reminding us of the purpose of the sacrament as a symbol of the union of Christ and His church, a remedy against sin and fornication, and to provide the mutual comfort, help and society for the two people so conjoined.

At this I thought of my beloved grandparents, whose union had lasted so many years until only death had sundered it, and yearned that ours would be the same.

'Therefore,' the words of the ritual continued, 'if any man can show any just cause why they may not lawfully be joined together, let him now speak, or else hereafter forever hold his peace.'

At this, I felt every person in the chapel tense, bracing themselves as if against another interruption.

Yet none came.

He gestured then to John and to myself. 'I require and charge you both as ye will answer at the dreadful day of judgement, when the secrets of all hearts shall be disclosed, that if either of you do know of any impediment why ye may not be lawfully joined together in Matrimony, ye do now confess it.'

I thought then, with a sudden chill, of Master Manners and felt an overwhelming gratitude that he and I had never formally been betrothed, for such would indeed have stood as impediment to this present union.

At last the longed-for moment came when we were to be forever joined.

'John Donne, wilt thou have this woman to thy wedded wife, to live together after God's ordinance in the holy estate of Matrimony?'

In the flicker of the single candle, I watched his beloved face, full of tender, protective passion, looking speakingly at me, and knew that if souls had voices, his would now be answering. 'Wilt thou love her, comfort her, honour and keep her, in sickness and in health? And forsaking all other, keep thee only unto her, so long as ye both shall live?'

I almost smiled at the thought of Master John Donne, creator of so much verse that sang of the joys of the flesh, confining himself to but one woman, yet the sombre sternness of his expression bade me keep my features as solemn as his own.

'I will.'

Then Samuel turned to me.

'Ann More, wilt thou have this man to thy wedded husband, to live together after God's holy ordinance in the holy estate of Matrimony? Wilt thou obey and serve him . . .' Behind John's shoulder I saw my sister Mary bite her lip at that. '. . . love, honour and keep him in sickness and in health? And forsaking all other, keep thee only unto him, so long as ye both shall live?'

'I will.'

'Who giveth this woman to be married to this man?'

Samuel's brother Christopher stepped forward.

At that he ordered John to take my right hand in his and repeat the words I had heard so often and yet, in some deep place in my soul, heard here and now for the very first time.

'I, John Donne, take thee, Ann More, to my wedded wife, to have and to hold from this day forward, for better for worse, for richer for poorer, in sickness and in health, to love and to cherish, till death us do part, according to God's holy ordinance. And thereto I plight thee my troth.'

He loosened our hands and bade me take John's hand in my right one. 'I, Ann More, take thee, John Donne, to my wedded husband, to have and to hold from this day forward, for better for worse, for richer for poorer, in sickness and in health, to love, cherish, and to obey, till death us do part, according to God's holy ordinance. And thereto I give thee my troth.'

'Who hath the ring?'

Christopher handed it over and John solemnly took my left hand in his, his eyes still holding mine. He slipped it onto the fourth finger of my left hand, repeating, 'With this ring I thee wed, with my body I thee worship, and with all my worldly goods I thee endow. In the name of the Father, and of the Son, and of the Holy Ghost. Amen.'

I could scarce breathe with relief and happiness when Samuel joined both our hands and stated gravely: 'Those whom God hath joined together let no man put asunder.'

He then pronounced us man and wife and at last John swept off his black hat and kissed me.

It was not the wedding I had dreamed of, with bells pealing and kith and kin toasting and feasting through the night, and yet my heart sang nonetheless.

For John Donne was the man in all the world that I had truly chosen for my own, and whom I loved, body and soul.

'Well, Ann,' said Mary as she held me tight in her arms, 'you have what you wanted at last and I hope you will be eternally happy.'

I returned her embrace. 'None can be eternally happy this side of paradise. Yet I know one thing: without him I would have had as much chance of contentment as a blackbird prevented from building her nest.'

'And now the only shadow in your blue sky is when to tell our father.'

At that I sighed. 'True enough. Yet I will not think of it now. We have decided that I must return today and prepare the way, that the blow when it falls, should be cushioned with the straw of my daughterly devotion.'

'You will need a cartload of hay for that, if I know my father's temper. So, what do we do now? Disperse without even a toast to your health and future? Bett's marriage had too much in the way of ancient custom yet yours, it seems to me, has not enough . . .'

Henry Goodyer, to whom I felt no great love, since he had sat silent throughout all like a great brooding owl, portending nothing but doom and disaster, suddenly awoke and spoke. 'I have bidden a room above the Angel tavern not two steps from here. I mentioned nothing of a marriage to the landlord, since John wished all to be discreet and silent. Instead we are celebrating my return from a long sea voyage.'

'I hope it was a successful one,' my sister laughed, the feather on the top of her hat nodding saucily, 'with much treasure and booty?'

Sir Henry smiled at that. 'It was indeed. Enough for good food and much wine to launch this auspicious occasion.'

As we sat, all seven, around the oaken table my new husband raised his goblet to me. 'A toast to my sweet wife, Mistress Ann Donne, the only woman on God's earth that ever I wanted to wed.'

'Aye,' teased his friend Christopher under his breath, 'though there were plenty you didn't.'

I stood then, to raise a toast of my own. 'To my dear husband, John Donne. Better, in my contention, to be the last love than the first.'

'Amen to that!' chorused all.

'There will be no seeing you home to bed, then, as we did with Bett?' asked Mary, a dangerous glitter in her eye from the wine. 'Yet I forgot. That is a fruit you have already tasted.'

I reddened then, and did not answer her. 'We will have a lifetime ahead enough for that. I must go to Charing Cross soon, before my father wonders what detains me.'

Though I kept my voice light, the pain of leaving sat like a stone upon my heart. This night should have been, by all usual accounts, my bridal night.

I was hoping to seize a private moment with my husband when his old friend Sir Henry, to whom I had spoken little, laid his hand gently upon my arm. 'Mistress More?' He laughed at that. 'Or rather, I should say Mistress Donne . . .'

This first use of my new name sounded strange even to my own ears.

'I wished to say that I am humbly sorry for what must have seemed to you churlish behaviour when you came upon us.'

'You worried that your friend would do an unwise thing in marrying me,' I stated simply.

'Aye,' he admitted, stroking his dark beard and smiling. 'Yet when I remembered what manner of lady you are, how wise, how nimble of mind, what learning you have, and how well you understand that rare and clever soul, Master John Donne, I could not but change my mind.'

'I have reason to be grateful to him. He woke me from a sleep that had lasted all my life.'

'Mistress Donne, Ann . . . I also saw that it was not *he* who was risking much to marry you, but *you* who were ready to hazard all in marrying him.'

'An equality of souls, then? Is not that what matrimony is instituted for?'

He laughed at that. 'If so then I have seen few successful marriages.'

'Then ours will be the pattern.'

'Mistress Donne, you are wise beyond your years, perhaps even beyond John's.'

'My grandfather told me I was born with an old soul. And indeed I do sometimes feel older than the people around me, be they twenty years on this earth before I was.'

'You will need courage in the days ahead, when Sir George discovers the truth about your marriage to John.'

'Indeed.' There was no denying it.

'If there is aught I can do, I will ever wait in readiness.'

I saw that I must alter my bad opinion of the man who stood before me. 'He has a good friend in you, Sir Henry.'

'And a good wife in you, Mistress Donne.'

And now I had to take my parting of my husband. He stood across the crowded chamber, his eyes fixed on me, as if he would detain me by power of his will alone.

'I must go, husband.'

'Aye, wife, yet I wish with all my soul it were not so.' He dropped his voice so that only I might hear him. 'And that instead I held you within the circle of my arms and naught—world, masters, fathers, none—had the power to reach us. I would take off that silken gown and claim you as my own.'

Deep inside me I felt a ripple of desire, as if some small, hidden tremor had begun its dangerous and lethal action, and that nothing in our lives could ever be the same.

'It will not be long before we are together, as God ordained, man and wife.' I unpinned the rose from my headdress and pressed it into his hand. 'We must keep the faith, no matter how hard the road ahead.'

'I will do so. You are my destiny, Ann.'

'As you are mine.'

I kissed his forehead. 'Hold me there in your mind. And in your heart. It will not be so far a time until I am in your bed also.'

At that he drew me into his arms and I felt his mouth on mine. 'For me it cannot be soon enough.'

I could see the pain of loss went as deep with him as it did with me. 'Let me come with you now,' he suddenly demanded. 'We will find your father and tell him the truth, that we made a contract when first we met and have honourably kept to it, as well as any man and wife.'

'He will not see it as honouring a contract but that you took advantage of my youth and innocence. I need to show him that it was not so. Let me find the moment and speak first.'

'In that case, farewell, my love, and God speed the time we may be together.'

'Wait until the day after tomorrow, then send Wat. I will have a letter ready to tell you how the wind blows. Farewell, my John.'

I turned away from the candlelight, not wanting him to see the tears that glinted in my eyes. He was friend, counsellor, lover, poet. He stirred my mind, my soul and my body as none had ever done before. Beneath the witty ambitious courtier, in him I had seen a sadness and a solitariness that echoed with my own. Both had lost a beloved parent at a tender age, and by great good fortune had staunched each other's long-felt pain.

To leave him now, when we had just joined our hearts forever, was like a mother having her child ripped untimely from her arms, when most she needs it.

And yet I must. And I must be strong also for, married though we might be in the eyes of God, we were not so in the eyes of my father.

Chapter 24

I HAD JUST regained the street and begun to run, holding my skirts up from the mud and the mire, when a voice, full of laughing venom, stopped me. 'Mistress More, what do you do abroad alone and unaccompanied?'

It was the Countess of Straven, on horseback, with several retainers carrying her parcels.

'I have been visiting my sister.'

'Ah. The useful Mary. I hear she has been doing a little visiting of her own. You seem very strangely dressed for a sisterly visit.' She studied me carefully.

My hand flew up to my head and I knew the cause of her amusement. How had I forgot I wore my bridal flowers still? Hastily, under cover of my cloak, I pulled off my wedding band, though it pained me sorely so to do.

My mind ranged desperately for an answer. 'My sister plans a Twelfth Night masque and has cast me as Persephone bringing spring back to the winter world.'

'Indeed? Yet, if you are Persephone, who then is your dark lord Hades? Or can I guess?'

I ignored the cruel laughter in her voice. 'Goodbye, my lady. I must get home before my father worries.'

'He has much to worry about, from what I hear.'

I turned my back on her and ran, conscious that she watched me still.

She was an uncomfortable enemy. And would be the worse when she saw that I had got what she so wanted.

I was entirely out of breath by the time I reached my father's house.

'Ann, where have you been all these hours? I have looked for you since dinner and that stupid girl who waits on you knew nothing. And are those leaves in your hair?'

His voice bristled with annoyance that I would somehow have to pacify. I had thought he would be caught up with his business not watching out for me all afternoon long.

'I am sorry, Father, the time passed so quick.' The answer I had given the Countess was as good as any I could devise. 'Mary is planning a Twelfth Night masque. That is why I am wearing the green dress with the ivy for she wishes me to play Persephone.'

'Ah.' He seemed to accept my story, and replied with his usual concern for naught but his own self, 'You will have to tell her you cannot. We will be at Loseley for Twelfth Night. That is why I am waiting for you. I wish us to leave tomorrow. The new picture gallery is ready and I must supervise the hanging. Now, go and pack up your belongings.'

I knew we were bound for Loseley, and yet it was a blow that our departure was so imminent. How long would I be absent from my husband? And was I deluded by some mad dream that the manner of my father's discovering my marriage would alter his acceptance of it?

With a troubled heart I packed my belongings into trunks and baskets and went to tell my father they were ready.

He watched me as I put a match to the tapers in the withdrawing room, a faint smile lighting up his features. 'The green becomes you, Ann. You could indeed be Persephone coming back to light up the world with the freshness of a new year.'

And then to my surprise he did a generous thing. 'Do you greatly wish to act in this masque of your sister Mary's? Perhaps we might spare you somehow if you do.'

'No, no, Father,' I answered quickly, seeing a trap opening up before me since this masque was a figment of my own fantasy. I wished to be near him, the good daughter waiting for the right moment to break my news. 'I am happy to come with you to Loseley.'

'We will have a happy Christmastide, then.'

I wondered then if I should make the most of his softened humour to break my news to him. After all, the deed was done, I was wed, and surely he would have no choice but accept it?

Yet I had no chance, for in walked an usher to announce the arrival of the Lord Keeper. 'God's blood, George, do you know whom I have just seen, bold as brass upon the public street? Mistress Barnes, who married young Aston in secret to get her hands on his fortune. She was with another young lad, stroking his downy chin and kissing him. And she just released from a year in the Fleet prison for her pains and looking for all the world like an old woman!'

I blenched at his words, feeling suddenly faint. If this young woman had paid for her secret marriage with a year in the Fleet, would the same happen to me when it was discovered that we had wed in secret and without my father's consent?

The Lord Keeper noted my sudden paleness. 'Are you ill, Ann? You look as if a ghost had walked across your grave.'

'No, no. A little light-headed with hunger, no more. I left early to rehearse for a masque.'

'Her sister would have her play Persephone,' explained my father with a touch of pride.

'I loved to play in masques when I was younger. Though Hercules was more my line than some Greek goddess.'

While my father and the Lord Keeper conferred on some matter for Parliament, I wrote a note to my sister explaining the reason she was now preparing an unexpected Twelfth Night celebration.

The next day I would have all the coach journey with my father and perhaps then an opportune moment would arise.

Yet the morning dawned cold and wet, with a chill east wind that brought on his cough and put him a vile temper. 'Now I shall have this throat to tease me all over Yuletide,' he complained.

Even my offers of herb tisanes or making him a vest lined with goose grease met with a barked reply that it would be bolting the stable door after the horse had flown, so I kept my peace and waited.

The one unexpected joy was that Mary and Nick sent word they would also come to Loseley for the Christmas feast. I had known that Margaret and her husband came often, for Peckham was not so far away, and this year Sir John Oglander, betrothed to my sister Frances, was also bidden. Mary also had chosen us over her grand Throckmorton relatives.

I had to pass a whole week yet before Mary arrived with all her children, and a coachload of luggage. I had wondered if Nick might stay in town, not wishing to kick his heels in the country away from all his usual pleasures, but instead he came with Mary and the children and in great good humour too.

'Has not little Nick grown apace since you last saw him, Ann?' he asked me, proud as a peacock with his little son. Mary had the goodness at least to flush, for I had seen him not long ago, when his mother took him on an assignation, as cover to meet her lover.

'Look not so superior,' Mary chided me sulkily, when she and I slipped away from the others, claiming we must hunt for ivy swags, and holly berries to decorate the hall. 'For my sin is a drop in the great wide ocean compared to yours. Since all is passing calm at Loseley I assume you have not yet informed our father that you are a wedded woman?'

I shook my head.

'Aye, I guessed as much. Then wait till after the feast is over for the sake of all the rest of us. Nick and I are reconciled and I would welcome a day of calm before another storm.'

I had thought that they seemed content in each other's company. 'What happened? You did not confess nor he discover?'

She shook her head and smiled her slanting smile. 'Neither one. And I have no intention of telling him. Especially now that he has had the nod he will inherit from his uncle Francis, who owns the manor of Beddington and great estates to boot. All he must do is change his name to Carew and lead an honest life and he will be a rich man!'

'And you a rich woman?'

Mary shrugged. 'I will not be a rich woman since all will belong to Nick. I will be a woman married to a rich man.' Her wicked laugh shook the air. 'Still, it is better than a poor woman married to a poor man, with a rich father who refuses to help her.'

'Mary,' I meant what I said, 'I am truly happy for you.'

'As long as he keeps it. A fool and his money, as they say.'

'Yes, but Nick is no fool. This may be the making of him.'

I could see the clear blue sky reflected in my sister's eye and was glad for her.

'He says he is turning over a new leaf and this time I credit it. He has not been to the bear baiting or the bowling alley for a month. He even chooses to stay at home rather than gamble at cards, so I have had no time or chance to meet the other gentleman.'

Although she admitted it not, I could see that Mary was happy to have her husband back and that her dalliance had been in part to distract herself from their many worries.

We took our booty of ivy and berries back to the house and offered them to Constance, who told us to give them to the groom since she had already completed her decorations.

And, indeed Constance, for her part, had decorated in a manner which led one to wonder if the Queen were coming on an unexpected visit. Her berries, not good enough in nature's red, were painted with gold leaf and fixed behind every picture in the new gallery. The vast fireplace in the Great Hall was draped in red taffeta and cloth of gold, billowing together, and the same festooned over beams and banisters throughout the house until the effect was one of Christmas in the cathouse. At any moment I expected ladies of dubious virtue to appear, like those from the Castle upon Hope Inn, to drape themselves half-clad all down the stairwell.

Yet though my family was about me, I could not enjoy myself, but sat staring out of the great windows at the path from the turnpike, in case any message came from London.

It was almost Christmas when Wat rode up to the front door. I was on my feet in a flash and ran out to meet him, laughing, yet stopped when I saw how doleful was his face.

I took him round to the kitchen door and found him food and sustenance. 'How does your master, Wat? Is he in good form?'

Wat shook his head. 'He languishes. Between your absence and the war between the Lord Keeper and the Countess, the joy is all drained out of him. He has been to Court once or twice and still works hard for his master, yet never smiles. I wish you could be with him, mistress.'

I glanced behind at that, hoping none overheard us.

'I will, Wat, as soon as ever I can.' The sharp longing for him made my heart ache. 'Tell him that my father is all good humour and I but wait for the moment. He should be at the ready to come.'

'I will tell him.'

'Give him this.' I kissed Wat on the cheek so that he reddened to the colour of the westering sun as it sank over the river.

'I hope he would not mistake me, mistress, if I gave him such a token.' Wat grinned.

'Wat,' I laughed heartily at that, my mood lightening from the heavy burden of its worry. 'There are scarce few certainties in this life of ours but my John loving men is not amongst them.'

Finding a chance when my father's mood was light and he was without company turned out to be like opening a thousand oysters and finding not a single pearl. If he was alone he was ill-tempered, and, in company, unapproachable. And over the twelve days of Christmas there was more company at Loseley than I had ever witnessed. It was as if, now the house was finally his, he would show all its finery to every person in the county above the rank of yeoman, and even a few of those. The clerk of the kitchen was forever slaughtering more sheep and oxen till I wondered if anything that could low or baa was left in all Surrey.

He asked me what had befallen my sister's masque and startled me by declaring we should have it here. In the end when Twelfth Night had come and gone and I had not yet spoken, I vowed to screw up my courage at last, no matter what the portents for his mood. The house had been quieter for the last days and I had hopes that my father planned no more entertaining.

Today he had seemed in a passing good mood. He had praised Frances' stitchery and said that Sir John Oglander was a lucky man, then complimented his wife on the variety of her table, and even offered Mary's husband a game of backgammon, which my father won, though whether Nick allowed him this distinction I know not.

This, then, should be the night. I would wait until he was mellow after supper, with wine taken, and his admiring family all around him, then request a private word. However much he hated my disclosure he would have the night to sleep on it and I my sisters' help to protect me from his ire.

I dressed with extra care, wearing all the jewels my mother had willed me, both to give me courage and to remind him of her whom he had lost, trusting he would not want to lose me also by his final banishment.

The gown I chose was the one he had told me I looked well in, and so that I might also solicit the support of our Saviour, I added the small gold cross which my grandmother had given me.

As I walked slowly down the great staircase, willing myself to have all the courage I could muster, I met with William, my father's yeoman of the buttery. 'William,' I smiled at this ancient gentleman, 'I have a matter of some moment which I intend to tell my father of this night. Could you make sure his glass is never empty, for I have a favour to ask of him and am sure he will be the more accepting with the help of Bacchus.'

'Do you, Mistress Ann? Then I will do all I can to assist you. Yet your father is no great drinker, much though he fills up the glasses of others.'

'Do your best!'

'Yes, mistress, I will that.' He winked broadly at me. 'And good luck with your favour.'

The one enlivener of my gloom was the arrival of Sir John Oglander, who had come only this evening after staying with his brother in London.

He had dressed for dinner in the unusual ensemble of an Indian prince, complete with yellow silken turban, sent him by a trader friend. 'Know you, Mistress More, the natives who wear them in that great continent never cut their hair and it grows nigh on six feet long. Imagine.' He pointed to his own thinning locks. 'To think I have trouble hanging on to six inches.'

'Depends where you put them, John,' remarked my brother-in-law, Nick, with a cackle.

Sir John glanced at him wonderingly, not understanding a word, simply looking puzzled and a little wounded for he knew he was the butt of Nick's joke yet knew not why.

And kind Sir John went on to compound his sin still further by informing all that his brother was a tradesman. 'Aye, Martin is a mercer, at the sign of the Hen and Chicken in Cheapside, and a good one too. You must go to him if you need aught in that line, Mistress Ann.'

He did not notice the sniggers that were spreading amidst the other guests. 'Do you not think it sensible, Mistress Ann, that even a gentleman should have trade to prevent him becoming too high?'

I looked down the long table at the well-fed faces that had eaten more at this one feast than many had in a month, and how they laughed at the idea of working for their living. And I thought also of my secret husband, whose father had been an ironmonger, be it a great one, and how they would wrinkle their brows in distaste at such a low profession.

'An honest day's work would do you no harm, Nick.' My brother-in-law stayed his goblet halfway to his mouth and looked at me in surprise.

'Now Ann becomes a moralist also.'

'She is right, husband,' Mary seconded, though her voice was teasing. 'A week in a mercer's shop, so you had to keep to the clock and not go cocking or to the Globe would hurt you not at all.'

'God's blood, Mary!' Nick banged his goblet onto the table spilling his wine.

In the midst of all the sound and fury Sir John leaned closer to me. 'And were you in town yourself not long ago, Mistress Ann?'

'I was, Sir John. My father and I were staying in his lodgings at Charing Cross.'

'Then it was indeed you I glimpsed! I thought as much! I saw you one day coming out of the chapel hard by the Savoy Hospital when we walked homewards from the Convent garden. I said, "Martin, look, there is Mistress More, Sir George's daughter, sister to my betrothed." I meant to come and greet you but you were talking to some great lady astride her horse.'

At his words I felt drops of sweat gather in my palms and my throat closed over so I dared not trust my voice to answer.

And before I could think of how to pass the question off, my father answered for me. 'Indeed, you interest me very much, Sir John.' I felt a sharp breath of fear at his words, as if a crypt had been opened and the foul air released. 'For I cannot recall, Ann, any reason why you would need to go to such a scandalous place as the Savoy Chapel.' I felt his eyes upon me flaying away the skin until my innermost being was exposed. 'Unless it were to contract a secret marriage which had been expressly forbidden by your father.'

Chapter 25

'WELL, ANN,' MY father demanded, his face contorted like one of the evil spirits carved into Loseley's great chalk fireplace, 'have you no answer for me? For if you have indeed dared to do such a thing, make no bones, I will have so immeasurably unwelcome a marriage annulled! Speak!'

At my continued silence he raised his hand as if to strike.

Mary stepped in front of me, shielding my body with her own, as poor Sir John looked on in horror at the consequence of his innocent question. 'And this is the gentle treatment you apportion to your daughters, sir! If so, no wonder they seek protection elsewhere!'

'And you are hardly better!' My father tried to push her away so roughly that her husband had to leap forward and intervene.

'You should control your wife, sir!' he hissed at Nick. 'She does you no credit.'

Nick shepherded Mary protestingly away. 'This is a Christian country, Father, and may our Lord Jesus Christ have mercy on your soul for such behaviour.'

'Look to your own soul, daughter. It is your sister who needs God's mercy if one hundredth of this tale is true, for she will have broken every law of church and custom. I thank God that such a marriage, performed in secret without my knowledge or permission, would certainly never stand.'

At his words I heard a great ringing in my ears as of water tumbling over me, twisting and drowning me, so that I had to gasp for air.

'See, Father, the effect of your threats on Ann, she is fainting away.'

'Your sister is not so feeble as to pull that woman's trick.' He took my chin in his hand, the parody of a lover's gesture, and pinched it hard. 'Since you have denied nothing, go now to your chamber where you will stay, speaking to none, not even your sisters, while I discover the truth of this matter. Go!'

I ran up the stairs, past the startled stares of the yeomen of the dining chamber, my throat closing over and my heart beating so hard it pained my chest. What other than this fury had I looked for in my father when he found the truth? No two men more different could be found on God's earth than he and my new husband. My father so narrow and restricted in his thought, a lover of things remaining as ever they had been, a firm believer that all should know their place, from the lowest to the highest. How could he not distrust a man like John, the son of an ironmonger, clever, ambitious, with a ready wit and a dangerous reputation, who dared to believe that merit should be rewarded for its own sake?

Once inside I did not wait for my father to come and lock the door but took the key, made of black iron and so heavy it would make a hole in any pocket, and locked the door myself.

I threw myself upon my bed and wept bitterly. Yet not for long. I was not one for weeping, which had no end other than a wetted pillow. Instead I must act. I must get a message to John that thanks to poor Sir John my father now knew all. Our only remaining hope was to show my father that our love was honourable, and that he would make a worthy son-in-law.

This task seemed like that of a mahomedan trying to reach Mecca by walking there from Loseley, yet there was no other choice. Perhaps his master the Lord Keeper would vouch for him. Tomorrow my father would go to London to stir up trouble.

At once I knew I must go before him and warn my husband of the storm that raged around us.

I heard a quiet knocking at the door, too gentle to be my father.

Of my sisters only Mary would dare to defy my father's edict.

And indeed it was she. I pulled her into the room.

'What do you do now?' she whispered. 'Our father storms like some miser whose treasure has all been stolen. Nick and Thomas try to calm him, but they are making him madder. Nick's spendthrift ways are overlooked now there is a savage wolf that has descended on his poor innocent lamb.'

'God's blood, I am no weeping virgin. I went to his bed willingly enough.'

'Not an argument that will placate our father. He would liefer believe Master Donne dishonoured you than that you dishonoured yourself.'

'Mary, I must go to my husband now and warn him of my father's intentions.'

'It is six of the clock on a winter's night. Are you mad?'

'I know the way well enough and even you allow I ride better than a man. You must find me some food and water and I will do the rest. Father will leave himself on the morrow and you can say I will neither speak nor eat.' I smiled at that. 'A story he will believe, since it has the ring of truth.'

'Ann, I dare not. Something might befall you.'

'Unless I can get to John my life is over. He must be warned so that he can ready his defence.'

'Then send a messenger.'

'No, I need to see him myself. To stoke our strength for what comes after.'

'It is the last thing I do for you, Ann.'

'You have done much already.' At that I held fast to her as if she were the last tree left standing in a flooded landscape. 'Thank you, sister.'

She brought me some plain warm clothes an hour later, with a parcel of food stolen from the kitchen. 'Good luck, and come swiftly back. I cannot keep others from your door for long.'

It was but nine of the clock when I at last crept out, locking the door behind me and hiding the great key in an alcove behind a thick curtain on the staircase.

I knew which horse to take, the best chestnut mare, and saddled her quickly, as I had watched the groom do a thousand times.

I opened the stable gate and led her out. To my great good fortune a full moon was lighting the sky and I could see my way almost as clear as day. With a swift glance behind me to make sure none witnessed my departure, I began my journey.

God must have been on my side for the rutted way stretched out ahead of me like a shining river, quiet and empty.

Tess the mare and I were old friends and we rode as one.

She only reared once, startled by a fox that ran suddenly into our path, but I soon calmed her, talking to her softly, and calming myself at the same time.

From I know not where came the strength to keep me going hour upon hour, stopping but once to give her water and some oats I had stolen from the stables. By three of the morning we approached the outskirts of London long before day was beginning in that great heaving city. Hiding my face under its borrowed cap, I joined the stream of carts, horses and flocks of cackling geese that crossed London Bridge. It seemed not so long ago that I had done the same on horseback with my father, yet it was two whole years past, two years in which I had passed from childhood to being a woman and now to my strange state of being a secret wife, with none of those dues or comforts which wifedom promised to accord.

Did I regret it, alone in my deepest silent contemplation, that I had taken so grave and dangerous a step, one that I had hidden even from those who loved me?

I had not noticed, so deep was I in thought, that my cloak had blown back from my face, revealing my true nature to the grey, damp morning world. 'Ho, there, mistress!' A rough, leering man tried to grab my reins, jerking back poor Tess's head. 'What does a pretty maid like you do alone in London town? Looking for trouble, I'll be bound.' I felt his hot stinking breath as he tried to pull me from the saddle. 'I'll give you trouble, and more . . .'

At that I spurred Tess on, and she leapt forward, dragging the man with us.

'Leave the wench alone!' shouted a bedraggled woman laying out her few paltry wares on the broad pavement. 'You be no good to any woman, Jeb Smith, least of all a young and comely one!'

He turned at his name and loosened his grip for an instant. It was long enough for me. I drove my horse through the complaining crowd, my head down and cloak pulled over my face again, until it parted like the Red Sea, mumbling and spitting, but at least giving me road until I was safely across the river.

Heart racing, I turned left and made my way towards my husband's lodgings, not allowing myself the thought of what I would do were he not within.

To my great relief I came upon Wat, sleeping like a faithful dog on a pallet outside the door.

'Good morrow, Wat.' I shook him gently. 'How is your master? Still asleep?'

Wat sat up, looking troubled. 'Not good, mistress. He strides about his chamber all night long, never sleeping. And last night I heard him pray out loud, begging God's forgiveness that he had done wrong, and most of all wronged you, an innocent young maid, by marrying you.'

'Hush, Wat.' I knew one thing, that if my husband was thus weakened it would be down to me to steel him for the fight ahead. 'Go, buy bread and beer and leave it by the door.' I handed him some coins. 'I will make it my business to raise your master's spirits.'

He dropped to one knee and kissed my hand. 'Mistress Ann, you are as one sent from Heaven.'

I looked rueful at that for I did not think God would bless me at this moment, especially for the means I had in mind of cheering my husband, but I let it pass. 'Go.'

And, very gently, I opened the door of the chamber.

He was sleeping on his back, one arm flung behind him. His dark hair was spread upon the pillow. Quietly I slipped off my borrowed clothes, shivering at the sudden cold, and climbed onto the bed, pressing my naked flesh against his.

He woke and looked at me, startled. 'Ann? Is it truly you and not some vicious vision come to taunt me?'

'Wat thought me an angel sent from God,' I teased.

He laughed, and taking in my naked state I saw his eyes narrow with desire. 'I prayed yesterday that I had not wronged you and selfishly led you down a path of my own desiring.'

'John. Husband. I may be young in years but I know that which I desire also. And it is this. And it is you.'

After that all was obliterated.

All but the feel of his bones on my bones, his skin on my skin, in the true mystical union of bodies and souls, with desire and love mixed equally. And in the white fire of our passion I saw that all his doubts were unfounded, that no matter what trials we had to face, the reward would be worth the struggle.

Yet we had to take action now before others than Master Manners blackened his name still further.

'You must tell my father of our marriage at once, before others make the disclosure worse. I thought perhaps I could do it, yet I see now that it must be you who tells him yourself, and you must do it honourably, not humbly nor borne down by a sense of guilt, but with an honest face and sincere reasoning.'

He kissed my face, his own lit by a sadness that made me wish to shake him, for whatever happened he must not lose his resolve. 'I am not sure it will matter in what manner I break the news. He will never accept me as your rightful husband.'

'Then persuade him! Where is all that strange irresistible art your champions talk of?'

'That is in my verse.'

'Then put it also in your face and conversation. Charm him! Show him you are well regarded by your peers and your masters alike!'

'Ann, Ann, would that I had your youthful optimism!'

I hit him with the pillow at that. 'Cease! Stop talking as if you were an old man when you are but nine and twenty!' The light was shining brightly through the windows now and I must get up and go or I would make things the worse for us by the discovery I had come to visit him.

I jumped from the bed and dressed at speed, helped by the cold air nipping at my naked flesh. The bed, our rightful home, had never looked so inviting.

'Farewell, husband. Promise me that you will come soon. It will be for the best, I know, that he hears it from your lips instead of those of snakelike traitors and evil wishers who care not a jot for our happiness and would like to see you brought down and trodden underfoot. Goodbye.'

I gently stirred Wat, sleeping again outside, and bade him also farewell. With the great intelligence he always showed he had fed and watered my mare and she was ready to go.

And go, we did. Wat had bade me cross with her by water, and though she shied at first, being led into the small craft, she afterwards stood straight and proud. We alighted on the south side, gaining half an hour at least, and since I now had brought bread and a flask of small beer, we continued down the grey-streaked road stopping only once for rest, and by ten of the clock had reached the outskirts of the town of Guildford, which my father represented in Parliament. Here I kept my head well down, lest my face be known, and cantered on across country until I gained the quietest entry to our land. At last I dismounted, and not wanting to risk taking Tess to the stables, instead left her tethered to a tree from which I would untie her later, when all were busy at the midday meal.

Now all I had to do was get myself once more back into the house unrecognized, and pray that my disappearance had been well hidden by that consummate actress, my sister Mary.

I scuttled like a mouse to the side door and thence down the kitchen passage, wishing with my whole heart that my father stood not so on his ceremony, and employed not fifty servants but five. For each time I stopped, hiding in some darkened nook, I heard the laughter or chatter of more of my father's men. It took me all of twenty minutes to safely gain my chamber, where I tore off my sweat-soaked clothing and quickly dressed in my proper attire, just as the bell sounded for dinner. Still banished to my chamber, I of course would not be joining them.

And then a surprising thing. A knock, and Frances stood at the door, smiling as if she were the bearer of a message twixt God and his creations. 'Father has found no further evidence of your forbidden marriage. He says you may join us at the table.'

My heart raced like the bellows at this news. For I knew all too well the truth of the matter.

Indeed my stepmother Constance told me with surprise that I looked well today and that my eyes were unusually bright.

'And your cheeks uncommon red for one who has spent so long confined to her chamber,' Mary added, one dark eyebrow raised in my direction.

'Ann,' my father's tone bore a humility I had rarely heard before, so unexpected it pained me exceedingly, 'sit down. I have an apology to make to you. I have sent a message to the Lord Keeper himself on this matter and he denies it.'

At this I felt as if a piece of jagged glass ripped at my heart. Surely I could hide my secret no longer? 'Father, speak not so, it is I who must ask your humble apology.' I spurred myself on to tell him the whole truth. 'For you see . . .'

'Ann, will you so soon spoil my good opinion of you? Be seated!'

After that, all I could do was wait for my husband's arrival and the axe to fall. Which happened three days later. Yet not at all in the manner I expected.

Chapter 26

EACH MORNING AS I waited for the storm to break I knelt and said my prayers, beseeching the Lord to help us, while my conscience asked if we had not committed too great sin to ask for His assistance. After I prayed I sat up on the window seat of my chamber watching for the moment my husband would appear.

On the third day my heart flew to my mouth when I saw a black-clad figure ride up the road and turn his horse through the wooden gate that separated the front court of Loseley from the parkland beyond.

Yet it was not he! I saw, with sinking spirits, that it was indeed a not-too-distant neighbour of ours, no less a personage than the Earl of Northumberland, whom some called the Wizard Earl on account of his outlandish interests in alchemy and astronomy. And yet why came he thus alone, without retinue?

And then I gasped, seeing at once the truth of why so great a man might come alone and unannounced, to see my father. He was also a close acquaintance of my husband. Had John, knowing my father's reverence for those above him, bidden this man to intercede to him on our behalf?

And I saw also in the same instant what a terrible error this would prove.

The truth was, my father hated to defer to any, and here came one who was higher than he in status to announce, before he officially knew himself, that his own daughter had wed herself in secret to a man that he despised!

I watched his grace of Northumberland go in through the great front door and waited, my body taut, listening for a shout or the crash of breaking glass when my father heard the dread news.

Yet there was nothing save an unaccustomed silence. Perhaps it was my fear or fancy yet the great house seemed to me as still as the grave, as if all the bustling servants held their breath and ceased their daily duties. Even the horses in the stables and the partridges in their coveys were stilled.

Waiting.

And then my sister Frances burst through my door, tears coursing down her pious features. 'Ann! Say it is not so!'

Waiting for no answer she turned away, eager perhaps to spread the forbidden news to other ears, shouting as she sped that our father bid me come down to the hall at once.

I threw back my head, breathed deeply, and straightened my shoulders as one might who was going into battle.

My moment had come and I would not use it lightly.

It was chill in the Great Hall, save for the warmth of the logs in the great stone fireplace. My father stood in front of it, as still as an effigy, his ancestors massing on the walls above him, as angry and affronted as he was. Ranged at either side were my three sisters.

He held a letter sealed in red wax with a sheaf of snakes, written in that familiar neat and sloping hand.

His face was as grey as rancid whey. 'So it is true, then, you have married him and lied to me, time and time again?'

I could play the effigy also, and so I stood before him, proud and silent.

'Since you were first at York House, this matter has had foundation, so your . . . *husband* writes to me.' He spat out the word 'husband' as if it were a deadly insult he would not keep within his mouth. 'That it was there you promised yourselves to each other.'

I nodded.

'How old were you at that time, remind me?'

'Fourteen years.'

'And this man, your *husband*, thought nothing of taking advantage of one so tender in years and innocent as you were then?'

My eyes met my father's, warm brown locked onto chilling grey.

'He took no advantage of me. From our first interview I was lost and wanted none other than he, though I did not at first perceive it. Indeed it was often I who did the persuading.'

At that he could contain his fury no more. Silently he approached me and hit me hard across the cheek, with all the strength he could muster, so that I reeled and almost fell.

Behind me I saw Mary start forward.

'Want you that I should strike you also? Go home to your spend-thrift husband and be lucky this is not you who transgresses for I will not take you in. Nor you,' he turned to the unfortunate Frances who cowered back. 'Nor you either!' he lashed at Margaret. It would have been almost a jest, the thought of Margaret sinning against her Thomas, but for the terrifying anger in my father's eyes, as he stood here as pitiless as the Archangel Michael casting out Lucifer and his band from Heaven into the fires beneath.

"'At her lying in town this last Parliament,'" he read, waving the letter at me, '"I found means to see her twice or thrice; we both knew the obligations that lay upon us and we adventured equally . . ." What about the obligations to your father or your family?' He turned towards the Earl, including him in his all-encompassing fury. 'How could a libertine and an innocent maid adventure equally? He tries but to cover himself against the accusations he knows will surely follow.'

'He does not, Father,' I spoke at last. 'We did indeed adventure equally. We are two souls joined into one by love.'

'Hah, this is the kind of versifying nonsense he has bewitched you with, two souls in one. Two dowries in one, perhaps, for it is more like your inheritance that he covets than your eternal soul. That he will leave to God.'

He turned back to the letter. 'Yet I must be grateful to him, for here he assures me the reason he did not tell me of this outrageous marriage was because he stood not well in my opinion. Indeed, sirrah! I wonder why it should be that I think not well of a debt-ridden Papist, a scurrilous poet and a deceiver of gentlewomen who wishes to advance his own prospects by marrying into my family?'

'Father,' Mary intervened, 'that is not just!'

'What hand had you in this, Mary? More than you are saying, I'd wager. Your own husband is thick enough with Papists himself. Did Ann paddle in this felon's palm when she stayed under your roof? Perhaps you brought them spiced ale and plumped their pillows?'

Wisely Mary said naught, but this incensed my father yet further. 'Go! Back to your weak-willed husband. Leave!'

'I will not abandon Ann with you, defenceless, when you are in such a disposition!'

'Indeed, yes,' his voice rose shrill again in fury, 'her husband shares the same concern, that she should not feel the sudden terror of my anger.' I recoiled in fear he would strike me again. 'Worry not, daughter, for she comes to London with me. I would have her tell her uncle the Lord Keeper face to face how she crept between the sheets with his secretary when his own wife was dying of the smallpox . . .'

'Father, do not say so . . .' I cried in anguish at so cruel an accusation.

'Do you deny it?'

'I do absolutely, Father. I loved her like my lost mother. When she was so cruelly taken I sought solace with Master Donne yet there was no impropriety between us. Indeed he would not have it so . . .'

'Yet you would have lifted your skirts willingly?'

He did not wait for me to defend myself. 'See, there is one final insult in this choice letter from Master Donne. He wishes I should not incense his master, the Lord Keeper, for that would destroy both him and you—as if seducing his master's niece in his own house were not enough to do it! Well, I have a plan.'

Of a sudden my father smiled, and yet his smile was more chilling than his anger. 'If he fears losing his position so much—then I will do all I can to deprive him of it. I will have him dismissed from his employment.' He looked narrowly at me, showing no pity. 'And fear not, Ann, I will get this marriage decreed null and void. You may be Mistress Ann Donne today, but you will not be so for much longer!'

He thrust the letter into my shaking hands. 'Here, read it, see the letter your husband sends me—too much the coward to come in person, he dares only to write!'

I ran back to my chamber, tears blinding my eyes, attempting to read the words even as I stumbled up the stairs. I knew at once that my clever, witty husband had erred in conveying such news by letter.

In person he might have charmed or reasoned or shown the true sincerity of his intentions. The letter sounded bold and defiant, as if the act were all complete and naught my father could do to help it. Could my father indeed overturn our marriage as he threatened?

I gathered up an armful of clothing and thrust it into a pannier, not caring what I chose, for what did it matter since, married though I might be, I was not to be allowed to join my husband?

We could have gained London at much greater speed on horseback, yet my father had ordered his coach, and summoned liveried grooms to accompany us. It occurred to me that London might be gossiping about me, the spiteful Court ladies enjoying the spectacle of my public ruin. I cared not a jot, for I hated the life they led, pampered and yet tied like servants in their service to the ageing Queen. Yet my father cared greatly. And so we would approach the city with all the pomp and ceremony befitting Sir George More of Loseley, Knight, Sheriff of Surrey and Sussex, and Chamberlain of Receipt in the Exchequer.

The journey was a silent one. The servants had not come out to see us off, and the grooms accompanying us looked deliberately away from me, lest their gaze locked onto the red weal across my cheek.

I could have worn my vizor but chose not to. Let my father and others also see the glorious effects of his paternal hand.

Mary waved to me, silent for once. I knew she feared for my safety and the future of my marriage yet I felt naught but a cold, hard anger. I would not let my father break me.

At last we were at York House, and alighting here was almost my undoing for all the memories of our courtship overwhelmed me, the amorous doves, our stolen hours together, and at last the deep love which led us to that secret assignation before Christmas, and made us man and wife. And yet for how long?

We were greeted, with some surprise, by my uncle's groom of the stranger's horse. And while he saw to the team, my father insisted on seeing his master the Lord Keeper with no delay.

York House rang with the shouts of merry laughter, the sweet sound of lute songs from the musicians in the minstrels' gallery, and the buzz of chatter from the Countess, her daughters and all their great entourage as they sat, dazzling in their expensive finery, around the supper table.

My uncle, usually the most serene of men, looked like one who has been on his feet all day and sees no sign in his own home of a peaceful fireside.

'What is this urgent matter, brother-in-law, which takes me from my supper table? I must tell you, you have not chosen the most auspicious day to bring me your difficulty. My wife entertains her newest acquaintances from Court with roast swan painted with gold when I have often bid her ban such gross extravagance.'

'I think you will grant me your precious time when you hear the import. For the matter is one that touches your honour also.'

The Lord Keeper sighed and rubbed his tired brow. 'Tell me, then.'

'It concerns my daughter, Ann, and your own secretary.'

'Not Gregory Downhall?' A small smile played about the Lord Keeper's lean face, which had grown leaner and more lined with care since his marriage. 'I would have thought him too old and studious to make a young girl's heart race.'

'No.' My father's voice rose shrilly, so that one or two of the revellers glanced in our direction. 'Not Gregory Downhall. Master John Donne. And he has not just made her heart race, but wooed her and bedded her under your very nose while my sister, your wife, lay in her bed, her face covered in pustules, gasping for her dying breath!'

At this Sir Thomas's face paled and grew waxen, so that he had to hold onto a chair for support.

'And worse still than that . . .'

'What could be worse than such betrayal?' the Lord Keeper demanded, his eyes stricken. 'Worse than so cruel an abuse of my sweet wife's trust and generosity? She is not with child?'

My father cast me a look of venom. 'That at least we have been spared. Yet he has secretly married her three weeks since in the liberty of the Savoy Chapel, against all the canon laws and in breach of every rule of honour and decency.'

He thrust the letter confessing it into the Lord Keeper's hand.

The blood rushed from my head and thundered in my ears until I thought I must faint away. Yet I must be strong. And so I willed myself to speak.

'My lord uncle, it was not thus! We did not betray your beloved wife so! We two fell in love almost since ever we first met, some three years since. And yet we acted not upon our strong desires, but waited patiently to see if this was a flower that would bloom or wither on the stem. And despite all, respect for you, difficulty of meeting, the difference between our ages and our estates, our love grew stronger and more blessed and so at last we sanctified it but a short time ago.'

'Never say sanctified,' cut in my father. 'This union is not blessed but cursed! An aberration!' He grabbed the Lord Keeper's embroidered sleeve. 'Master Donne must pay. He abused your sacred trust. You must deprive him of his office! Indeed, he should be flung into the Fleet and the key be lost forever.'

'Calm yourself, Sir George, you were ever too passionate.' Sadly he turned to me. 'And yet, Ann, if he is indeed in breach of my confidence and the law there is no choice in the matter: Master Donne must indeed face a sojourn in the Fleet.'

Chapter 27

I WAS NOT present when they took him to the Fleet Prison.

Thanks to the good offices of the Lord Keeper he was not escorted in front of the crowds at Chancery, but quietly from his chamber.

Wat told me after that he went proudly, and was polite to his jailers, yet I could but imagine the pain and fear that beset him. Did not his own brother, Henry, die of the plague in Newgate Prison but eight years since?

When I heard of his imprisonment, I threw myself upon my father's mercy.

'How can your conscience allow this, when you know he will languish and even die in such a place?'

The Fleet Prison, as he well knew, was greatly feared for its nearness to the plague districts.

'Talk not to me of conscience!' My father's fury lashed at me, as painful as a whip across my still-reddened face. 'You, who pretended sweet innocency while all the while crawling into his bed like a stewhouse drab!'

'He is my husband. May I at least send food or clean linen to him in this frightful place?'

'No!' I thought he might strike again and stood my ground, unflinching, my eyes level with his, if not somewhat above, for I am taller by some inches. 'He is no husband of yours until the Archbishop of Canterbury himself decrees it at the High Commission. And since I have applied for an annulment, he may never be such!'

'Do not say so.' I tried to keep my eyes from letting me down by weeping. 'He is my husband before God and none, not even you, can undo God's holy ordinance.'

Of a sudden he laughed hollowly. 'And you are his destiny, or so he has told the Lord Keeper. Until he met you his life was no more than a waking dream. Well, now it will be a nightmare. And if ever he is released that will be an end to his advancement. The Lord Keeper has dismissed him.'

'I will not listen to this venom. He loves me and I love him in return. I care naught for worldly advancement and no more does John.'

He laughed in derision. 'All men care for worldly advancement, your husband more than most. You believe your hearts to be so strong? That you will live on love and air?'

'If need be. Yes.'

Though it pained me sorely, I dared not try and visit my husband in the Fleet, for I knew that it would bring but greater ire upon his head from my father. Yet I did get a message to Wat that he must go and take some small necessities.

The tale he told fairly broke my heart.

My husband was detained in dank and cramped surroundings not many yards from the Shambles, where my aunt and I had bought the suet for my uncle's malady so long since. Now he was in a cell choked by the stink of the tanneries, next to the foul Fleet river which was full of refuse flung into the stream by furriers and butchers alike.

And for this privilege, Wat explained, he must pay £3. 6s.d for his commitment and 20 pence to be allowed to feel the fresh air on his face by walking the yard.

'He is not alone, mistress. His friends visit, and he writes to the Lord Keeper and your father, hoping that one or the other will show him mercy. And also, mistress, he sends you this.' He handed me a parchment, scrawled in the familiar beloved hand.

My husband's letter bid me keep my spirits up and said that he knew, in the end, our love would triumph over all adversity.

Yet it was his postscript that made me wipe away a tear for he had added the mournful message: *John Donne, Ann Donne, Undone.*

And I swore that to my last breath I would not allow it to be so.

Six whole days had passed since my husband's imprisonment in the

Fleet and hourly I waited for the news that he had succumbed to some dread sickness or affliction.

Another letter arrived from him addressed to my father, this one as humble as the first had been bold and defiant.

'Master Donne learns some humility at least,' my father shrugged.

At that my heart soared with sudden hope. 'What will you answer him?'

'That his fate lies not with me but with the Lord Keeper.'

I had almost to remind him that it was he, and not the Lord Keeper, who had caused the imprisonment a week ago. Indeed the Lord Keeper bade him think it over, yet my father would have none of it; Master Donne must be imprisoned and his livelihood lost. And now here was my father washing his hands of my husband's fate, like Pontius Pilate.

And then, unexpected and unannounced, with only her groom to bid her company, about her neck the double chains that made her resemble the Lord Mayor of London, my grandmother arrived from Surrey.

My father had decided to sup early for the day's business in Parliament had been long and tiring. The servants had already begun to clear away the dishes when in she strode, riding crop in hand, just as Mary had come into the church on the day of my marriage. Yet where Mary was all lithe beauty and elegance, my grandmother had the bustling strength and courage under fire of a great warhorse that naught, not even vast cannons packed with gunpowder, could alarm.

'Well, George,' she thundered, stopping not even to remove her overgarments, 'I am come to discuss this nonsense of throwing Master Donne in prison.'

My father jumped up from his gilded seat. 'My lady mother, you know nothing of these proceedings.'

'I know enough. I know that this man has married Ann.'

'Precisely. In secret, without my consent and in breach of canon law, and she a minor.'

'Thousands marry in breach of canon law. The Lord Keeper for one, who has come to richly regret it, and serve him right for wedding that shrew with my dear daughter hardly cold in her grave.'

'Mother, you forget, Ann was but a maid of fourteen years when he began this cursed courtship. The libertine abused her innocence.'

'They had no relations until she was near seventeen, Ann swears, and the law allows marriage at twelve. Indeed, you betrothed her sister Frances when she was twelve years old without her even meeting the gentleman.'

He turned angrily away. 'The present case is different. They courted secretly. They had relations.'

'And for how long has this courtship run its course?'

'Three years.'

'And after three long years, and many separations, one beyond a twelvemonth, they still risked all to marry secretly, knowing the weight of your displeasure would fall upon them. Is that not proof their love endures?'

'She is but a child, what knows she of such things? And she has chosen a man who some suspect of coveting her portion or her position, a man sullied by gossip, from a family of known Papists, who has few prospects, and you wish me to celebrate such a union?'

'Ann is no mewling babe in arms, she is a woman, yet you have failed to see it. She has made her choice and proved the steadfastness of her love through much adversity. She even starved herself to show you. Have you not marked how she lights up like the summer sky when Master Donne's name is talked of?'

'I have no time for such women's nonsense.'

'You refuse her own choice, tried and tested by time, yet offer her to a man who would have defiled her if he could, and would do worse to punish her when they were wed, because it suits your ambitions for this family?'

'Mother, I . . .' He seemed at last defeated as if he could think of no further arguments.

She dropped a hand onto his shoulder. 'George, you are a man of extreme passions, yet you love your daughter, do you not?'

'How can I hand her to a man who has taken advantage of her innocence, of whom all London gossips, the air beating with all their wild surmisings like the flapping of some evil bird?'

'Is it not your daughter's life that matters more than idle chatter, which will last no longer than a puff of smoke in a strong wind? Besides which, the race is run. She is married to him, for good or ill.'

'That has not yet been established.'

'My son, he proves it with a petition lodged at the Court of Audiences which they say he is very like to win.'

At that my father seemed suddenly to hunch up, his shoulders sagging as old men's do. 'What world is this, then, when a father's consent counts for naught and a girl of ten and seven years can marry whom she pleases?'

'A changing one, my son.'

'I love him, Father,' I said in a voice of humble submission. 'He is my lawful wedded husband. And yet he languishes in a stinking prison cheek by jowl with death and pestilence.'

He turned his head away and I could see that he struggled between pride and anger and the love he bore me.

My grandmother, never one to lose an advantage, blustered onwards. 'If this nonsense over keeping Master Donne in prison ends not, then I shall never return to Surrey.' Her hawk-like nose, looming above us in the shadows, seemed twice its usual size, and the grim unsmiling line of her lips could swallow a man whole. 'Indeed, if you persist in your usual blockhead fashion, George, I shall be as fixed as that oak newel post.' She pointed to the solid block that formed the base of the banister. 'And never shall you rid your house of me. The choice is yours.'

Next to God, I knew my grandmother to be my best ally, and while I helped her unpack her trunk that night, I thanked her for it.

'I hope your father will see the light, yet he is a stubborn man and thinks too much of the world's opinion.'

'My lady grandmother, God bless you for coming here and for taking my part.'

'Ann, mind this. I have opposed this marriage as much as any have, but life has taught me that it is idle to cry over milk that has been spilt. Since the deed is done, better that you prove it was worth the doing.'

'I will, Grandmother, as soon as ever I am given the chance.'

Chapter 28

EARLY ON THE morrow I slipped out before the rest of the household awoke and took myself to St Bride's Church to pray for my husband's release from that terrible place. I could not but think of what had befallen his brother Henry in Newgate, and I pictured a similar fate beckoning to my own husband. If I by the end of this day had not changed my father's mind, I would go to the Fleet myself, no matter what the risk.

Even at that early hour the churchyard seemed more like a market than a place of peace and penitence, bustling with vendors setting up their wares, at one side a tavern offering ale to busy guildsmen, right there in the sight of God, and at the other a printing shop where pamphlets and bills were being noisily prepared amidst a group of arguing writers.

I stole past, my vizor protecting me, and into the back of the church. Matins were halfway through and the familiar sound of voices raised in worship soothed my sorry heart.

For many minutes I knelt, my head bowed, begging God to have pity on our lot. We had committed a sin of the flesh, I knew, and yet was it so great a sin to love as we did and to sanctify our union in the hope of a true and loving marriage?

I know not how long I knelt there, head bowed, until the cold had overtaken me and I could no longer feel the life in the fingers of my hands. I looked up then to find an empty church, its worshippers departed.

And there, in the deathly silence, a terrible solution came to me.

'Forgive us, Lord,' I spoke aloud, my voice ringing out through the chill darkness. 'Yet if you must punish us for our sin, punish only me. Release my husband from his prison cell before disease can ravish him and I will oppose my father's wishes no longer, even though it means that he whom I love most on this earth is denied to me and that we will only be united in the next. Amen.'

Outside the sudden sunlight blinded me and I fell back into the shadows to make my way back to Charing Cross. And yet, if my father would do naught for us, why did I not appeal myself direct to my uncle the Lord Keeper?

I found him just rising from his own morning prayers and not yet departed for the council chamber. His kindly face wore the crease of annoyance and bad temper it had worn ever since he married the Countess of Derby. It was said she crossed him in everything, no matter how small, and that their angry words could be heard right down the Strand. How different from the sweet peace he had shared with my beloved aunt.

'What can I do for you on this cold morning, niece?' He shook his head sadly. 'As if I knew not. It concerns Master Donne no doubt.' He waved a letter at me. 'I have received this missive from him this very morning.'

'Then let me add my appeal to his. My lord uncle, his own brother died in Newgate of a plague.'

My uncle shrugged. 'It is a common fate.'

'Uncle, listen. If it saves him from sickening in that place I will renounce the marriage.'

He saw what this cost me, yet stared straight ahead, making no answer.

'Is your Master Donne so dear to you that you would give up all for love—family, position, even your good name?' The Lord Keeper turned away, staring out at the cold grey river. 'Love can be an illusion, Ann.'

I wondered if he thought of his new wife, so harsh and shrewish.

'Ours is not such,' I said simply. 'It can also, as you well remember, my lord uncle, be the greatest solace and delight God gives to his creatures on this earth.'

'Aye.' His sigh was deep enough to launch a fleet from Tilbury. 'I will release your Master Donne.'

I gasped, unable to keep in my delight.

'Yet, niece, I cannot reinstate him in his former place here.'

I bit my lip, knowing how hard that would go with John, how difficult it would be for him to get another place. Our future together would be a lean one.

Yet I cared not for that.

He would be released and I thanked God for it.

'Remember, Ann, I will have him freed, yet I can do no more. Your father is your father and I will interfere not in family matters. I lend no approval to this marriage.'

'Yet it is a step to our reunion. If he is freed I ask naught else.'

His face softened into a wintry smile. 'Ah, the optimism of youth. I have always valued Master Donne's talents, though his ambition sometimes makes him blind, and while I would have wished you another husband, yet I can see the merits of this one. You will have a rough road, if ever you are allowed to walk it together.'

'Yet each will have the other to watch and guide them. It is enough. Thank you!'

'Then go and good luck. I will have him released to his lodgings this day. The rest is up to your father. And the decision from the Court of Audience.'

Though the weather was now foul, and the stinking mud caught on the hem of my gown, and my best red shoes were spoiled, yet my soul soared. He was to be freed this day! The road to our reunion might be long and hard but at least it would be possible.

I judged it better not to tell my father I had been behind his back to visit the Lord Keeper.

When Wat arrived with the good news of his release I pretended ignorance along with my joy.

Wat stood, his face beaming like a cat at Christmas when it is given its share of festive goose. 'I bring you word from my master,' he announced. 'He is confined to his lodging, yet that is so great a change for the better that it is not to be complained of.' He dropped suddenly to his knees and grasped my hands tightly. 'Oh, Mistress Ann, I did truly fear for him, so sharp was his decline in that dire place. Yet now he is released, the Lord be praised.'

All day I bided my time and played the dutiful daughter, yearning to see him, yet knowing I must not if I were to win round my father, agony though it was. Instead I bid Wat tell him God had blessed us and that surely now it would not be long till He smiled on our re-union.

I was surprised when my father returned early from Parliament and asked if I and my grandmother wished to take the air abroad with him at Whitehall.

In the Whitehall Gardens we felt the first feathery fingers of spring dance across our faces and although it was madness, for I knew him confined to his chamber, I yearned to catch a sight of my husband. Many fine gentlemen promenaded through the gardens, dressed as he would be in lace collars and deep black hats, yet none was he.

Next to the gardens stood a small graveyard where, to my surprise, we spied the Countess of Derby, the Lord Keeper's new wife, contem-plating tombstones.

'Sir George!' She greeted us like long-lost kindred. 'A pleasure to see you! I am glad indeed to hear of Master Donne's release. He is a man of myriad talents. Indeed I intend to commission some verse from him to mark my daughter's wedding feast.'

My father, ignorant of the speed of events, looked as if struck by a bolt of lightning that had deprived him of his speech.

'Has the thought struck you, Sir George,' the Countess mused, 'that Master Donne's verse might live on long after the rest of us have spun our last thread? That it may be *his* tombstone future generations seek out?'

My father fell quiet at that, not even railing against the Lord Keeper allowing his release.

My grandmother nudged me in the arm. 'Your father has been struck by the notion of immortality, and whether having Master Donne as his son might offer it more securely than a month of mumbling pa-ternosters.'

Yet what caused the wind truly to change was the rumour that our marriage was to be declared valid after all. Mary came to visit and said that, since we were to be husband and wife after all, all the talk now was that my father had behaved rashly and to his own disadvantage, and seeing this my father had asked the Lord Keeper to reinstate my husband.

For my own part, I dared not hope, but played the dutiful daughter, as quiet and obedient as my sister Frances, and I prayed.

Easter came early, with its penitential stations of the cross, which suited my sombre mood. My grandmother, restless and eager to be back with the chickens she had left in the care of Hope and Stephen, grumbled, 'Will he never unbend yet stick as stubborn as some old-fashioned schoolmaster to the rules others have long since abandoned?'

And then, on the twenty-seventh of April my father called me into his closet and, looking up from his parliamentary papers said, 'Daughter, there is one below who wishes to speak with you.'

Slowly, lest the dizziness in my head should send me sprawling, I descended the steep staircase towards my father's small library.

A man stood in it, alone, his face hidden by a large black hat.

He turned at the sound of my step.

And there, after so many long months apart, a smile of joyful longing lighting up his features, stood my husband.

Chapter 29

AFTER THE PAIN and the uncertainty, even the fear of death in that
dank cell, when the limits of my courage and resolve had been tested,
I had thought this moment would have been our crowning glory.

Yet now my spirit deserted me and I felt a sudden shyness.

We had overturned so much convention, and angered so many who
were close to us, caused such scandal and gossip, risked so much for
love, that the prize must be worth the cost we had paid for it.

What if he found me wanting, regretted the loss of his ambition or
feared our fate would be too narrow and impoverished?

He stood before me, his beloved face more careworn, wearing a
borrowed doublet for the occasion in thread of gold, his familiar black
cast away.

And yet I found no words to speak to him.

Indeed I felt a strange relief when my father came into the room,
strutting as usual, and no smile to bid us good luck on our way.

'Well, Master Donne, you have your Ann. Be good enough to let
me know your situation when you are settled in lodgings for I take it
you have no property of your own?'

Even now, at this late hour, my father could not but twist the knife.
Graciousness was not his way, especially in defeat, and he would do
all he could to sour our joy.

To me, he reached out a hand as if I were for all the world a yeoman or a groom of the household leaving his employ.

'Farewell, Ann. I have done well with my daughters, have I not? Mary married to a noble spendthrift and you to a penniless poet?'

I shook the hand, though I would rather have dashed it away from me. 'Farewell, Father. I am sorry I am not the daughter you wished for. Yet you have a goodly wife in Margaret and Frances may yet prove the cream of us all. Perhaps she may still speak to you in your dotage.'

At that I turned and walked from the chamber. I had not even readied my possessions for my new life, yet I could not wait another moment in that mean and narrow house. My grandmother could send on all I needed.

Yet there she was, waiting in the hallway, a look of tender sadness softening the fierceness of her features. 'Pay no mind to your father. He confuses love with blind obedience. He cares much now, yet his rigidness will soften when he hears the good things I know will be spoken of Master Donne.'

'He may relent. I am not sure that I can.'

She pressed a bag of coins into my hands. 'A wedding gift from my poor hens. They wish you very happy.'

At that I felt my throat close over, and tears begin to sting my eyes.

Prudence appeared behind her, with a basket containing a few of my possessions. She delved into her apron pocket for a small bundle which she handed to me with humble apology. 'For your new home. Tis not much, mistress. A pillow slip I have worked with your initials and your husband's.' I looked down at the letters 'A M' entwined forever with 'J D' in scarlet silk, and the truth of my new situation enveloped me.

'Thank you, Prudence. You have been a good friend.' The tears began to run down her face at that, for servants rarely felt their employers' kindness.

'Thank you, mistress. We will miss you sorely.'

And then we were out in the muddy street. I was grateful that he had hired a coach for our departure, even though we could not afford it, for I wished to leave the house in Charing Cross, and my father in it, with all speed.

A thought struck me and I turned to John.

'But where will our home be?' I had sudden visions of us thrown onto the street with our meagre possessions around us. 'Will Master Haines allow a wife to share your lodging?'

He shook his head.

'Your cousin Francis bids us come to live at his house in Pyrford. It is not far from Loseley and your grandmother, and Francis promises there are many spare apartments. I will have peace and quiet for my writing and can help him with his accounts and any tasks needful of doing around the estate. Perhaps he is being kind, yet he says we will be the greatest help to him and Mary.'

'Poor John.' I touched his face gently. 'You who hate the country so, and see it as the root of all boredom and all evil.'

'That was without you. Now I shall gaily walk the meadows, adorning the cows with ropes of wildflowers and writing verse to sing the praise of farmyard fowl.'

I laughed at that, relief flowing through me that I appreciated his company as much as I had done before. 'Mock not farmyard fowl.' I chinked the bag of coins. 'For they may be paying for this coach we ride in! Do we go to Pyrford now?'

At that he smiled a secret, lazy smile. 'On the morrow. Tonight shall be our bridal night, so long awaited.'

'And where will we spend this long-awaited bridal night?'

'Wait and you shall see.'

I looked out of the window as we passed down the busy thoroughfare of the Strand and into Fleet Street up towards Ludgate Hill. I could see him shudder at the nearness to the Fleet Prison and was glad when the coach turned away towards Smithfield, drawing up at last outside the Rising Sunne, a quiet inn in Cloth Fair, hard by the church of St Bartholomew the Great.

I felt a certain disappointment at surroundings so modest and discreet for our first wedded night, yet told myself our luck was in being together at all.

The innkeeper, a decent-looking man, answered our knock and led us upstairs to our chamber. As he opened the door I almost gasped aloud, for the chamber was one of the most beautiful I had ever beheld, panelled in wood from floor to ceiling and everywhere I looked were Turkey carpets in bright shades of indigo, blue and crimson, not just on the walls but on the floor also. The curtains were of great swathes of silk in russet and green, tied back with thick knotted ropes as if we were for all the world in a playhouse.

And everywhere were strange and unfamiliar objects, a pipe attached to a silver stand on which incense or some other spice burned; a spinning globe with all the new world marked upon it; and all round the bed hung small lanterns, their sides of coloured glass, with star-shapes cut from their silver holders so that all the room was jewelled with coloured light.

Yet the eye was caught most of all by the vast canopied bed, adorned with rich brocades and glowing velvet coverings edged with ermine and white fox.

He saw me look and then my eyes shyly turn away.

'The chamber belongs to a sea-captain who stays here only between voyages.'

'I have never seen aught like it before.' I felt suddenly the need to chatter, to postpone the moment when, at last, we two would be truly man and wife. Instead I picked up a huge shell in dazzling iridescent blue.

'From the Indies. The room is full of such treasures.'

My eye caught something familiar laid out upon the bed and then I smiled, my fear departing, for it was my own white linen nightgown.

'Your tire-woman Prudence summoned Wat and sent it on before us.'

'Yet, Master Donne, if I remember your verses aright, I should not need such a garment. Is it not full nakedness that is required to taste whole joys?'

He laughed and took my hands.

'Was there ever such a one as you, my Ann?'

'No, never. And I am sure if there was you would have found her, since you seem to have undressed every lady in London. And some, I fancy, who were less than ladies.'

'Tut tut, such boldness in one so young. Sir George is well rid of you, I think. No wonder he relinquished you so easily in the end.'

I stopped laughing then, remembering the fear and the loneliness of these three long years. 'No, John, he did not relinquish me so easily. I had to fight him every step of the way.'

'My sweet Ann, I know that. And now after all your struggles I have transported you to a meagre fortune.'

'No, say not that. Our fortunes will be joined together from this moment hence. No such future could be meagre. Indeed it will be rich beyond imagining.'

He caught me to him then and lifted me onto the bed.

'You are right,' he told me merrily, 'we will not need this chaste garment.' At that he flung my nightgown to the floor and looked back at me, his smoky eyes darkening yet further. 'Come, let us indeed remove that girdle and that spangled breastplate.' And so we unlaced one another's clothing until we lay side by side, each to each truly a new-found land.

At that my hand strayed downwards until I found out what I sought. And I whispered, 'Husband.'

And he, his eyes seeking mine, answered, 'Wife.'

That night, our first alone when none could spy on us, nor stop us enjoying the fruits of one another's bodies, passed like the wink of an eye and I awoke to find the sun's rays lighting the motes of dust that danced all around us in our great curtained bed.

'Pay no mind to the sun,' my husband told me. 'We went not to bed last night because it was dark, so why should we arise now because it is day?'

So we passed another hour in great delight until Wat and the innkeeper banged upon the door to tell us that our horses were ready and waited down below to carry us to Pyrford and my cousin Francis.

It was late in the day when we arrived there, each smiling and dreaming of the night before. Francis, his young wife Mary upon his arm, a babe and springer dogs playing about their feet, waited outside his timbered manor house.

IN ALL THE time we stayed there Francis was never less than welcoming and, although our fortune was indeed a narrow one, our days at Pyrford were happy ones. The next year the Queen died after so many on the throne that many had known no other monarch than she, and with her death came the end of an era.

The Scottish king succeeded her and all scrambled for honour and position. I was truly happy that Francis was made a knight, along with the husbands of both Mary and Margaret and my brother Robert. Mary's naughty Nick did indeed inherit a great estate and became a worthy citizen and eschewed his gambling ways. My father had a greater honour still, being made Treasurer to the Household of the Prince of Wales. And though I knew my husband envied their advancement, and sometimes sighed at the life he had lost, yet he was content for their sake.

When the new King James set out on a summer progress with his Court, his first night was spent here at Pyrford, and after that two nights with my father at nearby Loseley, where the works were finished just in time with a fine new chamber entitled the King's Room, complete with painted ceiling in his honour.

Our beloved daughter arrived that year also.

Our life here is quiet, yet my husband fills it with study and writing letters to his many friends on divers topics of the day. At times they try to summon him back to the city and the Court, yet he says he prefers to spend his time here in the country. He even wrote to his old friend Henry Wotton that God is near him here. Perhaps it is to comfort me.

And most of all, we each have one another.

THE SUN RISING

Busy old fool, unruly sun,
Why dost thou thus,
Through windows, and through curtains call on us?
Must to thy motions lovers' seasons run?
Saucy pedantic wretch, go chide
Late schoolboys and sour prentices,
Go tell court-huntsmen, that the King will ride,
Call country ants to harvest offices;
Love, all alike, no season knows, nor clime,
Nor hours, days, months, which are the rags of time.

Thy beams, so reverend, and strong
Why shouldst thou think?

I could eclipse and cloud them with a wink,
But that I would not lose her sight so long:
If her eyes have not blinded thine,
Look, and tomorrow late, tell me,
Whether both th' Indias of spice and mine
Be where thou left'st them, or lie here with me.
Ask for those kings whom thou saw'st yesterday,
And thou shalt hear, All here in one bed lay.

She is all states, and all princes, I,
Nothing else is.
Princes do but play us; compared to this,
All honour's mimic; all wealth alchemy.
Thou sun art half as happy as we,
In that the world's contracted thus;
Thine age asks ease, and since thy duties be
To warm the world, that's done in warming us.
Shine here to us, and thou art everywhere;
This bed thy centre is, these walls, thy sphere.

Postscript

'WE HAD NOT one another at so cheap a rate, as that we should ever be weary of one another,' wrote John Donne in 1614, twelve years after he and Ann were married.

Their marriage lasted fifteen years and produced twelve children, ending only when she was carried off days after a final still-birth by 'a savage fever' at the tragic age of thirty-three. Highly unusually for the time, John Donne never remarried, writing:

> *Since she whom I loved hath paid her last debt*
> *To nature, and to hers, and my good is dead,*
> *And her soul early into heaven ravished,*
> *Wholly in heavenly things my mind is set.*

Materially they did not have an easy time. After their marriage was declared valid Sir George More handed over his daughter with bad grace, refusing until some years later to pay any of her dowry. They survived thanks to a legacy from her aunt, swiftly granted by Lord Keeper Egerton, who seems to have forgiven more easily than Ann's father the sins they had committed against canon law and social convention, although he did not restore Donne's employment. Fortunately Ann's cousin, Francis Wolley, offered them a home at Pyrford, not far from Loseley in Surrey.

Some of John Donne's most moving poetry was almost certainly inspired by Ann, verse that was different in tone from the defiant, sexy, occasionally misogynistic poems of his youth. The poems with Ann in mind are still witty, sensual, challenging, full of the old cleverness and enjoyment of sex, and yet there is a sense that he is sharing the experiences with another person rather than writing simply about himself.

Only with Ann does Donne seem to have achieved the longed-for union of body and soul.

One explanation is that, unlike most women of her time, Ann was 'curiously and plentifully educated', according to Donne's biographer Izaak Walton.

It was while he was married to Ann that John Donne wrote 'A Valediction Forbidding Mourning', containing one of the greatest images ever written about a loving relationship, recognizing both the lovers' interdependence as well as their individual differences. He imagines that he and she are 'twin compasses' and when one roams the other 'hearkens after it', growing erect as it comes home.

> *Such wilt thou be to me, who must*
> *Like th' other foot, obliquely run;*
> *Thy firmness makes my circle just;*
> *And makes me end, where I begun.*

John Donne was both ambitious and clever and undoubtedly life away from London and the Court must have frustrated him, yet this frustration also fuelled the angry distinctiveness of his poetic voice. At times he longed for both career advancement and masculine company, yet his unusual empathy and concern for Ann are clear and constant. Theirs was no fairytale romance with an easy happy ending. Yet there was true tenderness and deep affection in their life together.

To the shock of some he took holy orders in 1615 and after Ann's early death he did indeed focus himself on 'Heavenly things', eventually becoming Dean of St Paul's Cathedral and delivering the most famous sermon in the English language: 'No man is an island.' He was also reconciled with Ann's father, Sir George.

Frustratingly, no letters from or portrait of Ann survive.

It is often pointed out what John Donne gave up for Ann, yet rarely acknowledged what she, superior in social status and financial position, willingly sacrificed for love of him.

The Lady and the Poet, based on fact and also on imagination, tells an extraordinary and little-known love story and attempts to paint a picture, my picture, of the Ann who is absent from history.

ACKNOWLEDGEMENTS

JOHN DONNE has been my lifelong passion but it has taken the immense help and enthusiasm of my agent, Judith Murray, and my delightful editor, Imogen Taylor of Macmillan, and Charles Spicer of St. Martin's Press, magnificently assissted by Allison Caplin, to turn that passion into a novel.

I would like to thank the Surrey History Centre, a model of preserving local documents; the Surrey Archaeological Society for their original work on 'George More's Other House'; the staff at Loseley, especially Nicola Cheriton-Sutton, and of course its owners, the More-Molyneux; M. Thomas Hester for his insightful introduction to *John Donne's Marriage Letters*; to Patricia de Vekey for first lighting the spark; Valerie Clayton, for nagging me over three years to finish the book; Professor Neil Rhodes, Director of Postgraduate Studies at the School of English of St Andrews University who directed me to the Oxford Authors edition of John Donne's work, edited by John Carey, which attempts to publish the undated poems chronologically, and of course to John Carey's own seminal *John Donne: Life, Mind and Art*.

I greatly enjoyed listening to Donne's love poems read erotically or abrasively (sometimes both at the same time) by the late Richard Burton and to the delightful musical collection 'O Sweet Woods' featuring Donne's love songs and sonnets set to the lute by Dowland and others, which Donne himself would probably have hated.

A final thanks to my family who have become fed up with me quoting Donne on every occasion, and to my friend Carol Kelly for the gift of the seventeenth-century sampler which has found its place in the novel, and to Professor Dennis Flynn of Bentley University for reading and correcting my manuscript.

The following books have been incredibly useful in re-creating this fascinating period: John Oglander: *The Commonplace Book of Sir John Oglander*; R.C. Bald: *John Donne: A Life* (OUP 1970); Hilary Spurling: *Elinor Fettiplace's Receipt Book* (Penguin 1986); Izaak Walton: *The Life of Dr Donne Late Dean of St Paul's, London* (written 1640, OUP 1946 edition); G.R. Elton: *England Under the Tudors* (Routledge 1977); Lytton Strachey: *Elizabeth and Essex: A Tragic History* (Chatto 1930); Anna Beer: *Bess: The Life of Lady Ralegh* (Robinson 2004); Henry Shelley: *The Inns and Taverns of Old London* (Wildside Press); Alison Sim, *The Tudor Housewife* (Sutton 2005); D.J.H. Clifford: *The Diaries of Lady Anne Clifford* (Sutton 2003); Joyce Youings: *Sixteenth-Century England* (Pelican 1984); James Shapiro: *1599* (Faber 2005); Liza Picard: *Elizabeth's London* (Phoenix 2003); Derek Parker: *John Donne and His World* (Thames & Hudson 1975); Anne Somerset: *Ladies in Waiting from Tudors to the Present Day* (Weidenfeld 1984); John Stubbs: *Donne: The Reformed Soul* (Viking 2006); M. Thomas Hester: *John Donne's Desire of More* (Delaware 1996); A.L. Rowse: *The England of Elizabeth* (Macmillan 1951); Malcolm Airs: *The Tudor and Jacobean Country House* (Bramley Books 1995); M. Thomas Hester, Robert Parker Sorlien & Dennis Flynn: *John Donne's Marriage Letters* in the Folger Shakespeare Library (Folger Library 2005).